'Haunting and so exquisitely written'

Michelle Davies, author of *Gone Astray*

'*Fragile* is as devastating as it is beautiful. Very few writers possess the skill to make a story as immersive as this . . . a perfectly crafted read'

Lucy Dawson, author of *White Lies*

'Wonderfully twisty and atmospheric. Kept me second-guessing right until the end'   Sam Baker, author of *The Woman Who Ran*

'Extraordinary . . . affecting, unflinching, so atmospheric, and the pin-sharp characterization is as good at it gets. Sarah has produced a novel that feels contemporary and socially important, yet somehow other-worldly . . . executed beautifully'   Caz Frear, author of *Sweet Little Lies*

'A stunningly written, deliciously dark and immersive thriller full of atmosphere and depth. I absolutely loved it'

Roz Watkins, author of *The Devil's Dice*

'The writing is so elegant, so restrained, that it brings to mind Patricia Highsmith. *Fragile* is a very fine and very creepy psychological thriller'

Lucy Atkins, author of *Magpie Lane*

'Tremendously atmospheric! *Fragile* will tangle you up in a house full of secrets and broken lives. Beautifully written, its dark secrets reveal themselves with a deft hand'   Rachael Blok, author of *Under the Ice*

'I have long been an admirer of Sarah Hilary's work, and *Fragile* is an exceptional novel. The writing is superb, and every page glitters with dark brilliance. I loved the Gothic quality of the book, the twisted plot, and the sense of peril that pervades the story'   Kate Rhodes, author of *Hell Bay*

'A beautifully written exploration of the damage people do to each other and the lies they tell themselves along the way'

Cass Green, author of *In a Cottage In a Wood*

Fragile

Sarah Hilary's debut novel, *Someone Else's Skin,* won the 2015 Theakston's Old Peculier Crime Novel of the Year award and was a World Book Night selection. The *Observer's* Book of the Month ('superbly disturbing') and a Richard and Judy Book Club bestseller, it has been published worldwide. *No Other Darkness,* the second in the series, was shortlisted for a Barry Award in the US. Her DI Marnie Rome series continues with *Tastes Like Fear, Quieter Than Killing, Come and Find Me,* and *Never Be Broken. Fragile* is her first standalone novel.

Also by Sarah Hilary

DI Marnie Rome series

Someone Else's Skin

No Other Darkness

Tastes Like Fear

Quieter Than Killing

Come and Find Me

Never Be Broken

Fragile

SARAH HILARY

PAN BOOKS

First published 2021 by Macmillan

This paperback edition first published 2022 by Pan Books
an imprint of Pan Macmillan
The Smithson, 6 Briset Street, London EC1M 5NR
EU representative: Macmillan Publishers Ireland Ltd, 1st Floor,
The Liffey Trust Centre, 117–126 Sheriff Street Upper,
Dublin 1, D01 YC43
Associated companies throughout the world
www.panmacmillan.com

ISBN 978-1-5290-2946-8

1 3 5 7 9 8 6 4 2

A CIP catalogue record for this book is available from the British Library.

Typeset in Arno by Jouve (UK), Milton Keynes
Printed and bound by CPI Group (UK) Ltd, Croydon, CR0 4YY

Visit **www.panmacmillan.com** to read more about all our books
and to buy them. You will also find features, author interviews and
news of any author events, and you can sign up for e-newsletters
so that you're always first to hear about our new releases.

To Alison Graham

1

London looks so different in the daylight. Undressed somehow, indecent. And that's before you count the people, those who belong here and the ones who never will, the lost and the found.

I'd been watching the street for over an hour when I saw her, coming out of the house. I hadn't even known there was a house here – thinking it was all offices, restaurants and coffee shops. When last night I'd followed Joe only to lose him on this street, I'd said to myself he must have slipped into a late-night restaurant, expecting the bill to be paid by the stranger who'd picked him up earlier in the evening. Joe always attracted strangers. I'd said to myself they were hungry – Joe was always hungry – and they'd stumbled on this strip of West London with its bright lights and dirty pavements, the hot smell of cooking from kitchens. In daylight, it all made another sort of sense.

The street looked grey and tight-lipped. The girl leaving the house was the only colourful thing in it; so colourful, she hurt my eyes. I watched her swaying down the steps from the house, yellow pigtail bumping at her shoulder. Twenty-three or so, in a lilac coat and scarlet jeans, an easy smile on her lips. One of those world-at-her-feet girls, every birthday with a cake baked and candles burning, unwrapped presents lying in a welter of red ribbon. No one had ever abandoned her, or turned their back. She'd never know loneliness, never find herself without friends or hope. Hard not to feel a sharp little stab of anger at her complacency. Her life was so easy and she didn't even know it, how suddenly the world could cave at your feet, swallow you whole.

I wondered what had happened inside the house to put that smile on her lips. Such a strange house to find hidden away here, so narrow it was nearly invisible. Three storeys of brown brick with a white wreath moulded to its door below a window of wrinkled glass. No bell to be rung; she'd raised her fist to knock. I hadn't seen who opened the door since a lorry blocked my view, as it had last night. But now I'd seen the house, it seemed obvious to me that this was where Joe had disappeared last night. The woman who'd picked him up – she must live here. They'd been hungry, I'd got that much right, but it wasn't food they'd wanted. In the nightclub, she'd singled Joe out, imagining he was alone. Well, he was. I'd been there in the background, but we weren't together. Joe hadn't noticed me following him to the club. He hadn't noticed me in days. As for the woman, she'd had eyes for no one but Joe. The girl coming down the steps from the narrow house could be her daughter, they were so alike, each so blonde, like an over-exposed photograph. Joe's woman had worn a belted black satin coat and high heels, showing enough skin at her throat to make you wonder whether she was wearing clothes underneath, her hair pinned up out of the way. This girl wore a pigtail tied with a black bow. She'd spent half an hour inside the house; I'd noticed her going in, and I'd seen her coming out. Six shallow steps led up to the front door. More steps led down to a basement but that was hidden behind railings, hard to see from a distance.

I'd had time to study the house from my seat in the window of the coffee shop that called itself a diner. Hungry's, the name painted above an ancient awning. The faces of celebrities stared from the walls, actors and singers who'd gorged here on toasted sandwiches and lemon meringue pie. I couldn't afford the pie or even a plate of toast. I'd scraped together the last of my loose change for the cup of tea I was sipping as slowly as I could. The diner was warm and greasy, smelling of bacon fat and coffee grounds. They let me sit in the window undisturbed. It's possible they thought me a good advert with my grumbling stomach and pinched face, the face of Hungry's. Traffic trundled past the window, indifferently. I might have been invisible for all the notice anyone took. I was used to that, it didn't bother me, but the street did.

This street and I were old enemies. I'd walked it many times but never spied the narrow house, too busy being the eyes in the back of Joe's head as he scored whatever he needed to get through another night, or another day. He couldn't stand to be cold, he said, as if what he was scoring was a woolly scarf rather than a Class A drug. We'd been homeless for six weeks. It'd been all right while the summer lasted, but the year was turning and Joe with it, turning away from me. We were sleeping on the Embankment, not far from this street which was home to dealers and addicts, and well-heeled West Londoners. I'd thought it had no houses, only places to eat and work, like the restaurant with its mirrored tiles, the office block with its smoked-glass windows. Between these two, the narrow house was slipped like a lover's note, long forgotten. It must have been a listed building to have survived the surrounding development. Five ornate plaster letters ran across its face, 'Starl', edited by the loud red front of the restaurant where last night I'd expected to find the woman in the satin coat buying Joe his supper. But it was the house that had swallowed them. Last night, after I'd given up searching, I'd retreated to our spot on the Embankment, missing Joe's warmth at my back. This morning, I'd gathered the last of my change and come here to keep watch for him, not knowing what else to do. I was responsible for Joe, that's how it felt, that's how it was. And he was in the narrow house across the street, I was sure of it. But just as sure he wouldn't want rescuing, not by me who hadn't the cash for a second cup of tea, let alone whatever was on offer across the road.

The girl with the pigtail was coming towards me, swerving through traffic. Away from the house, towards the diner. My teeth twinged from the tea. I had to steady my hand on the cup.

She dragged the door open, letting in a lick of wind and litter.

She was younger than I'd thought, acne spoiling the beige mask she'd made of her face, and achingly pretty with big blue eyes and a plump pink mouth sitting open over white teeth. At the counter, she ordered a skinny latte in a sleepy voice. Did anything ever put a crease in her nose, or make her curl her hands into fists? Did she sit up in the night as I did, icy sweat on her shoulders, straining to see in the darkness whatever it was that'd scared her awake? I couldn't imagine it.

Her coffee was served in a takeaway cup. She sat at the table next to mine and took out a phone, pecking at it with painted fingers, her free hand stroking her throat. 'It's me.' She stretched the personal pronoun to two syllables. 'I got it, but I turned it down . . . No, listen, it was weird. Like the whole set-up, just really weird.'

She was talking about a job. In the narrow house, across the street. Could this be my way in?

'Dr Wilder.' She lowered her voice to a lazy purr. 'Robin.' A pause, her fingers walking up her neck, before she laughed. 'God, no. He's ancient!' More laughter. 'Later, okay? Yes, yes I will.'

I stood as she ended the call, cocking my head. 'I couldn't help overhearing,' I said.

'Excuse me?'

'I work for Gazelle, the recruitment agency? Our offices are just up the road.' I gestured vaguely then gave what I hoped was a conspiratorial smile. 'I've sneaked out for a coffee break!'

She blinked to bring me into focus. Girls like her never noticed me unless they made a special effort. I had a useful face, the kind that gets me out of trouble, now. When I was younger, it gave me away, over-sharing my sadness or rage. My face left me nowhere to hide, that's what Meagan Flack said. But I'd trained it to be a good face, a mirror face, giving back what people wanted to see.

'Oh . . .' The girl perked her lips into a smile. 'Sorry, are you recruiting on your coffee break? Only I've just turned down a job offer. I need some time to regroup.'

'Of course. But you did say Dr Robin Wilder? From—' I nodded towards the narrow house.

'Starling Villas,' she supplied. 'Yes. Why?'

She was frowning finally, the smallest dent in her self-confidence. Had she taken the trouble to study me, she might have questioned my alibi. For one thing, my hair needed washing and my teeth a good brushing. But she didn't take the trouble. I calculated she didn't need the job she'd been offered in Starling Villas; she'd walk into another easily enough. I indicated we should sit, making a gesture of confidentiality of the kind I'd seen from social workers, and the police.

'I probably shouldn't be telling you this, but we've had a little trouble over there.' I lowered my voice, forcing her to lean into me. 'Dr Wilder . . . Let's say he isn't the kind of employer I'd want for my sisters.' I was going to say *for myself*, but judged *sisters* to be better.

Her face stayed smooth, untroubled. 'Why not?'

'He can be a hard taskmaster.' She remained blank so I tried, 'He's not the best boss. He doesn't always pay his bills.' I was warming to my theme. 'And he has a temper. We've had . . . complaints.'

I put a pause there, for her to fill in the blank.

She blinked her indignation. 'They didn't say anything about any of that, at my agency.'

I sipped at my cold tea. 'He's clever at covering his tracks.'

'I still think they should've said something. I was alone in the house with him. I mean, he *said* he was alone.'

'You didn't see anyone else in the house?'

She shook her head. Had I made a mistake?

'I felt I had a duty to speak up when I overheard you on the phone.' I looked her over, taking care to be impressed by what I saw. 'You know, my agency has a lot of good vacancies for young professionals.'

'Oh, it's not that.' She tossed her head. I'd always imagined that was an expression people used in books, but she actually did it. 'It's not like I'm desperate.'

'That's what I thought. Let someone else be the one he pushes around and doesn't pay!'

'You should tell the police what he's like.' She sipped at her coffee. 'Seriously. I knew it was weird but not everyone has my instinct.' She was psychic, on top of everything else.

'The job offer. Was it for . . . ?'

'PA. He has like a ton of boxes and books. He said it needs sorting out but frankly it's a mess in there.' She inspected her glossy fingernails. 'I'm going to make a complaint to my agency. They said it was different to an office job as he's working from home or whatever, but they didn't say anything about him being a pervert, or not getting paid.'

Nor did I say anything about him being a pervert. She'd made up a story in her head, admittedly with my help, a tale to tell her friends. She was shiny with it. I'd given her something better than a boring job shelving books and sorting boxes, ruining her nails into the bargain.

'I'd rather you didn't say anything to your agency.' I frowned, as if thinking it over. 'I mean, you could, but my agency is working with the police and HMRC to gather evidence. I'd hate anything to get in the way of that.'

'Oh, right.' She nodded, bored with me now. 'I wish I'd known about all this when I was over there, that's all. I'd have told him where to stick his job.'

'I thought you did tell him.' I switched on a big smile then dimmed it to a frown. 'Are you sure he understood you turned it down?' Had she lied about it, told him she'd think about it? Under the table, my feet danced with impatience.

'I'll make it clear to him now.' She tossed her pigtail over her shoulder, reaching for her phone.

I listened while she made the call in a freeze-dried version of her voice, all the warmth iced out of it. The voice she used to break

7

up with men. She'd broken up with plenty of men, I could tell. She took pleasure in disappointing Dr Robin Wilder, killing whatever hope he'd had of her accepting his job offer. She'd be dining out on my story for months.

We left Hungry's together, the girl sipping her coffee as she swayed towards the tube station. I waited until she was out of sight before I crossed the road to Starling Villas, climbing the six steps to the door with the plaster wreath.

Setting my nylon rucksack at my feet, I lifted my fist and knocked. I told myself this was it, my one chance to get inside the house which had swallowed Joe last night. I knocked and then I stepped back with the morning's traffic running behind me, waiting for him to answer.

2

I swear the house shivered as I stepped inside. A passing lorry would be the logical explanation. Starling Villas was built long before any dream of cars or lorries. It had the stifled chill of a museum, shadows marking the places where furniture once stood and paintings hung. Its hall was tiled in black and white, doors leading to rooms left and right. A spiral staircase with banisters like bars climbed up to the bedrooms and down to the basement. It was exciting to be inside the house. My heart tapped in my chest. The girl with the pigtail hadn't exaggerated the boxes: dozens snaked about the hall and again in his library where he led me. I wondered briefly what was inside the boxes, but decided it didn't matter. What mattered was that I was inside, out of the wind and rain, away from people's feet. Right at that moment, nothing mattered more, not even finding Joe. The house smelt as I did, of neglect. I'd washed in Hungry's lavatory, doing what I could with my hair and clothes, but homelessness has its own scent. In the diner, my smell was masked by the odour of fried food. There was no such reprieve here.

Dr Wilder, to give him credit, did not wrinkle his nose. 'I wasn't expecting any other applicants.' He had his phone in his hand, fresh from her break-up call.

I waited to see if he would recognize me. I had the strongest sense we had met before. Was he in the club last night, with the woman in the black satin coat? I hadn't seen anyone else, but all of my attention had been on Joe, who'd been restless for days. I had been on high alert for his desertion. As soon as the cold weather came, I knew, he'd start looking for a place to lie low. Joe didn't always make the best choices, even he would have to admit that.

'I came on the off-chance. A friend of mine at the recruitment agency mentioned you were looking for someone?'

Someone blonde and pretty, over-exposed. I was nothing like that. I saw him gathering the right words with which to dismiss me without causing affront. Manners mattered to him, as did privacy. He hadn't wanted to conduct this conversation on the doorstep. Since answering the door, he'd avoided looking directly at me but it was possible he had excellent peripheral vision. As I did.

'Do you have secretarial training?' he asked now.

'Of course.' I had the idea he was checking the air for the flavour of my lie. Lies taste different to the truth. I'd conducted my own checks, catching a whiff of burnt toast and brown dust as we'd walked through to his library. It was tidy, if you looked beyond the boxes littering the room, but it needed a deep clean. The whole house did. 'I can cook, too. And clean.' I didn't smile, in case he thought I was joking. 'I'm a quick learner.'

And you've just been let down by someone who thinks you're a pervert.

'I don't know . . . I wasn't expecting anyone else.' He frowned, thrown. 'I like things in order and right now this is a mess. I'm sure you understand.'

I understood. He didn't care for surprises or strangers, people who knocked on his door without an appointment. I wasn't what he'd wanted. Nor was he what I had expected, Dr Robin Wilder of Starling Villas, London W8. For one thing, he wasn't ancient, no more than forty. And he was attractive, at least to my mind. His eyes were grey, under straight black brows. His dark hair curled in feathers across his forehead. His nose was broad at the nostrils, his mouth curved by a long upper lip. His hands were lean and long-fingered, the kind that could be clumsy yet precise. Men's hands fascinated me. If I shut my eyes, I'd see Joe's hands, slim and sunburnt. But I didn't shut my eyes.

'I'm a quick learner, and a hard worker. I've worked in houses before. Is it just you here or—'

'It's just me, now. In the Villas.'

I waited for him to qualify the statement. Given his age, had he grown-up children, a dead mother, an estranged wife? But he nodded as if he'd said everything necessary for me to understand the set-up here. Just him, in the Villas. I said, 'It's a beautiful house.' Let him taste that lie.

He didn't seem able to tell me to leave, any more than the staff at Hungry's who'd let me sit so long in the window. He should be sending me on my way. Instead, he looked at the boxes as if they intimidated him. It was the mess, I decided. Some people can't stand mess. Everything else in the room was neat and – what were the words he'd used? *In order.* His desk had a pot to hold pens, a tray for letters. The bookshelves were full but not crowded, each spine turned the correct way. Lamps were angled here and there, pointing light precisely where it was needed. Only the boxes spoilt the impression, dumped on the floor and in the chair behind his desk. He was a meticulous man, besieged by boxes. As we stood there, he reached a hand to rest it on the nearest box, the same brown cardboard cube as the others, sealed right round with tape. The kind of box that held important papers. His hand lay on the spot where packing tape criss-crossed the seams. Private papers, confidential.

'I can see there's a lot to be done.' I made a point of looking at the bookshelves and desk, letting him know I saw his tidiness underneath the mess. 'I know you're looking for a secretary but I could also take on the cooking and cleaning, if you'd like. That would free you to organize things in here.'

His fingers slackened as if I'd loosened a screw inside him, a small but vital adjustment. 'You mean a housekeeper? I've had one or two, in the past.'

'But not recently.' I smiled an apology.

It was an oddly charged impasse; I could feel my fingers fizzing. I still expected him to send me on my way, but something was stopping him. Politeness? Or another reason, one I couldn't see.

'I suppose . . .' His hand fell free of the box. 'I could show you the rest of the house.'

I followed, close enough to catch his scent; it was like green ferns growing in the shade. He wore grey flannel trousers and a blue shirt, brown leather lace-ups. His shoulders were broad, the rest of him narrow. When he turned the corners in the house, his shadow shrank to a thin blue line.

The rooms in Starling Villas were stacked one on top of the other, three on the ground floor and three on the first. Tall, square rooms, plagued by panelling on the walls and across the ceilings and in the shutters of the windows. I'd need a broom to reach the worst of it. The dining room had an elaborate ceiling rose from which a naked bulb was strung like a laddered stocking under a ball gown. His tour had an odd effect on me, simultaneously repelling and attracting, I suppose because I was being shown how much hard work was here. But I'd wanted to be inside the house as soon as I'd spied it hiding on the high street. I'd recognized Starling Villas, and it recognized me.

Hello, it whispered as I followed Dr Wilder through its rooms, *Hello, you.*

I grew giddy standing beside him in room after room, seeing the scale of the task I'd be taking on. Each room he showed me was empty. But Joe had been here, I was certain. The house reeked of the kind of warmth he craved, indulgent, decadent. It would take weeks to search every shelf and cupboard, and even then I might not find the evidence to prove it. But Joe might come back here. And while I was searching, I could hide. Thanks to Meagan Flack, I needed to hide.

'It's three floors,' he said, 'four, with the basement. But the top floor is an attic. You won't need to clean there.'

Where the servants once slept, I said to myself. Starling Villas had been grand in its day. The living room had a marble fireplace with urns carved at either end. I'd seen similar urns in funeral homes, but those served a purpose. These were ebony, he said, warning me to be careful how I cleaned. His tour was full of warnings. I listened to each one but it didn't alter the fact that I knew I was going to live here in Starling Villas, with him.

'My bedroom.' His hand was on the door handle.

I met his eyes. There it was again, that loosening in him. Easier this time, as if I'd oiled an internal working. He didn't see me as a threat; why should he? This was his house, we were playing by his rules. The muscles in his wrist and forearm shortened as he opened the door.

His bed was made, but I could see the shape of his head in its pillows. Bedside cabinets to either side, a paperback book on one, a lamp and an alarm clock on the other. The furnishings and bedding were pale and looked pricey, but the sheets hadn't been ironed and the carpet needed vacuuming. Long jade-green curtains hung either side of the sash window. A mirror was mounted on the wall at the foot of his bed, so extravagantly ugly it could've been a prop from a horror film, its frame a nightmare chiselled with crouching mice and pointed ears of wheat. He saw me staring and said, 'I like the glass to be cleaned using white vinegar and newspaper,' which explained the strange smell in the room.

He shut the door, moving on with the tour. 'Two other bedrooms . . . The bathroom, of course.'

Tiled in white, cobwebs on the ceiling and behind the lavatory. Why had he advertised for a personal assistant when it was a housekeeper he so badly needed? But what we need and what we want are rarely the same thing. What I knew of Dr Wilder's wants could be written in the palm of my hand. I could come to know them, in time. If I stayed, if he let me. I'd make him let me. The house had shivered as I'd set foot inside. Had he done the same? Did he possess that much sense?

'And this is the garden room.'

We were on the ground floor again, in an extension at the back of the house. The garden room was cold, and mostly made of windows. Green-black plants grew into the glass, spidering in all directions. Waxy-faced orchids lit the edges of the room. A clock ticked behind us. I'd heard it from the first floor and feared I'd hear it in whichever room would be mine, its ticking keeping me awake at night. My skin pricked in alarm. Insomnia and I were old enemies. I'd stolen so many of Meagan Flack's sleeping pills, I'd lost count. *Tick-tick-tick.* Was it possible I was the one making the mistake here? I was aware of him watching me, measuring my discomfort.

'The kitchen's in the basement.' He stood with his hand on the banister rail. 'Let me show you.'

I followed him down the spiral steps.

The kitchen was large and its ceiling low, with built-in shelves and a blackened stove shackled to one wall. A scarred table ran the length of the room. The sink was a porcelain trough below a window that looked out onto the shallow yard where stone steps led up to the railings I'd spied from across the street.

'I like my housekeeper to keep things clean and in order.' Dr Wilder glanced around. 'I'm sure you understand.'

'Of course,' as if I couldn't look at a dirty surface without reaching for the bleach, had never slept in doorways or begged for food or stolen it from bins outside restaurants like the one next door to Starling Villas.

The kitchen floor was grouted by grease. The whole house was miserly with its dirt, making an obstacle course of cleaning, the kind requiring ritual and patience, and a battery of bottles and cloths. Hard work, top to bottom. But I'd never been afraid of hard work. Of many things, but never that. Traffic swept the street above us. The kitchen held on to the sound as if each bowl and cup was filled by it, even the spoons. The traffic might have been miles away, or it might have been carriages and traps. I felt as if I'd stepped out of London, and out of time. Over the table, an ancient bronze lampshade hung from a frayed flex. A fire hazard, if ever I saw one. I'd seen plenty.

'Everything you need should be here.' He frowned, but it was a footnote to the decision he'd clearly made somewhere between his bedroom and the garden room. He was going to take me on. I was here to stay. I nearly smiled.

'The housekeeper role would be on a trial basis,' he said, 'to see if we suit one another. I hadn't really thought about anything other than employing an assistant. To be honest, I am not sure I want a housekeeper.'

'Of course.' I was going to make Starling Villas shine, he'd see. In no time, I would be invaluable. And I was going to find whatever was hiding here. I knew so much about hiding.

'Will you have far to commute?'

His question stung me from my fantasy.

'I've only just arrived in London.' I pre-empted his next question: 'My references might take a few days. But at the other houses where I was housekeeper, I always lived in.'

Dr Wilder shook his head. 'I'm afraid that won't be possible here.'

We eyed one another. He'd forgotten the boxes, being down here in the kitchen, but to escort me from the house he'd have to walk back through their havoc and be reminded of the task he was facing, alone, without me here to help.

'It's out of the question,' he said.

16

'Then I'm very sorry.' I held out my hand. 'I'm very sorry that this won't work out. It was a pleasure meeting you.'

My prediction proved accurate. One look at the boxes in the hall and he withdrew his objection, taking me to the top of the house, to a chilly little cell of a bedroom with tiled walls and a bathroom across the landing.

'You would have this floor to yourself. There's the bedroom and bathroom, and an attic room too if you're able to do anything with it.' He opened the attic door, glancing inside. 'It could use a good clear-out.'

He wasn't joking. The attic was mess and work when there was enough of that downstairs, an entire house to keep clean, meals to cook and no fitted kitchen, not even a dishwasher.

You're the dishwasher, I reminded myself. But a thrill ran under my ribs at the sight of the attic, my first proper feeling in a long time: *I could do something with this.*

Meagan Flack was in the back of my mind, my first taskmaster. She'd put me to work in a house far less orderly than Dr Wilder's, filled not with boxes but with brats, to use one of her nicer words about us. Not only cleaning and cooking but cuts and bruises, cradling and rocking to sleep. I'd managed that house from the age of eight. By comparison, Starling Villas was a piece of cake, and a place to hide. Because I might wish Meagan in my past, outclassed and outpaced, but she was out *there* – looking for me. Hunting me, because of what I'd done. Everything I'd done.

Dr Wilder shut the attic door. He hadn't looked directly at me, not once. Had I beaten him unconscious and robbed him, stolen his papers, set fire to his bed and the towers of boxes, he would not have been able to give the police a proper description. Perhaps my height, 'Five foot three or four', and my colouring, 'Dark hair, pale skin', but not my age (eighteen) or my eyes (indigo blue) or the deep star-shaped scar editing my right eyebrow.

'Well then, Miss . . .'

'Nell. Please.'

He made a movement with his head, not quite a shake. Distaste in the shape of his mouth; no first names. 'Miss . . . ?'

'Ballard. Nell Ballard.'

'Well, then. Welcome to Starling Villas.'

3

A fly was stalking the window towards a spider web which'd appeared overnight, unless Meagan Flack was only noticing it now. She'd missed a lot of things, lately. Like the mould growing at the back of the wardrobe that'd turned her clothes green, or the mushrooms in the airing cupboard, skinny and pale as upturned fingers. Every inch of the flat was riddled with damp, and dirt. You stopped seeing it after a time. Had to, when you'd bigger things on your mind, like finding the little bitch who'd put you in this dump where even the flies were suicidal.

She lit a cigarette, 'First of your five a day,' shaking out the match before it could ignite whatever poisons were lurking in the cracked flooring under her feet.

In films and on television, spider webs were combustible, catching fire at the brush of a match. In reality, it was the dust they collected and not the silk itself which was flammable. People fell into the trap of thinking all spiders made webs, but plenty preferred to hunt their prey. Even those with poor eyesight that relied on touch and smell when hunting. Some species cared for their young, far better than they were given credit for. Like Meagan, who'd run that big house as a tight ship until they'd stopped her. Alarms to get you up, curfews to keep you in, penalties if you flouted the rules. Kids needed boundaries, and discipline. The police were no strangers at Lyle's but they knew how tough her job was, trying to turn around kids who'd had their hearts broken, or their bones. The unloved, and those who'd been loved too much. Angry kids, sad kids, sly kids. They came to her in all shapes and sizes. She never once turned a kiddie away. Not even one like Nell Ballard, with trouble written right through her. 'Little Nell,' Meagan called her, even after she filled out and there was no little about it. 'Little Nell, my success story.' If she found her – *when* she found her – she'd give that girl a curfew she'd never come back from.

The window wouldn't open, sending her cigarette smoke straight back into her eyes. She was watching the street for the postman, or postwoman with her musclebound calves and peaked cap. Mostly what they delivered was junk and bills. Final reminders, the one thing that never changed. Not even Nell Ballard had been able to change that.

'This is Nell. Nell, this is Mrs Flack, your new foster mum.'

Ten years ago, that was. The day before Nell's eighth birthday, no one thinking to let Meagan know this latest kiddie needed a cake and balloons and a present wrapped in paper. She'd have bought a card, at any rate, if Social Services had been doing their job properly. As it was, the paperwork arrived a week after Nell, too late to make a fuss. Fuss never helped anyone.

'Well, say hello.'

She was a quiet one, was Nell. That should've put Meagan on her guard from day one. Better they came in kicking and screaming, since she'd a cure for that. Those like Nell who stood in silence, fixing her big eyes on everything, those were the ones who gave her the worst trouble.

'It was your birthday,' she said when the paperwork came through. 'Day after you got here. You should've said. I'd have baked a cake.'

Eight-year-old Nell watching the smoke rise from Meagan's cigarette, as if she knew she'd never baked a cake in her life. 'Next time, eh?' She tapped ash into a saucer, nodding at the child.

Nell accepted this, as she did everything in those early days. The room she had to share, sheets that brought her out in a rash, food that did the same. Never once complained. Meagan had a cure for complaining, but she hadn't one for silence.

'You should've said' – turning the girl by her shoulders so she could see how bad the rash was – 'I'd have given you something for it.'

Nell waited to be released before dragging her dress back over her head. That look again, as if she didn't believe a word coming out of Meagan's mouth. But she knew to keep her lip buttoned. Fast to follow orders, slow to take fright, keen to be needed. She'd tried to make it work with her stepdad, Meagan read that much between the lines of the social worker's report, tried to make herself wanted and when that didn't work, to make herself needed. An eight-year-old who knew how to iron a man's shirt? That wasn't any more normal than the rest of it.

After a week or so, she tried to get the girl to open up, out of idle curiosity and because it helped to know what she was up against. 'Put you to work, did they?'

'I didn't mind.' Nell was folding clothes from the washing line. 'I like to help.'

21

'That's good. Plenty to be getting on with here. I do what I can but . . .' She shrugged.

That look again: *Liar*. Nell kept folding clothes as if she could make everything small and neat, tidy it all away. She didn't flinch when Meagan snapped at her over the iron – 'What's this death trap doing out?' – just tucked away her new knowledge about Meagan's temper as if it were a clean vest. The house had never been so orderly. It set Meagan's teeth on edge – things the girl found as she sneaked around clearing out cupboards and drawers. Overdue library books, final warnings from the vampires trying to drain her dry, letters from mums and dads she'd never passed on, all left like reproaches on Meagan's bedside table. 'What's this then?' Flapping an envelope at the girl.

'It looks like a bill.' Eight-year-old Nell gazed back at her. 'It was at the back of the airing cupboard.' She watched Meagan as if her anger were a live thing she was learning, waiting to see where it would land. 'I'll put it in the bin, shall I?'

Some of the kids amused themselves turning stones in the garden, inspecting their undersides for insects and worms, whatever was wriggling underneath. Nell was like that, only with people.

Sharp little thing, Meagan had thought.

She hadn't stopped thinking it, until Joe Peach arrived on the scene.

The thought of the pair of them, Nell and Joe, made her crack her hand at the window. She opened her palm to see a fat black smear, before scraping the dead fly onto the windowsill where the wood was crumbling, rotten as the rest of it.

The flat was temporary, a concession from the council. They'd had to rehouse her after what happened at Lyle's. They'd have rehoused her in a prison cell, if they could've made it stick. Plenty thought she deserved that. Even the police, who used to respect her for the way she handled the kids in her care. She was lucky, that's what she was told. Lucky to have escaped a murder charge, even with no body to be found. Manslaughter would've been worse, with its implication of neglect and stupidity. Meagan was many things, but stupid wasn't one of them. And if she'd been neglectful, it wasn't in ways they could measure. Lyle's had been held up as an example of how to run a good foster home. Until Little Nell decided to bring it all crashing down.

Meagan smoked to the filter, grinding it out on the underside of the windowsill.

Where was the spider?

Her web looked empty, still vibrating from the shock of Meagan's hand swatting the fly. The spider was hiding, keeping out of sight in case she scared off her prey. Spiders could wait for weeks, or months. This one would re-spin her web each day if she felt like it, perfecting the design to attract what she was after, when she was good and ready.

4

Now it was just the two of us in Starling Villas, me and Robin Wilder.

'Settle in,' he said vaguely, 'and we'll talk about a rota.'

I was to work for him off the record, cash in hand, no references or National Insurance number. London was full of desperate people without official identities; he could've had his pick of us. Not the pretty girls but those like me, ready to try anything for the chance of a roof over her head and a hot meal inside her. It was easy for him to rationalize my readiness to take this job. Rationalizing his own reasons was trickier but I told myself that's what the rota was for, to make our arrangement feel more formal. He had boxes to sort, and he'd had housekeepers in the past. How many others had stood in his hall, hearing the hard ticking of his clock and fearing they'd go mad from lack of sleep or the way he looked right through you as if you weren't there?

I counted the steps as I climbed to the attic. There were thirty-nine.

In my new bedroom, the old mattress creaked and sagged. I had to shut my eyes not to see those who'd slept in the stale sheets. A spider was crouched in the corner above my pillow, a furred black scrawl on the white tiles. But the pillow was mine, like the bed and the bathroom. Everything on this top floor of Starling Villas was mine. Tomorrow, I'd start searching. Every cupboard and shelf, each drawer of his desk. For the drugs that had lured Joe here, or some sign of the woman who'd taken him from the nightclub. Or evidence of another kind to explain the strangeness of the house, and of him. Dr Robin Wilder. If he'd been part of the scheme to lure Joe here, I'd make him pay.

He stayed in his library, buried in his boxes, most of the day. Shirtsleeves rolled back from his square wrists, dressed in grey flannel trousers two shades lighter than his eyes. My only change of clothes hung from the shower rail in my bathroom, waiting for the creases to fall out. Dr Wilder didn't care what I wore, or how I looked. It was peculiar how little interest he showed in me, this stranger he was allowing to live in his house and cook his food.

'Start with the kitchen, please. That needs the most work.'

His rota was long, pages and pages of it, bound inside a clear plastic wallet. He'd typed the rules using a bold font. Had he typed it quickly, while I was settling in? Or had he taken the rota from a drawer in his desk (one of those I would search), wiping it clean of his previous housekeeper's fingerprints before handing it to me? 'Say if anything's unclear. I've tried to use plain English. This, for example.' He reached to point at the page. 'You do understand?'

I read the rule out loud, about a certain drink to be served at the same time each night. It was hard to concentrate with his wrist resting on mine. Reciting his instructions slowly, I placed an equal emphasis on each syllable. He didn't pull away and nor did I, until I'd reached the full stop.

'Good,' he said then, and paused. 'You can always ask if there's anything you don't understand. I'll expect you to ask. Otherwise, just get on with it. I find that's best.'

My wrist felt chilled without his and seemed to be all bone, as if a layer were missing and I'd find it later when I was sweeping. That's what dust is, after all: the sloughing of skin. His nostrils flared, catching my scent. I'd washed off the worst of the streets. What was he smelling? Orange energy drinks and cheap soap, sleepless nights and sorrow? I was certain my skin told my secrets. So often I woke with a rash on my throat as if every one of my lies was written there, for anyone to read. Each sour black word and deed, branded on my body.

'I'll expect you to ask,' he repeated, stepping away.

How can I describe that first contact, his wrist on mine, a moment which came and went with the reading of his words? Such a small thing and so painfully, impossibly tender.

My afternoon was elbow grease and bleach, battling the dirt that had settled over everything since he last had a housekeeper. I managed a third of the work before it was time to cook his supper. After serving the meal, I returned to the task. The house was dark around me but it was comforting to work in the light from his lamps. The sooner the house was clean, the sooner I could get to my real work. When at last I stood, my back stabbed and my legs shook. I had to grip the banister as I climbed to the top of the house. Below me, I heard the small sounds of Dr Wilder going to his bed.

In my attic, I leaned on the lip of the window, looking out at London. Not the city seen from the tops of skyscrapers where the danger dwindles to a neat grid of roads, but here where the houses once stopped, three or four floors above the pavement. High enough for birds to come edging along the ledges, near enough to see the bald spots on passing businessmen. The city was lit by neon and the sulphurous yellow of street lights. I propped my aching wrists on the windowsill, watching the Thames as it ran through the city, away and away. Mapping my journey in my mind's eye, the way I always did, no matter how far I travelled from the three of us. Joe and me, and Rosie. I'd take a train and then another. Shutting my eyes, I smelt the bitter brakes and sour bodies as the windows filled with stations north and west. At last, the breaking sky, secret.

Wales is castles and princes, the strongholds of centuries. It gives up its shorelines to holiday crowds but the mountains are ours. True Wales is deep pockets and welts, pools where water lies flat and green, waiting. In summer, your toes grip the weed coating the stone ledges that reach into water so cold you bite the inside of your cheek. Wales is mist stealing your hand from in front of your face, the sea hoarding the summer's heat long after the land has surrendered.

Under my grip, the attic window peeled its paint, scabbing my palms.

I kept my eyes shut. I wasn't in London, I was in Wales. A train and then another. I'd walk the last mile, the ache of the incline in my shins, blue knots of gorse on all sides, slate slipping under my feet. I'd crouch and take a slice of it, blade-thin, into my hand, waiting for my heat to creep across its smoothly whetted surface. There at the side of the lake, so deep between the rocks, drawing down the sky and all its stars, spreading the yellow moon like butter on its skin. My favourite place in the world, but I could never go back.

Below me, Dr Wilder slept in the bed whose sheets I'd smoothed and drawn tight. I wondered if he understood what he'd let into his house.

5

The postman brought his usual dribble of bills, thin brown envelopes that Meagan fed to the swivel-lidded bin. Nothing which'd help her find that little bitch. But the world was turning, summer on its way out. The first cold night would change everything. The stove wouldn't light, so she ate beans cold from the can, watching the road through the kitchen window, its tarmac twisting away like an oily river. It led to Lyle's, that road. She'd not been up it in months. Hardly dared show her face outside the flat, even at this safe distance and after all these weeks. The beans shed their skins against her teeth. She picked at them, thinking about cake and broken plates.

By her ninth birthday, Nell Ballard was doing all the baking at Lyle's, letting the littler ones decorate the cakes, cleaning up their mess without being told. Meagan took a tough line, the only line. Her kids didn't trust kindness; why would they? Look what'd happened to Felicity Barrow, 'Call me Fliss', with her nose in the air and her homemade dresses. She didn't look so proud after little Tallini seduced her husband before running off with their credit cards. No one ever robbed Meagan Flack, and it was common knowledge she took in the worst of them. So what if she turned a profit on the nuisance of keeping house for kids whose parents had babies not because they wanted them but just because they could? She thought she'd seen it all, from teenage pregnancies to benefit fraud, but Florence Ballard set a new record. She had Nell when she was too young, then wanted shot of the kiddie when it was time to get married – not to Nell's dad, who'd never been in the picture, but to a man after a family of his own thank you very much, not leftovers from anyone else. He'd expected Nell to appreciate his point of view. To top it all, she was made to admire the fat baby that came soon after they'd packed her off to Lyle's.

'We can arrange that, yes?'

Playing the proud dad, insisting Meagan bring Nell to meet her new half-sister. Except the baby wasn't that, was she? No *half* about it, since they'd turned Nell's bedroom into a nursery, stuffing it with plush bunnies and bunting. He'd been boasting all week about his new baby, wetting its head with his mates down the pub, showing photos to anyone who'd look. Running short of people to impress until he remembered the girl who should've been his stepkid, the one he'd dumped on Meagan so he could start his new family. Social Services saw a chance of reconciliation, but Meagan knew better. If Nell had been a bit older, maybe – useful as a babysitter. Social Services dug their heels in, all the same.

'The weather's nice enough,' Meagan had compromised. 'We can meet up the park.'

Give Nell the chance to run off, she'd thought, *without it looking like a scene.*

Nell said nothing when Meagan told her the plan, just pulled on her coat and shoes. She didn't take Meagan's hand, the way some kids would've done. Not fearless, just too used to living with fear. Chances were she didn't even know she was afraid. It took them that way, kids raised with fists or without love. It rewired their brains. They never got better.

In the park, Nell looked for her mum but Florence had stayed home. It was just him with the new baby. 'Come and see how beautiful she is!' Standing there in his pricey parka, full of himself.

Nell walked to the pram and looked inside.

'She's sleeping right now. Sleeps through the night already! Mum said she can't believe it after you, says I must have the magic touch, ha-ha!'

On and on, as if Nell was one of his workmates, happy to hear his boasting. She stood, staring into the pram. The baby had a halo of yellow hair, and rosy pink cheeks. Picture perfect, tucked up to her fat chin in snowy folds of blanket. 'Isn't she gorgeous?' Bouncing on his toes, beaming.

Meagan got a chill, thinking back on it. Silent, skinny Nell with her dark eyes fixed on the baby. She didn't say a word on the way home to Lyle's, or for days after that. Meagan told Social Services it was a one-off, no more visits. It wasn't fair on the girl, and it made her own job harder.

A week after the park, she told Nell, 'Table needs laying.'

Nell laid the table without complaint, but two plates got smashed along the way. Two plates and a baby mug she'd brought with her to Lyle's, painted with angels and bows. Meagan didn't hear the smashing, only found the pieces later, razor edges wrapped in newspaper and put out with the bins. She'd thought of those sharp edges seven years later, the day Rosie Bond went missing. Nell was fifteen by then, all fresh curves that snagged the eyes of the dads who came to Lyle's, and the boys who lived there. Boys like Joe Peach. All that summer long, Nell was in vest tops and shorts, and, *My God*, Meagan had thought, *this is going to end with someone getting hurt.*

She'd missed a trick, all the same. Too busy watching the men and boys when she should have been watching Little Nell, no little about it now. Florence Ballard and her beau had moved away the summer before. Another fat baby had followed the first, and of course the local schools weren't good enough. Social Services delivered the news, leaving Meagan to break it to Nell, only where was the point in that? They were gone, and good riddance. Nell had troubles of her own, filling those shorts the way she did, her neck suddenly so lovely. Eyes for no one but Joe Peach, and the little girl who looked a lot like the one in the pram. Rosie Bond, with her big blue eyes and pink pout of a mouth.

From her kitchen window, Meagan saw a car turn onto the ribbon of road, coming from the direction of Lyle's. It wasn't coming for her, not this time. She was out of those woods, as far as it went. Exiled to this damp dump of a flat, empty of everything but spiders and flies. She ran a tap to rinse the spoon, still picking her teeth free of beans. When she'd finished, she lit a cigarette; first thing she'd done after they'd handed her the keys to this place was take the batteries out of the smoke alarm. She watched the car until it was out of sight, leaving the street empty again.

Nearly five months they'd been gone, Nell and Joe Peach. Since just after the memorial service, which everyone called a funeral. They'd gone to ground, in London most likely. Nell would've promised to keep Joe safe but her promises were worse than worthless, he'd know that by now. The first cold night would bring them back to her. All Meagan had to do was sit tight, and wait. Because she wasn't done with Little Nell, not by a long stretch. She hadn't even got started.

6

Our life together in Starling Villas was dictated by his rota, the plastic-sleeved leash on which he kept me in those first few days. It was such an odd way to run a house. Not even Meagan Flack, who'd kept me on her own leash long enough, had bothered writing down the rules. In Starling Villas, I was kept busy below stairs, too busy to search the house the way I wanted to, but there was time. I was prepared to wait.

Breakfast, the rota said, was to be served in the library. An omelette made from eggs beaten in a bowl then tipped into a hot pan where a sliver of butter was browning. No seasoning, just a grating of hard cheese. His diet was austere, to the point of being penitential. For what, I wondered, was he punishing himself? The omelette smelt good. I tore a corner of bread and wiped up the froth of butter, laying it on my tongue to savour its sweetness.

In the library, he'd cleared a passage for me through the boxes. Already he'd emptied a couple of them, flattening the cardboard for recycling. He ate at a table under the window, away from his desk. The cutlery was silver, worn with age. Worth something, but not much. Not enough.

As I laid the plate in front of him, he said, 'Thank you,' but didn't speak again.

I'd nearly set fire to my sleeve, making the omelette. His old stove didn't like the cleaning products I'd used on it last night, spitting flames at me. I thought of the old joke, 'What did your last slave die of?' Dr Wilder's last slave hadn't cared about cleaning his stove, or being turned out onto the streets. It made me uneasy, for a reason I couldn't name. Her neglect, and her departure. He'd had one or two housekeepers, wasn't that what he'd said? Where were they now?

While he ate his omelette, I sat at his kitchen table to write out a shopping list. He'd left cash in an unsealed envelope, £120 in ten-pound notes, more money than I'd seen in a long time but still not enough, certainly not to risk losing this new roof over my head. His rota said, 'Shop locally and stay within budget but don't compromise on quality.' It sounded like a test. What were the penalties, if I failed? There are always penalties, Meagan taught me that. All those years under her roof, when I was in charge of meals and shopping, along with everything else. I'd been on the streets for only six weeks, but I'd known how to make someone else's small change stretch to two meals. Poverty, like misery, sharpened my wits. But you can only plan for so much. Hadn't Meagan taught me that, too?

Forty minutes after serving breakfast, I returned to the library with a fresh pot of coffee. Thanks to the rota, I knew where in the house I would find him at any given hour, although (in theory anyway) it armed him with the same knowledge about me. Setting down the pot of coffee, I saw he'd opened another of the boxes and that it held large white envelopes with black barcodes, each envelope stamped 'Private and Confidential'. He was back at his desk, bent over his work. A sleek silver MacBook was set to one side, sitting among the papers like a spaceship in a vintage car lot. His rota said the MacBook wasn't to be touched at any time. The same rule applied to his phone and sound system. It made me wonder if his last slave died of an electric shock.

'How is your room?'

I was surprised he'd spoken, and more surprised to be asked a question implying an interest in my comfort. Was it a reward for how well I was following the rules? 'Thank you, it's fine.'

'I expect it's cold.' He didn't look up from his work. 'You'll find hot-water bottles in the airing cupboard, and blankets.'

When I didn't speak, he raised his eyes to look at me, blinking as he did so. I'd fastened a white tea towel as an apron over my charity-shop black dress. Max Mara, it fitted me perfectly, its length modest but flattering, its neckline the same. I'd been told I had good legs, and that my neck was lovely. I'd put my hair up, his old stove lending a clean sheen of sweat to my skin. My only jewellery was a red woven bracelet, damp from the sink. Joe had made the bracelets to sell on the streets, back before his fingers grew too shaky for the knots. He and I wore matching bracelets, always. I wondered where he was, and whether he was wearing it now.

Dr Wilder withdrew his gaze, bending back over his book. His left hand reached for his coffee, finding it without looking because I'd placed the cup with its handle turned towards him. I waited, but he'd said all he wished to say. Carrying the tray from the library, I closed the door behind me, soundlessly. I had a great deal to be getting on with.

I'd heard of fake houses in London and New York where a dignified facade was needed to hide a sewage works or electrical plant. Starling Villas was like that, telling lies with its elegance and age. I wanted to bury my hands in the house – bring up its secrets. For now, I could clean.

His bedroom was my favourite in the house. In the morning, if I was quick, I'd catch the heat of him, hiding like a cat under the covers. I searched both bedside cabinets and in the suitcases under the bed, finding nothing of interest. No photos of blondes in black satin coats, smiling from silver frames. He slept alone. I don't know why that was such a comfort. Only the ugly mirror unnerved me, its gilt fraying under my duster. It had a flaw, a bubble trapped inside the glass that swallowed my reflection, snuffing me out. If I stood in front of this spot and turned my head from left to right, my face vanished, reappearing on the other side of the flaw. Blink, and you missed me. I stood in that spot on my second morning in Starling Villas, making a solemn promise to myself to see this through. Like the one I'd made to Joe when I was fighting for our lives in Lyle's, trying to make him see why it wasn't safe for us to stay there any longer.

'She knows, Joe. She knows and she'll tell. She hates us.'

It wasn't a lie, but nor was it the whole truth. Meagan hated me, but she loved Joe. It's why she fought so hard to keep him. She didn't care about Rosie, or even about what had happened to Rosie, but she cared about Joe. And she hated me, with every bitter wire-wool fibre of her being.

In Dr Wilder's bedroom, I turned my head and let the mirror take me, just the mist of my breath on its old glass. 'He doesn't know,' I whispered. 'He thinks I'm nothing, no one. He has no idea why I'm here in his house. He imagines it happened by accident, that his job fell into my lap.'

Nothing had ever fallen into my lap.

Back in the kitchen, I searched for evidence that Joe had been here. I knew his weaknesses: the pills he'd stolen from Meagan when we lived at Lyle's, and the harder drugs he'd bought on the streets. I found an old mobile phone buried in a drawer, its charger attached, but it wasn't Joe's. Meagan had given him a phone, and sometimes pills; he hadn't always had to steal. There were no pills in any of the drawers or cupboards I searched. The only white powder I found was flour, churning with weevils. I sealed its paper packet and dropped it into the pedal bin. Everywhere, I found signs that his last housekeeper had left without warning. Had they fought? Did he fire her or did she simply stop coming? I considered the envelope of banknotes; he trusted me. Had he trusted her? My heart beat oddly, slipping in my chest. What had happened here, before I came?

On the windowsill, a fat pigeon was walking on gnarled feet. The grey smell of cigarettes drifted through the gaps around the ill-fitting frame. Next door's office workers liked to smoke in the street, discarding their butts down our area steps. Given the state of the stove, it was a wonder their cigarettes hadn't started a fire. I reached to close the window, stopping when I saw a spider sitting there. It had spun a web, tacky with dust and grease, a perfect trap for anything coming into the house from outside. The web was clotted with small black bodies. Shivering, I pulled the window tight, locking it shut before pocketing his cash and my shopping list.

Outside, it was squally, a whip of wind warning that autumn was on its way. I buttoned my coat over the black dress, instructing my heart to stop speeding. It was Joe's fear I was feeling, he was the one who couldn't bear to be cold. I loved the autumn, its colour and crispness, but Joe just saw trees stripped bare, earth frozen under his feet. It was why he left me that night, seeking shelter in the club where *she* was drinking, in her black satin coat cinched with a belt. She didn't see me, only Joe. She liked what she saw so she took him, leaving me alone. I couldn't be alone, any more than Joe could be cold. He knew that but he went with her anyway, never once looking back.

Dr Wilder's favourite cheese shop was next to an art dealer with a sculpture in its window of rusty coins welded into the shape of a woman's body. A glazed pot sat at her feet, sea-green with a lick of white running through it. It made me think of our lake, all those miles away. A pool, Meagan called it, but to us it was a lake. She said it should've been condemned. It probably was, now.

The cheese shop stank of churned earth and abattoirs. I had a sudden craving for burnt fish fingers, Rosie's favourite: 'Black and orange fingers!' The only food she really loved, apart from cake and warm milk. She'd have lived on cake and warm milk, if we'd let her.

'May I help?' A man in a white coat and vinyl gloves stood poised behind the cold cabinet.

'Yes, please. I'm after . . .' I searched my pockets for the shopping list, reading out the name of the hard French cheese from Dr Wilder's rota.

The man corrected my pronunciation, gently. How thin he was, the bones in his face like knives. He placed the cheese under a wire, quizzing me with a cocked eyebrow as to how much of it I wanted. I gestured with my hands, having no idea how much the cheese weighed. It looked like a stone, and was the colour of an old woman's heel. I saw Meagan sitting with her feet propped on a stool, waiting to be pedicured. Me kneeling, Joe on tiptoe with tweezers in his hand, searching the crown of her head for white hairs. The pair of us scared silly, our skin stinging with yesterday's slaps, not wanting worse. I could smell her vinegary skin. It made me shiver.

'Is that all?' The cheese man wrapped the cheese in wax paper.

'Eggs. No, I'll get those elsewhere.' I needed to be out, away from the cold cuts of meat with their strong stink of death. 'That's it, thank you.'

'Dr Wilder likes his eggs from here.'

'What?' I stared, seeing him properly for the first time, the way his hair grew in a widow's peak, one eye set higher than the other in his face.

'You're new. At Starling Villas, yes?' His smile was patient. 'Dr Wilder is one of our best customers.' He nodded at the cheese he'd wrapped for me. 'Shall I box up the eggs?'

'The supermarket,' I started to say, until he stopped me with a shake of his head.

'Dr Wilder wouldn't want you to cut corners.' He began to fill a box, slotting in white-shelled eggs. 'He's very particular about his food. These are only a little more expensive than eggs from the supermarket. We're really very good on price.'

'Do you have pressed cod's roe?' I wanted to put a wrinkle in his nose. 'Or tinned salmon?'

'Ah, no. That is from the supermarket.'

'What is cod's roe?'

'Fish eggs.'

41

'Like caviar.' I nodded at the glass jars on the shelf behind his head.

'A little.' His smile didn't slip. 'Roe is the fully ripe egg masses in the ovaries of fish and certain marine species such as shrimp, scallop and sea urchins.'

We eyed one another across the cold cabinet.

'Sea urchins.' We were sharing a joke now but at whose expense I wasn't sure. 'I'm Nell.'

'Bradley.' He nodded, his sharp chin touching his shirt collar. 'Pleased to meet you, Nell.'

'Thank you.' I paid for the cheese and eggs with the first of Dr Wilder's ten-pound notes. Static passed from my palm to his, making the pair of us flinch. 'Goodbye.'

Outside, I sucked traffic fumes into my lungs. It was the first time I'd spoken with a stranger since accosting the girl in the diner. Talking with Dr Wilder didn't count, after two days. Funny, given all the other lessons she'd served up, that Meagan Flack never taught me how to speak to strangers, or warned me not to speak to them. Perhaps she was afraid I'd find my way out from under her thumb sooner than I did. She loved to lecture us about the dangers outside her front door, as if Lyle's was the tip of a terrifying iceberg and we should be thankful for her protection while it lasted.

Spying a park, I sat on a bench to catch my breath.

I'd walked too fast but couldn't sit for long. The cheese needed to be in the fridge, there was the rest of the shopping to get done and his stairs to be cleaned. Anger prodded at my ribs. *Hush.* I shut my eyes, thinking of our lake.

Joe and I used to say there was a drowned village at the bottom of the lake, that if we swam deep enough we'd touch the church spire. In divers' suits, we would walk through its streets, seeing anemones flowering, shoals of fish squatting in the houses, an octopus behind the grille in the post office. I tried to picture Rosie playing with the sea urchins but it hurt too much, squeezing my throat shut. Small fingers tugged at my leg. I scuttled sideways on the bench, smothering a yelp.

Not fingers – a greasy chip paper, blown by the breeze. I kicked it free, blinking the wet from my eyes. In the playground, a solitary child climbed on and off the roundabout. Out of a hundred children, not one would remind me of Rosie. Only sometimes, seated on a bus or standing in a queue, I'd catch a whiff of Savlon and feel that pressure building in my chest. Perhaps there was no escape. I'd run and run, and it would always find me, always hurt me.

Across the park, I saw the spire of a church splitting the sky, putting a path between the clouds where the sun was breaking through. A boy lay on the grass, propped on his elbows. At a distance, he was enough like Joe to hold my attention. My age or a little older, wearing faded khakis and a blue T-shirt, ancient All-Stars on his sockless feet. His face was tipped to the sun, his eyes shut. He lifted the fingers of his right hand to kiss a cigarette, sipping at its smoke. The pressure in my chest was like stones being stacked, one on top of the other. I was afraid to breathe in case I brought them all down.

Finishing his cigarette, not-Joe climbed to his feet and headed off, away. Where he'd been sitting, the grass righted itself, each blade unbending, shivering skywards. Cold crept into my bones as I stood. Time to get to work.

Starling Villas felt safe, silent on my return.

Down in the kitchen, I divided the shopping between the fridge and cupboards, pleased to know I could lay my hands on everything I needed for Dr Wilder's supper. Slicing the bread for his mid-morning toast, I slid it under the grill while I ate the discarded garnish from his breakfast, chewing the parsley to take the taste of the cheese shop from my mouth. When the toast had cooled, I loaded it with the hard salted butter he liked. I was hungry enough to wonder whether I could get away with eating a plate of toast myself. There was no time in his schedule, and no cash provision, for meals of my own. I'd be more use to him if I wasn't distracted by this nagging hunger. But I couldn't afford to make a mistake so soon into my apprenticeship. The thought of being back on the streets filled me with horror, my body soft and fearful after just two nights. As I cut his toast into triangles, I realized I'd used the wrong word. Whatever this was in Starling Villas, it was not an apprenticeship. Dr Wilder had no interest in my learning, of that I was certain.

In the library, he'd put a tweed jacket over his blue shirt. He wore more clothes than any man I'd met. Under the shirt, he was wearing a white cotton vest and blue boxer shorts. I knew this, being responsible for tidying the cupboards in his bedroom. In a slim box, I'd discovered a pair of elastic sock suspenders. Was he wearing them now, under his flannels? Surely not. I didn't know what to make of a man who wore so many clothes.

He'd cleared a space on his desk for the plate of toast. When I set it down, he reached for a slice without taking his eyes from his book, the cuff of his shirt riding to reveal the squareness of his wrist where yesterday it touched mine. Had I been poisoning him, he could not have made it easier. He took a bite of toast and then a second while I waited for the coffee press to work its reluctant magic. His teeth had left marks in the butter I'd spread according to his instructions, lavishly. I had longed to cut my own slice from the loaf, spreading this same generous helping of butter before spooning on strawberry jam. I'd eat it delicately, savouring every bite, not as he was doing, his jaw moving mechanically. My head fizzed with hunger. I was poised to pour the coffee when he put his hand across the cup. I faltered, coffee press suspended, worrying I'd made a mistake, deviated from the rota, distracted by my own emptiness.

'Thank you,' he said, dismissing me. 'That will be all.' He glanced up. 'Do please make yourself a meal. Whatever you need.'

What did I need? I was afraid to name it. If I did, he would throw me out, of that I was certain.

It was after midnight before I returned to my attic. I ran a bath, slipping down until the water cupped my chin, kissing the bruises I'd collected on his stairs. The woven bracelet at my wrist turned a darker shade of red in the water. For a while all I could hear was the throaty sound of the tank refilling, water battling air in the pipes before a long, luxurious silence. Nothing to indicate the tank reheating. I reconciled myself to the tepid temperature. No doubt Dr Wilder rationed the hot water, and I'd used my quota cleaning his stairs. I listened through the layers of quiet for the echoes underneath, taking care because listening for echoes was dangerous. The shadows of cars crossed the ceiling. On either side, I felt the spur of buildings that formed my new perimeter. A car backfired, too far away to frighten me.

Where are you, Joe?

I'd thought I'd find him in this house, but he wasn't here. Was he waiting, the way he'd once said he would, or was he too high or low to care? A promise made in the summer cannot count, I knew that. The promise we made was two summers old, but it was carved from a terrible secret. I couldn't believe he'd forgotten that, or forgotten me.

Next door's restaurant was emptying for the night; soon I'd hear the rattle of bottles in its bins. For now, there was only steam knocking in the old pipes, whistling as it fought its way through the narrow arteries of the house. It knocked and whistled and finally it sighed, meeting the air outside with a little swooping *whoosh*. If I listened long enough, it would start to sound like panting, each puff of steam followed by another in quick pursuit. I flexed my hands, making the water slop and slap in the bath. The other sounds, the echoes, came without warning.

Joe's breath as he slept, mouth open on my pillow. The tread of feet on the landing at the start of the day, the huff of her, 'Hello,' against my cheek. Sounds I'd lost by coming here. Hiding, here.

The bathwater was shallow, as if I'd pulled the plug by accident. It was rotting, the rubber plug cracked right across, leaking water while I lay there allowing myself to remember the things I ought never to forget.

Drying myself, I pulled on an old vest top and shorts before going into the attic.

The window should've let in the street light but it had to struggle past piles of old papers and sagging cardboard boxes. Too much of this house was boxes. Someone had spread old newspapers across the floor. I glimpsed a headline here and there, the name of a politician long dead or disgraced. The papers stretched to every corner, hiding something soft underneath.

Crouching, I uncovered a rug, rubbing my thumb across its

sooty surface. It was patterned with curling stems and thorns, and tiny starbursts the colour of pavements after rain. Stripping more papers out of my way, I followed a trail of crimson feathers and turquoise trees, yellow larks and lizards, to a border of copper links. The rug stretched from wall to wall. I sat back on my heels, surprised and delighted. A whole room of silken rug shining like glass, buried under rotting boxes stiff with pigeon droppings. I wanted to set to work restoring it, brushing the weave to bring up its colours – I'd use the soft-bristled brush I'd spied in the cupboard under the stairs. Not tonight, as I was too weary, and the noise might wake Dr Wilder. But soon.

I climbed to my feet, kicking the papers back into place. The rug would keep. It would be my secret, a piece of the house which was all mine. It felt good to have a secret. The rug had been hiding up here for years. I stood with my thumbs pricking, eyes searching. What other treasure was hidden here? His childhood toys? Photo albums of Dr Wilder as a young man in cricket whites, or racing across a beach on the skinny legs of an adolescent?

I thought I'd known what I was hunting for here but now I let myself imagine a different plan, one where I restored his beautiful house and in return he gave me shelter and food and kindness.

A ripple ran across the floor, finding my fingertips. Her ghost, or Joe's? I stood very still, listening, but Dr Wilder had gone to his bed, and the house was quiet.

7

I woke not knowing where I was, mattress springs prodding my ribs. For one long skin-pricking second I was terrified, slick with sweat, eyelids quivering against the rough ticking. Then I sat up, shaking the fear into anger. I hated being scared, shouldn't be – *couldn't* be – after all the things I'd done to escape it, the bridges I'd burnt and hearts I'd broken, including my own.

Last night, I'd dragged the mattress to make a bed under the attic window. My throat was full of damp, my skin gritty. Why hadn't I changed the bedding? I'd been too busy washing his stairs and shopping for his stinking cheese. This was his fault, Dr Robin Wilder who wanted his breakfast in an hour and would not tolerate any deviation from his rota. Hauling on my clothes, I cursed him, not stopping until I was down in the basement struggling to light his ancient stove.

Breakfast was scrambled eggs. The beating of eggs in a bowl helped to rid me of the rage. By the time I set the tray at his elbow, I no longer hated him. His hair was damp from a shower. I could smell his shampoo, and last night's wine working through the pores of his skin. He was reading a book, his thumb keeping his place

49

as he waited for me to unload the tray. The library curtains were drawn against the day. It was my job to open them after he'd finished his breakfast. Was it superstition underpinning his rituals, or had something happened to make him fear change? Death or disaster, or heartache of another kind? I shook the puzzle away. What did his heartache matter to me? I was going to search the library as soon as the rota said it was safe to do so.

Dr Wilder plucked the parsley from the eggs and set it at the side of his plate. The rota insisted on the garnish, even if he never ate it. He liked a teaspoonful of Dijon mustard whisked into his eggs. What bliss it'd been to lick that spoon, my tongue shivering from the mustard's heat. Behind me, the library clock *tsk*ed its tongue. I'd search inside it, behind the cogs and wheels. Perhaps I'd break it, by accident of course. Dr Wilder didn't speak a word, eating my eggs and drinking my coffee with the curtains closed. I waited in the hall until it was time to return and uncover the windows to a white sky where the sun crouched out of sight. Rain was coming to relieve the pressure, I could feel it in the joints of my fingers. I reloaded my tray with his empty plate and cup, the French press with its grounds silted inside like a black clot of earth.

In his bedroom, I took up each pillow in turn, hitting it with the heel of my hand. His sheets wouldn't need changing for another two days but I wanted to strip the bed and remake it with the linen in the airing cupboard. The sheets needed ironing but I'd been doing that since I was seven. Meagan shouted the first time she saw me with the iron, as if she'd thought me helpless, a child like all the others. I wasn't sure I'd ever been a child, unless it was with Joe, the summer before we kissed. I was nearly fifteen then. It seemed a lifetime ago, but it wasn't even four years.

In his bathroom, I rinsed the basin, polishing the taps and tidying bottles of shampoo and shaving cream. When I ran my finger around the rim of the basin, it squeaked.

None of his clothes were lying out in the room but I opened the door to his wardrobe anyway, slipping my hand between the hang of jackets and shirts. His suits were smooth tweed and glassy flannel, the rail overloaded to the left where an evening jacket hung, black with peaked lapels. Sliding it along the rail, my fingers met the sudden chill of satin. I reached to remove the plush hanger, its wire neck wound with pink ribbon. Hanging from its padded shoulders was a silver evening gown. It slinked from the wardrobe, flooding my feet.

Sleeveless with wide shoulder straps of satin, its neck low and cowl-shaped. I turned the hanger in my hand. The back of the dress was slashed in a deep vee where the shoulder straps met a diamond clasp stitched onto the high waistband. A stern little circle of stones which would imprint itself on the wearer's skin when she sat, or lay down. It was an achingly sexy dress, slim at the hips, with the whisper of perfume in its heavy folds. I brought it close, the satin grazing my lips. Under the perfume, it carried a woman's russet scent. His mother's? The style made that a possibility, but it felt too new. The gown had been made to measure, for someone narrow, snake-hipped and small-breasted. The sort of woman who might wear a belted black satin coat, naked underneath. The sort of woman who picked up stray young men in nightclubs and took them home with her.

I crossed to the ugly mirror, holding the gown in front of me. It would never fit my curves, but it was beautiful. The silver shuddered against me, as if the satin were breathing. I looked taller and more remote, unreachable. My hair was suddenly darker, my lips redder, my eyes darker. I ran my palm down the dress where it lay along my hip.

'What are you doing?'

I swung to face him, the gown against me, clinging to my thighs.

Dr Wilder stood in the doorway to his bedroom. 'I asked you a question.'

I didn't recognize his voice, it was so altered by anger. But I recognized the rage in his eyes. I'd seen it in other men's eyes, and women's too. The room slipped sideways, away from me.

'I'm sorry, I was tidying—'

'Put it back.' He took a step towards me, his body rigid, teeth together. 'Now.'

I gathered the cold folds and shoved the gown inside the wardrobe, snagging the hanger at the rail as I fought the slipperiness of the satin. I felt his eyes on me, burning and freezing at the same time. My heart filled my whole chest.

As I shut the wardrobe door, he said, 'Now get out.'

His anger was so familiar, far easier to navigate than his calm. I drew a breath, holding on to it for a long moment before I said, 'I'm sorry. It won't happen again.'

He expected me to run from the room, but I stood my ground. Counting time in my head, the way I'd learnt to do when Meagan's anger bubbled over. Running only made her worse.

Slowly, my heart unclenched. The room stopped tilting, and settled into place.

Dr Wilder stared at me, his face pale and carved.

I saw him struggling to find a way back from anger to coolness – the distance he'd put between us with his rules. He flexed his hands, forcing his fingers loose from the fists they'd formed. I wanted to tell him it was all right, I understood. His anger made sense to me, perfect sense. I was even a little relieved to see it, it was so familiar to me.

'I made a mistake,' I said. 'I'll learn from it. It won't happen again.'

After a long moment, he nodded. He stood aside to let me leave the room, the blades of his shoulders against the door. We passed so close, I thought we'd touch. But he was too careful for that, standing very still with only the adrenal scent of his skin to give away what had happened.

I was afraid as I went ahead of him down the stairs, afraid he'd hear the triumphant hammering of my heart: *I was right I was right I was right.*

A woman lived here. *She* lived here. This was the house she and Joe had disappeared into that night. After the club where she stole him from under my nose, not knowing we were together, bound together by a secret so black its stain would never wash away.

Starling Villas was the house.

It happened here. *I was right.*

8

The Spar would be closing soon. Meagan should get going if she didn't want a supper of mouldy bread. The memory of Nell's fruit cake pricked the inside of her mouth with saliva. The little bitch could cook, whatever her other failings. She poked inside the fridge at nothing very much of anything at all. It was the Spar, or starve. She'd have to run the gamut of the town's attention but she was used to that. After the funeral, it felt as if all of Wales knew what'd happened at Lyle's.

She pulled on her coat and hat, dragging the door shut with the key in its lock to be sure it stayed closed. Good luck to any fool who thought to rob the place. The left sleeve of her coat was green from the wardrobe, stinking of damp. She lit a cigarette to get rid of the smell. Curtains twitched as she went up the road. What did they see? Just an ordinary woman at the wrong end of middle age, going about her business.

A pair of teenagers sat on the wall outside the Spar, kicking their feet, hands hunched in the pockets of their parkas. Summer had slunk away, almost overnight. *Good.* A day closer to settling her scores. The girl on the wall gave Meagan a vacant glare as she went into the shop, her boyfriend muttering, his elbow in the girl's ribs, the pair of them spoiling for a fight. The whole town was spoiling for a fight, a slag heap of disappointments held together by grudges. Pick at any part of it and the whole lot'd come sliding down to bury you. There were days when Meagan would've welcomed that, but she wanted them home with her first. Nell and Joe Peach.

Funny to think they fought like cats, the first time they met.

Joe hadn't been in Lyle's five minutes before he sat in Nell's space on the settee. One of the little ones went to him, climbing into his lap. Rosie Bond, it must've been, who was welded to Nell day and night. Joe didn't make a fuss, just lifted his arms out of his lap to make room for her, sitting with his console held over her head, his eyes on the game, but mistily, as if he wasn't serious about playing or winning. He was asking for it, and Nell told him so. Told him with her feet, and then with her fists.

In the Spar, Meagan added a bottle of cider to her shopping basket. After the pram in the park and the smashed china, she'd kept an eye on the girl, of course she had. But she'd failed to see it coming, even with the fight to flag it up, Nell flinging herself at Joe. She caught him off guard. He hadn't figured her for a threat. In a room of kids, it was the adult he watched out for, the man in the priciest suit or the woman in the tightest dress. He'd learnt to spot his predators, had Joe. Nell taught him a lesson that first day. Rosie slipped to the floor as they fought, her thumb in her mouth, watching every move they made. She wasn't frightened by the fight, it wasn't hurting her. Nothing phased Rosie, unless it was the loss (always temporary, thanks to Nell's sharp eyes) of her best bear.

When the village gathered to say their goodbyes, the wreath was white roses with blue forget-me-nots spelling out her name:

R-O-S-I-E. People brought toys and balloons, the way they do when a kiddie dies. That day, Nell hid her face in Joe's shoulder, the pair of them so tragic it was nearly comical. Meagan knew to nip it in the bud: 'Shape yourselves. People are watching.' The press and Social Services, Rosie's parents who'd caught the whiff of money coming off the scandal of her death. And Nell and Joe with their arms twisted together, all the long way home to Lyle's. You'd've taken them for newly-weds, never guessed they'd fought like cats before they were even introduced. Never guessed at the rest of it, either. Meagan saw to that: 'Shape yourselves, you two.'

No one broke up their battle, that first day. There was only Meagan and she'd enough on her plate. 'You like us to fight,' Joe accused her, weeks later. 'It keeps us busy. And it uses up our anger and energy, so there's none left for you.' He was smarter than he looked, Joe Peach.

'I'll put a stop to it when I see fit,' Meagan told him.

Fostering was a fool's errand. She hated kids and she hated Lyle's but she didn't stop there, hating the whole town. 'Pig's Knuckle, Arkansas', she called it. But she should've seen what was coming down the line. For Joe Peach and Nell Ballard, and their precious Rosie Bond.

That first day, after Rosie was put to bed, the pair of them took up camp in the bathroom. Nell showed Joe where the plasters were kept. She'd found a tin of antiseptic cream, smearing it onto his bruised cheek. Meagan stopped to watch, standing in the corridor with an unlit cigarette in her fingers. Neither of them noticed her, too wound up in one another. Joe sat on the side of the bath, his hands between his knees, chin tilted under the light. Nell stood on

SARAH HILARY

one foot, bare toes crooked around her calf as she concentrated on his face, treating the marks she'd left with her fists. When Joe shut his eyes, Nell's toes curled tighter.

Trouble, Meagan had thought. It'd stirred at her stomach. Nell Ballard and Joe Peach were going to be trouble. Six years Nell had been with her by that time. She'd settled into Lyle's so deeply it would've hurt Meagan to root her out; she counted on the girl for too much. Her idea, she'd thought, but now she wondered whether it hadn't been Nell's plan from the off. She was the one who kept it all ticking over, feeding those who wouldn't feed themselves, stockpiling ways to soothe the kiddies when they were fretful or sick. 'Cheaper than Calpol,' Meagan called her. She'd stopped Rosie Bond's tantrums, when nothing else would. Rosie was a chubby cherub with a talent for winding herself round whichever finger was your weakest. Tied Nell up in knots, she did. With Rosie in tow, Nell dug herself deeper into Lyle's. By the time Meagan noticed, it was too late. By the time Joe arrived, it was terminal.

'This isn't like other places,' Nell said as she smeared the cream onto the boy's bruised face. 'It might look the same, but it's not.'

Meagan stood outside the bathroom, listening to her telling him all the unwritten rules, how to navigate his new home. She didn't know Meagan was listening, or she didn't care. She'd recognized Joe, the way Joe recognized the men in expensive suits and women in tight dresses. Only Nell fancied she'd found an ally, not an enemy. He was sweet, was Joe, and soft. 'Soft lad,' Meagan called him.

'She's mean,' Nell told Joe as he sat on the side of the bath. 'And she hates us. But she needs me. You can make her need you, too.'

Joe held his hands between his knees, listening. He wasn't the only one. Meagan listened with her ears pricked, shivers running up and down her spine. Until that moment, she hadn't been sure how much Nell understood about Lyle's, and about her. But Nell understood all right, naming every one of Meagan's buttons, giving soft lad the inside track. Hard to forgive her for that.

When Joe asked why she stayed with Meagan, Nell told the story of the Egyptian plover and the crocodile. 'The Nile crocodile has a lot of teeth, and most of his food gets stuck in his teeth. When that happens, he sits very still in the water with his mouth wide open. The plover sees this invitation and flies down to clean the crocodile's teeth, making a meal of the trapped food.'

It was a story she'd read to Rosie, from a picture book. Joe listened in silence. Then he said, 'You're the plover bird, and Meagan's the crocodile. But who's the food?'

Nell put the lid on the tin of antiseptic cream, shutting it up in her fist.

Joe said, 'Is it Rosie?' He shifted his shoulders, wincing from her bruises.

He wouldn't make the same mistake twice, Meagan thought, letting the kiddie climb into his lap. But Rosie might. Rosie would. *Who's the food?*

'It's all of us.' Nell put the tin in the bathroom cupboard and turned to face Joe, seeing Meagan standing in the corridor. Her hands closed into fists, lips pressing together. 'Every one of us,' she told Joe, but her eyes were fixed on Meagan.

In the Spar: 'That everything, is it?' The woman on the till didn't bother looking up.

'And a packet of Silk Cut.'

Every one of us. Meagan had shuddered in spite of herself. She was not a religious woman but, *God help anyone*, she'd thought, *who comes between Nell Ballard and the thing she loves.*

Outside the Spar, the teenagers had moved on. A boy of about ten was hanging from the rail, grubby blond hair falling over his face, skinny jeans ratted at the knees. He fired a look at Meagan from brown eyes flecked with amber, like a tiger's. He wasn't a pretty boy, but something about him reminded her of Joe. She held out the packet of cigarettes, watching as he came upright towards her. The cellophane sizzled as he stripped it from the box. 'Take two,' she offered.

He did, handing back the box. 'Thanks.' His voice hadn't broken, thin as a girl's.

The cigarettes went into his pocket. For his mum? Meagan had hoped he'd smoke them, warm himself up a bit. If she'd had enough food, she'd have invited him home. She was lonely, and he looked the same. He needed a decent meal inside him, and a hot bath. She could make up a camp bed on the couch. But he'd never have come. Like the rest of the town, he knew to keep away from the flats at the end of the estate. She took her own cigarette from the packet, propping it between her lips.

He pointed at the sleeve of her coat, where the damp had done its worst. 'Green,' he said.

She snapped her lighter at the cigarette. Green was what her old ma had called newborns, or those who couldn't see which way the wind was blowing even when it was blowing a gale. 'Not me, sunshine. I was born with a full set of teeth.' She bared them, nodding her approval as he backed away. 'Born and raised.'

9

The next morning, autumn was touching its teeth to Starling Villas. The summer had lasted six weeks. A fortnight ago, Joe and I sat sunbathing on the Embankment, only shivering after it went dark. But even then the days had been getting shorter. Cigarettes weren't enough; it's why he went to the club to get warm, in the only way he knew how. We'd found places to stay when we first came to London after leaving Lyle's. For three months, we slept on strangers' sofas or in their beds, before we ended up on the streets. Joe blamed me for that, our hard landing. He hated London, that's what he said, the cold crouching in all the cracks. I told him it was the same everywhere. Sun turned to mist in a moment, especially by water. All summer long, our lake was green as glass but in the winter it was white, the hard months ahead showing in that first yawn of fog. 'Don't you remember?' I said. 'How Rosie thought it was smoke, that the lake was on fire?' But Joe didn't want to remember. He was sick, he said, of remembering.

In my attic bathroom at Starling Villas, I dressed in jeans and a long-sleeved T-shirt, fastening my hair away from my face. Rosie was like Joe, I remembered, hating the cold but refusing to wear a hat or gloves, saying they made her look lumpy. Her mum and dad had called her Doll and Princess, dressing her in designer clothes, piercing her ears while she was in nappies. Then they bored of her, because princesses shouldn't cry or shriek or bounce on your bed when you've a hangover. They gave their doll to Meagan Flack, or the social workers did. Rosie cried a lot at first, weeks of weeping before she crawled into my lap for a cuddle. It made Meagan laugh. 'Turned you into a proper little mum, hasn't she? Should've got her months ago, spared myself some trouble.' Meagan with her hard palms and quick fists. It filled me with rage, to remember. Long before the funeral she was telling me to move on – 'Plenty of others needing a cuddle. Pick one of them' – as if all the kids at Lyle's were the same and there was nothing to choose between us.

Dr Wilder was working in the library, head down over his papers. A lick of shaving foam sat behind his right ear, creamy against his neck. A wife would lean across and wet her finger, wipe the cream away. I set the plate of toast at his elbow, with a fresh press of coffee. His cardigan smelt of paraffin lamps, a safe-dangerous smell. At supper last night he'd said nothing of the silver gown, his anger like his work, tidied away for the day. I hadn't taken fright, and that puzzled him. As I laid his cup and saucer on the desk, his eyes were on me, wondering. If he'd asked, I'd have said it soothed me, his anger. But he didn't ask. He'd been working hard, emptying more boxes of their envelopes marked Private and Confidential. I missed his anger, locked away inside the puzzle of his loneliness. It made me want to wipe the shaving foam from his neck and rest my fingers on the pulse that beat there, to mark my place.

After breakfast, I searched under the stairs for a hard-bristled brush. I filled a bucket at the kitchen sink, adding disinfectant and hot water from the stove. The fat pigeon was on the window ledge but she clattered away when a plume of steam rose from the water.

Carrying the bucket to the hall, I knelt on the tiles with my back to the library, soaking the brush until the hot water hurt my hands. Pushing it at the floor felt primitive, Dickensian; where was my steam mop? But there was a pleasure to the labour, the scratch of the bristles, the slow staining of the water in the bucket. I worked towards the front door, thinking of the silver dress hanging in the wardrobe where I'd left it. I'd expected him to move it to a new hiding place, but he'd warned me well enough. He didn't understand – how could he? – that his anger was a comfort to me. Fear had been flitting just out of reach since I'd set foot inside Starling Villas. Yesterday, he'd let it in. I understood the house and him a little better now.

'How long until you've finished?' He was standing in the doorway to his library, holding his cup of coffee in its saucer, his face brisk with enquiry.

'The tiles?' I sat back on my heels. The cuffs of my T-shirt were wet, clinging. In the steam from the bucket, my hair curled loose from its ponytail. 'I can try to be done in forty minutes.'

He studied the length of the hall, from his feet to the front door. 'Forty minutes.'

'I can try.' I balanced both hands on the brush, leaning my weight into it. 'Is the noise disturbing you? Would you rather I started upstairs?'

'There's the kitchen.'

'I finished that on my first night. Before I went to bed.'

'And the shopping?'

'That too.' I lifted the back of my hand to wipe my hair from my eyes.

How much longer would he stand there with me kneeling at his feet, dripping dirty water? What did he want from me, really? I was so focused on what I wanted, it was easy to forget he too had a motive for letting me live here. I searched his face, finding nothing to help me. Dangerous to think I understood him because of his anger over a dress. Is this what his last slave died of – beating her fists against the rock face of his indifference, looking for a way in? I was tired. My back blazed, and my eyes. I wanted to lie down. To eat, and sleep. I wanted to finish scrubbing his floor.

'Forty minutes.' He nodded. 'Of course.'

Back in the kitchen, I caught sight of myself in the window above the sink, hollow-cheeked and dark-eyed. From the flat look on my face, I might have been born and raised in captivity, in this house. I turned away, taking a bottle of wine from the rack, slotting it into the fridge to chill.

A movement at the window brought my head back around.

The fat pigeon sat there, cocking her eye at me like Bradley in the cheese shop, 'You're new,' recognizing Dr Wilder's slave as clearly as if I wore a yoke and bridle.

In the afternoon, he vacated the library for the sitting room, allowing me an hour to dust the spines of his books, and to polish his desk with a block of beeswax. Each drawer in the desk had an ornate brass handle, a perfect excuse to linger. One drawer wasn't shut, so I opened it in order to smooth the passage for its runners. Another excuse. The drawer was full of papers; why did that not surprise me? A slim box rested on top, its lid loose. I took it from the drawer. Inside was a paintbrush and a black dish with a stone etched in Japanese characters. Another stone sat alongside, with a loop of blue thread fastened to it. A paperweight? I dredged the information from a recess in my brain, nights spent reading library books at Lyle's in defiance of Meagan's mockery. It was a calligraphy set. The ink stone silked black onto my fingers, smelling of soot and far-off places. I traced the characters on the paperweight with my fingertips, wondering what message they held. My chest was hot and tight. The box moved me, in a way I'd not anticipated. I repacked the stones in the drawer, not wanting to be caught red-handed a second time in as many days.

One of the envelopes marked Private and Confidential was sitting out on his desk. I slid my thumb along its broken seal, peeping inside, glimpsing a royal coat of arms and the word 'Court', before a sound in the hall made me jump.

I returned the envelope to its resting place, hurrying to finish the task of dusting his shelves. The boxes got in my way, nearly tripping me twice, as if they'd moved by themselves in the time it took to polish the brass handles on his desk.

Dr Wilder wasn't in the hall. The sound I'd heard was the post being delivered. I collected it from the mat. Another envelope, for his eyes only. *Dr R. Wilder JP*. I made a new promise to myself, to find out what was inside one of these envelopes. There was no such thing as useless information, Meagan Flack was right about that much.

As supper was cooking, I changed into my black dress, putting my hair up. I was coming back down the stairs when a key grated in the front door. It froze me, panic slipping up my spine.

Dr Wilder was in the library, bent over his books. Who then was on the other side of the door? The grating stopped then began again, as if a different key was being tried in the lock. I gripped the banister so hard it hurt my fingers, catching a flash of myself from above, standing at bay. Ready to run, my black dress clinging to my curves and the slim muscles in my thighs. Who was it? His old housekeeper, back to challenge me? Who else had a key, whom did he trust enough for that? I was the only one, surely. But I hadn't even been here a week. What did I know about him really, what did either of us know about the other?

Light shoved its way inside the house.

The woman that followed was small and neat, bright gold hair swinging above the collar of her black satin coat. Just as I remembered her from the nightclub, her cat's face looking satisfied and curious at once. In her early forties, but very well preserved. She wrested the key from the lock, the struggle showing in every line of her body. Dressed all in black, expensive, putting my Max Mara castoff in its place. Her coat was a piece of sculpture with its narrow waist and flared hips. Her hair moved as she did, a bell of hair, perfectly cut and coloured. High black heels, stockings. Some women find heels more comfortable than flat shoes; I hadn't believed that, until I'd seen her stealing Joe from me. She moved the same way now, effortlessly. Her face turned towards the light, showing her skin cool and smooth, eyes flickering as they found me on the stairs, blanking for a second before coming into sharp focus.

'You're here already!' Her voice was like her skin, creamy.

The silver satin gown belonged to her. I could see it clinging to her slim hips. I'd known, of course, as soon as I'd found it in his wardrobe. *I was right I was right I was right.* But even so, I was shocked. She scared me. I hadn't thought it would feel like this, seeing her face to face.

It's just me, now. In the Villas.

That's what he'd told me.

'Robin said you were starting this week.' She dropped her key into the bag she carried. 'I'm Carolyn.' Her smile ate me up. 'Carolyn Wilder. Robin's wife.'

10

The council estate was crawling with schoolkids. Not just teen-agers bunking off, little kiddies too. Meagan watched them from her window, weaving about on their bikes or standing in gangs, huddled around whoever had the smartest phone. They all wore the same black padded coats, whatever the weather, hair greased flat to their heads. One or two had the glassy look Joe Peach wore after the first wave of trouble died down, before Nell launched her final offensive. Meagan knew that look, how expensive it was. The kids on this estate were the same as Joe, needing a sniff or a smoke. Pills, if that was all that was on offer. She'd made sure to get herself a prescription for anxiety and another for insomnia; if the worst came, she could sell the tablets on the estate. Keep them from kicking in her windows, at any rate. Pills had kept Joe quiet, and plenty of others too.

'Doing your bit for community relations.' She lit a cigarette. The boy from the Spar who took her smokes – he was the one she'd sell to, if she got to choose. He had Joe's eyes, tiger's eyes.

On the estate, the huddle parted enough for her to see a yellow-haired tot in their midst, propped in a grimy pushchair. Someone's sister? Or daughter? Lots of the lads down there were old enough to have kids of their own. Odd not to see Granny in tow, often just a strip of a lass herself, looking bewildered by the speed at which her life was running through her fingers. The tot in the pushchair was sucking on a bottle of purple juice, rotting her teeth on her drug of choice. Where were Children's Services when they were needed? Poking their noses into foster homes, that's where, because it was easier than getting off their arses and doing any real work.

'What we don't understand, Mrs Flack,' wearing a pained expression, 'is how Rosie Bond came to be out on her own at that hour of the day.'

That's not all you don't understand, she'd thought at the time. *That's just the tip of the iceberg, love.* She'd fought to keep it that way, since the damage was already done.

No one took less pleasure in Rosie Bond's disappearance than Meagan Flack. She didn't bake cakes or make dresses but she knew how to keep kids safe, prided herself on it. Pride didn't come easily; she'd grown up with a man who thought it meant lowered voices and a raised hand. But there'd not been one teenage pregnancy under her roof. More than you could say for Felicity Barrow or Dilys Morgan. Kids came and went, but enough of them stayed. Like Joe would've stayed, if they hadn't shut her down. It began as a review, an inspection.

'Emergency inspection,' they said. 'Serious case review.'

She'd been vetted back at the beginning, so thoroughly they knew her knicker size and lavatory habits, and reviewed on a regular enough basis ever since. This was different, though. Because of what'd happened that summer, two years ago now. Because of Rosie.

The Bond Baby, Social Services called her when they first brought her to Lyle's. She came in screaming, a fat lump of a thing, red-faced, fists waving. It wasn't until she'd cried herself to sleep that you saw what a beauty she was. Golden and pink, well-named. Two years old but she ruled the house from the off, using her blue eyes to get what she wanted and when that didn't work, using her lungs. She'd a scream that could loosen your teeth. It was why her parents wanted shot of her after they'd ruined her with their fussing, dressing her like a gypsy bride. Some of it stuck, too. Rosie was forever climbing in front of mirrors with her lips pouted, admiring herself. 'Little madam,' Meagan called her.

Nell fell, badly. She'd always been good with the little ones. Most of them loved her and those that didn't, needed her. Nell needed to be needed. When Rosie climbed into her lap, patting at the girl's face the way she did at the mirrors, Nell would tell her how pretty she was and how special, how much she loved her. And Rosie would purr like a kitten. That's how it was, at the beginning.

Something about the Bond Baby had needled at Meagan from the off. The thorn under the rose, her old ma would've called it, pricking at her tough hide. She couldn't shake the memory of the pram in the park, *that* golden baby, and how Nell had looked at her. That fool of a father bouncing on his toes, demanding her approval even after he'd shut her out. Nell loved Rosie, no doubt about it, but love could twist you in knots. Love could turn you inside out, make you sick and selfish and vicious. Look at the kids who came to Lyle's. Look at Nell, thrown over by Florence Ballard for the new man in her life.

'Little madam kept me awake last night. What's she mithering about now?'

Nell was putting out cereal bowls for breakfast. 'Her teeth are hurting.'

'So're mine, after last night.' Meagan lit her cigarette. 'What?'

'Nothing.'

Nell hated her smoking in the house, but she had the measure of Meagan's mood. She fetched the cereal boxes from the cupboard. Rosie's highchair was at the head of the table next to Nell's place so she could feed Rosie while eating her own breakfast. Rosie's third birthday was coming up but she liked to be spoon-fed. Twelve-year-old Nell was baking a cake in the shape of a fairy castle.

'You're ruining her.' Meagan slitted her eyes. 'Making a rod for your own back.'

'She's little. She needs a lot of looking after.'

'Meaning what?' Meagan was spoiling for a fight. It took her that way after a sleepless night; the bruising tension in her jaw only knew one way out. 'That I'm not pulling my weight?'

Nell retreated to the other side of the table, taking her time with the spoons. She tucked her chin in, making herself smaller. Her hands shook slightly, spoons tapping together.

'Well?' Meagan demanded. Her palms itched to slap the girl.

'I just meant she's a baby. I like looking after her, it's no trouble.'

'Look at you! Up all night, late for school. I'll have Social on my back for that, you wait and see.' It rankled how the girl kept laying the table as if she could cope better than Meagan, as if she *was* better. 'I'm keeping an eye on the china, you know. I've not forgotten those smashed plates and that baby mug you broke into bits.'

Nell's hands faltered, her face flickering. She looked up at Meagan then away, eyes darkening, lips turning white.

Meagan should've stopped but the meanness was between her teeth, like a string of old meat. 'I've not forgotten that baby, any more than you have. She's like her, is Rosie. Could be her twin.' She curdled her mouth. 'I'm watching you, lady.'

'I'd never hurt Rosie.' Nell took a breath that sounded like a sob. 'I love her.'

'I saw you.' She flicked ash. 'Brushing her hair. That's what set her off, last night.'

'It – snagged in the brush.' Nell's eyes were black buttons in her face. 'She's got so much hair, it gets knotty. I was getting the knots out.'

Meagan snorted. 'You'll never get the knots out of that one. She's too greedy and ungrateful. She'll suck the life out of you, if you let her.'

Nell went to the fridge for a jug of milk. She set it on the table, keeping her fist around the handle. Meagan could see she wanted to throw her words back at her, about who was sucking the life out of who, around here. She didn't dare, though.

'She's a bottomless pit.' Meagan turned the cigarette in her fingers. 'Got you dancing to her tune with that bloody cake and its turrets and towers! You're a fool.' She tapped her foot on the tiles. 'I thought you were smarter.' Tougher, was what she meant. Nell had been a tough nut since the pram in the park. Rosie was making her soft. It'd do her no good in the long run. Kids like Nell needed to be tough to survive. 'She'll eat you alive, if you let her.'

'She's just a baby.' Nell released the jug's handle, stepping back to study the table.

Everything was in place, ready for the kids to come down and eat their breakfast before school. Princess Rosie in her throne, pouting for the next mouthful, and the next. Nell smoothed her hands at her school skirt until they stopped shaking.

'Babies grow up,' Meagan warned. 'I was a baby once.' She sucked at the cigarette. 'You need to shape yourself, lady. You're getting soft.'

Two years later, those words came round to bite her. When Joe turned up on her doorstep, and Nell fell head over heels all over again. They made an odd triangle, Nell and Rosie and Joe. Like a family with an absent father; Joe was never quite there. He needed Nell, like Rosie did. Needed her to make his bed and bring him blankets and squeeze the oranges his social worker left behind, handing him the juice in a tall glass. Of course he fell for her too. It was the fight that did it, those fists and feet on the first day. He fell in love with the girl who'd defend her patch at any cost. Joe needed a champion.

'God help anyone,' Meagan said, 'who comes between Nell Ballard and the thing she loves.'

On the estate, the kiddie in the pushchair had thrown her bottle on the ground. A growling came out of her, like a motor starting up. Meagan remembered that noise bouncing off the walls in Lyle's as Rosie worked herself up over nothing. She'd shout for Nell, 'Get yourself down here!'

Once Joe joined the house, it took Nell longer and longer to get herself down the stairs to deal with Rosie's tantrums. It was like the boy had flicked a switch inside her, turning her from a little mum back into an adolescent girl. 'I'm watching you two, lady!' Only she wasn't, not properly.

All she saw was Joe taking Nell's protection for granted, another one set to suck the life out of her. Rosie sensed the threat, plain as day. Four years old, and greedy with it. Whenever Nell had a pound to spend it was Rosie who got a bag of sweets or a bracelet. Joe didn't want presents (unless they came in pill bags) but he wanted Nell to himself. When the summer came, it was worse.

'Come to the lake, Nell. Please.' Turning those tiger's eyes on the girl.

That's when Rosie would suddenly develop a stomach ache. 'I want my mummy!' meaning Nell.

Joe hissed at the child. Meagan could smell the animosity in the house, like ammonia. Then Rosie changed tack, welding herself to Joe's leg instead of Nell's.

'I love you, Joe.' Pouting up at him. 'You're my daddy.'

After that, it was the three of them. A love triangle, you might call it. Meagan called it that, looking back. Knowing what she did about love, how it turned your guts into a tangle of greed and jealousy. Of course she couldn't use those words after Rosie disappeared, when the emergency review reared its head. She couldn't talk about the strange shape the three of them made, and how she'd failed to put a stop to it. But she snapped to attention soon enough, seeing how the review was going to do for her. No Nell to keep things ticking over. No Joe to smile and say how great Meagan was, how life at Lyle's had saved him. Because Joe was the problem. He was with Rosie when she went missing. Nell, too. Meagan couldn't tell the case workers that, could she? Leaving a six-year-old in the care of teenagers made her look worse than useless. So she covered for them, making it clear they were to cover for her in return. Scared out of their wits, the pair of them. Nell shaking, Joe spaced out like he'd taken something. Meagan searched the house every other day for anyone else's pills, or for knives – anything that might come back to bite her. Except she hadn't thought of death, had she? You couldn't search for that under pillows or in the backs of cupboards. Soon as she heard the police cars, she knew it was up. No more Lyle's, no more money. The best she could do was dodge charges. She'd covered for the pair of them, but it hadn't stopped that little bitch doing what she did.

On the estate, the kiddie was bawling in her pushchair. Tipping over, trying to reach her dropped bottle of juice, hand outstretched, fingers starfishing. None of the others took any notice, busy on their phones.

Watching her, Meagan remembered another kiddie from years ago. A girl she'd gone to school with who'd tripped on the pavement walking home, hit her head and died from it.

That's how easy it was to kill a kiddie.

You took your eyes off for a second, and it was all over.

11

Three of us now in Starling Villas.

Carolyn Wilder and her husband, and me. They were in the sitting room, where I'd been instructed not to disturb them. They'd go out, Carolyn said, for supper. I was to find a way to preserve the meal I'd cooked; surely it could be frozen for later in the week. Wasn't that why I was here, to make myself useful?

'I'm assuming you're resourceful.' The switch of a smile, a flash of her perfect teeth. 'Yes?'

It had taken her less than a minute to establish this new world order, as I'd stood frozen on the stairs. Crossing the hall, high heels tapping at the tiles I'd scrubbed, instructions reeling off like ticker tape in her wake: 'Freeze the supper, won't you? We're going out.' She only stopped speaking when she reached the library, opening the door and disappearing inside.

I waited for some sound from the room, his voice raised in anger, or surprise. Hers, cajoling. Nothing. I shivered, feeling the cold in the house, and in the city sprawled outside. London lies so still on the water, its long jaws open in invitation. You see its scraps, the promise of a meal. All the gaps and hollows, and people hiding, unknowable, in each one.

I'm Carolyn Wilder. Her scent stained the hall. *Robin's wife.*

The living couldn't touch me, that's what I'd told myself. Only ghosts could do that. Carolyn was what I'd been waiting for, the whole reason I was here. Stealing Joe from me, leaving me alone. I'd told myself I'd find Joe here and if I didn't, I'd take my revenge. On this house and the people inside it. So why wasn't I glad she was finally here in the house? I had what I'd wanted, and she had no idea who I was. I could get to work properly now.

It's just me, now. In the Villas.

I touched the red woven bracelet, remembering the warmth of Robin's wrist on mine. He'd been happy without her. With his rota, and me. Should she be allowed to ruin that, too?

From the kitchen windowsill, the pigeon watched me search the cupboards for a container to hold the meal I'd been ordered to freeze. Carolyn hadn't asked what it was, wrinkling her nose in the direction of the kitchen, deciding they'd dine out. I'd made ratatouille, nothing fancy, but it smelt good. I'd planned to warm a hunk of bread for him to soak up the sauce. I didn't think he'd mind getting his hands dirty because that's the kind of dish it is. Rosie called it red stew.

Pulling a plastic lidded bowl from the back of a cupboard, I banged it onto the counter by the sink. The pigeon took flight. When she spread her wings, I saw the soot inside. She'd looked white but she wasn't, London's dirt lining her feathers.

Carolyn Wilder. His wife. Her silver satin gown in the wardrobe, perfume lingering in its folds. Lime, with a twinge to it like artificial sweetener. Her scent, I knew now. Tomorrow, his bed would smell the same, its pillows indented, sheets ratted. Did Joe smell of her? Or had he been a one-night stand, soon forgotten? Sitting on her high stool at the bar in her black satin coat, naked underneath. I'd seen their heads together, hers and Joe's. What had she promised when she whispered in his ear? I'd been telling myself it was drugs or money, but maybe he liked the way she looked, her lime scent, her cool creaminess. Robin must have liked it, too. He'd married her, even if they no longer lived together.

Leaving the ratatouille to cool on the stove, I rinsed the lidded bowl. Sweat sat in the armpits of my black dress. I'd planned to warm a hunk of bread for myself, a rough crust to wipe around the casserole dish after I'd served his helping. The zest of lemon had been on my tongue all afternoon, appeasing my hunger with the promise of this treat to come. I should eat it, the whole casserole dish of it, while they were dining out. Let Robin come home to find me curled over his kitchen table with two hunks of his bread in my fists, red juice running down my chin.

The library door stayed shut.

I climbed the stairs to his bedroom, armed with white vinegar and a fistful of newspaper. The room looked the same, his bed as I'd left it, tightly made. Facing the mirror, I saw a dark figure with her hand a crumpled grey fist, her lovely neck knotted with distress. I sprayed the vinegar, watching her face run down the glass in wet white streaks. The newspaper smelt ashy. I bunched it in my fingers, pushing it at the mess where my face should have been. My breath was coming in hisses, damp against the glass. I took a step back, pressing my lips together to keep the noise inside, my chest tight with tears. I wanted to smash the mirror and crawl inside, to hide. I wanted Joe. He was the reason I was here, the reason I was trapped.

He'd left me alone in the club, following Carolyn as if he'd known her all his life. He had, in a way. Or women like her. All his life.

Darkness fell into the mirror, dimpling there in a hot little bubble.

Carolyn was standing at the foot of her husband's bed. She moved, and our eyes met in the bruised surface of the old glass. 'Oh . . . !' She laughed. 'Now I see what Robin means.'

'Robin?'

'Dr Wilder. Your employer.' She came closer. 'My husband.'

In her heels, she was taller than I was, and slimmer, her face symmetrical in that classical way we're taught to call true beauty. Her eyes were a cat's, though. Yellow-green like her scent, and just as narrow. We stood shoulder to shoulder, two women dressed in black, as different as could be. One tall and golden, made of symmetry. The other dark, her eyes evasive. Next to Carolyn, I felt crude and clumsy. Her grey dress, cinched at her waist, whispered against her skin. Like her coat, the dress was all about how naked she was underneath. She'd retouched her make-up, her lips newly red. She watched my face for a second then dropped her stare to my hands holding the bottle of vinegar and scrunched-up sheet of newspaper. Her own hands were empty but she didn't need a weapon, with her eyes like knives.

'Well, get on with your work. It's what you're paid for.'

A stab at the end of the sentence, as if the full stop were a drawing pin.

Before we were homeless, in those first three months after leaving Lyle's and coming to London, we'd lived for a while with a man called Brian. We met him in the Shunt Lounge, where Joe and I went often. One night, Brian hired a masseuse to come to his house. She wore acrylic nails, each press of her fingers punctuated by a crescent of pain. Carolyn's stabbing sentences reminded me of that woman's fingers, her sharp acrylic nails.

I turned back to the mirror but I must have been at the exact spot where the flaw lay, because I wasn't there. There was only Carolyn in an empty room, with her eyes on me.

After supper, they went to the garden room to drink champagne.

Carolyn had brought a bottle back from the restaurant, ordering me to find an ice bucket. There was no such bucket in the house. I explained this, as simply as I could. She stood and listened and then she said, 'You really are hopeless, aren't you?'

'Perhaps they sell ice in the newsagent's?'

'Oh, never mind, we'll just have to finish the bottle before it loses its chill.' She wrung the champagne bottle by its gilded neck. 'Can you at least find a pair of flutes?'

Dr Wilder used two kinds of glasses, one for water, another for wine. Both were kept in the kitchen cupboard, but neither was a flute.

'For goodness' sake, there must be some purpose to you. Champagne flutes.' She sketched the shape with her free hand. 'You can manage that, surely.'

I found what she wanted in a cabinet in the drawing room. I washed and rinsed the flutes before carrying them on a tray to the garden room where Carolyn made an acidic joke about warm glass and cold champagne. Dr Wilder didn't look at me. He wore a suit of dark flannel over a white shirt and crimson tie. He looked very handsome, and unhappy. Lonelier than I'd ever seen him look.

I wanted to bring him a mug of warm milk, but she was busy filling the flutes with champagne.

My attic was warmer than the garden room.

I closed the door and changed into leggings and a T-shirt before sweeping the newspapers from the rug. I'd brought the soft-bristled brush with me. My neck ached with the work I'd done in the house but I was wound too tight for sleep. Kneeling, I brushed at the rug, taking the soot and dust from its silk, working a small section at a time, raising the pile until its colours glowed.

The light was going from the sky, the ceiling bulb stingy. I worked in a swill of light but it was enough, my fingers knowing when the silk was clean by its heat under my hand. The sound of brushing soothed me, rhythmic, raising the smell of chimneys and woodsmoke so that while I worked I was able to imagine the mountains rising up around me.

When at last I straightened and stood, the moon was watching me, waiting. I opened the window to see street lights pitching their slew of colour into the road. Traffic hushed either side of Starling Villas, the scent of petrol strong enough to taste. Was Robin awake to taste it? Was he watching the moon, the way it bloomed like a flower in the night sky? No, he was with her, tasting champagne and *her* . . .

Forcing the window wide, I leaned out, remembering the way the moon hung over the lake that night, two years ago. The night I stayed, the day Rosie disappeared. Afraid to leave her alone, out of my mind with fear. It'd filled every inch of me, curling my toes and squeezing shut my eyes, its black fur thick in my throat. No one could help me, not even Joe. The lake was like tar, sucking at my feet.

In Starling Villas, I fell asleep with my cheek pressed to a clean corner of the rug, the soft-bristled brush tucked like a child's toy under my chin until dawn came, chilling me awake.

For a long time I didn't move, watching as the sky grew stronger, seeing more and more of the attic as the day asserted itself. I knew what I must do. Where I'd found myself, and how to fix the problem of Carolyn Wilder. As if last night's industry had emptied my skull of everything but the solution, as clear-cut as the diamonds she wore on her fingers and in the soft pink lobes of her ears.

12

'Do your shopping, missus?' No one ever knocked on Meagan's door. Yet here he was, bold as brass, fixing his ten-year-old tiger's eyes on her face. 'I do hers.' Nodding in the direction of Meagan's neighbour. 'She pays me two quid.'

'Do I look like a charity?' She'd not slept well, plagued by dreams about Nell, about stones and broken china coming through her windows. 'Clear off.'

'Do yours for fags.' He cocked his head at her. 'Paid me for nothing, last time.'

Another good deed coming back to bite her. She bared her teeth at the boy. 'Clear off before I call the police.'

'Had enough of the police, you have. And anyway, they won't come out here. Can't be arsed, can they?'

She tried to stare him down. When that didn't work, she said, 'Does your mum know you're bothering respectable people when you should be in school?'

'What respectable people? Not you.'

'Know all about me, do you?'

'Know you killed that kiddie. Everyone says so.'

'Everyone's wrong.' But she opened the door, wide. 'Come on in, then. Since you're not scared of the kiddie killer.'

He hesitated, long enough to let her know he believed the gossip. In his padded coat he looked half-starved, smelling of gutters. But he swaggered in, hands in pockets, eyes all over the place, making up the stories he'd tell his mates about being in the killer's flat.

Meagan took him to the kitchen and gave him a packet of biscuits and a glass of milk, because she could be like that when the mood took her. Even after Little Nell's best efforts to make her into a monster. 'What's your name, then?'

'Darrell.' Mouth full of biscuit. 'You ran a home. What's that like?'

Meagan lit a cigarette. 'Better food than your mum cooks by the look of you.'

'Fuck off talking about my mum.' He drained the glass of milk, wearing a white moustache. 'For real, though. What's it like?'

'Nothing special.' She shrugged smoke across her shoulder.

Strange to have someone in the flat with her, after all this time. Stranger still that it should be a child. She was telling the truth for what it was worth – Lyle's was nothing special, just another big red lump of a house with no central heating, top to bottom hard work. Filthy, no matter how much you cleaned it. Cold, no matter how many jumpers you put on. The kids always hungry, always missing their mums, even the mums who'd battered them. Crying and mizzling, catching every germ going. She wasn't paid nearly enough for the work. Stood to reason she needed help from the likes of Nell and Joe, not that Joe was ever much use on his own. Social Services sticking their oar in, every few months. Police, Meagan could handle. She'd grown up with them. Social were one long moan, from their home perms to their sandalled feet, prying and preaching, poking their noses, muttering about soft play and art therapy. Soon's she saw that perky Fiat 500 parked up outside, she'd shout for Joe: 'Get your arse and eyelashes down here, that cow's incoming!'

No point pretending life wouldn't be tough when it was already tough, that's how they'd landed up with Meagan. She'd fostered over eighty kids before it got on top of her, after the trouble with Rosie Bond. No coming back from that. She'd tried, because God knows they needed her. Lyle's was the back of beyond but there were always kids in need of a home. It wasn't just cities or towns that made a mess of families, it was slag-heap villages like Pig's Knuckle Arkansas, the fag end of an old mining community. Hard winters that kicked your windows for six, trains bringing tourists five weeks of the year. Londoners mostly, kidding themselves they were getting away from it all, having a big adventure. Until they discovered how hard it was to cook authentic rye bread with Calor gas, and that septic tanks took exception to a diet of kale and quinoa. She watched them come, shiny-eyed and patronizing, and she watched them go, loading their camper vans with recycling bins and the wetsuits they'd bought for their kiddies to swim in that bloody lake which was an expensive joke – a dirty green pool that should've been sealed off years ago. Deep enough to drown in, riddled with caves to carry you out to sea, and all a stone's throw from Lyle's.

'Stay away from that bloody pool!'

How many times had she shouted that at Nell and Joe? They never listened, too in love with the place. Hiding towels under their clothes, pretending they were going to catch the bus to the beach, but Meagan always knew. They came home damp, smelling of clean coins. She watched from the window as they trailed up the path, heads together. Saw the way they held one another, feet moving in step, like one kid not two. A flash of light from inside the house – Rosie's bobbles bouncing in her hair as she raced to greet them. Nell reaching to scoop her up, Joe petting Rosie's cheek. The three of them clinging together, wet towels dragging in the dust, the kiddie's head buried beneath their chins. Seeing it, a shiver moved up Meagan's spine. Nothing to do with the stubborn chill in the house. Fear, for the three of them. Their closeness, that selfish happiness like a kite flown too high to come down. You couldn't survive on closeness. As for happiness, it was just another way of getting your fingers burnt. The three of them so tight together, the smell of the pool getting into Rosie's hair, her dress damp from their T-shirts. Scowling, 'Take me next time!' Kicking at the pair of them with her sandalled feet. 'Take me or I'll tell!'

'Give us one of those then.' The boy, Darrell, reached for her cigarettes.

She passed them across the table. It was nice to have company for a change, someone who wasn't scared of her, or not enough for it to get in the way of his hunger or his curiosity. He had Joe's eyes. But this boy was a lot sharper, she could see that. Give him time. All the boys she'd ever known turned to mush as soon as they fell in love. And Joe hadn't been the brightest brick in the bucket even before Nell got to work on him.

All that summer, two years ago now, black rot had sat on Lyle's windowsills. No matter how hot it got, those windows let you know it'd be winter soon enough. Burst pipes, fights over breakfast and extra blankets. Nell and Joe thought the summer would last forever, that they could sneak off to their bloody pool whenever they wanted and never find it frozen over, a pit of cold that'd suck the heat from your bones and spit it back in bubbles.

'Take me next time!' Rosie kicking at the pair of them. 'Take me or I'll tell!'

Nell and Joe with their arms wrapped round her, the sea off somewhere behind, its tides tugging at the beach. When winter came, it'd be chucking waves over the railings onto the prom, rusting the hubcaps of cars.

Back at the beginning, Meagan thought Nell was like the sea. Wild and choppy but you could learn its tides, chart its patterns. That summer, she'd started to see the girl was more like their precious pool. Deep and treacherous, full of caves where currents flowed to an ancient rhythm, stealing through the spaces in the stone, taking fish and rocks and anything lost, sucking it into a place no one could ever follow or find.

Meagan wouldn't have minded, but for Joe.

All those years of not caring tuppence for any of the kiddies they landed on her, but he was different. Got under her skin, did Joe. She missed him when he ran from Lyle's, missed him like he was part of her. She'd broken a toe, years ago it was now. But she felt the weather in that toe before any breath of wind or rain on the way. It surprised her, feeling the same pain over Joe. Kids had come and gone from Lyle's, dozens of them, and never so much as a twinge. With Joe it was like he was her blood. And he picked Nell over her, that's how it felt. Even though Nell wasn't the one keeping his secrets, the shoplifting and the rest of it. It was Meagan he'd to thank, for everything. That little bitch stole him away, after Rosie's funeral. Upped and went in the night, leaving Meagan to face the music all over again. Stories in the press, stones through the windows. It was Nell's doing – to keep Meagan too busy to hunt them down. Not just busy either. *Ruined*. No Lyle's, no livelihood. A hole inside her like a missing tooth where Joe'd been. She'd missed Nell too in those first few weeks, with all the work to be done in the house and kiddies crying, the sound of it jagging on and on until Social Services came to take them away. Then she was left alone, cursing the girl who'd arrived on her doorstep all those years ago. Little Nell handed to her like a stick of dynamite and she took it, old fool that she was, and nothing was ever the same again.

'D'you do it, then?' Darrell smoked like a woman, his thin fingers fussing at the cigarette. 'That kiddie.'

Meagan was choosing her answer when she heard the phone ringing. Not the one on the wall. The pay-as-you-go phone, in her handbag. Only one person had that number.

'About bloody time.' She heaved herself to her feet, leaving Darrell at the table.

He watched her as she dug the phone from the bag, answering the call.

'Well?' she demanded. 'What've you got to say for yourself?'

'I'm sorry,' Joe Peach said. 'Can I come home?'

13

Hungry's was my lookout post in the days after Carolyn came home, where I retreated with enough money in my pocket for a cream cheese sandwich and a cup of tea as I sat watching the house, waiting for her to arrive. There was work to do in Starling Villas, but I carved out this free time because I needed to think about how I was going to deal with Carolyn.

She was an infrequent visitor in those first few days, always managing to take me by surprise. I hoped to learn her habits and routine, but she didn't make it easy. Most mornings it was Robin I watched in the hours between breakfast and lunch, his shadow at the library windows, or anchored to his desk. His loneliness had a colour, pebble-grey. I'd have watched him all day if I could. How his cheek thinned as he was thinking, the whiteness at the edge of his mouth, the slope of his left shoulder when he wrote. She'd laughed at his boxes, pushing them aside with the pointed toe of her shoe. Whose bed had she used the night she took Joe home with her? Not Robin's, unless it was revenge. I understood revenge, better than I understood her.

I ate my sandwich slowly. The bread was fresh, butter melting into the cream cheese, but I was too distracted to enjoy it. As I finished, Hungry's proprietor collected my empty plate, returning with a wedge of lemon meringue pie topped by a swirl of cream.

'For our regulars.' He smiled.

'Thank you.' I was touched to tears by his kindness.

The pie was perfect, its pastry thin and sweet with sugar. When my fork met the cream, it collapsed in a cloud of air. I shut my eyes to savour the lemon's tartness. Rosie loved lemon puddings, said they made her teeth shout. Red stew, and yellow pudding – made with condensed milk and three whole lemons. Meagan couldn't touch it. She'd a sweet tooth, she said. If that was true, it was the only sweet thing about her.

'Yellow pudding!' Rosie would wrap herself around my legs as I carried it to the table.

Joe liked it too. I hadn't known he had a sweet tooth until I caught him cleaning the tin, sucking condensed milk from his thumb. It made me giddy, watching him. I was fourteen then, and he was only a year older.

In Hungry's, the menu said, 'Lemon Meringue Pie', but it was better than that. It was sunshine and summer and sweet, sweet sadness. I savoured it, watching the house, for her.

It's just me, now. In the Villas.

Robin had lied to me, betraying my trust. But when I tried to retrieve my earlier anger towards him, I could only find this ache under my ribs. Hadn't I lied, too? My presence in his house was a trick made possible by the lies I'd told about him to the girl I'd accosted in this diner. Carolyn, not Robin, was my enemy. She no longer lived in Starling Villas. The guest room was impersonal, its wardrobes empty. Why did she keep coming back? To torment

Robin, or to be close to him again? What unfinished business was there between them? Robin could have changed the locks, turned her out. Everything else in his life was so neatly nailed down. Why did he tolerate her trespass? And Joe's, too.

I'd failed to find any trace of Joe in Starling Villas but he'd left the club with Carolyn – where else could he have gone? Did Robin meet him that night, or was he absent from the house? He did on occasion leave Starling Villas, according to his rota. Perhaps that's why Carolyn chose that night, knowing she and Joe would have the house to themselves.

I licked lemon from the corner of my mouth, collecting pastry crumbs with my fork, one after another. I'd been wrong about Robin's bed. She hadn't slept in it the night she came home. What then did he get from her visits? Nostalgia? He smelt strange after she'd been in the house, but I didn't think it was arousal.

I paid for my sandwich before making my way back to Starling Villas.

The traffic wasn't hard to navigate if you knew its crossing points, the lulls created by lights further up the road. I walked between the cars and lorries, unharmed.

As soon as I entered the house, I smelt her. *Carolyn*. She'd slipped under my defences, as she kept slipping under his. The free pie soured on my tongue as I realized it was during that brief moment of pleasure she'd evaded my watch.

On the hall table, she'd dumped lilies wrapped in sodden paper. She'd brought them for me, not as a gift but a chore. I'd have to hunt down a vase, wipe up the water, trim the stalks and arrange the buds. The lilies were her way of putting me in my place. Had she played the same spiteful tricks on his last housekeeper – wearing her down, driving her out? What did Joe see in her? Only Meagan was worse. But he'd loved Meagan, I remembered. I'd had to fight to get him away from her.

Carolyn was in the library. I caught the pitch of her voice stabbing at the stillness in the house. I pictured Robin with his thumb marking his place in the book he was studying, a crease of concentration on his face, waiting for her to go so he could have his routine back. The rota with its pages so firmly bound – was it his defence against her, or the reason she'd left? Because of his rules, which allowed no space for spontaneity or risk. Risk was overrated, I wanted to tell her. Real risk wasn't worth it. She was playing a game, poking her perfect fingers at his life to see what would stir. Some people are addicted to making a mess. Order scares them, and they have to subvert it. For some people, chaos is a form of comfort.

'I need a rubber bath plug, please. The cheapest you have.'

The plug was my excuse for staying out of the house. I couldn't settle in Starling Villas while she was there. The hardware shop was the other side of the park, smelling of creosote and tar and rubber. The smell of summer. My skin rippled with remembered pleasure. I lingered on my way out of the shop, breathing Joe's name, my tongue touching the roof of my mouth.

Three summers ago, the weather had been perfect. The sea giving back a glossy sky, the sun's heat heavy on our heads. Joe had a job working on the boats in the harbour. He was fifteen, only a year older than me, but it meant he could get a job. I ducked my chores at Lyle's to watch him work, not caring about the punishments Meagan served up. He moved so smoothly between the deck and rigging, tying sailcloth and hitching rope without making a single mistake. He had a way of moving on a boat that made the sea look like solid ground. A different Joe to the one I'd known all winter, his tiredness and clumsiness gone, as if he'd outgrown it. He fitted in his own skin, now. We both did. Watching him made my blood run fast. Salt spiked his hair and spangled in his lashes, his skin golden, the whites of his eyes so bright they looked luminous. He loved working on the boats. He was horny, he said, the whole time. 'It's the heat.' Kissing me, hungry. 'And the sea.'

It was both of us, and the summer – so much skin on show. It was the way he lifted his face to the sun, the way he *shone*. I could taste him just by looking. Salt burnt my lips when I sucked the thin skin below his collarbone. It was the sea air, and being young. We were invincibly happy, so happy people started to notice. Out on the boats, and in the harbour. I still remembered the first day I knew we were being watched.

Joe was sanding old paintwork and I was sitting on the harbour wall with his lunch in the shade at my feet. The man's stare was like fingers in the small of my back. I didn't turn, not right away. Instead I let my hair loose, combing it into a ponytail with my fingers. When I looked, he was gone. It was a trick of the light or the dazzle from the water, but he was there one second and gone the next. I blinked at the wall where he'd been standing, knowing what I'd seen. A man with fair hair, tall and nearly as tanned as Joe. He'd looked like Joe. But everyone did, that summer. Everyone *was* Joe. Everyone and everything. When I woke from dreams of Joe, the day was Joe-shaped. At breakfast, the toast was the colour of his skin, our feet touching under the table. I washed his clothes separately to the others', lingering over them, wringing water with my hands before pulling his shirts into shape for the washing line. At bedtime, the stories I read to Rosie were of knights with Joe's eyes or sailors with his sun-bleached hair. Even her warm milk and cake were somehow Joe-shaped, Joe-scented. The man by the harbour wall was an older, tougher Joe. It was weeks before I would learn he was the one who first sold drugs to Joe. Down from Chester for the day, looking to hire a boat, throwing in the pill bag as an afterthought. I hadn't minded his stare on my skin, it had excited me. The sun and the sensation of being watched, the man's red shadow on the inside of my eyelids. I felt powerful, in control. All summer long, people stared at us. Some days it was Joe who attracted the attention and some days it was me, but mostly it was the pair of us, together. Our love, I'd thought, like a bat signal shouting at the whole world. Pheromones, I knew now. But what is love if not pheromones? Spicing our blood, making us reckless, stupid.

At the end of each day, I walked home in a fever of happiness. Joe idled barefoot at my side, boat shoes hanging from his crooked thumbs until we reached the turning where the path was pebbled. Sand gritted between my toes, sending little shivers of sensation up the backs of my legs. Sometimes we sat at the flat stone that passed for a seat, where Joe liked to smoke a cigarette. He stole them from Meagan, or she let him take them. She had a soft spot, a blind spot, for Joe. She would slip him cigarettes and later, pills. To keep him quiet, she said. Like the Calpol she slipped to the little ones when they had toothache, or when *she* did and needed her sleep. I didn't mind the cigarettes because it was an excuse to look at Joe's mouth and hands, his forearms newly roped with muscle from the boats. He moved his back to the breeze, flinting the plastic lighter. To shield the flame, I cupped my hands around his. He shut an eye against the smoke, thumbs stroking my fingers. 'Close your eyes.' I did. 'I made you a present.'

He knotted a red bracelet about my wrist. 'Now you're mine.' He showed me the matching bracelet around his own wrist: 'And I'm yours.' He was so intense, so serious. It scared me a bit.

He held the cigarette smoke in his mouth. Soon I'd taste it, the smoke and Joe's tongue. He tapped ash at his feet, leaning forward. I watched the loose shape of his fingers, wanting them on my neck, under my vest, inside my shorts. A blue crescent of sweat darkened the back of his T-shirt between his shoulder blades. Looking at it made me thirsty. I reached to touch the bare skin at the base of his neck. 'Paint,' showing Joe my thumb. 'You should get clean.'

He squinted down at his shirt. 'Shit.' He should've worn an old shirt, or taken it off.

Meagan's rules and her wrath seemed very far away, miles and miles from the cliff path. My thumb burnt where I'd touched him. I'd only wanted to touch, I hadn't meant to worry him.

'Better not let Rosie see.' He rubbed at the paint stain on his hem. 'She'll tell Meagan.'

'She won't.'

'You know she will.' He shot me a look. 'She's always doing it.'

I didn't defend Rosie again. Joe was right: she was jealous of the time we spent together and it made her mean. Telling tales was the only revenge she knew.

'Come on.' I stood, pulling Joe with me. 'Let's go to the boathouse.'

The boathouse was padlocked, but Joe had a key. He said the man he worked for hated getting up early so he'd asked Joe to be the one to open up in the morning. I suspected Joe stole the key but it didn't matter, because being inside the boathouse was the best thing that'd ever happened to me. It was made of slatted wood with a felted roof like a garden shed. It bolted shut on the inside where the only light was the sun spearing through the slats. Inside, it smelt of wetsuits and buckets and spades, paint and tar and bitumen. The best smell in the world. I took a big gulp of it as Joe put a hand under my elbow and pulled me close enough to kiss.

'Nell. Nell . . .' Breathing my name into my neck, into my mouth.

A scorched taste from the cigarettes, but it was Joe's taste. I licked it from the underside of his lip, then sucked it from his tongue. He let go of my elbow and put both hands on me, on my neck and shoulders and my breasts before pushing a hand into my hair, tipping my mouth to more of the kiss, fingers teasing at the waistband of my shorts. The waistband was loose, shaped to the width of his palm. He could fit his hand inside, easily. If I sucked in the curve of my stomach, his fingers would slide inside. My mouth was wet from the kiss, tender at its edges, fiery as sunburn. I could feel the grit of sand between my toes, a separate sensation to all the others. I'd shut my eyes when he started kissing me but I opened them now to see the blunt head of a hammer hanging from the slatted wood, part of a rack of tools – spanners, screwdrivers, saws, a rubber-necked torch.

The wall was dry, dusty under my fingers. I propped my hands behind me in case I touched too much of him, too soon. I didn't want this to be over, never wanted to go back to Lyle's or Meagan or even Rosie who would tell on us, I knew. Anyone who saw what we were doing would tell.

Joe was licking my neck, teeth sharp under the softness of his lips. His mouth moved lower, the paint smell in his hair making me rub my face there. A splinter from the wall found my thumb and I flinched, making Joe lift his head to look at me. I worked my hand up between our bodies and he lifted it to his mouth, sucking the splinter from my thumb, using his tongue and teeth to draw it free before spitting it sideways from his mouth. Sweat wet the small of my back. I wanted him worse than I'd wanted anything in my life. When he knelt, everything fizzed and danced, the sun striping the back of his neck and the backs of my hands holding him there. The heat was going out of the day. It would break up soon, light lifting a bar at a time from our skin until there was nothing but darkness and the throb of Joe's pulse against mine.

A taxi honked its horn, traffic trailing the road in front of Starling Villas.

Was that how it was with Carolyn, that night? Darkness and the throb of them, together. No, because that Joe was gone, long before she picked him up in the club where he was selling himself for drugs, trying to stay warm the only way he knew how, and maybe it was the same for her, the only way she knew, but that didn't mean I wouldn't make her pay in any way I could.

Someone had to pay. Why not her?

Back inside the house, her scent was muted. The library door was shut. She'd gone again. Had she?

I climbed the stairs to Robin's bedroom, taking a handful of newspaper as an excuse. His mirror looked back at me, indifferently. If I took a hammer and hit it, again and again until my shoulder burnt and blood ran down my cheeks from flying shards of glass, my wages couldn't begin to cover it. Seven years' bad luck, just for starters.

Shutting the door behind me, I stood beside his bed.

A week ago, his bedroom door had creaked, like all those in the house. I'd rubbed petroleum jelly into the hinges, a cure-all learnt to silence the doors in Lyle's – the quieter the doors, the more often I could sneak out to watch Joe working on the boats. It was how we were able to leave the house unheard that day two summers ago, the day that changed everything.

In Starling Villas, the door to the sitting room was the worst offender, until I'd treated its hinges. My second favourite room in the house, its windows hung with rose linen curtains, floorboards softened by matting, a deep planter in its empty fireplace, filled with pink and cream hydrangeas. Carolyn stayed out of the sitting room, declaring it too cold and dull, but I knew the real reason. Under its pendant lamp, her blonde hair showed its brassy highlights. The matting trapped the high heels of her shoes, making her stumble like an old woman. I'd seen her consulting the mirrors in Starling Villas, one after another. But she wasn't here any longer, didn't she know that? She'd left and she couldn't come back, I wouldn't let her. I'd chase her from this house if I had to.

'You're not here any longer,' I whispered. 'It's only me in the mirrors now.'

I bent to smooth Robin's bedsheets, tucking them tighter than usual around the mattress, my palms chasing away the night's creases. It was my morning routine, and my proof he slept alone. Without her. Pushing my hands deep under the mattress, my fingers caught on something snagging there. I tugged it free, seeing a slim red ribbon fall from the sheet. No, not a ribbon.

I reached down, knowing what it was before my fingers closed on its familiar knots, before my eyes had time to relay the information to my brain.

A red woven bracelet. Joe's bracelet.

I wore its twin around my own wrist. We'd sworn we'd never take them off. Joe's bracelet was knotted, not cut. It must have come loose, worked itself free from his wrist while he was—

'There you are.'

Carolyn Wilder was standing in the doorway, watching me. No warning creak from the door, since I'd silenced it so effectively. She moved until her reflection was in the mirror, two of her, mocking me with their smiles. 'What've you found?' Her eyes went to my hand.

I hid Joe's bracelet behind my back, a childish reaction but I couldn't help myself. I didn't want her seeing what I'd found in the sheets of Robin's bed. She'd probably put the bracelet there herself. Or else they'd used this bed that night, she and Joe. Robin didn't know. He mustn't know.

'Haven't you worked it out yet?' She turned to admire her reflection, sleeking her hands at her hips. 'And to think he imagines you're intelligent.' She pouted, touching the tips of her fingers to the arch of her mouth. 'He likes you to be intelligent, for whatever reason. The girls he brings here.'

She twisted to face me. 'Well, it was his turn. I'd had my fun, and without his scruples. My boy didn't have any brains to speak of.' She gave a narrow smile. 'I expect you've found his bracelet in the bed. He was upset about it when we were saying goodbye, upset he'd lost it. I couldn't see it mattered, a cheap thing like that, but he was attached to it.'

'Dr Wilder didn't bring me here.' I felt punched, out of breath. 'That wasn't him.'

'True, he said you sprang yourself on him. But you came about the job advert.' She took a step nearer to the bed. 'Another of his scruples. He can't just pick you up in bars. I expect it's the magistrate in him – you do know he's a magistrate? – needing to play by a set of rules. Well, you've seen his rota.' Her eyes pinned me in place. 'You're not his type, either. He likes them blonde, as a rule.' The repetition of *rule* made her laugh. 'Men are peculiar, don't you find? I expect that's why I prefer boys.'

Joe, she meant. My Joe. And *my* Robin. I wanted to run at her and scratch the smile from her face. My head was beating so blackly, I feared I'd pass out.

'It's what we do.' Her voice was bored but her eyes were alert, watching for my pain. 'Robin and I. We take turns bringing you back here. You're his latest, although he seems to be struggling to move past the scullery maid fantasy to the real reason you're here.'

'You're lying.' My tongue was furred, thick in my mouth. 'He doesn't – that's not why I'm here.'

'So much for his theory about your intelligence.' She took another step, smiling. 'You really haven't figured it out, have you? You didn't see anything odd about him letting you walk in here and demand a room for yourself. Or were you planning to seduce him?' She put her head on one side, sizing me up with her stare. 'You're up to something, I thought that the first time I saw you.'

'I'm here to clean, and cook. He has work to do, the boxes—'

'Have you looked in the boxes?' She was close enough now to put her hand on his bed, crimson fingertips grazing the white covers. 'You should.'

'It's none of my business.' My hand was sticky around Joe's bracelet, my fingers closed so tight the knots bruised my palm. 'I'm here to cook, and to clean.'

'You're here because he chose to let you stay. He does that sometimes. When he's playing at being the master of the house.' She flicked her fingers at his bed, dismissively. 'A boring game, it's why I left. But it always ends the same way . . . He's waiting for me to help him finish it.' Her eyes were on mine, glittering. 'You liked my dress, he said. The silver one.'

I felt sick, trapped. I needed to get out of the room, away from her. She was an evil, perverted liar. Robin hadn't done anything other than trust me and give me a roof over my head. This story she was weaving – it was *my* story. The story I'd made up to scare off the girl in the diner. It wasn't true, it wasn't. I wanted to be up in my attic, safe from her stabbing eyes.

'The dress isn't your size.' Her stare swept over my hips and breasts. 'But I'm sure I can find something to suit you. Better than that ridiculous homemade maid's outfit.'

I wanted to scream Joe's name at her, summon him with a shout. I'd tried texting but he was ignoring me or he no longer had the phone Brian gave him, or the one Meagan did. To keep in touch, he said, as if that made any sense. I'd rescued him from Lyle's, and from her. Where was *my* rescue? Like a fool, I'd followed him here to this trap of a house where nothing was what it seemed and everyone was a liar. A magistrate, she'd said. The master of the house.

'Robin sets the pace,' Carolyn said. 'Those are the rules. He likes to play a long game. I wanted to warn you. Since there's a chance you've fallen for his act, or for him. I wouldn't want you getting hurt.' Her eyes dug at my face. 'That wouldn't be right.'

14

'You look like something I drew with my left hand.' Meagan sat Joe Peach in her kitchen with its broken stove and spider webs. 'What've you been up to?'

He'd begged on the phone for her to take him back. 'Oh no, sunshine,' she'd said. 'Oh no you don't.' But then he'd found his way to her flat, asking those nosey neighbours where she was, and she'd weakened. Shivering on her doorstep in his filthy T-shirt and anorak. She'd run a hot bath then put him to bed, no questions asked for a couple of hours. Now, though, she wanted to know how he meant to pay his way.

'I don't know. But I will.'

'What about madam? Where'd she end up?'

'Nell?' Joe pushed a finger at the kitchen table, looking hazy. 'I don't know.'

'Thought the pair of you were joined at the hip.' She lit a cigarette, keeping the savagery out of her voice. If Joe was here, Nell couldn't be far behind. She was the one Meagan was after, Little Nell who'd spread the stories that put stones through her windows

105

and hounded her to this dead end of a flat. 'I'm not having you here for free,' she told Joe. 'I can't afford it.'

He searched the pockets of his jeans, dredging up a plastic fiver that flipped itself over in the heat of his palm. 'I can get more money.'

'Oh yes? How're you going to manage that, then?' Because he looked half-starved but not enough to beg on these streets, not in a nice way. He'd need a dog for that.

'I've begged before,' he told her. 'We both have.'

'So what happened?'

Joe shrugged. They both knew what had happened; the first cold night, just as she'd predicted. Nell was tough enough to last a winter on the streets, but not Joe. Nell must've known that when she was planning their escape from Lyle's but he'd have promised her, saying he was off the drugs for good, and she'd needed to believe it. As if addiction was a hobby he'd had in the holidays, or a pet that didn't need feeding to stay alive. Nell had never understood Joe's addiction, not the way Meagan did. Little and often, that was the way to keep them quiet.

'No filching,' she told Joe now. 'I'm keeping my head down. Last thing I need's the police on my doorstep.' He nodded his agreement. 'And no heroin.' Because she could see what this was, where that half-starved look came from. 'This isn't bloody Aberystwyth.'

Nodding again. 'I just need to get warm for a bit.'

'You and me both, sunshine. You and me and the rest of North bloody Wales, but you've a short memory if you think the winters round here are a picnic.'

'I know.' He shivered. 'I'm sorry.'

She took pity at last, lighting them both cigarettes. 'What was wrong with London?'

'Nothing, I just needed to come back for a bit. I missed you.'

He meant it, she could see that. Nothing to do with sentiment – he'd missed having a place to lie low with someone who knew the real Joe Peach. Not the boy who'd worked the boats and made bracelets, the lad Nell fell for. The real Joe, who was with Rosie Bond the day she disappeared.

'Well, you'll earn your keep. I'm up to my backside in debt. Tempted to sell my story to the papers, that's how bad it's been. "The Lies Inside Lyle's . . ." Make a change from me being the one on the ducking stool.' She narrowed her eyes at him. 'Nell wouldn't like it, though. Wouldn't do either of you any good, come to that. But maybe I shouldn't care. Where were *you* when I was up against the wall? Buggered off to London, that's where. Whose idea was that?' She knew, but she needed him to say it. Penance, for picking the wrong side when he picked Nell.

'Nell's idea. She said we couldn't stay after the funeral.' He mentioned the funeral without hesitation, his expression unchanging. 'I'd turned eighteen. They'd send me to an adult prison, that's what she said.'

'Maybe that's where you belong. After Rosie.'

She watched him but he just smoked the cigarette she'd lit for him, and didn't speak. She might've been talking about an old sock he'd lost. It froze her blood.

'Still using that phone I gave you, though. Remembered my number when it mattered.'

'You put it in the phone,' he reminded her. 'But I've a new phone now. A present from someone we stayed with in London, before Nell got us kicked out.'

'Why'd she do that?'

'We couldn't afford to get comfy.' He took a drag of smoke. 'And we didn't deserve it.'

'Meaning what?'

'Like you said.' Joe rubbed his eyes with the heel of his hand. 'After Rosie. We don't deserve to be happy, ever again.'

Little Nell wasn't done, then. She hadn't rescued him at all. Or only from Meagan. She meant to make him pay, the same as she'd meant the stories and the stones that'd driven Meagan from her home. It wasn't Meagan's problem, none of it should have been her problem. Joe had been about to turn to eighteen when Rosie's sandal washed up. He'd have been out of Lyle's at eighteen, that was the rule, and Nell not far behind him. The pair of them would have been out on their ears, even without Nell's escape plan. But the girl had to make Meagan pay, taking Joe because she knew it would hurt, seeing through Meagan's tough old hide to the softness she felt for the lad.

'Hand it over then, this new phone. We'll call it a week's rent.'

He gave her the phone, as easily as that. Darrell would've put up a fight, but not Joe. After he'd gone back to bed, Meagan plugged the phone into the wall and switched it on, and there it was.

A text from Nell, asking for his help. 'Please, Joe. I need you.'

Something about a woman he'd spent time with in London. No address, not yet. Just a first plea but there'd be a second, and a third. Nell wouldn't give up on the boy that easily.

If Joe had seen the text, he'd ignored it. Meagan could text back, if she felt like it. Pretend to be Joe and ask for an address. One thing was for certain: no help was on its way for Little Nell.

She ground her cigarette into the sink with a savage satisfaction, remembering the day the girl came home with Rosie's teddy bear. She'd not been above asking for Meagan's help that day, scared out of her wits by what she'd seen down at that bloody pool.

'Where's Joe?' Meagan had demanded.

Nell had stared up at her, the way she did back when she first arrived at Lyle's. Black eyes burning in her face, shaking so hard Meagan could hear it in her teeth. Her hair was wet, clothes too. She was throttling Rosie's bear, hands around its scruffy neck. Rosie went everywhere with that bear. Inseparable, that was the word in Meagan's head as she watched Nell wringing its neck.

'Don't tell me what happened,' she decided. 'Just tell me how bad it's going to be, what we need to do.' She tapped ash from her cigarette. 'The police are coming. They'll search the house. When they don't find anything, they'll widen their net. They'll want to know where Rosie likes to go. Someone'll say the pool.' She pointed the cigarette at Nell. 'Someone'll say she loved going to that bloody pool with you and soft lad. So where is he?'

'He's ch-changing.' A whisper between chattering teeth. 'He got wet, in the lake.'

'He was born wet.' Meagan narrowed her eyes. 'Was he swimming, or what?'

'Searching, in case . . . In case she fell in.' Bringing the bear to cover to her mouth, eyes huge and hot with tears. 'In case she was in there.'

'In the pool. Your so-called lake.' Meagan smoked to the filter then scrubbed the cigarette out on the stone window ledge. 'Rosie. She drowned, you mean.'

'No.' Nell shook her head, fiercely. 'No.'

'But soft lad jumped in, just in case? You followed suit, judging by these rat's tails.' She pulled a strand of Nell's hair, watching the girl wince and curl away. 'You lost her, in other words.'

She let this sink in, saw blame take shape in the girl's face, altering it. She'd always look like this now, shadowy eyes and sharp cheekbones. It suited her. Men'd look twice, not knowing they were seeing shame and guilt. Imagining intrigue, or an erotic invitation.

'She wasn't with us,' Nell insisted. 'We told her not to come as she was poorly.'

True enough. Rosie had been whingeing all week, clinging to Nell and Joe the way she did when she was sick. No wonder the pair of them had tried to shake her off.

'So what's that, then?' Meagan pointed at the bear between Nell's hands.

'We found it.' Tucking the teddy under her chin, a wedge against the tremors. 'By the lake shore.'

'So she wasn't with you, but her bear was.' Meagan drew a second cigarette from the pack. 'You're a bad liar, love. You'll be better off sticking with silence when the police come. One word out of your mouth and they'll know you're lying.' She tapped the cigarette on the box, thinking about her options. Wondering whether it wasn't better to let Nell talk to the police, weep all over them if she had to. Confess whatever she had to confess, get it off her chest.

'Joe,' Nell whispered, her lips moving against the bear's ratted fur. 'Joe found it.'

'Joe?' Not just the girl then. If the police got hold of Joe—

'He found the bear, by the water.'

'Right. That's why he dived in and got wetter than usual.' She waved out the match. Furious at Joe, and with herself for caring so much. 'Neither of you can lie to save your life.'

Nell gave her the big eyes. There it was again, that difference. Her hair framing her face, the swell of her upper lip. Blaming herself, which was good. Not blaming Joe, and not Meagan.

'Keep quiet,' she instructed. 'To the police. They've a job to do, we'll let them get on with it.' She picked a fleck of tobacco from her lip. 'When'd you last see her?'

'First thing. Before – before breakfast.'

'And she was sick, so you told her to stay home. No matter how much she likes going with you and Joe to that pool or lake, whichever you want to call it. Today, she stayed home.'

Nell was listening, but she didn't seem to hear. 'She was at the lake.' Her fingers tightened on the teddy bear. 'She must've been.'

'Did you see her there?'

'No.'

'Did soft lad?'

'No.' A flicker of doubt in her eyes. 'He said – No.'

Meagan's scalp clenched, remembering how Joe had hissed at Rosie, how he hated her telling tales. She drilled Nell with her hardest stare. 'The police won't want to know what you *imagine* happened. They'll want facts. You saw her at the house, that's the last time—' She broke off because the girl was weeping, her face ruined by it. It made Meagan stiffen her own face, and her voice: 'That's the last you saw her.'

Nell knelt, bending double on the floor, sobbing into the bear. Meagan picked another shred of tobacco from her lip and waited, needing to know which way the girl was going to go. Hysterics might help, with the police.

She thought: *I'm not a monster, I don't want that kiddie to be dead but I've the others to think of. What happens to them if they shut me down?* She smoked to settle the worry.

Bloody Joe. What'd he done?

Nell was making an inhuman noise. Fear and pain and panic, an unholy noise, frightening. It frightened Meagan. She leaned and put a hand on the girl's dark head. 'There,' she said. 'There.'

Nell's noise separated into words: 'I won't let anything happen to her. I love her. I'll kill anyone who tries to hurt her.'

Too late, Meagan thought.

A crumb of tobacco clung to the corner of her mouth. She scraped it free with her thumbnail, tasting ash.

Nell shook the hand from her head and sat up straight. 'If they try to hurt her, or us?' Rosie's old bear was buried in her lap, neck twisted, scruffy face hidden by her hands. 'I'll kill them.'

15

'Are you on your period?'

'What?' I stopped at the foot of the stairs, stupid with shock.

Carolyn was rearranging lilies at the hall table, turning their stems this way and that in the vase. She wore a long satin bathrobe over a matching nightdress, the colour of oysters. Barefoot, with her hair loose, the morning's light resting on her shoulders in red lines.

'Are you on your period?' Fixing me with her cat's eyes.

I was paralysed, my face flaming.

'You are, aren't you? I can smell it.' She wrinkled her nose. 'You should wash more carefully. Especially given the reason you're here. Didn't you listen to a word I said?'

She finished with the flowers, sending me a smile that had me cringing closer to the wall, afraid of what she'd say or do next. One of the lilies turned until it was watching us. Carolyn reached a hand and prodded the bud into place. The lily stayed, its head meek. She rested the heel of her hand on the marble table, her smile toying with me. Then she lifted her fingers and inspected them, rubbing each pad against her thumb. 'And dust more carefully.'

She wasn't wearing heels but my toes curled as she approached, afraid she'd tread there, pierce my foot to the floor with hers. Her walk was swaying, as casual as her cruelty. I'd been wrong about her being more comfortable in heels. Barefoot, she walked as if she owned this house, the street and all of London. When she passed through the library door, a faint backdraught set the lily shivering but I was quick, crossing the hall to still the stem in its vase, keeping the bud obediently facing the wall, where she'd put it.

My face was scalding. I pressed my palms to my cheeks and shut my eyes. I wouldn't cry, but I felt as if I might crack wide open. Everything she did, each word she flung, was pressure on a bruise I hadn't known was there. She magnified all my worst fears, making them monstrous. My just-washed hair was greasy, my pimples were boils, my aching ankles elephantine. And Robin. She'd made him monstrous, too.

I hate her, I told myself, *I hate her.*

But it wasn't really hate, not yet. It was fear and shame. I was ashamed. The lilies' scent was crushing. I took my hand away from the vase, waiting for my fingers to stop shaking. I kept seeing Meagan's face, smoke snaking from one of her many cigarettes: *You lost her, in other words.*

Last night, I'd slept clutching the phone from the kitchen drawer, longing for a text from Joe, some sign he was out there, alive. I'd given up hoping he'd ride to my rescue. No man had ever done that for me. The men in my life reject me or betray me. Abandon me. And Joe had form. Hadn't he left me, that night he went to the club? Wasn't that how I'd found myself on this street, stumbling on Starling Villas while searching for a trace of him?

*

In the garden room, Dr Wilder's plants were thirsty, soaking up the water I tipped into their earth, drinking until the soil was black at their roots. I trickled more water, wiping dust from their leaves before spraying a tar-based fungicide solution, in accordance with his instructions. Following his rules helped, in spite of everything Carolyn had told me in his bedroom. The real reason I was here, she said. This game he was playing – I'd believe it when I heard it from him. Women had lied to me all my life. She wouldn't be the one to make me run. I was tired of running. It made no difference, that's what I'd learnt. But all the same I stayed away from him, in the garden room, tending to his plants.

At Lyle's, the garden took all the water it could get in the summer months. The hosepipe ban became a blessing, no more hauling watering cans around. The garden was a feature of the house, in the eyes of the social workers. A big lawn for kids to play on, flower-beds to lend colour and give the impression of a caring presence at work. As long as the begonias were in bloom, they could pretend Meagan's was a good home for lost or lonely children. I tried to imagine the child Carolyn and Robin Wilder might have. Spidery like this orchid, or twisted out of shape like that bamboo shoot. A daughter with her mother's fair hair, snapping the stem of every flower in here, or else ticking off tasks against Daddy's rota. I tried to see their child but instead I saw Rosie, winding herself around Joe's leg as he begged me to put down the watering cans and run away with him, to the lake. 'Please, Nell.' Pushing Rosie away. 'Please.' My fingertips chilled with the memory.

Looking down, I saw I'd buried my hand in the wet soil where the orchid was rooted. I pulled free, shaking the worst of it away before wiping my fingers on the thigh of my jeans. More mess for

Carolyn to remark upon. I'd been stupid to let her see how shocked I was by her words. I should've let her say her piece and scratch her claws, giving nothing in return. You couldn't feed a creature like Carolyn, it only made her hungrier. But I blushed so easily, shame too near the surface of my skin, running its rash along my neck. 'Rosie, and Rosier,' that was Meagan's joke. How I'd longed for Joe's sunburnt skin that never paled, until I brought him to London and we found ourselves on the streets. My fault, Joe said, because I'd wanted the pair of us punished. Did I still want that?

In the empty hall, her scent hung over everything, making me hold my breath.

I went down the stairs to the kitchen, my hands shaking as I prepared their coffee, so much I nearly smashed his china.

When I set the tray on the library table, Robin lifted his head and looked at me. His shadow was on the bookcases, smaller than usual because she'd tied back the curtains and switched off the lamps, shrinking the room. Even his books seemed smaller. My heart ached for all the learning he'd ever done, and all the learning he'd yet to do. I tried to smile but my face wouldn't cooperate, obeying some instinct of its own to keep my distance from this man.

Carolyn sat at the edge of his desk, swinging one bare foot. Without make-up, she was unrecognizable, as if she'd removed her face. She watched as I unloaded the tray, setting cups and saucers on the desk between her and Robin. My skin crawled from her scrutiny. I looked away but she was there, at the edge of my eye, her face wiped clean. She was like one of the white hairs we were made to pluck from Meagan's head. She'd hit us when we took too long, or else she'd kick us, the flick of her hand or foot somehow worse than if she'd laid into us because it was so casual, too easy for her to hurt us. What recourse did we have? Worse than none, after Rosie. How she loved to remind us of that. *Who's in charge, eh? Who exactly is in charge?*

'We've decided we'll paint you,' Carolyn said.

I straightened from the coffee press, looking between the pair of them. Robin avoided my eyes, rubbing at a mark on his desk, a white frown at the bridge of his nose.

'I don't understand.' I kept my hand on the press.

'Paint.' Carolyn made a wand of her hand, waving it at me, the way Meagan used to wave her cigarettes. 'We're attending an art class together and we need a model to practise on.'

My skin twitched under her gaze, repelled.

'As you're in the house anyway, we thought why not? You'll do.'

I pictured her, Juno in a tunic, making leisurely marks on a canvas as I cowered at her sandalled feet, naked and exposed. 'I'd rather not. There's such a lot to do in the house—'

'Oh, we'd pay you, of course. A model's fee. You need the money, I'm sure.'

I looked to Robin, needing him to rescue me. I was his house-keeper, not hers. Not her model, or her slave. He said nothing, polishing at the imagined mark on his desk. Ashamed of her, or had this always been his plan? Just as she'd told me, yesterday. My throat hollowed, my stomach cramping.

'We'll start at the weekend,' Carolyn said. 'I need to buy in the supplies, brushes and so on.' Her stare raked my body, knowing its secrets. 'That should give you the time you need.'

*

117

In a single week, I'd learnt the shape of Starling Villas. Every corner, every shadow. But since Carolyn came, the house was changed, shutting me out. Dirt crept back as soon as I finished cleaning. I made no difference and never would, no matter how long I stayed or how hard I battled. His house could never be my home. Like Lyle's, after it all unravelled.

As I washed their cups, I thought of Lyle's as it had once been. The amber glass in its front door, above the brass bell and letterbox which Rosie grudgingly polished once a week. She'd been happy in the house, that's how I chose to remember her, back when none of us knew any better. Meagan wasn't in the business, she said, of making happy memories. But we defied her, making them in spite of her. In summer, the porch filled with buckets and spades and shells and sand, all the jumble of seaside living although we were a long way from the nearest beach. We'd catch a bus down to the coast on afternoons when Meagan wanted us out of the house. She'd let me pack a cheap picnic of white bread sandwiches spread with ketchup, and orange squash in a big bottle to be shared. We'd have money for the bus fare and a lolly for the little ones. There were always at least six or seven of us in Lyle's, sometimes more. Joe carried old towels in a woven bag with bamboo handles, Rosie and the others humping buckets and spades. Up the cinder path at the back of Lyle's, down the winding path to the bus stop. How I loved the scratch of the bus seats against the bare skin of my legs, the driver letting Rosie sit at the front because he liked kids. Not like Meagan, lying in an eye mask, simmering with resentment until our return.

In Starling Villas, the fat pigeon alighted on the windowsill.

I rubbed my thumb at the marks Carolyn had left on the cup. She wasn't wearing lipstick but I could feel the tacky imprint of her lips at its rim. She was everywhere in the house, shedding her skin like scented dust. Starling Villas was hers again. Everywhere I'd cleaned and polished and tidied – put back down in disarray. It wasn't my house any longer, it wasn't even his. She'd come to reclaim it, poisoning me against Robin, whispering her lies in my ear. Should I be grateful to her? It gave me no pleasure to realize how far I'd fallen for him. I'd lost too much to love to consider it anything other than a punishment. Perhaps that's why I cared so little for Carolyn's warning; what could he teach me about punishment that I didn't already know? But perhaps, too, I wanted to believe him capable of change, as I longed to be. Freed from the past, from the terrible things I'd done or allowed to be done.

Shutting my eyes, I held my hands under the hot water, thinking of how Lyle's was a hundred different houses all at once. Some kids hated every second of their lives with Meagan, couldn't wait to get away. And others like Joe grew to love Lyle's. The stairs we were made to brush, the broken banister wound with Sellotape that had turned brittle and brown. The garden where we lived in the hot months, hearing the throb of bees in the hollyhocks; if summer had a sound, it was that. I could smell the grass parching, soil baking all about me. Face down under a blanket of sun, Rosie put to bed after lunch, worn out by the heat. Joe and I side by side, taking turns on the only lounger. We were slaves to the sun, that summer. I was fifteen and fearless, filling my palms from a stolen can of Meagan's suncream, its thick foam smelling of skin and sex, Joe stretching his arms and legs for me to stroke the cream there. Later, when the heat was gone from the day, we'd shiver as we crossed the stone threshold to climb the stairs. Rosie would wake, wanting to play, grabbing at our sunburnt ankles, making us yelp. Meagan would be snarling, the sound peppering the house like shrapnel. I'd pour her a glass of cider and take an icepack for her head, and another sleeping pill. If I could keep her quiet until suppertime, it'd be all right. The nights belonged to me and Joe. Rosie wound herself at my waist, all sticky kisses. I had to peel her free, warming a cup of milk to keep her busy. Joe had gone to his room. I'd find him later, face down in the sheets, the day's heat rising from his brown skin. In the twenty minutes it took to deal with Meagan and Rosie, I'd missed him so much my heart felt battered, beaten flat. What was love but pain, and punishment?

In Starling Villas, I set Carolyn's cup in the rack and pulled the plug, watching the water as it drained away, the gulp of it startling the pigeon into clumsy flight.

What did they want from me, the Wilders?

He'd told at least one lie I knew of – *Just me in the Villas* – and now he wouldn't look at me. There was nothing good in the house, just this new suspicion, this fear. I'd been so certain I'd find Joe here. I'd searched for drugs, thinking if I found them I'd take my revenge in whatever small way I could. Thinking revenge was all I had left. Joe and I should be together, forever. Not love, not now. What we had was darker and dirtier. Joe thought he could outrun it, but I knew better. Carolyn knew nothing. She'd fed his addiction without knowing its consequences, the terrible thing it had done. She knew nothing of Joe, or of me.

I shook the water from my hands, drying them on the waist of my dress.

I'd built a castle once. A fairy palace of sponge turrets and towers, glittering with sugar. I'd saved up to buy the food colouring and edible glitter, working all night to sculpt stars in the windows and fix tiny flags in the turrets. I stood the finished cake at the head of the table, tying balloons and foil streamers to Rosie's chair where she scrambled the next morning to demolish it all, sucking sponge and sugar roses from her fists before grabbing a turret and cramming it into her mouth, screaming a muffled warning at the other kids that it was *her* cake, her birthday, all hers. Icing in her fair hair that was so like Carolyn's, streaked with gold. And Meagan at the foot of the table, laughing and smoking, one eye on the mess Rosie was making, waiting to tell me to clear it all up and hadn't she warned me it would be like this, hadn't she told me so?

16

Twelve hours. That's how long it took Meagan to regret letting Joe Peach move in with her. The morning after he'd turned up shivering on her doorstep, she was woken by voices outside the flat. She dressed, putting an unlit cigarette between her teeth as she went to the front door.

Joe was on the walkway, leaning one hand on the rail, his back blocking her view. She saw the tension in his spine through the cheap cotton T-shirt he was wearing. Whoever he was talking with, they'd dropped their voices to whispers when they heard her coming.

'Oi,' she said. 'What the bloody hell's this?'

Joe straightened, half turning in her direction. Enough for her to see the boy, Darrell, with his hands in his pockets, grinning at her. The sight of him standing so close to Joe gave her gooseflesh. The walkway was a sheer drop down to the tarmac, eight floors below.

'You'd better not be doing what I think you're doing.'

Drugs, because wasn't it always drugs with Joe? Forget the promises he'd made to Nell, and to Meagan last night. She'd been a fool to try and extract a promise; better off doing what she'd done at Lyle's – dealing him the bloody things herself. At least that way she knew how much he was taking. And it kept him coming back to her, kept him quiet.

Darrell said, 'He was fixing me a fag, that's all.'

Joe looked down at the boy. Did he see what Meagan saw – his likeness to Darrell? No, he just saw a kid who knew who was dealing on the estate. He'd always been good at spotting his predators, had Joe. As for Darrell, he'd no idea what he was seeing. No idea how this morning chat might've ended, had Meagan not shown up when she did.

'You, get your arse inside the flat.' Nodding at Joe. 'And you, bugger off.'

Her heart was beating a tattoo in her chest. Joe was standing so close to the boy, close enough to pick him up and drop him over the side. She couldn't stop herself seeing Rosie in his arms, lifted over that bloody lake. It was a sharp drop over the side of the walkway; Darrell's head would crack open like an egg.

Joe slipped past her, into the flat.

'Don't come round again,' she warned the boy. 'Not while he's here. Understood?'

Darrell met her stare, his eyes hooded, before he turned on his heel and walked away.

Joe was in the kitchen, filling the kettle.

'State of you!' she hissed. 'What'd I tell you?'

'No heroin,' Joe shrugged. 'He wasn't selling heroin.'

'He's ten years old!'

'I was ten years old. Once.'

'Before my time, sunshine.' She reached for her lighter. 'This isn't bloody Lyle's. Stay away from the kiddies. I told you, I've seen enough of the police to last me a lifetime.'

Joe took the sugar down, licking a finger to dip in the bowl. 'What happened to Lyle's?' He sucked the sugar from his finger. 'After we went, I mean.'

'Ask your little girlfriend. She's the one who started the stories. Not just to the papers, to the whole town.' Rage clouded her vision. 'Every one of my windows smashed! Every bloody one. It took the council three weeks to send a man to nail boards over.'

She knew some of the vandals, recognized their faces inside the hoodies they all wore. She'd had a bird's eye view, being inside Lyle's as the windows were exploding, picking up the stones in the morning, clearing the worst of the broken glass from the floors. When the 'For Sale' sign went up, it was spray-painted with obscenities in no time. By kids she'd once fed and kept warm. All that might've died down but for the papers chucking oil on the fire, thanks to Nell feeding them a story. Speculation and rumours and outright lies about what was done to the Bond Baby on Meagan Flack's watch.

'Lost girl sold at sex parties,' shrilled the headlines, with Meagan named as the pimp. 'She treated us like slaves,' the sources always anonymous.

She knew which kids were selling their stories; the pixelated photos gave them away, like their choice of lies. Greedy kids claiming she'd starved them, rowdy ones saying she'd gagged them. Plenty made money out of selling their stories. Well, good luck to them. Meagan knew she'd done nothing wrong. She'd followed the rules to the letter – let them try and prove otherwise. She'd braced herself for a story sold by Nell or Joe but they never breathed a word, letting others do their dirty work. And because they knew the truth. Guilt had a way of gagging you, better than any threat.

'Your little girlfriend stitched me up.' She made a fair fist of keeping the fury from her voice as she boiled the kettle for tea. Joe was a mess but he'd protect Nell, even now. Old habits die hard. 'To think I fell for her tears after they called off the search. All that fake crying the pair of you did.'

'It wasn't fake,' Joe said mechanically. 'We loved Rosie. Nell loved her.'

Catching himself in the lie. He'd stayed wide during the police search. It was Nell who parked herself by that bloody pool, keeping watch. For weeks, all the divers came up with were bottles and balls, a rusted pram dripping green weed. She'd told the girl to buck up: 'It's starting to look like you've something to feel guilty about. You don't want the police getting the wrong end of the stick.'

Rosie was in that pool, no doubt about it. Meagan hoped the child went quickly. She wasn't a cruel woman, no matter what anyone said. She was hard because *life* was hard. She'd seen others spoil the kiddies they took in, making promises they'd never keep, talking about unconditional love as if you could buy it off the shelves in Poundland. 'Your new family, forever home,' as if anything was forever but debt and death. At least her kids came up fighting when life kicked them down. She was proud of the ones who sold their stories and made themselves a bit of money. For a while, every week brought a fresh theory about what had happened that day. Meagan stopped reading. The sea took Rosie. You couldn't prosecute the sea. Everything else was just flapping mouths.

Oh, but the stories about that kiddie! You'd think she'd grown a pair of wings and flown to heaven. Funny how death did that.

Took ordinary kids – lazy, spoilt, or just plain nasty – and turned them into angels. Rosie Bond was selfish from top to toe, same as all six-year-olds. Meagan had warned Nell and Joe to stop spoiling her. She was getting too big for her boots.

'I'm the favourite,' she'd started telling the others. 'Nell's like my mum. Joe loves me the best.'

Meagan had broken up friendships before, when she saw fun and games turning to long silences behind bedroom doors, fumbling eyes at the breakfast table. Nell was too smart for that. Sneaking round behind Meagan's back, biding her time, bringing Meagan sleeping pills to be sure they weren't disturbed. Joe was the hopeless romantic, that's how she'd read the situation, Nell was the one with the head on her shoulders. But look how she'd fought for Joe, wanting to believe the best of him never mind all the evidence pointing in the other direction.

In the flat, Joe dipped his finger back into the sugar bowl.

'You'll stay away from that estate and those kiddies while you're dossing here, understood?'

He nodded and handed her a cup of tea, made strong the way she liked it. He knew her, that was the problem. They'd recognized one another, from the off. He wasn't like the other kids at Lyle's, and not just on account of his looks. Meagan hadn't trusted him, not at the start. Made sure he knew it too, treating him roughly on account of those looks, as if they were a trick he was trying on, or else trouble in store. No one was that pretty without it warping him. She was right, too. Joe's social worker had fallen like a bag of bricks: 'Such a sweet boy, so lovely!'

Meagan's first thought was, *You're not pulling any wool over my eyes, sunshine.*

She'd have preferred a kid with scars, or big ears. The ugly ones were easy to manage, didn't get too many bright ideas about themselves for starters. She'd expected Joe to lord it round Lyle's like a little prince, bagging the best seats, demanding the biggest helpings. She gave him the box room, to cut him down to size. 'Not a lot of space but you've not a lot of things, have you?'

Rubbing his nose in it, but the boy needed to know who he'd to thank for the new roof over his head, and that his tricks wouldn't work here. 'It'll do you.'

The box room was at the front of the house, just enough space for a single bed with a shelf over it, no desk or chair, no bedside cabinet or chest of drawers. A miserable, narrow cell of a room that all the kids hated. Joe went straight to the window, not more than four steps from the door. The sun was out and he stood in it, his fringe lit gold, shadows from his eyelashes lying along his cheeks, looking like a young Paul Newman. He picked the spot on purpose, striking a pose to help her see how handsome he was, that's what she'd thought. But by the end of the first week, she'd learnt what was going on with Joe.

He liked his little cell of a room because it got the sun. He was a slave to the sun, was Joe. 'Sunshine,' she started calling him, tongue in cheek. The social worker outstayed her welcome, giving tips on how to care for young Master Peach, warning of his sensitive stomach and the need to get him out into fresh air on account of a vitamin D deficiency: 'The sunshine vitamin!'

Meagan listened and pulled the right faces, and let the silly cow leave a bag of oranges after getting her to say she'd put in a good word at the next review. Day one and Joe was earning his keep, but it was too easy, like ripe plums dropping in her lap. Meagan didn't trust easy. She felt better after Joe fought with Nell. Fighting was normal. Standing around striking heart-throb poses was neither normal nor useful, unless that smitten cow happened to be around.

'You'd better share those oranges, sunshine.'

He did as he was told, at any rate. But nothing Meagan said could stop him seeking out the sun. He followed it around the house like a cat. When she wanted to punish him, she shut him in a room without a window. Winter was hard work, Joe slowing down like a toy with a flat battery. Nell did most of his chores in the winter months, covering for him because she'd fallen so hard.

'He needs to clean the bathroom.' Meagan didn't like the boy getting away with it, and was surprised the girl let him. 'It's filthy.'

Nell was packing lunch boxes, ready for school.

'I said he needs to clean the bathroom. Have you seen the state of it?'

'He'll do it. He's helping Janine with her homework.'

'I don't have to wash my face in Janine's homework. Tell him to get it sorted.'

Later, when the bathroom was clean, it wasn't Joe that smelt of bleach and scouring powder.

'So much for feminism,' Meagan mocked. 'You'll be dressing him next.'

Or undressing him. She watched them that summer. Nell was fifteen and abruptly lovely, the way it took some girls. Joe looked more than ever like Paul Newman. The social worker had said something about unwanted adult attention, this being all the rage with social workers at the time. In Meagan's experience, the fact he'd been groped by grown-ups meant there was an even chance Joe Peach was a pervert, or would grow into one. So yes, she watched them. But there was no warning Nell. Meagan tried to tell her there was something up, but she wouldn't hear a word against Joe.

'He's not right in the head, you know that? Something's missing.'

'He's just tired,' Nell would say.

'No.' Meagan wanted to spell it out. 'There's something missing.'

Three years of that – of Joe living like a prince in Lyle's – before Rosie Bond went missing.

Rosie who told tales, bringing her stories to Meagan like a kitten delivering a string of dead birds – 'Joe didn't pay for the sweets he bought' – saucering her eyes as if she didn't know she was dropping the boy in it. 'And he's got a new phone.'

'He's not right,' Meagan told Nell. 'He'll have the police on us, is that what you want?'

It was Joe she wanted to bawl out but he'd slipped off somewhere, leaving Nell to shoulder the blame and take the punishment.

'I suppose he's got you in on it. The pair of you'll end up in that unit down in Abergele. That's if he doesn't wriggle off the hook. You're a fool, girl. He's got you round his little finger like the rest of the women in Wales.'

'Except you,' Nell said under her breath.

'Too bloody right except me. You think I'm falling for the golden boy act at my age?' Or any age. 'I've had it up to here with batting bloody eyelashes. His tricks don't work on me.'

Joe came to Meagan's room that night, to apologize. He didn't bat his lashes, standing there in an old T-shirt, goosebumps on his bare arms. 'I'm sorry, I'll stop. Let me stay.'

'And have the police on my back? Not bloody likely. I'm calling your case officer in the morning. You can bugger off back to Barmouth.'

130

'I can't. They won't have me.'

'Come off it. That old bastard with the busy hands? He'd love to have you back.'

'No.' Joe looked straight at her, eye to eye. 'He wouldn't.'

The way he said it sent a shiver up her spine. It was the first time she'd seen him look straight at anything. His eyes were always sliding about, or else he was blinking, going into soft focus like someone'd put Vaseline on his lens.

She'd been partial to a bit of Paul Newman in her youth, that sulky mouth and chin, the way he turned his eyes into lasers. *Cat on a Hot Tin Roof* was her favourite. Scowling about on his crutches, making Liz Taylor weak at the knees until she ran up the stairs, 'Yessir!' in the end. And here he was in front of her, not blue eyes but golden brown, sharing something special with her, that's how it felt, something he'd shared with no one else, not even Nell. Trusting Meagan with his truth. No one had ever trusted Meagan that way before. It wove its way into her gut, warming her.

'You bring the police in here, I'll skin you alive. Is that clear?'

'Yes.' He crooked his mouth, shrugging his shoulders to make himself smaller. 'I don't know why I do it, not really.'

'Don't get deep with me, sunshine. I'm a foster mum, not a psychiatrist.' But she narrowed her eyes at him. 'D'you have a psychiatrist?'

He shook his head. 'Just you.'

'Suppose I don't tell your case worker about the shoplifting.' She smoked for a bit, thinking about her options. 'Where's my incentive?'

'I'll stop. Or . . .' He watched her face, picking his way through the words, searching for the right ones. 'I'll lift other stuff, better stuff.'

They stared at one another for a long moment.

'You're a piece of work, Joe Peach.' She tapped ash into a cup. 'Did anyone ever tell you that?'

He said again, 'Just you.'

Standing there in his T-shirt, making a gift of his guilt and his confession. Seducing her with the idea she was special, the only one he'd ever confided in. Oh, he was good, was Joe Peach. Rotten to the core with it and, God help her, she fell.

Now, he was sitting at her kitchen table in this dump of a flat where she'd been run to ground, thanks to his little girlfriend's lies. Well, it was her turn this time. Joe could earn his keep. He owed her, the debt two summers old.

Dry as dust it'd been that afternoon, the kind of dry that stuck in your throat and made your armpits itch. The lawn was yellow, ladybirds crawling in the cracks. Bees were dying, it was all over the news. Not just nature at work; vandals broke into an orchard and destroyed the hives. A man wept on the TV news, saying he couldn't understand why anyone would do such a thing. Police said the vandals would've been stung badly during the attack. Meagan was surprised anyone cared that much about bees, dead or living. Rosie and the others dug graves in the flowerbeds to bury those that fell out of Lyle's hollyhocks. They had to soak the soil before it was soft enough to dig, it'd been that long since they'd seen any rain. The sheets Nell pinned to the washing line crisped in the heat. All the kids had rashes. Meagan would've prayed for a storm if she'd been the praying sort. A headache was poking a black rod of pain behind her eyes.

'Keep them quiet,' she warned Nell. 'I've a migraine coming on.'

Nell fetched a glass of water and a sleeping pill, drawing the curtains. Meagan lay down, shutting her eyes.

She was a good girl, Nell. A shame she was falling for Joe but she could've fallen for a lad in town, the one with the freckles and forearms who washed the hearses for the funeral home. They had it good at the funeral home, no noise or fuss, no kids. Air-conditioning. Meagan would've killed for air-conditioning that summer, the way the heat crept around the house.

By mid-afternoon it was squatting outside her window, thick as soup through the curtains. She woke in a stupor, her face stiff from the migraine, hearing the clatter of kids in the house. Nell was supposed to be keeping them quiet. The weather made them scratchy, starting fights they hadn't the energy to finish. Her eyelids felt as if coins were pressing there. She'd dreamt of the funeral home, lying in the dark listening to the trays slide in and out of the walls around her. Heat held her to the bed until she couldn't bear the smell of her own skin, sweating cigarettes and cider. She pulled herself upright, keeping her eyes closed, feeling for the glass of water Nell left. Here – lukewarm, soapy. She reached for her cigarettes, swinging her feet to the floor. The curtains were hot to the touch, sun inching past hers to the narrow window of the box room. Joe's room. He didn't spend any time in there other than to sleep, preferring to sit with Nell in the big drawing room, or in the playroom where an old mattress was upended against one wall. It was a bit cooler down there, but not much. Heat had stuffed every corner of the house. This summer was hell on earth. She pushed the window wide to let the smoke out. That's when she saw them, trailing home. An hour before the alarm was raised and the police turned up, shedding their respect for Meagan faster than a whore sheds her knickers. Nell and Joe, coming back from the pool. Where else would they go? But she said nothing. What could she say?

'I reckon the three of them were at the pool while I was taking a nap. Not the swimming pool in town, the one at the old quarry. They call it a lake. Trespassing, yes.'

That would've gone down like a bag of bricks. She told no lies, and asked no questions. Too many the police could've asked in return: 'Have they ever gone off like that before, the three of them? Or the two older kids. Nell, is it? And Joe. Have you ever had cause to wonder where they were, or what they were up to?'

'Well there was this one time, officer. With the blood.'

'The blood, Mrs Flack? How much blood are we talking about?'

'A lot of blood, but I didn't like to ask any questions.' She could hardly have admitted that.

She'd caught Joe trying to bury the bloodstained towel in the airing cupboard. He'd invented some lie or other, the tips of his ears pink as a rabbit's. She hadn't the energy to pursue it back then; the heat that summer made everything an effort. She'd assumed it was Nell's monthly, or else they'd been experimenting.

'A lot of blood, officer, but I kept quiet about it.' How would that have helped anything?

She said nothing to the police that day or since, because she could see the stories coming down the line as soon as the kiddie went missing: Neglect. Shameful. Criminal.

She'd lit a cigarette, was shaking out the match when she spied them. Heads together, so close they looked welded at the hip.

Nell in last year's sundress, faded to the colour of milk and too tight, showing off her new curves. Joe with his legs brown and scuffed at the knees. The sun on their heads, hair wet from the water.

She looked for Rosie, following behind. But it was just Nell and Joe, moving in step, holding hands so hard she could see the whiteness of their knuckles from the window.

17

'You're holding back.' Carolyn's hand was poised, paintbrush hovering over the canvas, her face freighted with accusation. 'We're painting you, not putting you on trial for murder.'

I was on trial, all three of us knew it. There hadn't been a day since I'd arrived at Starling Villas when I wasn't being judged, against his standards or hers. What was his rota, if not a trial?

Carolyn threw down the brush and crossed the room to put her hands on me. My shoulders, elbows, waist. Twisting me two inches to the right, prodding me an inch to the left, as if I were one of the lilies in her vase. Her fingers were hot through my clothes, the fever in her like Joe's.

'There. No, keep your shoulders down.' A quick press of her palms as if she'd rather be using a cattle prod or wearing rubber gloves. 'And your chin up.' The tilt of two fingers.

Robin didn't speak. He was using charcoal, its flavour like ash in the back of my throat. I'd seen his eyes when her hands were on me, the blood-swell of his lips. I wished I hadn't seen that.

We were in his bedroom. They could have painted me in the garden room or the sitting room, or shackled to the stove in the basement. Instead, she'd posed me by his ugly mirror, her choice of background. The glass licked coldly at my neck. If I took a step back, it would swallow me.

'And show some emotion, for God's sake.'

She crossed the room to her canvas. Her scent stayed in my nostrils, somehow shrill and green.

Which emotion did she want from me? Shame? Rage? Guilt. Sweat soaked the armpits of my dress, the apron starchy at my waist; of course she had to paint me in my servant's uniform. The light was in my eyes, I'd see its ghost for the rest of the day, an oblong shaped by the window's frame. It would be there when I cooked their supper, and washed their dishes. I'd see it as I climbed the stairs to his attic and lay down on the mattress under the eaves. Even asleep it would be there behind my eyelids, waiting.

'Better . . .' Carolyn touched her brush to the canvas in short, dismissive strokes.

Robin moved his charcoal across the page, the sound of it like whispering. I was grateful for the light blinding me, blanking out the room. He wet his thumb, rubbing at his sketchpad as if to wipe me out. *Please*, I thought, *wipe me out. Make me less.*

My head filled with Rosie. Rosie and her crayons, one of the rare times she could be persuaded to sit still. Her crocodile with its basket of blue eggs, Meagan poking fun because it wasn't an Easter bunny. How angry she'd been when Joe pinned the picture to the wall. The house wasn't ours, we could be moved on any time she pleased. 'Take that rubbish down!' Rosie's crocodile with its teeth studded by stars and flowers because that's what Rosie loved to draw, that's who she was. Meagan tore it from the wall, screwing it into a ball for the bin. It was Joe who rescued it. He smoothed it flat and ironed it between sheets of greaseproof paper, testing the heat of the iron by holding it to his cheek. I'd never seen him take such care over any task. I think that's when I fell in love with him, my terrible Joe.

In Starling Villas – the whisper of his charcoal and the *shush* of his thumb, wiping me out. Her tongue *tsk*ing her teeth, taking me down.

At lunchtime, Hungry's had the radio playing, a cowboy ballad of love and grits. I sipped my hot chocolate, its sweetness kissing my lips. The cowboy was singing about the wind, how he was riding into it or against it. He made it sound like sex, a tussle with a dusty lover. I wanted Joe to come through the double doors, swinging them wide like saloon doors, his thumbs through the belt loops of his fraying Levi's, a duck feather in his fringe, framed by sunset. Every head would turn his way. Oblivious, he'd stand with his weight on his left hip, smoky eyes surveying the scene. Even Robin would look up from his books and stare. Lovely Joe, with everyone looking, lusting. And he'd walk through it all to my side. To us.

I set my empty glass aside and reached for the phone I'd found in the kitchen drawer in Starling Villas.

'Dear Joe,' I texted. 'I thought I could do this without you, but I can't. I need you and you owe me. I know you haven't forgotten. How can anyone forget a thing like that?' The words writhed on the screen. What choice had Carolyn left me? When I put up my hair, she laughed at my lovely neck. She hadn't laughed at Joe's, that night in the club. I could be free of her but I needed his help. If he'd kept his phone, if he hadn't lost it or sold it for drugs. 'Please, Joe. It'll be easy, I promise.'

I was only asking him for what he'd already done, that night he went home with her from the club. Carolyn would get a second helping of what she'd wanted that night, and then perhaps she'd leave me alone. I couldn't see further than that – to what I wanted, or Robin might want. First I had to clear Carolyn out of my way. Joe could do it, easily. A simple solution, if love or sex was ever simple, if desire made any kind of sense.

Back in the Villas, pollen scabbed the marble of the table and tiles. I fetched a damp cloth and knelt, the hard press of the floor finding old bruises on my knees. The afternoon sun poked shadows in the way of my work; I had to keep shifting to see the specks of pollen. When I stood, everything rose around me, rocking, so that I had to rest my head on the table until the dizziness passed. Strange, how quickly marble steals your heat for its own.

Robin was alone in the library. She'd gone again, for now. I set his tray down quietly to remind him of the difference I made, the difference I was. As I laid the spoon in the saucer, he raised his eyes. I'd seen into his wife's eyes this way when she was posing me for their pictures. His bedroom would need tidying, charcoal dust to be swept up, the mirror polished free of my shadow. Had she taken their artwork with her or would I find it in the room, left out for me to see? His drawing, and her painting. Would I recognize myself?

'Thank you,' Robin said. 'You're very good,' he said.

It sounded like an apology, although the pair of us knew there was no apology large enough to excuse his wife's cruelty. All the same, I looked back into his eyes.

'There's no need,' I said, as softly as I could. Everything about me in contrast to her. All my hardness hidden on the inside. He could dig and dig and he would never find it, never find me.

'Yes,' he said. 'There is.'

'Then . . . I'm worried.' I straightened. 'About the money, these extra meals. I've done what I can to make the allowance stretch but there's the roast on Sunday. I don't want to cut corners.'

'Of course. I'll give you extra cash, after I've been to the bank.'

He didn't trust me, then. Pretending he'd no money in the house when there was a wad of notes as fat as a house brick in the bookshelf behind him. I'd found it when I was dusting and if he hadn't wanted me to find it, he should've hidden it more carefully or asked me to clean less fastidiously. A week ago, I'd have been excited to find it – proof that this house was what I'd suspected, corrupt and rotten. Who keeps a wad of cash like that, unless it's to pay for something illicit? Drugs, or sex. But my priorities had changed in the past few days. And who was I to judge him, really?

'Will Mrs Wilder be here on Sunday?' I asked. He searched my face, as if looking for a way out. 'I need to I know how large a joint to buy.'

'It's just me.' He flinched, as if remembering his first lie to me, a week ago.

I stood a moment longer, letting him see my silence as well as hear it. The clock ticked behind us, measuring out the seconds while he stared and I waited. In that moment, I'd have given him anything, if only he'd had the courage to ask. Not because I loved him or wanted him but because I was afraid – of kneeling on that tiled floor forever. Afraid of his wife and what the pair of them had planned for me. He dropped his eyes, and the danger passed.

In the bedroom, she'd cleared it all away. Canvases and paints, sketchpads and easel. You'd never know we'd been there, unless you looked closely. The carpet held the shallow imprints of my feet, a greyness in the air from his charcoals and her brushes. She could have painted me anywhere in the house but it had to be here, six feet from his bed, the mirror making a gift of me, twice.

I climbed the stairs to my attic with my fist pressed under my ribs to keep the rage inside.

Neon stained my lovely rug, London's nightlife ramming through the window. I changed into dirty clothes and set to work, pulling trunks and boxes into the middle of the room. In a metal trunk, I'd found dozens of sepia theatre programmes for shows dating back decades. In the kitchen, I'd discovered a can of varnish and a Stanley knife. From the hardware store, I'd bought a pot of glue under the pretext of fixing a flap of wallpaper. Kneeling, I tore apart the theatre programmes, arranging their pages on the floor until I found a pattern I liked. The old paper took the glue well, the sepia shining through the thin layer of varnish I stroked there. At the skirting board and around the window, I used the knife, wickedly sharp. The fumes from the glue and varnish were heady, better than being drunk. I worked without stopping, losing myself in the rhythm of smoothing pages to the wall, brushing varnish back and forth.

My attic was taking shape, in spite of all my other work and my misgivings. Each night before bed, I cleared another corner. Whenever I emptied a box, I flattened it and stored it out of the way. There was so much cardboard in the cupboard under the stairs, I feared a fire hazard. I'd spread a trunk with a strip of tapestry found wrapped in red tissue paper. Along this, I'd stood a caravan of brass camels, each polished until she shone. An old lamp had been buried in one of the boxes, its shade made of coloured glass panes. One pane was gone but I'd folded a square of tissue paper to seal the gap. The bulb was blown so I'd brought a spare from the kitchen, propping the lamp on the floor next to my mattress. From another of the attic's boxes, I'd unearthed a collection of spoons, some with coloured beads threaded through their handles, others carved from horn. All these treasures – chipped or scuffed, stained by damp – I loved. At night, I touched my fingers to each in turn before climbing into bed, as if they might bind me more tightly to the house, its history and its truth. What other treasures had I found? Reading glasses, their lenses scarred and cloudy. Lipsticks still bearing the imprint of lips. Postcards of far-off places. Christmas baubles and a set of tree lights which I coiled inside a Kilner jar, plugging the lights into the socket shared with the lamp. A sketchpad full of line drawings, life studies and landscapes, one of a tree standing by a pool of water, its branches softened here and there with leaves. The reflection in the pool was perfect, as if another, stronger tree grew under the water. I framed the sketch in tissue paper before propping it between my camels, as if a mirage had visited the desert, a watering hole to make their journey less perilous. The phone from the kitchen drawer was plugged into the wall beside my bed, in case of a text from Joe.

After varnishing the newly papered walls, I stood and rolled the crick from my neck, opening the window to see the neon painting the city a dozen different colours. I stayed like that a long time. When at last I turned, the room was dark and its new walls dirty, scribbled by shadow.

That night, I dreamt of Joe, in my attic with amber varnish drying on its walls. I dreamt of the bedsit we'd promised ourselves in Brighton over a fish and chip shop on the front, our bathroom behind a beaded curtain under a skylight. We'd smell of vinegar and fish batter, all summer long. On warm nights, we'd walk down to the beach to lie in the empty pockets of shingle, looking out to sea and naming all the faraway places we'd explore one day, like Bouvet Island and Tristan da Cunha. On cold nights, we'd stay in the bedsit and I'd watch Joe shower, the water running over the peaks of his shoulders and into the hollows of his hips. Joe Peach, my forever summer, my freedom. In my dream, I sat on the bed and counted the rosary of the beaded curtain as he washed off the day. Through the skylight, the sun fell on him and his skin shone until it sang.

When I woke, Joe's song was gone. There was only the house holding its breath beneath me. What a fool I'd been to think I could hide here, squirrelling my shame under the eaves and into the corners when every one was taken, filled with the secrets Robin and Carolyn were keeping. The cupboard under the stairs, drawers in the kitchen, even the mean space between the back of the mirror and the bedroom wall. All of it taken up with their secrets, no room for mine, no room for me.

The phone buzzed so suddenly I bit my tongue in surprise.

I crouched for it, quickly.

A text from Joe. *Joe*. He wanted to know where I was, so he could come and get me.

'Starling Villas,' I typed back. 'You remember. The house you went to that night, with her. I need you to come back and help me deal with her.'

It took a moment for the response. Then –

'I remember, just not the address. Remind me?'

18

Joe was in the kitchen, loading a cup of tea with so much sugar it grated in the cup.

'Little Nell's been in touch,' Meagan told him. 'She's invited us up to London. Starling Villas. She said you'd remember.'

Joe shook his head, licking the spoon. 'I'm not going back to London, it's too far.'

'We can't leave Nell in the lurch,' she told him. 'That wouldn't be right.'

He looked at her then, and she could see he knew how it was. How long she'd been waiting for this chance, and how determined she was to take it. He hadn't the energy for a fight, not with her. She'd worn him down long before London and his life on the streets.

Rosie's sandal, that's what did it, washing up nearly two years after they'd stopped searching. A red jelly sandal, one of a pair missing from the house, Rosie's name painted on the sole; the paint was nearly washed away, but still distinguishable. The sea sent the sandal up like an afterthought to all the panic and pain of the investigation. The chances of that happening had been so small

Meagan hadn't even considered it, but the sea did as it pleased, a law unto itself. She'd lived close to it all her life and still the sea was a stranger, a puzzle to her.

Everything had started up again after the sandal, the questions and rumours, only this time Meagan wasn't in the mood. She'd covered for them long enough. Too long; she couldn't shop them without shopping herself but she could remind them what she was owed.

'Think I've forgotten?' Hissing at the pair of them, the meanness taking hold of her because she could see what was coming and it scared her. 'I'm never forgetting, and nor should you.'

They lived in fear of her after that. Jumping to do as they were told, whatever chores she threw at them. It was like it'd been at the beginning, back before they got too big for their boots.

Nell's hands shook as she laid the table, but she was plotting even then. Figuring a way to get them out from under Meagan's heel. She should've guessed as much. When that first stone came whistling through the window it might as well've had a note tied round it written in the girl's neat hand. Less than a month after the sandal washed up, they were gone, headed for London's bright lights. Well, that adventure had lasted less than five months and here was Joe, right back where he'd started.

'We can't leave Nell in the lurch,' Meagan said again. 'That wouldn't be right.'

Joe dropped the spoon into the sink.

At the train station, she bought him a bag of jellied sweets. It was freezing, the way stations always were. She could see the haziness coming over him, like mist pushing in from the sea.

'I need you awake, sunshine.'

146

Gulls lined up on the station roof, searching the crowd for sandwich crusts and chip wrappers. One had ketchup splashed up its beak. The same gulls that grew fat in the summer, invading the beaches, swooping for ice cream cones. Bloody Wales. It'd be the death of her.

'What's wrong with you?' she asked Joe. But she knew what was wrong. He didn't like her plans for Little Nell. He wanted to leave the girl alone in her new house with whatever security she'd found there. As if Meagan didn't deserve security of her own.

'Maybe she's found someone,' Joe said. 'Maybe she's happy.'

As if Meagan didn't deserve happiness.

'So? *You've* found someone. Haven't I looked after you?'

'Yes, but we've got a place—'

She lost her patience then, leaning to hiss in his face, 'It's falling down! What d'you want to do, paper the cracks with bills? You'll be back on the streets for Christmas, where you won't last a day without her to prop you up. And she's hardly likely to do that, is she? Since you ran out on her.'

She'd been digging the story of Starling Villas out of him, a piece at a time. She patted the pocket where he'd put the joints from Darrell's friends on the estate.

'We're not going to mess this up for her, that'd be daft, and, anyway, Nell's not stupid. She won't want to lose this new job, whatever it is, but she'll want to help. When she hears how hard things are for us. Hasn't she always looked out for you? Haven't we both?' He nodded, thirst in his face, wanting a fix. 'In any case, she asked for your help, didn't she? She's expecting you.' Just not with Meagan in tow, with her own ideas about who was helping who.

'Eat some sweets. I need you sober for tonight.' She handed him the bag of jellies. 'Stay off it, until tonight. Understood?'

He nodded, putting a sweet between his teeth to suck. His teeth weren't rotting yet, but the window was closing on Joe Peach's summer. Each day he was a little less tanned, less glossy.

'And watch her. Nell. She's smarter than you, always was, always will be. We're up against the wall, you and I. But Nell won't want you homeless. She's a good girl, she's a good heart.'

Lies, as far as Meagan was concerned, but it was what Joe needed to hear. He sucked the sweet, his cheek hollowing. He was scared, but he trusted Meagan to make it right. He was right to trust her, too. Hadn't she kept his secrets, all this time? The shoplifting and the rest of it. The worst of it.

When the train came, it was packed.

She took the last seat, instructing Joe to sit on the floor. He didn't mind, falling asleep soon enough. When they reached Euston, she had to nudge him awake, his bottom lip crusted with sugar.

She spat on a hankie and wiped his face.

'Right, sunshine. Let's see what our Nellie's up to, shall we?'

19

'There you are.' Carolyn arched her eyebrows at the attic. My attic. She hadn't knocked, opening the door and walking in while my head was full of last night's dream of Joe. I might've been getting dressed, or naked. She didn't care. As far as she was concerned, this was her room and I was the intruder. 'Oh, Robin, do look!' She laughed. 'She's papered the walls.'

Robin put his head around the door, having the decency to look ashamed. She'd dragged him up here and he'd come, but he knew it wasn't right. This was my room, he'd said so. All the rooms on this floor belonged to me. Carolyn swayed her way to my window, ducking under the eaves to exaggerate the lack of space. She drew a finger down the pane of glass and inspected it, turning like a wind-up doll to stand with her back to the light.

Robin nodded at the walls. 'You've done a wonderful job.'

'Yes,' Carolyn said, 'lovely,' as if she were mispronouncing *ghastly*.

But Robin wasn't paying any attention to her. He'd straightened, standing in the tallest part of the attic. 'You've transformed it.' He smiled at me, a real smile, straight from his storm-grey eyes.

And I smiled back, fully aware of Carolyn over by the window, watching.

Let her watch, I thought. Let her get the measure of what was happening. She'd brought him up here to humiliate me, or else to punish me in some way for some small thing, perhaps nothing at all. Eight rooms weren't enough for her bullying; she'd wanted to expand, hoping to recruit Robin to her cause. But he was smiling because of the spell I'd cast, transforming the attic into a home. Why else would he smile like that, as if I'd unlocked a secret seam of happiness inside him?

'This rug! I'd forgotten all about it.' He crouched to touch the floor beneath his feet. 'I used to play bear hunts on this when I was a child.'

My beautiful rug a magic carpet, transporting him to his childhood.

Straightening, he reached to smooth his thumb along the wall. 'Is this varnish? It's very clever. Découpage, is that what you'd call it?' He kept his hand on the wall, as if to reorient himself.

The house let out its breath. I lifted my head and looked at Carolyn, standing with her back to the light, the mocking smile dying on her lips. I met her eyes, and I did not look away.

The cheese shop was cold and gleaming. Bradley looked pleased to see me. Thanks to Carolyn, I was in here every other day, for eggs to bake a cake she'd declare too dry to eat, or for extravagant cold cuts – *capicola, mortadella, bresaola* – naming the meats as if they were body parts. Despite our conversation about money, Robin had made no additional allowance for her demands on his budget.

I was afraid I'd have to break into the money she'd given me for the modelling, a curling fifty-pound note offered on the hot palm of her hand. I'd been ashamed to take it.

'How are you this morning, Nell?' Bradley lifted the cheese onto the cutting board, manoeuvring the wire above it with a delicacy that had me holding my breath.

'It's a beautiful morning,' I said.

Autumn was here. The leaves were coming down, lying crisp along the pavements, my attic window furred by condensation. The scent of glue and varnish lingered at the top of the house; I could no longer smell Carolyn in Starling Villas. In the cheese shop, I was the first customer of the day. The steady thrum of the cooling system was comforting. I liked to watch Bradley work.

'We have a very nice Fleurie just in.'

'I don't know what that is.' I smiled at him. 'Is it wine?'

He reached for the waxed paper. I saw him running through a list of possible responses before he said simply, 'Yes.'

'Hedgerow fruits, brambles, a hint of granite and earth?' I quoted from a book I'd flicked through, in Robin's library.

'Exactly so.' He returned my smile, placing the wrapped wedge of cheese on the counter.

'I'm afraid Dr Wilder hasn't given me enough money for impulse purchases.' I wanted to see if my indiscretion would surprise him.

He busied himself with the rearrangement of the cold cabinet. When he looked up, I saw the thread of a frown on his forehead. 'You're staying safe, I hope?'

'In London?'

'In Starling Villas.' His stare was direct. He didn't drop the volume of his voice.

Both of us now, being indiscreet.

'Of course.' But his question raised the hairs on the back of my neck. 'Did you know her? His last – housekeeper?' He nodded and I struggled to make sense of the look on his face, searching beneath its surface circumspection for a sinister meaning, a salve to my nagging sense of unease. 'Why did she leave, do you know?'

'I'm afraid I don't.' Bradley peeled off his plastic gloves, one finger at a time. His eyes didn't leave my face. 'I wasn't aware she *had* left.'

The way he said it scared me, as if she were still inside the house, buried at the back of the wardrobe or hiding behind the heavy curtains in the library: *I wasn't aware she* had *left.*

'Until you met me.'

Bradley adjusted his expression to neutral, nodding. 'Exactly so.'

Starling Villas was silent when I reached home.

I caught myself thinking that – *home.* Pushing the key into my pocket, I scowled at my own stupidity. *Hi, honey, I'm home. With your stinking cheese and fresh eggs.*

I wanted so much to be fierce again, full of rage at my predicament, at the easy way his smile slipped under my defences. Ours was no fairy-tale but there had been the start of something, before she came. The shape of his hand hesitating as he reached for the coffee I'd poured. His offer of blankets, his insistence I cook myself a meal. The peace I'd found, washing his floors. There had been such comfort in our shared silence, the whisper of his wrist against mine.

I knew what Meagan would say: *Nell with a K. Death Knell.*

She hated me. Hated all of us in Lyle's but me more than anyone because I did her job, kept the house clean and fed the little ones, rocked them to sleep, taught them to read. I showed her up, and she couldn't forgive that. She'd hated me long before I set the local press at her heels with my rumours of what went on in the house. What would she make of my life here in the Villas? 'You're papering over the cracks, girl.' Not a metaphor. Up in the attic, I was literally papering over cracks, although I suppose you could say it was what I'd done all my life so, yes, all right, a *metaphor*. I was a prisoner in plain sight, given keys, allowed outside. But what truly traps a person? Debt. Death. Love. 'The ruin's in the blood,' Meagan used to say about Joe and me. 'The worm's in the apple.'

Every trick I knew, she taught me. If I was too good, she grew wary, too wild and she threatened to throw me out, too servile and she took advantage. I learnt to be a tightrope walker, agile-footed mother hen, acrobat, magician. Her tricks should have helped me here in Starling Villas where balance was the frail thing on which the house was resting.

'Two worms in one apple. I should throw you out. Disgusting, degrading.'

It was happening again, here in Starling Villas. Robin had begun to trust me. But then Carolyn came and I'd no way of knowing if this strange seduction was what the pair of them had planned from the start. No way of knowing if I was the one who'd walked into a trap.

I banged his rota onto the kitchen table, flicking through its plastic-shrouded pages. He had a rule for everything, except what really mattered. How To Treat Your Housekeeper With Respect and Dignity – where was that chapter? The pages were slick under my hands. I could feel the steel of the knives in the butcher's block, each blade slicing its shadow on the counter.

I drew a long breath, shutting my eyes. I mustn't lose my temper or burn my bridges, not so soon after the last time, after Brian and the masseuse. Reading the rota's bland instructions helped to calm me, and to remind me I should be watering his plants.

In the garden room, I fancied I heard the plants growing, the trickle of their roots through soil, the furring of their leaves. For a second I stood defeated by their industry, my neck creeping as if I'd disturbed a room of conspirators. His plants huddled at the edges of the room, a dense mass pricked by colour, and thorns. A moth orchid shuddered on its tall stem, turning its ghost's face away from me. I made a circuit, checking the moisture in the pots, trickling water where it was needed. Halfway around, I came to an abrupt halt, holding the watering can away from my dress.

Poking from under a terracotta pot – the pale corner of a sheet of paper. It hadn't been there yesterday. Setting the can down, I lifted the plant out of the way, pulling the paper free with a spattering of soil. It was Carolyn's painting of me, a blue watermark bleeding around my face. 'Show some emotion,' she'd said. She'd drawn me with downcast eyes, my mouth ajar. 'Half-cocked,' Meagan called it. 'Don't stand there with your mouth at half-cock.'

Blood beat in my ears.

In Carolyn's picture, my hair was piled into a black turban and my shoulders were weak, trailing to nothing. She'd painted me with no arms or legs, a head and torso floating in front of the mirror, grossly hunchbacked, an iron band of shadow around my neck. The slant of my eyes and the high angle of my cheeks made me look Slavic. She'd exaggerated the scar on my eyebrow, making it puckered and ugly. I didn't look like this, but I recognized myself in her painting. The darkening lines, the sense I'd bolt the first chance I got. She'd captured me, and I hated it. Rolling the sketch, I hid it up the sleeve of my dress before searching under all the other pots for his drawing.

Robin's charcoal sketch was nowhere in the room.

Instead, I found something else. Hidden under another plant – a keychain with a pink silk photo frame. It hadn't been here yesterday, or any day since I'd started working for him; I'd have found it before now. Photos of twin girls, aged about six. Asian, with big eyes and smiles. Water had crept into the frame, spotting their faces.

I shivered, rubbing my thumb at the spots. Who were they?

The keychain wasn't Carolyn's but she'd wanted me to find it, just as she'd wanted me to find her painting of me. The chain was a cheap thing, precious only because of the girls' faces. Had it belonged to his last housekeeper? Of the three keys, none would fit any lock in Starling Villas, their teeth were too wide for the doors here. Tucking the keychain into my pocket, I finished watering his plants. I searched every inch of the room, still looking for his sketch of me, but it wasn't there.

In his bedroom, I hunted again. Nothing. Carolyn had shoved the art equipment into the cupboard under the stairs where wicker hampers were gathering cobwebs alongside golf clubs and skis and an expensive rowing machine turned upright on its nose. Robin had liked to leave the house, once. He'd led an active life, sporty, holidaying abroad. Or had he only dreamt of it, buying the apparatus then abandoning his plans? Such a dull man by Carolyn's standards, unsocial and awkward. Why wasn't she with someone new? Young and glamorous, a trophy to hang off her arm as she flitted about London. For the first time, I thought how poisonous their relationship was. A squatting, swollen thing. For the first time, I wanted to run.

I carried the keychain up to my attic, sitting cross-legged on my mattress to study the little faces in the pink silk frame. His housekeeper's daughters, or nieces? Grandchildren, maybe. But why was the keychain here in his house when she was not? And why had Carolyn wanted me to find it today? She'd left her portrait in plain sight, knowing I'd search under every pot for his charcoal sketch. She'd wanted me to find the keychain, but what and whom did she want me to suspect? Twin girls, big-eyed. The chain was worn with use, its frame smooth from fingers or lips. I could picture its owner. Dark like me but bent with work, the soles of her feet polished to horn. How often had she kissed the pictures of her girls, reminding herself she was doing this for their sakes? She'd loved the frame, keeping it close. How then had she lost it, or left it behind? And why hadn't she returned once she'd discovered its loss?

I wasn't aware she had *left.* Bradley's expression was unreadable but he was warning me, I was certain of that now. Warning me of the need to take care here in Starling Villas.

I hid the keychain inside an old tea tin, pushing it to the bottom of my rucksack. When I straightened, I caught my reflection in the window, furtive and afraid. I should start keeping a record of what was happening in this house. For posterity, for the police. Then, when it was over and there was no one left to tell the truth about Starling Villas, they'd have something to go on. Proof. The wildness of the thought surprised me. The police had never been my friends and now, by any measure, would consider themselves my enemies.

I hadn't felt threatened here until Carolyn came. Even now, it wasn't a real fear but rather the ghost of one. Best to keep a record, even so. Robin would approve. Unless he preferred to pretend it'd never happened. His wrist on mine, the heat in his lips as she was prodding me into place or when I was kneeling on his tiles. In her sketch, I resembled a slave. Was I the same in his? He'd caught sight of himself in the mirror when her hands were on me. I'd watched him recoil, seen him thinking, *Who is this? Not me, not me.*

'Show some emotion,' she'd insisted when he was showing nothing but emotion, written all over him in hectic, betraying blood.

Was this what he'd hoped for, all along? The rota and rules his way of catching me off guard, and instilling discipline. *It's just me in the Villas.*

Liar.

I'd never have taken this job if Carolyn had been here that first day. But shouldn't the presence of a wife make a house less sinister, not more? The trouble was, I didn't know the rules, no one took the time to teach me. At school, yes, but I'd hardly attended thanks to my caretaker role at Lyle's. Meagan taught me ways to get out of trouble, not how to avoid it in the first place. She taught me to put on lipstick when Social Services sent a man instead of a woman, and to take notice of my body changing, as if its curves could be my camouflage. 'Just tell him you're happy here. You love Lyle's, the little ones. Rosie.'

Soon it would be time to make Robin's cocoa. I'd creep downstairs to battle with the stove, taking care not to heat the milk too long. When it was done, I'd carry the cup to the library where he'd ignore me, busy with his books, imagining because I was young I must be immune to pride or shame, patience or envy. If

I blushed, he dismissed it as shyness or at worst a fleeting humiliation, thinking I'd soon forget the barbs his wife flung at me, or his own studious disregard. But I was an old soul, with an old heart. At the age of eight, I was mother to a dozen kids. I grew up in a house where childhood was banished to the back of the cupboard. If Robin Wilder imagined his wife's stones only skipped the surface of my skin, he had no idea how deep I ran, what fears and furies I felt. *Nell, leave her. Come here.* I reached for my rucksack and held it close, shutting my eyes at the attic I'd transformed. Blood beat in my feet with the urge to run from this place, and these people. Starling Villas was stuffed full of money and history and character, but it was empty. Everything in here was hollow, including him. Including us.

You'll find out, I thought. *Dr and Mrs Wilder. If you push me, playing your games . . . You'll find out who I am and what I'm capable of.*

20

'Here.' Meagan handed Joe her cigarette lighter. 'And be careful,' she warned him. 'From what you've said, they're not the type for anything stronger than a smoke.' He'd told her all about Carolyn Wilder, his night of passion in her posh house. 'Wait for her to suggest it. Let her think she's the one making the decisions. Just like that first night, after she picked you up in the club.'

Joe took the lighter, pushing it out of sight into his pocket. He'd showered at Meagan's insistence. His fringe was damp, his eyes spacey. He'd bewitched that rich cow in Nell's new home, but only because Carolyn Wilder was fighting a closing window of her own. Meagan hoped the husband was the same, or that Nell had worked her magic there already. She'd not spied Meagan when she was out shopping, too busy buying overpriced cheese from a shop that made the Spar look like a food bank. She looked good, did Nell. Her skin like milked coffee, those haunted eyes. Guilt suited her, she wore it like a good coat. Meagan had thought she'd find the girl eaten up by it but here she was with her pretty feet under an expensive table, slipping between the cracks in that marriage as easily as last demands through a letterbox. Dr and Mrs Robin Wilder. The house reeked of money, and who owed Meagan more than Nell did? Who had run away because she was afraid of what Meagan knew about little Rosie Bond's death? No kiddies were living in Starling Villas, Meagan had established that much. It hadn't been easy to lay her hands on any better information. Very private, the Wilders. Well, good. They'd want to keep it private, what happened next. As for Joe and Nell, they owed her, after two years of keeping mum.

Meagan laughed, and lit a cigarette. *Keeping mum.* She wasn't without a sense of irony and she knew her faults, could count them on the fingers of both hands. She'd never pretended she was perfect, but she was owed. Time to collect.

21

On Sundays at Starling Villas, breakfast was served in the dining room. I opened the curtains and laid the table, after first polishing each plate and piece of cutlery. The sun sat in the centre of it all, striking the silverware. I was pleased with the effect, and that Carolyn wasn't here to see it. She'd left last night in her black satin coat, and she hadn't returned. I imagined she was in a hotel somewhere, with whichever Joe-shaped substitute she'd picked up for the night.

In the kitchen, I lit the stove. As it heated, I greased two ramekins to bake eggs before loading the coffee press, and frothing the milk. The smell of baking eggs brought the pigeon to the windowsill. She sat watching as I tidied my hair and smoothed the apron at my waist.

Carrying the tray, I climbed the stairs, crossing the hall to the dining room, where Robin was waiting, dressed for the day in his soft blue shirt and grey trousers. I set the tray on the sideboard, aware of his eyes on me as I brought the breakfast to the table.

'Sit with me,' he said.

When I hesitated, he added, 'Two eggs, yes? I can't eat two this morning. Sit, please.' He sounded sad, his thumb smoothing the handle of his knife.

'I'll need to lay another place.'

'Yes.' He nodded.

While I brought the place setting, he poured coffee into his cup, moving it into the space he'd reserved for me. We fell into a rhythm. As I set my plate, he settled the ramekin there; when I laid a side plate, he loaded it with toast. He moved the salt and pepper closer to me. 'Do you take sugar?'

'No, thank you.'

'Milk, then?' I nodded and he poured the froth from the jug into my coffee. Then he stood and drew back my chair, like a waiter. No, like a gentleman.

I was very aware of the weight of him, standing behind me. 'Thank you.' I sat, drawing my napkin into my lap, pressing it in place with the palms of my hands.

We reached for our coffee together, smiling at our synchronicity.

'This is nice,' he said.

He buttered a slice of toast, his wrist turning neatly. I thought about the strength in him which he kept hidden so much of the time. Had something happened to make him despise his strength, or fear it? All his energy went into sitting with his books and boxes. Did he put on the passivity, as armour against Carolyn? I'd never seen her look at a book, much less read one. I'd caught her poking a stockinged foot at a pile of his textbooks, toppling two of them to the floor. The look on her face – she hated his books, as if they were her mortal enemies. I had waited until she was gone before crouching to rescue them, smoothing their spines, running my thumb down the deckled edges of their pages. Rosie had hated books, saying on her sixth birthday she was too old for them.

'These eggs are perfect,' Robin said.

Did he ever think of me when I wasn't right in front of him? At night perhaps, sending his thoughts up through the house to where I lay in the attic. He'd called it wonderful – the varnished walls, the rug I'd restored from his childhood – but what would he say if he knew I thought of it as my home? His attic, mine. If he knew how much it meant to me to have rescued his forgotten treasures, the reverence I'd made of the ritual? My palms sweated against the linen in my lap, a flush of shame heating my skin. He crunched at the toast with his strong teeth, crumbs sitting on the cuff of his shirt. For the first time, I thought how human he was, and how handsome.

I broke the yolk of my egg with the point of my spoon. 'I found a set of keys in the garden room.' I licked the spoon, before dipping it into the hot heart of the yolk.

He frowned, fishing egg onto his toast with the tines of his fork. 'Did you?'

'I thought perhaps Mrs Wilder left them behind by accident. But the keychain has photos in it, of children.' I stopped, conscious of having crossed a line. The sentence was full of intimacy. His wife, clumsy or forgetful, leaving her keys behind. The faces of children when they had none. The word *childless* lay between us. 'I wasn't sure what to do with the keys.'

He chewed a mouthful of baked egg before he answered. 'I can't think who they belong to, unless it was Mrs Mystery.'

Mrs Mystery. Was he mocking me? I'd dreamt of the silk keychain, the twins' faces chasing me through the night until I turned and hissed at them to stop.

'Mrs Mistry was the last housekeeper.' He reached for his coffee. 'She left a few weeks before you came. As far as I know she took all her belongings with her. She has two little girls, I believe.'

'This must be them.' I nodded. 'Twin girls, very pretty.'

'I have her details somewhere.' He sounded vague. 'I'll find them, and we can return the keys.'

Neither of us asked why the keys had come to light only now. I'd been in the garden room every day. The keychain wasn't there, and then it was.

I finished my egg, wiping my mouth on the napkin but only after I'd licked every corner of my lips. Egg was horrible to get out of linen. 'More coffee?'

He nodded, 'Please,' and I rose from my seat to refill his cup. There was enough in the press for a fourth cup but I didn't refill mine, not wanting him to think I was taking advantage of his kindness. Did he even think of it as kindness, inviting me to share his breakfast? Did he know how long it had been since I'd eaten so much food so early in the day? How could he know? He'd wanted company, that was all. He couldn't eat the second egg and didn't want it going to waste.

'Have a slice of toast,' he said, upsetting my theory.

'It's yours.' Tears heated my eyes for a second. 'You always have two slices on Sunday.'

'I always have two eggs.'

I looked at the empty ramekin, my spoon rimmed with yellow. 'I'm sorry . . .'

'Nonsense.' There was an edge in his voice, of annoyance or impatience. 'I invited you to eat it. You know how I hate waste.' He moved the butter dish closer to my plate. 'The toast won't keep, so please. Take it.'

With my eyes down, I spread the slice, the way he'd buttered his. My mouth tasted of salt. Why was I crying? Carolyn wasn't here, it was just the two of us. I was warm and well-fed, enjoying his company. The room was wide with sunshine. It was a beautiful, beautiful morning.

'That's better.' He smiled at me, his eyes forest-dark.

As I ate his toast, he poured me a second cup of coffee, adding the last of the milk. We didn't speak again, finishing our coffees in silence with the sun moving slowly across the table to touch our hands with its easy warmth.

By noon, the sun had gone behind patchy cloud.

The day was mine, Dr Wilder was going out. He hadn't said where, just that he wouldn't be home for lunch and would eat sandwiches for supper. 'The day's yours.' Smiling again.

After finishing in the kitchen, I went to his bedroom, meaning to make the bed and tidy the bathroom, but it was all done. The sheets neat, the duvet folded at the foot of the bed. In the bathroom, everything gleamed, fresh towels on the rail. There was nothing for me to do. How little he needed me, I thought. He could look after himself, and no doubt he could cook too. But then I thought how we'd sat together at the breakfast table as easily as old friends. He'd had me here as a housekeeper, but he was keeping me for company. Mrs Mistry's children whispered to me. I couldn't make out their words, just the buzzing of their voices in my head. 'Hush,' I said.

His aftershave scented the room, making me see forests in

165

summer, the sun cooling as it fell between branches onto fronds of fern. I moved to lay my hand on his pillow and saw the charcoal sketch, his portrait of me with my back to his mirror. Trimmed to the size of a paperback book, propped against the lamp on his bedside table. He'd sketched my profile and its reflection in the glass, like the drawing I'd found in the attic of a tree mirrored in water. Two faces, neither one quite mine. The face in the mirror came closest, exposing the tension in my jaw and neckline. He'd used shades of silver and black, a stroke of charcoal for the shadows along my cheekbone and at the base of my throat. The scar on my eyebrow was a true star, silvered. I looked neither beautiful nor ugly, he'd been neither generous nor cruel, but there was a tenderness to the lines. Hesitation, perhaps, or reluctance; he'd lacked Carolyn's enthusiasm for the project. And yet he'd kept the sketch, propping it here at the side of his bed where he could look at it as he lay with his head on the pillow that smelt – I leaned in, breathing deeply – of lake water and autumn leaves, his skin. All last night while he lay here, I was with him. Mirror-me, with her neck angled away. Other-me, with her black eyes. Which did he see when he looked at me? Which girl had shared his breakfast this morning? The one with the lovely, youthful neck, or the girl who wouldn't give anything to the mirror other than her tension, her shadows and her scars.

That afternoon, I walked through London, chasing the sun as it wandered west. I was half-frozen from being inside Starling Villas for so long. Robin had told me to take the day off but it was strange to have idle hands, nothing to lift or wipe or whisk, no work to do.

By the side of the Serpentine, I stopped to watch couples in the boats they'd hired. Canada geese watched with me, their beaked faces somehow looking bloodthirsty. Soon they should be making spearheads in the sky, heading south for the winter, but for now they patrolled the park among the tourists. I was a tourist; I didn't belong in London or anywhere, unless it was with Joe.

On the water, a couple laughed, upsetting the pitch of their boat. The girl shrieked, her hands across her mouth. The boy wrestled with the oars, shouting happily, his face clenched with effort. Something shifted in the bushes at my feet and I fizzed with fear, moving away from the water to the sand path full of footprints. I had the sudden feeling I was being followed, but when I looked there was no one. The couple in the boat made me think of Joe and me, sharing a bed in Brian's flat.

We'd shared a lot of beds when we first came to London, nearly five months ago now. We would meet strangers in the Shunt Lounge, or in clubs like the one where Carolyn found Joe, and we'd go home with the ones who wanted us. Whatever we had to do, to buy a night off the streets. None of the strangers treated us well, but it was more than we deserved. Most of the strangers I'd forgotten. Only Brian's face came to me, thrust close to mine, 'You bitch.' The prickle of his wallpaper against my bare shoulders. The night before, he'd paid a masseuse to come and oil our backs. That morning, he'd found me going through his stuff, sitting cross-legged with his photos and papers spread over the floor where last night he and Joe and I had been spread. I'd made a pool of papers, giving myself no chance to hide my deliberate transgression when he walked back into the room. 'You bitch!' Grabbing me, shoving me up against the wall. We'd known each other nine days, intimately, carnally. I'd seen him naked from every angle. But I wasn't to see

167

his bank statements or school certificates, or the photos of him as a baby in his father's arms. That was where he drew the line. Everyone drew one, you just had to search and you'd find it. I'd spread his line all over the floor, waiting for him to return and find me there.

'What did you do?' Joe demanded when we were back on the streets, the slam of Brian's door ringing in our heads. 'Nell. What the hell did you do?' But he knew.

I'd done what I always did, sabotaging our safe place.

We didn't deserve to live well, when Rosie was dead. I'd thought Joe understood that. But he didn't seem to care that we were getting too comfortable with Brian, having too much fun. Eating good food, getting drunk every night. Joe was taking drugs for the first time since we'd left Lyle's, smoking and sniffing. It kept him warm, he said, helped him to forget. I didn't want him to forget. Brian liked to buy us gifts: clothes and jewellery, iPhones and sunglasses and cocaine. Joe knew as well as I did – we didn't deserve to live like that. 'Why d'you always have to ruin what we find, what we have?' He'd walked away from me, in disgust. I'd had to run to catch up with him.

The splash of oars on the Serpentine brought me back to the present.

People were coming up from the Underground with phones in their hands. A tide of people, pressing on the bruise of my aloneness. A man in a hi-vis jacket had attracted a tail of tourists. We're hardwired to follow the herd. Meagan hardly had to lift a hand to get her way. We jumped before she ever told us to. Each one of us trained to submit and obey, to be grateful for what little we had, living in fear of losing it.

Down in the Underground, trains scratched at the tracks. We

loved trains, Joe and me. The only time he slept easily was in the seat next to mine, rocked by the motion of the wheels. The night we escaped from Meagan, we took the train to London. Every detail of that journey was fresh in my head. The steamy smell of the carriage, cake crumbs on the seats, a filmy spot on the window where someone had rested his head. I was wearing the bottom half of Joe's tracksuit with 'Mathematics' printed up the outside leg. Joe wore the matching logo on his chest. He fell asleep almost instantly, his head on my shoulder and then in my lap. I dropped my hand to his hair, turning the silver ring in his ear, his latest piercing. Armour, he said, as if bits of metal could keep unwanted hands away. The ring was warm in my fingers. From an adjacent seat, a business-man watched, unable to keep his eyes off us. Mr Intercity, his shiny grey suit fitting like a second skin. I bent forward, my hair hiding Joe's face. The man's stare was hot on my neck. He couldn't decide which of us he wanted. He didn't know Joe and I were a package deal. Brian understood, it was why he threw the pair of us onto the streets after my act of sabotage. It was why I wanted Joe with me now, in Starling Villas.

'Excuse me, d'you mind?' A different businessman, uninterested in me. I was standing in his path, lost inside my memory of the train journey. The sun slunk over the park.

Where are you, Joe? Where did you go? Whose bed did you find, after Carolyn's?

We said we'd keep each other's secrets, take them to the grave. We made a pact, sealed in blood. Never to forget, never to forgive. How could he have forgotten that?

*

Starling Villas stood in sunset, all of its windows ablaze.

It felt good to be back. I'd tested the length of my leash, found the perimeter of my new home. But as I stepped into his hall, fear flared my blood. She was here. I could smell that siren scent, the lilies drooping in their vase – Carolyn was back.

I pocketed my keys, unbuttoning my coat, taking my time. Remembering our breakfast together, Robin and me seated at the table in the hush of the house. He'd given me the day off. I worked for him, not her.

Crossing the hall, I started climbing the stairs to my attic.

'There you are.' Her voice came from below me, on the spiral steps that led down to the kitchen. 'You sly thing . . . I thought you'd stay in, knowing you had guests.'

I continued up the stairs as if I hadn't heard her.

Let her call my name, if it was so important. Let her raise her voice, show her true colours.

'Your cousin,' Carolyn said, 'is in the kitchen.'

I stopped then, a thud in my throat.

Turning, I saw her on the lower step.

Light hit the underside of her jaw like a torch, showing every line and sag. When she spread her mouth into a smile, the light leapt to her cheekbones, carving her face into a jack-o'-lantern.

'Well?' she said. 'Aren't you coming to say hello?'

22

'It's fortunate I was in, since for whatever reason you weren't here to answer the door.'

'It's my day off.'

'Really?' Carolyn laughed. 'I didn't know you had those.' She stood at the kitchen doorway, as if guarding it. The light was behind her, all the betraying softness gone, leaving clean expensive lines of the kind I could never afford. Her dark red dress suited her, better than the black. She raised her eyebrows. 'What did you do?'

'Do . . . ?' I wet my lips.

She knew about our breakfast. My new happiness – was it written on my face, the way money was on hers? Or was she talking about something worse, from long ago? What had she heard?

'With your day off. What did you do with it?'

'I walked.'

Her eyes went to my shoes, then to my coat as if she could see the moth holes in its lining. She saw the flush in my cheeks, and the dampness in my eyes. I couldn't hide from her scrutiny. My stomach clenched, cold sweat stabbing at the back of my neck. All I could think was, *I have no cousin.*

'You've kept us waiting.' She swung the door wide with the flat of her hand. 'Luckily I was here to make tea, after such a long journey.' Her words made no sense, nor did the way she stood wide-armed, inviting me into the kitchen, where the bronze lamp was lit.

New shadows spilled on the floor. I was afraid to step inside, afraid of what I'd find.

Carolyn's face was masked by a smile, as if my fear thrilled her.

At the table, hands folded on the scrubbed surface, a cup of tea at his elbow—

'Joe.'

'Hello, Nell.' He smiled up at me, sleepily.

His fringe had grown long in the weeks since I'd seen him last, full of straw highlights. He wore a plaid shirt, faded pink and green, its cuffs fraying at his wrists. He'd brought the sun's scent in here. I wanted to touch his face, to be sure it was real. To be sure it was Joe.

I had to walk past Carolyn, to reach the table. For a second we were so close, a thread of static touched our cheeks. I lifted a hand to rub at its sharp, fleeting kiss.

Joe sat forward under the bowl of light. He'd taken all the studs and rings from his ears, naked without the piercings. It took me a second to see the tension in his shoulders, the warning behind his smile. But I'd smelt her before I saw her – iron slicing through the summer's sweetness like a scythe through a field of corn.

'Your cousin, Joe.' Carolyn spoke the words through her teeth. 'And your aunt, of course.'

At the foot of the table, hidden until I took two final steps forward. Grey hair at her temples, black coat buttoned to her neck.

Meagan Flack.

'Hello, love.' Her face cracked in a grin. 'Hello, our Nell.' Robin's rota was at her elbow, its pages open. 'This's nice.' Her eyes winked wetly at me. 'This is very nice.'

Five months had passed since I'd seen her, but it might have been five hours. The old danger dug its claws into me, as familiar as fear. She'd found me, run me to ground. The kitchen seemed to shrink around us, the floor tilting under my feet, light spiralling into the shadows. For a second I feared I would faint, fall and smash my head on the hard tiles. I forced myself to breathe and to stand still, meeting her stare.

This is nice. Starling Villas, she meant. And me, installed here. With Carolyn who stank of money, the one scent in the world that made her salivate.

How long had they been sitting, talking? How much had been said? Three cups of tea on the table, a fourth standing empty.

Stupidly, I thought of milk and sugar, shopping.

Meagan reached for Joe's hand, patting it with her stained smoker's fingers. He sat like a doll, head nodding under the lamp's heat. He'd taken something or it was stress, that strange lethargy that crept over him when he was scared; his brain shutting down for his own protection.

Oh Joe. What have you done?

'It's lovely to see you,' Meagan said. 'Isn't it, Joe?'

'Yes.' He was docile in her grip.

I wanted to pull him away from her. And I wanted to rescue Robin's rota. She'd no business looking at it, no business being here. Carolyn was tense with questions, her eyes like Meagan's hands – hooked on Joe. I'd done this, brought him back. And she was wondering why, with what purpose I'd brought him here. No matter how hard I wished him away, it was done.

Carolyn said, 'Lovely,' and it took me a moment to realize she was parroting Meagan.

When I forced myself to meet her eyes, I saw it was more than curiosity. Carolyn's body was always tight and her face too, but I'd learnt to read her. Fear sat in the shadow above her upper lip. This wasn't the way her game was supposed to be played. Joe was a one-night stand, a nightclub pick-up, someone she'd never see again. He'd fascinated her, the way he fascinated everyone with his sleepy sexiness, that sense you could take him unawares. Like the man on the train, Mr Intercity, Carolyn couldn't take her eyes off Joe. But Meagan was petting at him, so obviously in charge. And then there was me, the stranger who'd installed herself here while all along knowing Joe, knowing about that night. One step ahead of her game, from the start. I didn't need to panic, not yet. She was doing it enough for both of us. I reached for the pot and poured myself a cup of tea, adding a splash of milk. 'Did you come far?' I asked Joe.

It was Meagan who answered: 'From Bala. By train.'

'Goodness!' Carolyn laughed, and fear flavoured her voice too. 'I've no idea where that is.'

'Wales.' I drew out a chair and sat at the table.

Three of us now, staring up at Carolyn. I saw the soft spot under her chin. 'Bala is in North Wales.'

Her gaze shifted between Joe and me, avoiding Meagan. It struck me for the first time how the costly gloss of her skin aged her. It was such an obvious falsehood, like a child's clumsy lie.

'That's a long way!' Her voice was a pitch too high, falsely bright.

She was old enough to be his mother. For one night, she'd been able to pretend otherwise but he wasn't supposed to come back. That was my doing, mine.

I sipped at my tea, surprised to find a small measure of sympathy rising to the surface of my feelings towards her. Carolyn could afford so much, things I'd never have, but she couldn't buy the drowsy flush of Joe's cheeks. Meagan knew it, too. Sitting with his hand in hers, grey head cocked, soaking up every secret in the house, hoarding it as a miser hoards money and food and heat.

Meagan waited until I'd finished my cup of tea before saying, 'We should have a proper catch-up, Nellie. Just you and me. A proper natter.'

I took care to keep calm, although my heart was thudding and my throat was so tight I had difficulty swallowing the last of my tea.

'We must,' I said.

Somehow, I managed a note of challenge, meeting her eye so steadily I saw her face flicker. Unsure of her ground? Or excited at the thought of fighting me for a piece of whatever she imagined was on offer here? Money, it was always money with Meagan. And she'd never been afraid of fighting for it, getting herself dirty. She would bring up Rosie's death without a second thought, if she thought it would get her what she wanted.

What would Carolyn Wilder make of that? A six-year-old who died in our care, mine and Joe's, a drowned baby girl. What would Robin think? R. Wilder JP. Magistrate.

'We could have it now,' Meagan said, 'our natter.'

'Oh, but you must be tired, after your long journey.' I stood, and began clearing the tea things from the table. 'Why not leave it to the morning?'

I saw the smile crabbing her face. She was so sure she had me where she wanted me. She could taste my fear. I had to fight to keep my hands from shaking, the way they always shook when she fixed her attention on me. Through all of it, Joe sat immobile, his hands slack around his teacup, his gaze as distant as our lake. Carolyn didn't speak but she watched us intently.

When Meagan and Joe stood to leave, Carolyn made a joke about the spare room. Testing them or me, I wasn't sure, but Meagan was too smart for that. She knew to take her time if she was to inch her way inside Starling Villas. She wasn't going to rush and risk ruining it.

'Kind of you but we've a place not too far away. It's a flying visit.'

From the kitchen window, I watched their shadows bleeding up the street.

Not too far away. I pictured a small hotel, cheap because there was never enough money. Until now. I leaned into the cold slab of the sink. *Don't panic. Don't do anything stupid.*

Carolyn's shoes sounded on the steps, coming down into the kitchen.

I kept my back turned, busy with the cups. She'd seen them out of the house, insisting on it, following Joe as if sewn to him by threads. I thought of a dress I'd hemmed for Rosie, years ago. I'd put the dress in my lap as I worked and when I stood it stayed in my lap, because I'd sewn it into my own skirt. All those tiny, tidy stitches had gone through the thin cotton of her dress into the cheap fabric of my skirt. I'd had to unpick everything and start over again.

'Does Robin know you have visitors?' Carolyn perched on the corner of the table under the lamp, its heat lifting the silver scent of her hairspray.

'I didn't know myself.' I kept my back turned.

The darkened window gave me her reflection, watching, wondering.

176

'You must've known they might come when you gave out this address.' She coiled her body sideways, reaching to smooth a finger at her ankle. 'You must've known what you were doing.'

'I texted Joe, but only so he could text back.'

'You're not alike. As for your aunt . . . !' The lamp caught her laugh and hurled it at me.

I resisted the urge to duck. The cups were washed but I ran water to rinse the sink, putting off the moment when I would have to turn and face her.

'Oh,' she said then. 'I nearly forgot. Mend this for me, would you?' She reached for her bag, drawing out a piece of pale silk. Sewing, as if she'd read my mind. 'Invisible mend, isn't that what they call it?' She balled the silk and set it on the table. 'I don't want the mend to show, anyway.'

She slid to the floor, dusting her dress. Her movements were different since Joe, lighter and quicker, more self-conscious. As if she was telling herself, *Look, I'm youthful, full of life!*

Neither of us spoke of the fact Joe had been here before, in her bed. Robin's bed. Neither of us asked the other how it felt, to share that knowledge.

I waited until she'd left the kitchen before I picked up the silk she wanted me to mend. It was a camisole, frothy with lace and heated by the lamp as if she'd slipped it off her body seconds before. It was like holding a hot handful of cobwebs. To make an invisible mend, you had to steal a little cloth from the same garment, from a hem or seam, and work it into the spot where the damage was. Delicately, so it looked as if nothing had been added or taken away. The camisole smelt of her. I balled it in my fist as she'd done, pushing it into my pocket.

At least she was gone, the house was ours again for the evening, one last evening. But when I went upstairs to draw the curtains and light the lamps, she was in the garden room, waiting.

'Did you find anything in here?' She slipped her hands into the pockets of her dress, standing so narrowly against the windows I had trouble seeing her. 'The last time you cleaned?'

Her portrait of me, she meant. Or was she talking about the keychain? I couldn't detect any threat in her words or in the way she stood with her head tilted as if telling herself Joe must've found her fascinating, that's why he'd come back. Even though we both knew I was the one who'd summoned him. She needed to believe he'd come back because he couldn't resist her.

I could have told her about the things Joe couldn't resist, but I didn't.

'Why?' I asked. 'Have you lost something?'

There was a challenge in my tone. I heard it, and so did she. It wasn't my usual tone, nor was it an appropriate one in which to address the wife of my employer.

'You like Robin, don't you?' She cocked her head at me, pert as a bird, slim as a snake. 'It's why you don't want to look too closely at the way things are here, why you were so quick to dismiss my warnings about him.' She moved her hands inside her pockets, nails rasping. 'You should ask him about his old housekeeper, the one before you.'

'Mrs Mistry?' I spoke the name casually, as if I knew all about her.

'You saw the pictures of her girls.' Carolyn paused. 'I wonder what happened to them, where they ended up.'

She wanted me to believe the worst of Robin, to think him untrustworthy. Revenge, was that it? He'd been so different this

178

morning. Had he confronted her after her invasion of my attic, telling her that her behaviour was unacceptable, drawing a line under the last few weeks? He was ashamed of her.

I allowed that thought to bloom in my head. The sun touching our hands, his sketch of me by the side of his bed. But then I remembered the rota, all those careful rules.

Punishment. Joe said I was obsessed with punishment.

Why are you punishing us, Nell? When he knew. He *knew*.

'You should sleep with him.' Carolyn took her hands from her pockets. 'Why not?'

'What?'

'Robin. Sleep with him.'

I didn't speak. My mouth was dry and cracked.

'It would be a relief. I can't any more. Well, look at me.' She spread her hands as if she were so beautiful she dazzled even herself. 'How could I?'

I forced myself to speak: 'I'm the housekeeper. I'm his housekeeper.'

'Oh, I think we both know you're more than that.' She let her eyes glide around the room, at the specking of soil on the tiles under the plants, stubborn grime on the windows. 'And less.'

One after another, I lit the lamps in the house. Robin was particular about this, an extravagance in a man who hated waste. Unless he hated the dark more. Or, like me, he loved the Villas at night, its lamps burning like small fires.

As I switched on the last one, I paused in the doorway to his library before turning towards the stairs. He still wasn't home.

I wondered if he'd changed his mind about sandwiches for supper and was eating in a restaurant, or a hotel. Of the boxes stacked around the library walls, a few more had been emptied of their contents and flattened for recycling. Carolyn had told me to look inside and see what secrets they held. But Carolyn said a lot of things.

Sleep with him, so dismissively, as if she were making a gift of an old mattress she'd jumped on so often its springs were sprung, but maybe I could get a good night's sleep out of it. Hadn't I slept under bridges? An old mattress was five-star luxury to me. She imagined she was insulting me, calling me a whore on top of everything else, but if Robin was attracted to me it was because I'd made his house into a home, something she'd failed to do. I wanted her gone, for the house to be warm and quiet when he returned. Being responsible for another human being's comfort in the way I was for his can warp your sense of security, make you fear every little thing. I wasn't to disappoint Dr Wilder or I'd lose my home. His tea mustn't ever be too strong or too weak, or the bills too high, but nor must the house be cold or the lamps unlit after sunset. His meals must be edible despite the paucity of the allowance he tendered for their ingredients. For weeks, I'd lived in dread of breaking a cup or saucer, spilling butter on his soft furnishings. All that had changed, this morning. His kindness towards me, she knew nothing of that. Standing among the ugly plants, offering me sex with her husband while her unwashed camisole was festering in my pocket. *Sleep with him. Why not?* She picked that moment because of Joe. He'd done as I'd asked, riding to my rescue, seducing her a second time with his smile, all of it agreed in texts between the two of us. But I'd bargained without him bringing Meagan. He must have worked hard to find her, been determined to go back, in spite of everything she put us through. Had she intercepted our texts, or did she get the story out of Joe some other way? Because clearly she knew everything: the house, Carolyn, the night she and Joe spent here together. Perhaps Meagan sent the texts herself, forcing Joe to hand her the phone. No, not forcing him. He'd have given in without a fight. Without stopping to think what it would mean, for the four of us in this house. Meagan knowing everything. He'd brought her here, threatening all that I had. It was hard to forgive him for that. As I knelt to turn on my attic lamp, my hands shook.

Meagan, masquerading as my aunt. Carolyn had seen that lie for what it was, but she hadn't cared. I suppose we were beneath her notice and her contempt – just two cheap young people, easily bought. She used this house for sex, that much was clear. It had no other attraction for her. She didn't even seem interested in why I'd brought Joe back, except that it suited her purposes to be in a position to sleep with him again. And I was to sleep with Robin. She'd be able to make sense of it, then. My presence in this house, his toleration of it. We would be playing their game, according to their rules. I knew she longed for Robin to prove himself the preda- tor she said he was, longed for him to slip back into that role. She didn't believe him capable of change. I think the idea of it scared her, because it left her too exposed. Alone. As for me, she was prob- ably thinking that at last I was to be put to some proper purpose. Perhaps she even thought this had been my intention all along: a ménage à trois amidst the orchids and amateur artwork.

Show some emotion, for God's sake.

Clumsily, I dropped onto my mattress, knocking one of the brass camels. It lay on its side on the strip of tapestry, looking lost.

I reached to lift it back onto its feet, but what was the point? It didn't belong to me, nothing here did.

There was no lock on the attic door. Why hadn't I seen to that when I was bringing the lightbulb and varnish, cleaning the beautiful rug and papering the walls? A simple hook-and-eye lock would have screwed into place without the need for power tools. As it stood, Carolyn could come in here whenever she chose, in the middle of the night when I was sleeping, or when I was out at the shops. Perhaps she did exactly that, or Robin did. Standing under the eaves with their feet planted on the rug, eyeing the rescued lamp, angry at my scavenging or pleased to see how thoroughly I'd been trapped into believing I had a home here.

Nothing in the attic was mine except the clothes on my back. Damn Joe. He knew how Meagan hated me. She'd ruin everything, she always did. She already *had* – that look on Carolyn's face, gloating over the introductions, 'Your aunt's here,' when I had no aunt, or uncle. When I had no one but Joe. The springs in the mattress drilled like fingers. I ached all the way from the soles of my feet to the sockets of my eyes.

Pulling my hands into my lap, I studied the calluses left by hard work, honest work. A bruise discoloured the knuckle of my thumb, my cuticles ragged from hot water. I could count the places I'd blistered or burnt on his floors and breakfasts, the shallow scratch from a corkscrew as I'd opened a bottle of wine, a split fingernail. My hands were full of him, Dr Robin Wilder.

Joe had read my palms once. 'Your Fire Line is broken.' Sitting with my hand held in his lap.

'What does it mean?'

He folded my fingers. 'It can mean lots of things.'

'Which is the Fire Line anyway?'

He showed me. 'Most people call it the Fate Line.'

'Broken fate?' I squinted at my palm. 'That doesn't sound good.'

'It's not.' His face changed, as if I'd pushed too hard. 'It means you'll have a lot of accidents, one after another.'

From the attic window, the night's neon crept into my cupped palms. Joe was here in London, part of its night, but Meagan was with him. I couldn't sleep, knowing it. The house hung about me, altered and unfamiliar. Lifting a hand to the scar above my right eye, I traced its star shape with my fingertips, remembering.

23

That morning, three years ago, the lake was soaked with sunshine. I'd dared Joe to climb with me. He so rarely did, preferring to stretch on the towels at the side of the water, getting brown. The sun was high over our heads, the summer swollen at full burst.

'Come on!' I urged.

Joe twisted sideways on the towel before finding his feet. He was fifteen and I was fourteen, the pair of us invincible. Later, we'd swim, splitting the hot skin of the lake to find the cold beneath, but now we were climbing, slate slithering and skittering under our feet, seeing who could reach the summit first. It was my favourite game, scaling the slag heaps that lay around our lake. Three thousand men had mined the slate in these mountains but one by one the mines closed and now it was mostly slag, with gorse bushes erupting in prickly outcrops. You could pay to walk in the footsteps of the miners, deep underground where water dripped and the torch in your helmet carved tunnels through the dark. Joe and I preferred to climb, or I did. He was too lazy for the sport and never competitive enough to match me.

'I'll beat you!' Breath bursting in my chest, slate sharp under the soles of my sandals. Higher and higher up the heap, kicking my toes to find footholds in the slag, spying out the safe places to slot my fingers. Slate was easy to climb if you looked where to put your fingers and feet.

Joe was struggling, straggling behind. His legs and arms were longer, but he ran at the slag as if it were a hillside, planting the soles of his feet flat, the slate falling under him like the steps on an escalator. 'Shit!' Laughter panting from him, panicking when he slipped too far. 'Nell!'

'Come on! Keep going!' Nothing could've stopped me in that moment, not a goat flinging itself in my path or a gull wheeling out of the sky.

The sun struck the slate, blazing it back in a billion shades of blue. I shut my eyes to see better, using my fingers and feet, heat throbbing on my eyelids.

It was a gorse bush that caught me, jutting at a right angle, offering its thorny branches knotted with yellow flowers. I yelped and drew back my hand, balance lost, toehold dissolving in a flood of slate. I caught the blur of Joe's face as I fell, his mouth crooked with exertion. 'Nell!'

I thought the sound of falling slate would never end, clattering on and on, smashing and flinting, striking sparks from the mountain. We'd brought down the whole heap, that's what I thought, me by falling and Joe who'd dropped like a stone to reach my side as quickly as he did.

'Nell!' His voice was in bits. 'Nell, please!'

I'd struck my head on landing. My head and a dozen places all over my body, whispering savagely when I tried to move. 'Ow . . .' Everything was red, the sky wobbling behind Joe's head.

There was stickiness and it smelt bad, like something burning in a saucepan.

'Oh God,' Joe said. Then, 'Keep still!'

I'd only moved because he looked so scared. The whispering in my body turned to shouting, mostly over my right eye. 'Joe, it hurts.' Self-pity swelled in my chest, sobbing. 'It hurts!'

'It's blood. You're bleeding.' His hands held me down, the chill of panic in his palms. 'Stay still. Don't move.' He went away, leaving the wobble of sky and a harsh bleating of gulls above me.

I was lying on what felt like razors. Silly, it was just slate. But slate is sharp, it's old, hundreds of millions of years old, mud and clay pressed together by the movement of the earth, layered and hardened. When I moved my foot, it made a clacking sound like geese in flight.

Gulls brimmed overhead, wings dyed red by the blood filling my eyes.

Meagan said gulls didn't make their own nests until they were old, preferring to return to their parents to learn their best survival tricks. Stealing and attacking, all those vicious habits, the reasons we duck our heads when they come close.

Joe was back at my side with a towel.

He pressed it to my head. 'Here.'

I didn't move, scared by the pain. The cut was so close to my eye and so deep, as if a piece of me had been scooped out. 'Meagan'll have a fit,' I said, meaning ambulances and hospitals.

'I'll wash out the blood in the lake,' Joe said, meaning the towel.

'Stitches.'

'What? Nell, keep still.'

'I need stitches, it's deep.' I could feel the cut welling with blood.

'Joe, you have to get help.' He lifted the towel, speculatively. I was seeing in scarlet now, my lashes heavy with it. My blood raced through the towel, drenching the cotton. 'Ambulance . . .'

He stayed at my side, pressing the towel back into place, blinding me with it. He was afraid of authority, in any form. Afraid to raise the spectre of anyone else's curiosity. An ambulance would mean questions, probing, paperwork: 'What were you doing out here?' Hospital would mean no more lake, no escaping from Lyle's for an afternoon or a night. He was seeing closed doors, captivity, prisons. His fingers were shaking.

'It's okay.' I searched for his free hand. The bone in my eye socket was bruised by the press of the towel, my torn skin lifting and parting thickly. 'Joe? I'll be okay.'

'Lie still,' he said. 'I've got this.'

I lay under the circling of the gulls, letting Joe do what he could, even if it made it feel much worse. Because he was right: we'd be questioned and split up. It happened all the time to kids like us. And Meagan was looking for an excuse. She hated how close we'd become, her eyes fixing on us every time we were together. We were always together. She sensed trouble, not between us but for her. People in love were selfish, and proud. She was afraid I'd turn my nose up at her cleaning, the endless chores. I'd think myself better than that, *know* I was better.

'I'm okay,' I said it a third time to make it true. A promise, between us.

Slate slithered under Joe, splintering. All those layers, peppering into his skin. I'd see it later, back at Lyle's, a blue-grey tattoo on his knees, red at the edges.

Heat drilled down, the summer at full blast, but the pair of us were shivering.

I'd put a plaster over the cut when we got back to the house. The bleeding would stop, bleeding always did. There'd be a scar. Rosie would ask questions but she'd be the only one. I'd make up a story, let her poke the plaster to keep her happy. As long as Joe didn't give us away, we'd be safe. If Meagan pushed, he'd crumble. He couldn't do silence the way I could. His fear made him obedient, eager to please. He'd dance to keep her happy, because that's all he knew. How to dance, and how to dodge. Never to open doors until you had to, never to answer back or ask for help.

Lying there, it was all so clear to me. As if the fall had shaken something free in my head.

My mother, all those miles away and years ago, giving me up because she was to be married and there would be a new family. I was surplus to requirement, but that was okay. Better to be given up than kept by someone who couldn't love you. My father, long gone, uninterested or unknowing. The other one with the pram, his new baby tucked inside. It didn't matter. Better to live like this, with Joe, loved and needed. Rosie's fingers would hurt when she poked the plaster, but I'd let her do it. A black eye was the worst of my worries. I'd steal make-up to cover it or Joe would steal it for me, because he was good at that. I'd have to keep him away from Meagan until the mark faded because he could dance and dodge and shoplift, but he couldn't stand still when her eyes were on him, too quick to do whatever she asked. Her hand between his shoulders, pushing him at the door – 'That witch from Social Services needs charming' – and he let her, always he let her. He was trained to take orders, but it wasn't just that. Lying on the slate with my right eye swelling shut, I saw how it was with Joe and Meagan. He needed someone who showed him no kindness. One person who wasn't dazzled by his beauty, someone to bear witness without weakness to the actual fact of him. The rest of the world stopped looking when they saw his smile, as if he was nothing more than a mouth and a pair of eyes you could drown in. He was sick of people looking and not seeing.

The gulls came closer, tightening their circle above us, wings slicing the blue of the sky. In his last foster home, he'd told me, the woman fed him cream cakes, telling everyone those were his favourites when actually they made him ill. He hated cream cakes. She made up this story about the kind of boy he was, wetting her hankie to wipe cream from his chin. He was sick of always being the favourite, it set his teeth on edge, as he wasn't *Joe* at all. Meagan never fed him cream cakes, never gave an inch. She was like the stone under this mountain, unmoving.

'Nell . . .'

'I'm here, I'm okay.'

I loved Joe. Fiercely, proudly, selfishly. Meagan couldn't touch us, no matter how much she wanted to work her fingers between us, pull us apart. We were too tight. I'd stand between her cruelty and his need for it, and I'd keep us safe. Joe and Rosie and me. This blood would need a lot of lies. The blood and the plaster, my dizziness. I began inventing lies, as I lay there. Sunstroke and my period – the raging weakness that engulfed me once a month. It wasn't Joe's fault I'd fallen. I'd climbed too fast, so sure of myself.

Two gulls spun close, their wings curving like a mouth. For a second, Meagan's face leered down at me: *There's something up with him. Something missing.*

'Nell . . .'

'I'm okay.'

'You're crying.' The slither of slate under Joe's knees.

'It hurts.' My voice sounded faraway, further than the birds sweeping at the sky.

'I'm here. I won't leave you.'

'I know.'

No ambulance, no stitches. Just a scar, and this sickness lodged in my throat, alongside the lies we'd invent for Meagan. 'I know.'

24

'What happened yesterday?'

It wasn't yet 7 a.m. but Robin was waiting in the kitchen, sitting where yesterday Joe had sat, his hands folded on the table. 'My wife says you had relatives visiting.'

He used the word *wife* like a whip, punishing me.

'Shall I make breakfast?' I reached for the apron, tying it around my waist. 'Or coffee, at least.'

The table bore three rings from yesterday's teacups. Petroleum jelly would get rid of the marks, a trick Meagan had taught me. Where was she this morning, and where was Joe? I needed to speak with him, alone. I needed to know how much danger we were in.

'You gave out my address, to your aunt.' Robin turned in his chair to watch as I filled the kettle at the sink. 'Did you ask her to come?'

With my back turned, it was easier to hear the emotion in his voice. His anger wasn't the same as that time in the bedroom with the silver gown. This was less predictable, a real threat. I reached for the press, spooning in enough grounds for two servings. 'I don't have an aunt.'

'Then I don't understand.' He was silent for a second. 'Was my wife mistaken?'

'She was misinformed.' I lit the stove and faced him, the kettle heating at my back. 'Meagan Flack said she was my aunt so that Mrs Wilder would let her in the house.'

My turn to use the whip: *Mrs Wilder* made him wince. I was thinking of Meagan, hidden outside Starling Villas, waiting until I left the house before she knocked on the door. Wanting to take me by surprise on my return. Had I answered the door to her, I'd never have let her in the house, with or without Joe in tow.

'And your cousin. Joe, is it?' He rested an elbow on the table, his wrist hanging, fingers loose. I saw the effort it cost him not to make a fist. 'Was that also misinformation?'

'We're not related but we grew up together, in a foster home.' I held his gaze. 'Meagan Flack's foster home. That's where I learnt to cook and clean, and to do without.'

His eyes slid from mine, moving around the kitchen. He hadn't expected an argument, thinking to find me contrite, full of explanations and apologies. His quiet anger scared me, I could see its smoke rising behind his eyes. Smoke killed more people than fire, wasn't that what they said?

'If you're happy with my housekeeping, you have Meagan to thank. She left it all for me to do, from the age of eight. I had to stand on a stool for the cooking and washing up. She left me to look after the other children too, although that doesn't interest you. You haven't any need of those skills.'

He looked at me then, his stare darkening. 'Why are you so angry?'

'I'm not angry,' I thrust back. 'You're angry.'

The kettle screeched and I turned away, glad of the excuse to hide my burning face. How Carolyn would have loved this scene. How she'd have laughed at its squalid drama, its domesticity. I switched off the stove and was about to pick up the kettle when he reached around my shoulder to take it from me. 'Sit down.' He spoke quietly, but his voice was inflexible.

'I should make coffee.' My voice shook. 'I can do that.'

'So can I. Sit down.'

There it was then – he could make his own coffee, and no doubt his own meals. He could clean and cook and do without. My self-righteous speech throbbed in my throat. I wasn't needed here, not really. I sat at the table, folding my hands out of sight, watching as he worked the coffee press. He was in his shirtsleeves, the muscles in his shoulders moving as blue shadows, the nape of his neck narrowing as he bent over the coffee press. I felt the heat of tears in my eyes, like grief.

Rosie, I thought. *Little, little Rosie.*

It was so cold the night she disappeared, the night I stayed, looking for her. A shiver of stars crept across the lake but it was too dark to separate sky from mountains, or mountains from slag heaps. Waiting for the first breath of dawn to stir in the darkness like an animal waking. The lake breathing at my feet, as if it too were sleeping and might wake. All night I stayed, my eyes open on the water. When the first clouds covered the stars, the lake turned grey. So grey I could've reached out and twitched it away, caught it in my fingers and pulled and pulled until it was all gone except what lay underneath the surface, also curled, as if asleep.

I'd lost everything. Not only at the lake two summers ago but here and now, in Starling Villas. Everything I'd worked so hard to make, this small happiness, the frail living I'd scratched for myself under his roof. All lost.

'Drink this.' Robin set the coffee in front of me.

I drew my hands from my lap but didn't touch the cup. I didn't deserve its small heat, the pleasure of sipping to settle the queasiness in my stomach. Hard labour was what I deserved, a mattress that drilled its springs into my spine, an attic black with damp.

He set a second cup of coffee down on the table and sat beside me. 'Nell . . .'

'No.' I was afraid of sobbing or shouting, saw myself shoving at the table, spilling coffee and smashing cups. 'No.'

'No, that's not your name?' He took up his cup and drank a mouthful. 'Or no, you don't want to drink your coffee?'

'Don't be nice to me. It was better before.'

'I wasn't nice to you' – another mouthful – 'before?'

'You weren't anything. As if I were invisible.'

He frowned. 'And that was better?'

I nodded, setting my teeth. I was panicking, that was all. Joe and Meagan had made me jumpy and now Robin's sympathy, his curiosity, was making me panic. 'I'm all right. I am.'

He held his cup between his fingers. I told myself his anger was still circling, waiting for me to make a move.

'It upset me, seeing them here. I didn't ask them to come. Joe, perhaps. But not her, never her.'

'Meagan – Flack?' He tested the name, disliking it.

'She's not a good person. I didn't want her knowing where I was.'

'Why?' He asked the question with the bluntness of a scholar in need of facts.

'She does harm.' I curled my hand around my cup, drawing

his gaze from my face. 'A child disappeared from her foster home. Rosie Bond. She was only six, but Meagan let her go out alone. I couldn't watch her the way I wanted to, because I had so much else to do.'

'Cleaning and cooking.' He frowned. 'Caring for the younger children.'

'It was too much. Even though I was fifteen by then, it was too much for one person.'

'Joe didn't help?' He drank his coffee, as if Joe's name had left a bad taste in his mouth.

I told myself to take care. Robin wasn't judging Joe. He was judging me, the veracity of my answers. If I made a mistake, he'd decide the whole story – everything I'd ever said to him – was a lie. I'd never had to tell the truth so carefully before, to someone who listened so completely.

'He tried to help.' It sounded feeble, as if Joe were a halfwit.

'Carolyn's very taken with him.' His eyes met mine, a glimmer of humour there. 'With Joe.'

The red bracelet, in his sheets. In *his* bed. *Be careful, Nell.*

'I texted him.' I brought the cup to my lips. 'Which I wouldn't have done had I known he was with her. So I'm sorry for that.'

'It doesn't matter.' He moved his hand, dismissing my apology. 'Only that it's upset you.'

'And Carolyn.'

'Oh, she's not upset. Rather the opposite.' He smoothed his thumb at the table, the way he had in the library with Carolyn, as if there was a mark on the wood and he could wipe it away.

How strange we are, I wanted to say. You and I sitting here, discussing your wife's attraction to my friend who's young enough to be her son. Whose bracelet was in *your* bed. A week ago, you hardly spoke a word to me, nor I to you. Now look at us. And why? Because of Carolyn, or Joe?

'I'm sorry. I'll ask him to go home. I don't think they intend to stay in London long, in any case.'

'Really?' He wiped his thumb at the table. 'That's not the impression Carolyn gave. She said she offered them the spare room.' I flinched, and he frowned. 'I'm trying to understand the situation.'

But he would never understand, how could he? I had been there, and I didn't understand. Joe sitting at this table, at Meagan's elbow. Her crooked smile and smoker's teeth, his procuress. Taking his hand and smiling at Carolyn, seeing every year of her age under the expensive knives and acid, and seeing the vanity and loneliness and insecurity that spurred it. Everything she knew how to exploit. She'd made a living from manipulating weakness in others. I remembered her telling the Bonds just before Rosie's fifth birthday, 'She won't want cake or presents but it's a shame to see her in shabby clothes, such a little princess as she is,' and they handed over cash instead of toys. Rosie got a cake because I baked it, but she never saw a penny of that cash.

'Where are they staying in London?' Robin was refilling his cup. 'Do you know?'

'Somewhere nearby, Meagan said. A small hotel.'

'And they live in North Wales?'

'It's where the foster home was.' I paused to sip at my coffee. 'Joe and I moved away after what happened to Rosie.'

'You said Rosie disappeared.' He added milk to his cup. 'When was this?'

'Two years ago.'

He looked up, surprised. 'You were just a child yourself.'

'I was fifteen, nearly sixteen.'

'And Joe?'

'He was sixteen.'

'You were children.' He frowned as he stirred his coffee. 'You weren't put into new homes?'

I shook my head. 'We ran away.' Such a small sentence to describe our escape from Meagan, which had been desperate and painful, like the peeling of skin. 'We had no choice.'

Robin scratched at his eyebrow then stopped, self-consciously. I knew he wanted to ask about the scar above my right eye. I didn't think he'd allow himself to ask such a personal question but, 'You have a scar, here.' He pointed to his eyebrow. 'How did that happen?' He thought it was Joe, I could tell. That Joe had pushed me around, like Meagan.

'I was climbing. I loved climbing.'

'This was when you were living at the foster home? Was it dangerous?'

'The climbing? No. I was showing off.'

I touched the scar, remembering Rosie's fingers, her plaintive, 'I want a scar!' when she saw it. And Meagan's fury, her warnings. She'd known Joe and I were up to no good and no good would come of us, ever. 'You're scarred for life,' she'd hissed. 'I hope you're happy.' I didn't care about the scar but I hated her turning on Joe, 'You treat this place like a bloody playground! You need to grow up!'

Robin was watching me. 'I may be mistaken.' He turned his cup in his hands. 'But were you homeless for a time, before you came here?'

I imagined he might've been one of the men who walked past me, day after day, for six long weeks. Avoiding my eyes, stepping around my feet. It hurt to think that, putting me back on the defensive. 'Is that Carolyn's theory? Because I haven't many clothes, and I was desperate enough to take this job?'

'Did you need to be desperate to do that?'

'Are you serious?'

He studied me, unsure of his ground. 'I know the wages aren't great, but the room . . .'

So he *was* one of those men. Even if he'd never walked past me, he'd walked past others just like me, begging on the street. Picking up his pace when he saw us, taking out his phone so he didn't have to look at us. He hadn't any idea, living here with his books and papers, what my life, our lives, had been. It hurt to realize it, more than Carolyn's confession about their life together, more even than seeing Joe with Meagan yesterday.

'You let her paint me.' I set my cup down, resentful of the pain he'd put in my chest. 'Why did you do that? It was humiliating, horrible.'

'I thought you wanted the money.' He was unblinking, but I could see his anger circling, closer to the surface now.

'Like a whore, then. You think I'm a whore.'

He straightened in the chair, voice stiffening. 'I wouldn't have you here if I thought that.'

'Carolyn would. She thinks I'm a whore.'

'Stop – saying that word.'

'Because it makes you uncomfortable? You let *her* make me uncomfortable, without any good reason for it. You didn't enjoy sketching me, so why do it? This is *your* home. You could've told her no, that it wasn't right. You could have asked me what I thought, whether I wanted to do it.'

'And you could have said no.' He pressed the ball of his thumb to the table. 'Why didn't you?'

Something else he didn't understand. Power. All the power in this house rested with him, and with her. He was waiting for an answer. Truth, or dare.

'I was afraid of what you'd do if I didn't.'

'You're not afraid of anything.'

I laughed, incredulous. 'I'm afraid all the time! *Every day.* Afraid of being homeless, having to go back on the streets. Of breaking your plates or killing your plants, or cracking your horrible mirror. In case you throw me out. I'm afraid of your wife, what she wants from me. She wants me gone, I know that much. She won't leave me alone, she follows me round the house to insult and humiliate me. What does she want from me? What do *you* want?'

'I wanted a personal assistant.' His voice had iced over. 'You talked me into taking you on as a housekeeper.'

'So this isn't a game you play. You and Carolyn.'

He went very still, watching me.

'That's what she told me. Oh, and something else. She told me to sleep with you.'

I wasn't aware of raising my voice but the lamp took my words and flung them back at us. I swept an arm at the table as if I could sweep the words to the floor. Blood was raging in my cheeks. He studied me as if the colour in my face confirmed a theory he'd had about me from our first meeting. He was holding in a sigh, I could see its shape in his throat. 'You think I'm lying.'

'No.' He moved two fingers, putting my whisper to one side.

201

'But I did think you'd have the good sense not to pay attention to a word my ex-wife says.'

'Because of course you employed me for my *good sense*.'

'What else?' He challenged me with a stare.

'Someone with sense wouldn't work for a pittance, cash in hand, off the record.'

'Why not?'

'I know nothing about you. We're strangers, yet I'm living in here, cooking your meals—'

'You're a good cook.'

'—cooking your meals, spending your money, sleeping under your roof.'

'You're very good with money.' He wasn't paying me a compliment, simply acknowledging a fact. 'And I don't use the rooms at the top of the house.'

'You think it's normal?' I demanded. 'What we're doing? This . . . coexisting.'

'I think it's mutually beneficial.' He reached to refill my cup. The press only held enough for two but he'd been careful when he refilled his own cup; half-measures for the pair of us. 'Or it was.'

'That's it, then.' My throat hollowed. 'You're firing me. Because Carolyn slept with Joe.'

'I can't fire you.' His calmness was infuriating, like trying to dig my fingers into marble. 'We don't have a contract of employment.' He added the last of the milk to my cup.

'Then you're threatening me. "Or it was." What does that mean?'

'It means Carolyn will not stay away.' He moved the jug, clearing space on the table between us. 'And since you find that impossible,

I expect you'll have to leave.' He raised his eyes at the last second, letting me see the sadness there.

I didn't trust it, or him. 'Carolyn likes to play games . . . And you don't? This whole house is a game. I'm a game, to you. Although I expect you'd call it an experiment.'

He scratched at the side of his head, the movement so abrupt I tensed in my chair, measuring the distance to the back door, trying to remember if I'd locked it after putting out the rubbish.

'Nell,' he said sadly.

'You didn't want to know my first name, it made you uncomfortable. *Miss Ballard.* You didn't want any evidence I was in the house, only for me to be invisible. And I wanted the same.'

'You're not invisible.'

'Not to her,' I agreed.

'Not to anyone. Never to me.'

'I don't understand what you're saying. What are you saying?'

'I'm saying I'm ashamed of my wife and how she acts.' He bent his head, curling a hand to the nape of his neck. 'And of myself.' I saw his knuckles whiten. 'I can't judge her, I'm not fit for that. We were married and now we're not, but I chose her. We chose one another. Do you understand what I am telling you?'

Did I? I saw Joe at the side of the lake, his wrists wet with its darkness. Hadn't I chosen him? Over Rosie, over everything? Hadn't that been the start of this whole mess?

'You don't have to let Carolyn in here. You could change the locks. There's a locksmith's right around the corner.' He was silent. 'It will be worse,' I warned. 'Now Joe's back.'

'Yes,' he agreed.

It was why he was here in the kitchen, drinking coffee. Because

Carolyn had told him about Meagan and Joe. Because he knew what Carolyn was like, when boys like Joe were around. Things would get worse before they got better.

'Do you want me to leave?'

'You have nowhere to go.'

'That's true, but it's not your problem.'

'It is.' He looked at me then, the way no one ever had before. He looked into my eyes and said, 'It is my problem.'

25

Rosie was with us, in Starling Villas. I dreamt of her skin, the apricot fuzz of her cheeks. Each freckle on her arm was miraculous to me. She made being alive look so easy.

In Lyle's, I would study her as she slept, to try and learn the trick. Her chest sinking and lifting, wrinkles running across her nose and eyelids. Once or twice, her eyes would open and I'd smile down at her, but she was sleeping and didn't see. Joe slept the same way, deeply, easily. I'd hold my hand a hair's breadth above his chest to catch the rhythm of it. Heat came off him, harder than Rosie's, a real fever to it. When I looked back on those nights, it seemed I never slept, always awake and watching. That couldn't be true. There must've been times when I slept and they watched me but I couldn't catch hold of that memory, only of lying with my body tense between them, studying each small quiver of Rosie's face, feeling the fever of Joe at my back.

Now, Robin slept with his sketch of me at his side. What were his dreams? Was Carolyn there, was he dreaming about his once-happy life with her? Bare feet on blades of grass, idling by an infinity pool, wine chilling in a bucket where condensation crawled

205

like fat white lice. What did his naked feet look like? There wasn't an inch of Joe I didn't know, not even his dreams. Except now I wondered if that were ever true, if he'd ever belonged to me or if he was Meagan's from the start. It didn't matter, now. Not now.

'It is my problem,' Robin had said, looking at me the way no one ever had. 'It is.'

I knew why Joe was here. Summer was dying, winter on its way. At Lyle's, Meagan let him hibernate during the cold months. Rosie would burrow under his blankets, giggling. He let her, because she was so warm, but she didn't like him to sleep, prising his eyes open with her fingers, hoping to play. When the snow came, she didn't understand why he wouldn't race in it with the rest of us. She took his scarf and tied it around the snowman we built, 'This's Joe,' hugging the snowman until its head rolled free. After Rosie was gone, I sought out the cold. But Joe wasn't like me, and now I was different too. Because of Robin. I wasn't afraid of the winter the way Joe was, but nor did I believe any longer that I deserved to be out in the cold, away from any comfort or love. Because of Robin. Joe wanted a safe place to spend the winter. He'd do anything at all to find one. How could I forget a thing like that?

In Hungry's, Meagan was seated at my table in the window, alone. She'd summoned me with a text sent from Joe's phone, an unequivocal threat of what would happen if I didn't jump to her command, the way I once did at Lyle's. In the diner, she wore yesterday's shabby coat over a faded dress, her hair grizzled grey around her face. The white hairs we'd plucked had grown back, sticking up from her scalp like wires. Her eyes were hooded, their lids full of lines like the ancient awning folded above Hungry's window, a packet of fags at her elbow and a disposable lighter between her fingers. 'You've fallen on your feet,' she said.

'Where's Joe?'

'Sleeping. You know how he loves his bed.' She grinned, her teeth long and rotten. She was the reason I never took up smoking, even when I was on the streets and it would've been an easy way to keep warm. She'd chosen this table, my table, so she could watch the house. At her elbow an empty cup sat, stained like her teeth.

'I'll get you another tea, shall I?'

'All right, Lady Bountiful.' She relaxed, letting go of the stress that was squaring her shoulders.

I walked away from her, to the counter where Gilbert was polishing glasses with a tea towel.

'Coffee, please. And a cup of strong tea.' Strong enough to dye what was left of her teeth, that's how she took her tea. Strong enough to make the spoon stand up.

With my back to her, I replayed the details in my head. The shabby coat, her tension then her relief. 'Lady Bountiful', but she hadn't been sure of my role across the road, not until I'd offered to buy her a second cup of tea. She was hoping for a share of my good fortune, but she knew nothing about my life in Starling Villas. All she had was guesswork and a grudge.

I counted out the cash to pay for the drinks.

'I'll bring them over,' Gilbert said. 'The coffee, and the tea.'

'Thank you.' We smiled at one another.

With a twinge of pleasure, I remembered the lemon meringue pie, a gift for his regulars. Hungry's was *my* place. Meagan might be sitting at the table in the window but it was *my* table, just as Starling

Villas was my home. She was the stranger here. Let her be the one on her guard.

I walked back to her, holding my purse in my hand, setting it down on the table as I pulled out a chair. She didn't look directly at the purse but her head turned towards it, the way a gull's turns to the sound of chip papers. She was stony broke, as I'd been before I got my job with Robin. Worse, since Meagan undoubtedly had debts. She'd never been good with money. At Lyle's that had been one of my areas of expertise, making ends meet, scrimping and saving and budgeting for rare treats like my fruit cake. She'd always loved my fruit cake.

I scooped my purse into my pocket, saying brightly, 'So Joe's sleeping? Did you find somewhere nice to stay?'

'Not nice, but it'll do.' Her eyes pecked at my face, wondering at my good mood. 'For now.'

Gilbert brought the drinks, setting the coffee at my elbow and the tea at hers. He and I shared another smile. I saw Meagan's mouth tighten around the shape of her teeth as if a sour taste had flooded her mouth. 'How long are you in London?' I asked.

'Depends. Not long, I expect.'

'Joe won't want to stay once the weather changes.' I stirred my coffee, froth lacing the handle of my spoon. 'You know how he hates the cold.'

'Everyone hates the cold.'

'Do they?' I lifted the spoon from my cup. 'I don't.' Licked the spoon clean. 'I like it.'

'You didn't like it on the streets.' Her voice was sharp, stabbing at me. 'Joe said.'

She smelt of mildew, like Lyle's.

208

'Joe hated the cold.' I settled the spoon in my saucer, picking up the cup. 'I didn't mind.'

I punctuated the sentence with one of Carolyn's polished full stops, letting Meagan know that I'd learnt new tricks since the ones she'd drummed into me all those years ago.

'We're both pleased for you, how you've fallen on your feet. It's a long way from Lyle's is London.' Her lips creased at the rim of the cup. 'A long way from that pool of yours.' She pressed her lips together. 'You always wanted a place to call home, didn't you? Somewhere you were needed. Plenty of my kids were happy to be spongers, but not you. Not in your nature.' Summing me up in a handful of words.

I'd forgotten how good she was at that, reducing each of us to a nickname. Sunshine. Death Knell. Rosie, and Rosier. My mind skipped to the lake, dipping under its surface into the darkness. I let it go, to give myself time to think. She intended to blackmail me, I'd known that as soon as I saw her in Starling Villas. She hadn't forgiven me for the stories I'd started, the rumours that ruined her. Least of all for stealing Joe from under her nose. And she imagined I was onto a good thing with the Wilders. She'd seen money in the house, never mind the ancient stove and cracked tiles. She knew how much a house was worth. One like Starling Villas, in a street like this, was worth millions. She'd smelt money as soon as she set foot inside, wanting her share.

'It's a long way from the lake,' I agreed. 'And a long time ago.'

'It's back in the papers.' She'd reached the crux of it now, settling in the chair, sucking at her tea. 'Some rich bitch from Surrey bought Lyle's, thinks she can turn it into a holiday home. The shops are opening back up. Regeneration, they're calling it.'

I tried to imagine Lyle's turned into a holiday home. Farrow and Ball'd to within an inch of its life. Fireplaces with their original tiles restored, silk flower arrangements in place of coals. Sash windows curtained in pale linen, Welsh blankets on the beds, sea-scented candles almost masking the smell of mildew. Almost.

'Never thought I'd see the back of it,' Meagan said.

As if Lyle's had belonged to her, and she'd been trying to sell it. Baking bread to entice viewers, changing the flowerbeds as seasons came and went. What would attract someone to a house like that? You could sense the kids as soon as you stepped through the door, their neglect and sorrow.

'This's a nice place.' She nodded across my shoulder towards Starling Villas. 'You've done well for yourself. Especially if he's as handsome as her.' Robin, she meant. 'More money than sense if they're employing live-in help; that's a risk around here. A stranger in their home? You could be anyone.' She chuckled. 'I'm guessing they don't know the half of it.'

She'd intercepted my texts, I realized. She was the one who'd texted back, pretending to be Joe. He'd never have acted on his own. This 'rescue' was all Meagan. She didn't know the Wilders were divorced, she thought the pair of them were living in Starling Villas, with me. I waited to see how much more she knew.

Information was power, she had taught me that. I saw Robin bending over his books, boxes all about him. Carolyn had said I should take a look inside the boxes.

'Of course, they're strangers too.' She showed her tombstone teeth. 'It cuts both ways. That book of rules? Did you know what you were getting yourself into?'

Robin's rota. She'd read it while she was waiting for me to come home from the park. She'd seen his instructions so neatly typed, page after page of them, and drawn her own conclusions. The coffee was bittersweet, exactly how I liked it. I sipped it, not answering her question.

'Whose rules, exactly?' She tapped a thumb at the table. 'Well, no need to tell me. I've seen enough women like her, so brittle you could snap her in two. She's been broken, and she's put herself back together again. From what Joe told me, that's not a happy marriage. Not by a long shot.' Measuring me with a stare. 'He'll do the same to you, girl. A man like that? From what Joe told me, you need to watch out for yourself.'

I smiled, but didn't speak.

In response, her mouth made a sour shape.

'What happened to your common sense? Left it on someone's settee, did you? Joe's told me all about the games you got up to. Sleeping around, you wrecking every good thing you found. That's what you're doing over the road, I expect. Punishing yourself. Letting him punish you.' Her eyes slitted on my face. 'Found yourself a gaoler, girlie?'

Gilbert was watching from the counter, polishing the inside of a coffee cup. Meagan kept her voice pitched low. I was certain my face gave nothing away.

'She's back in the papers.' Meagan reached for her lighter. She couldn't smoke in here but she could play with the lighter, turning it in her fingers. 'Little Rosie Bond.'

She pushed her free hand into the pocket of her coat, pulling out a folded square of newsprint which she smoothed flat on the table. The light snagged on Rosie's smile, that gap between her front teeth. I didn't need to look at the photo of her face. Every day I lived with it, with her.

'The other kids are selling their stories again.' Meagan kept her thumb on the edge of the photo where Rosie's pigtail brushed the tip of her shoulder. 'Making money out of it.'

I cradled my cup in my hands. 'And you'd like to make some money too.'

She narrowed her stare at my calmness. 'There're stories I could've told. Still could.'

'Well, there you are then. Make some money.'

Calling her bluff.

We looked at one another. Meagan moved her thumb, sliding Rosie's face out of the sunshine. I thought she was going to screw the press cutting in her fist but she folded it along its old creases, returning it to her pocket. 'Bloody towels,' she said then.

I fixed a polite smile on my face, swallowing the urge I'd had to strike her when I thought she was about to crush the press cutting.

'Joe tried to hide them in the airing cupboard. Soft lad should've chucked them. I'd hardly've missed a couple of old towels. It was you did most of the laundry in any case.'

'Not just the laundry. I did most of everything.'

'Little mum.' Meagan twisted her mouth, mocking me. 'That's what she called you. "She's my mum! I'm her favourite!" You were, too.' She made Rosie's voice sound whiny, spoilt.

It was what she thought, I realized, even after all this time. That Rosie was just a brat. Noise, and a stomach to be filled. Nothing more than that, nothing special or precious.

'Why did you do it?' I asked.

Her face guttered, mouth sinking into its wrinkles. 'What?'

'Why did you become a foster mum when you hate kids so much? Why did they let you?'

She barked a laugh. 'Have you seen the state of the world, of Wales? Girls your age having babies, everyone having babies, thinking it'll fix things. Bad marriages or boredom, or benefits.'

She leaned to drill her stare to my face. 'Rosie's family wanted a doll, someone they could dress up and trot out to get attention. Piercing her ears, putting her in those dresses that scratched the skin off her, remember?'

I remembered. Frosted lace petticoats under shiny pink satin, Rosie lost under the stiff puff of it all, scars on her little hips from the weight of the dresses, when she wasn't even three years old.

'I took her in.' Meagan's eyes flinted. 'That was me. You might've coddled her and tucked her up in bed, read her those nonsense stories of yours. But it was *me* saved her from that pair.'

'And look what happened.'

'Oh no!' She screwed her thumb at the table. 'No, lady. Because he told me, didn't he? Joe told me what happened that day at the pool. Took him two years, but he told me.'

I finished my coffee with my heart thumping in my chest.

Oh Joe. Joe. *What did you do?*

'So there it is.' Meagan nodded, satisfied. 'Now you know. Why I'm here, and what I want. Justice for Rosie, and some bloody justice for me. I've spent years with the curtains twitching, being called all sorts in the street, stones coming through my windows. And for what? Your dirty secret to be safe.' A grim smile lit her face. 'Well, lady, it's not safe now. It's a long way from safe.'

I'd have challenged her then, demanded to know what proof she had. Joe could have lied, or she could've coerced a false confession.

I'd have called her bluff in spite of my throat closing up, the air suddenly too solid to breathe, but I didn't get the chance.

The double doors opened and there was Joe – two tiny reflections in Meagan's eyes, like golden chips of glass. No feathers in his fringe, no cowboy stance. Just a swirl of dust from the street, scurrying leaves into the diner.

Meagan nodded across my shoulder. 'You're late.'

'Sorry.' He slid into the seat next to her, hiding his hands in the pockets of his jeans.

I said his name but he wouldn't look at me, keeping his head down. He smelt sickly sweet. The pain in my chest deepened. I thought of the black foliage growing across the windows in Robin's garden room. That's how it felt – as if my lungs were infected, mapped by poisonous branches. If they X-rayed me, they'd see a map of all my rottenness.

'Get a fresh round in.' Meagan pushed our empty cups at Joe. 'Nell's paying.'

Joe looped two fingers through the handles of the cups and stood, swivelling towards the counter where Gilbert was watching. I kept my eyes on Joe, expecting him to come back for my money to pay for the drinks. But he pushed his hand into his pocket and fished out a plastic tenner. It sprang to life like a party trick. Gilbert took it from his palm.

'Thanks,' Joe said. The strip lighting gave him pink sideburns, his profile pale and wavering.

He wasn't even nineteen, but he looked ten years older. When he held out his hand for the change, light filled it and spilled over, staining the counter with the shadow of his knuckles. He fed the coins into the pocket of his jeans, fumbling, his free hand pressed to the counter as if otherwise he'd fold at the knee and never get back up. I stopped looking, focusing on Meagan instead.

She nodded as if to say, *He's not your Joe any more. He's not been yours in years.*

It was true, I finally admitted to myself. He belonged to her, not to me. She'd been slipping him pills at Lyle's long before he met a proper dealer. Laying the groundwork for his addiction, stealing him from me in stages. He'd not been my Joe that day at the lake when we lost Rosie. And all through the police investigation, he'd been out of it. Giddy from the fear she'd put into him, or pacified by her pills and promises to keep him safe.

I'd dragged him to London to get him away from her poison, but it had been too late. I'd been too late.

'What's wrong with him.' I didn't frame it as a question, afraid of the answer.

'He's sick. Been sick for months, I'd say.'

'What is it?'

'Lots of things.' She looked tired suddenly, picking at the dried crust in the corner of her eye. 'Drugs, mostly.' She flicked the crust away, hardening her tone. 'And guilt. I'm surprised you're not the same, but you were always the tough one. He may as well be made of wet paper.'

Joe was waiting for our drinks. The curve of his spine moved me in the same way. I still saw summer and freedom. I still wanted to raise mountains to protect him, a hollow where gorse gave way to grass and he could sleep for hours, sheltered from the wind, soaking up the sun.

'You were always the tough one,' Meagan repeated.

It was an accusation, and an order. How she'd loved to give me orders. *Toughen up, show them who's boss. Don't let anyone take you for a ride.*

'How long's he been like this?'

'Since before you talked him into running away. You didn't want to see it. Too busy laying your traps for the press, making sure I'd be up to my eyes in it after you'd gone.' Her face buckled under the weight of her hate. 'But he came and found me. I didn't go looking, in case that's what you're imagining. I'd've been better off never seeing hide nor hair of either one of you ever again.'

Yet we both knew what he meant to her. And here she was, blackmailing me.

She hadn't forgiven me for the stories I'd leaked to the press. She talked about money but it was revenge she really wanted. She wanted to see me suffer.

'What is it you want me to do?' I wasn't looking at Joe but I could see him at the edge of my eye, and not just him. Rosie was there too, her blonde head lolling at his knee.

'You've fallen on your feet.' Meagan picked up her lighter. 'Seems fair I have a part of it.'

The flame sprang up then died. She dropped the lighter onto the table, not wanting to attract any more attention. She'd never liked attention, despising anyone who craved it. Some kids at Lyle's had craved hers, making her gifts, pandering to her moods, telling her she was the best mum in the world – hard to believe anyone had ever done that. Plenty had clung to her, the way you'd cling to a rock face to save yourself from falling.

'What kind of man is he? Dr Wilder.' She nodded towards Joe. 'The kind of doctor who can help with that?'

I shook my head. 'No.'

'From what I saw of his wife, he's not likely to do *your* health much good either.' She hooked her mouth into a smile. 'Are you so lonely you'll take comfort from a man like that? But I'm forgetting.' Her smile broadened. 'You don't mind the cold. It doesn't bother you.'

'The bloody towel was this.' I touched the ends of my fingers to the star-shaped scar on my forehead. She'd brought up the towels, as if they were proof of some kind, instead of ancient history. 'Joe was afraid to call an ambulance, afraid of the fuss. He didn't want you to be angry at us.'

'And the teddy bear?' She tapped a finger on the table. 'The bear *you* brought back from the lake that day.'

'You gave it to another kid,' I reminded her. 'After the service.'

'I didn't want the police finding it. I was looking out for you, the pair of you.'

'Oh please,' I said. But she nodded as if the story was something I had to learn, as if we were rehearsing for a visit from Social Services. I remembered those rehearsals: *You're happy to help out, you love the little ones. You'd like to be a nanny when you're older. I don't let you do the dangerous stuff, but you love playing mum.*

'I'm looking out for you,' she repeated grimly now. 'Someone has to.'

'By blackmailing us.'

'It could be the police coming to your new home. Asking awkward questions, making that snooty cow look down her nose at you.'

'Instead of Joe, you mean? But then your plan wouldn't work, would it? Carolyn wouldn't want to sleep with a policeman.'

Joe was coming back towards us, a clutch of sugar sachets in one hand, concentrating on not bumping into chairs.

'More than one way to skin a cat.' I looked at Meagan. 'That's a trick you taught me.'

'I taught you more than that, lady.'

Joe sat at her side, his leg brushing mine under the table.

What did she teach me, Meagan Flack? To be miserly with my affection and my trust. To cut corners. Lie and dodge, never answer a question directly, never stay in one place too long, shrug and move on without looking back. And to carry whatever burden she chose to hand me. Shame, grief, guilt. My body was heavier than it'd been in years, as if she'd reached across the table and stuffed my hands with wet sand and rocks.

'Joe,' I said, but he still wouldn't look at me.

Yesterday's sleepy smile, the tilt of his head in the kitchen, had been for Carolyn, not me. No part of Joe was for me now. I ached all over. There was a burning at the back of my eyes, like unshed tears, grieving for the boy he'd been, for the pair of us.

Gilbert brought the fresh drinks. I didn't want mine. Joe tore the tops from the sachets of sugar and emptied all four into his cup. He drank tea now. Strong, the way Meagan drank it. He smelt like her too, of cigarettes and old jumpers. Were they living together? I pictured the house, small and dirty, plates crusting in the sink, blankets kicked to the bottom of the beds. In spite of the blackmail, I wanted to help them. My need to serve was so deeply ingrained; hadn't Meagan raised me to make myself useful? I longed to take the train home with them to Wales, wash and clean and cook a decent meal. All the things I was doing for Robin, I wanted to do for Joe. But I was too late. And besides, Meagan had drummed more into me than subservience. Self-preservation, for starters. I wouldn't survive this latest challenge of hers simply by following orders. I needed to be a part of it, exerting whatever small control I had over the situation.

'I want you to invite us for supper,' Meagan said. 'Tonight. A farewell meal to your family. You can cook your ratatouille, Mr Wilder won't mind that. Tell him you'll pay for the ingredients yourself. We'll eat in the kitchen. He'll understand why you want to give us a good send-off.' She paused. 'Will she be there, tonight?'

I nodded, 'Yes,' although I'd no way of knowing whether or not it was true.

'That's nice. It'll be nice to see her again. Won't it, Joe?'

'Yes.'

His leg moved against mine under the table. Its heat seemed more real than the rest of him, perhaps because I couldn't see it.

'On second thoughts . . .' Meagan ran her index finger around the rim of her empty cup. 'It'll be cosier without me. Just you and Joe.' She fixed her eyes on my face. 'The pair of you, and the pair of them. That'll be better, won't it?'

'Yes,' Joe repeated. He'd have said yes to anything she suggested.

'And then what?' I forced myself to ask the question, wanting at least one of us to challenge her.

'He can pay you for services rendered. That's the usual way of things, isn't it? And they can afford it.'

'Why would they pay? I'm already in his employ.'

'As a housekeeper.' She smiled flatly. 'I didn't see anything in his rota about . . . personal services. From what soft lad here's told me, you'll need paying. They've got very specific tastes, the pair of them. Very specific.'

219

Master of the house, Carolyn had called him. I remembered the rest of her speech from that day: *You do know he's a magistrate?* Meagan was right. Robin would pay for my silence. He'd have to.

'One night,' Meagan said. 'One payment. She was generous enough with Joe that first time, gave him the price of a first-class ticket home to me. I'm not greedy, given they're so generous. You'll see the back of me by this time tomorrow. Won't that be nice?'

I neither trusted nor believed her, but what could I do? Joe had handed her all the ammunition she needed. I had nothing left.

We sat in silence after that.

Meagan finished her tea, and Joe drank his.

When they got up to go, I tried one last time to stop what was going to happen. 'Joe—' but his eyes slid away from me. He stood, waiting while Meagan buttoned her coat.

They left together, my worst enemy and the boy I'd loved best of anyone in the world. The cafe door opened and closed, letting in a draught that ran up my legs and into my lap. I brushed it away with the palms of my hands as I climbed to my feet. I felt numb with cold, frozen inside. I needed to be moving, to get the blood to my brain. My body was heavy and clumsy, as if I'd been drugged. If I hadn't been watching her so carefully, I'd have suspected Meagan of slipping something into my tea. But it was just her old poison – fear. I was afraid of what was going to happen next.

In the cheese shop, another crowd had gathered in anticipation of a deli lunch.

Bradley was making up a box of pie and pickles. I went to the back, where cartons of eggs were stacked. Opening a carton, I inspected the shells for imperfections. It was normal to check for breakages before purchasing eggs. I wanted to hold something fragile in my hands, to think very hard about what I was about to do. Lifting an egg from the box, I cradled it in my fist. If you apply pressure to the top and bottom of the shell, finding the points of greatest resistance, you can't crush an egg no matter how hard you try. I held it to the light to see the place where life could be suspended, bound by a narrow cord to the skin of the shell. As I looked, I felt such a rush of love for Rosie it frightened me. I wanted to soar with her out of reach of everyone, to a place where the air was too thin to breathe, the land below us black and distant.

Starling Villas was quiet on my return.

Outside the library, I listened for the noise of voices then listened again outside the garden room. She was in the house, I could sense it. Carolyn and Robin were both in the house. My blood was hot; an image in my head of a rabbit skinned in a single scarlet piece, exposing its knobbly blue skeleton. I held on to the edge of the table where Carolyn's lilies were overblown, petals peeled obscenely open. Bruising my hand on the marble, afraid of letting this moment pass without censor, without mark. What I was about to do, what Meagan was making me do . . . A wail was in my throat but I couldn't let it out. I hadn't wailed that night at the side of the lake. Only later in Lyle's, my hands and face pushed into a stack of towels to muffle the banshee sound.

The library door opened to my right.

'Nell.' Robin stood watching me with his serious smile. 'I thought I heard you come in.'

I straightened, making a pretence at tidying the vase. 'They're dead.'

221

'The lilies?' He came towards me.

I wasn't ready, it was too soon. Supper, Meagan said. 'May I have the evening off?'

'This evening?' He put one finger on the marble, collecting a spot of pollen which he studied before looking at me. 'Why?'

'Joe's going back to Wales tomorrow. I'd like to have supper with him.' I summoned a smile. 'Actually, I'd love to cook for him, here. But you might not like that. After what I told you, and because it's not my place to invite guests here. It's your house, I'm just the housekeeper.'

I'd have kept on, stuffing the space between us with words, but he stopped me. 'Of course you must cook him supper. We'll eat out.'

'No. Please. I wouldn't want that. Let me cook for you both, too.'

He scratched his cheek with his thumb. 'What would you cook?'

'Ratatouille. It's the first dish I learnt to cook. We'll eat it with crusty bread like – like French peasants.' My smile was better this time. 'If you don't mind being a French peasant for the night.'

He laughed. 'I'd love it.'

'That's settled then. I'll serve supper in the dining room for both of you. Then I'll eat with Joe in the kitchen later, if you're sure.'

He hesitated, on the brink of inviting us to join them in the dining room, but it would never work. The two of us, perhaps. But not Joe and not Carolyn, not together. 'Perfect. Thank you.'

I dropped my head under the pretence of unbuttoning my coat, the press of tears in my eyes. His gratitude shamed me. When I looked up, he was walking away. Back to the library, to her.

I wondered what she'd wear to supper knowing Joe was in the

house. I would wear my black dress because it was all I had, but Carolyn had a suitcase full of dresses, silks and satins, crimson red and black, and shimmering silver.

I listened again for the sound of voices from the other side of the door, but there was only silence made sticky by the pollen and the lilies' dying scent.

26

Supper was a lie, like everything else. I didn't cook ratatouille, I didn't need to. It was in a lidded bowl in the freezer, put there the first night Carolyn came, after she instructed me to save the meal I'd prepared. Emptying it into a casserole dish, I set it on the stove on a low heat. I'd made a generous amount, planning on keeping some back for my meals. The bread at least was fresh. I wrapped a cloth around the loaf and set it aside to be warmed.

After that, I climbed the stairs to my attic to change my clothes.

Hungry's smell clung to me, and Meagan's smell too. In Lyle's, once Rosie had finished her warm milk and was asleep, Joe would stretch on the bed. I'd lie next to him, breathing in his salted honey scent. Now he stank of Meagan, dry and stale and bitter, but even that wasn't the whole truth. I was going to spend the rest of the day lying to myself, one way or another.

As I washed my hands and face, I allowed myself the truth in small measure, to appease the nagging of my skin. When I shut my eyes, Robin's smile was there. I wanted so much to lean into it but I couldn't, not now. Joe didn't smell of Meagan, or not only of her. He stank of vinegar and ammonia, with the floral scent of weed at the back of it all. Joe had been an addict since he was fifteen. After Rosie disappeared, he'd promised to quit. I'd let myself believe it because it suited me. I knew Meagan had been slipping him cash and pills to keep him dependent on her, and it pleased me to think he'd broken away. That he was *my* Joe, not hers. I'd been fighting her for him, and I'd wanted so much to believe I'd won.

A gull skittered on the attic roof.

I held my breath until I heard it again, edging along the tiles. Traffic droned below me. For the first time, I noticed its vibration, each brass camel trembling on the tapestry, tissue paper trembling in the broken panel of the lamp.

Starling Villas was old, too old to survive the onslaught of traffic and London's relentless expansion. In another five or ten years, it wouldn't be standing. I had no future here. The gull barked, wings thumping as it flew from the roof in search of litter.

'What happened to your common sense?' I repeated Meagan's words aloud, looking around my narrow attic room. 'Letting him punish you. Found yourself a gaoler?'

Nine days ago, when I'd first set foot inside, I'd known what I was in his house. A slave, his slave. How often had I called myself that as I went about my business, obeying his every rule? Then he'd smiled at me, inviting me to share his breakfast. No – *ordering* me to. Was Meagan right? Had Robin broken Carolyn, and was he hoping to do the same to me? His sadness was such strange bait, but wasn't that what first attracted me to him? The idea that I might be the one to assuage his sadness. Needing to be needed. *You always wanted a place to call home.*

My black dress was limp at the hem, tired of being washed and worn. I longed for a gown like Carolyn's, blood-red, with lipstick to match. Meagan's plan called for a temptress, a siren.

In the mirror, my eyes were hot and huge. Brilliant, as a book might say, with unshed tears. But it was a lie, like everything else. I had no tears, I was pitiless. Lifting my hair, I tied it in a knot, staticky against my neck. My throat was long and creamy, my lips blueish pale. I searched the rucksack for one of Joe's stolen lipsticks, painting an arch.

It was getting late. I had to set the tables, in the dining room where Carolyn and Robin would eat, and in the kitchen. Glasses for wine, red tonight. Shiraz, or Bandol Rouge, I pretended to know which was best, pretended all I needed was to stand the wine to breathe, polish the correct glasses. Carolyn would hate the supper, 'A French peasant! She actually said that?' so it hardly mattered, but it kept me from thinking of what came after the meal, when the house was settling towards night, all its rooms lit by lamps and the low chiming of its clocks.

Over the black dress, I tied a clean white cloth. When I turned to the mirror, I met a stranger. A girl with tumbling hair and fathomless eyes, who leaned towards me to whisper, 'Hello, again. I thought I'd lost you. After the Shunt Lounge, after Brian. They said you left, no way of contacting you. I didn't expect to see you again, but here we are. Just like old times.'

I shut my eyes at the mirror, blocking her out.

Closing the door to the attic, I went down the stairs, trailing my hand along the wall, finding out its imperfections. To live in an old house is to live with death, isn't that what they said?

After dark, the house was different. More solid, somehow. The shadows stood and stretched as if they'd spent the day as he had, cramped over a desk. The evening's noise slipped away as night prowled in, poking its muzzle into all the corners, seeking something to hunt.

Only at night did the house feel real, ready.

And I was its keeper.

I found a wound in the wall where a ladder had leaned, pressing the tip of my ring finger there, as if I could staunch the wound. The house was very still about me, waiting for my next move. I stayed where I was, sealing the scar in its wall with my crooked finger, the stairs winding away below me to the kitchen where supper was defrosting, and four fragile glasses waited to be filled.

27

That night, Carolyn had a new streak in her hair, an expensive platinum stripe running from root to tip on the right side of her face, as precise as a blade. She must have left the house after Robin told her of my supper plans, taking a cab to her hairdresser. The platinum streak made a statement, bold and brave. She'd stolen a march on time, that was how it looked. I admired her for it, the emotion alien, a metallic twinge on my tongue.

The ratatouille smelt good. Zesting a lemon, I winced as its juice found a paper cut at the tip of my little finger. Sucking at the sting, I thought of the brick of banknotes in their hiding place on his library shelf. Wouldn't that be easier than this? Fairer, surely. Robin's pride mattered more than his wealth, but either way it was a betrayal. Meagan imagined I could walk away from tonight unscathed. That, or dig myself deeper into Starling Villas. She thought this a transaction like any other. The scent of bread filled the kitchen, lofty and seductive. Hunger flipped my stomach. The light moved in red pinwheels, making a carnival of the kitchen.

Fear was everywhere in Starling Villas, now.

Not hiding any longer but sitting in the sun like a cat, stretching as the sky stretched, greedy for its heat. I was doing this thing, Megan's transaction. No, *we* were doing it. Robin and Carolyn, and Joe and I. My motive was fear – of what Meagan would say or do if I didn't obey her instructions. But at the same time it felt inevitable, as if the house had always wanted it. As if it'd only ever been a place where couples came to kill a lonely hour or to stop hunger in its tracks, the rubbing of bodies like the rubbing of sticks to make fire. I told myself we were keeping warm, that was all. That was everything.

In the dining room, Carolyn had arranged herself at the far end of the table where the light struck the new note of silver from her hair.

Robin glanced up when I brought the drinks, a smile warming his eyes. I smiled back. Then I smiled at her, as if tonight I could afford to be generous.

The banknotes were burning a hole in the wall one room away. I could leave the room and take them, a short detour on my way back to the kitchen. Then when Joe came, I could hand him the money and send him away.

I'd lose my job. If the police were involved, I'd be arrested and sent to prison, a warm place for the winter. All for what, Joe? For you? To tie you more closely to that old witch who scalped us for years, and will scalp us again if she can?

'Thank you, Nell.' Robin's smile was too much, I had to turn away.

Carolyn caught my eye as I turned, pinning me with her stare as if she could see through the threat of my tears to the promise I was keeping to Joe, and myself. A promise made two years ago, as

I knelt at the lip of the lake with Rosie's teddy in my arms, weeping her name into the water.

Enough. The rubbing of sticks. That was all.

The Wilders were spearing butter onto bread when Joe knocked at the front door. I answered without speaking, to let him inside Starling Villas, the house hollowing at my back.

Joe followed me down to the kitchen where I'd placed the props for our meal, bowls of congealing stew, oil in yellow chevrons across the surface, crusts of bread on side plates.

'There's no wine.' I pulled out my chair to sit at the table.

Joe took the seat opposite.

He was dressed in a white shirt and dark Levi's. New jeans. Meagan must be very sure of the evening's success. Unless she'd stolen the Levi's. Once upon a time, Joe would have done the stealing, back before the tremors in his hands.

'You'd better eat something,' I said.

'You sound like Meagan.'

'You smell like her,' I shot back, stung.

He nodded, picking up a spoon. 'That's what happens when you share a bed with someone.' He wasn't trying to shock me, simply stating a fact. He shared a bed with Meagan, her grey hairs on his pillow. 'Not for sex,' he added through a mouthful. 'Just because it's cheaper, and warmer. S'good,' he refilled the spoon, 'I'd forgotten what a good cook you are.'

'That's not all you've forgotten.' I wanted to claw at his face in my frustration. I wanted to cling to him, and beat him with my fists. 'Meagan said you *confessed*. About Rosie, that day at the lake.'

Joe was silent, eating the food, wiping his bowl with bread when he was done. My words slid off him and the light did the same, gliding from his shoulders like syrup. I couldn't keep hold of him, couldn't make him *still* the way I once could. How weak he was. The thought stabbed through my anger like new knowledge, but it was old. Joe was weak, and I was strong. I'd always known it.

'Remember the Shunt Lounge,' he said through a mouthful of bread.

'You remember that, then.' He wasn't going to talk about Rosie, or whatever he'd confessed to Meagan to give her this new hold over the pair of us. Instead he wanted to remind me I'd once played tonight's game readily, even happily. Swapping sex for security. 'It was a long time ago, Joe.'

'Since the Shunt Lounge? It was four months, not that long.' He sucked his fingers clean, looking around the kitchen. 'This's a funny house. I almost couldn't find it the second time around.'

'It hides, like a fake house.'

He nodded, as if he knew what I meant. 'You're not eating.'

'I'm not hungry.' I moved my helping to his place, clearing his empty bowl out of the way.

I'd loved him once, more than the whole world.

'Red stew, yellow pudding.' He ate as if making up for a month of starvation. 'And what was it she called fish fingers?'

Or was it the memory of my happiness I'd loved? My happiness, and my freedom. Afraid to let it go, knowing what lay underneath. I'd thought we had to be together, Joe and me, because of what was done. Not love, not now. Penance, or punishment. I'd been on my guard against love, ever since the lake. Because of what it'd cost us, what it cost Rosie. But that was before I found Robin.

'What did you tell Meagan?' I waited. 'Joe. What did you tell her?'

'Black and orange fingers, that was it.' He bent over the bowl, a smile in his voice. 'Burnt fish fingers, her favourite.'

'Don't talk about her,' I said savagely. 'If you've told Meagan – don't you dare talk about her.'

'Meagan doesn't care.' He slowed over the food, picking at it now. 'She wants to pay the bills, that's all. We liked it once, her straightforwardness, how she didn't care what we did.'

'This isn't indifference.' I gestured at him, the new jeans. 'She's making us do this.'

'She said you'd want to help.' He put his spoon down. 'You'd want to help me.'

'I tried to help you, Joe. For years I tried, but you wouldn't let me. You wanted something else. Drugs, oblivion – nothing I could give you. Not at Lyle's, not in London.'

'You stayed.' He sat back in his chair, knuckling his right eye. 'In London. You got it together. I couldn't do that. So I guess you're right.' He let the hand fall. 'You're right about me.'

'But now you're going to let her blackmail us into ruining what I have. You're not happy so I'm not allowed to be.'

'Like at Brian's, you mean. Like you ruined that for me?'

'You were never this cruel.'

'I'm not cruel.' He drew his hands into his lap. 'I'm just sad, and lonely. At least she cares enough to take me in, even after everything you did, the stories in the papers, all of that.'

'She doesn't care. This isn't care.' I leaned towards him, hissing. 'She's not capable of it.'

'You don't know.' His eyes glazed over. 'You're safe, you've forgotten how it feels to be cold.'

'I've not forgotten. How could I? After what happened.'

'It's one night.' He turned his head away. 'Then we'll go, and you can stay. He won't blame you, why would he? And if it gets rid of her, then that's good, isn't it? You'll have him to yourself.'

I looked at him sitting under the bronze lamp, flushed with food, and I thought: *You burn too bright, Joe, you always did.* That quick fever under his skin. I'd coveted it once, but it couldn't last. He'd never grow up, because he didn't want to. He was afraid, the same as anyone, but he couldn't mend because he didn't know he was broken. There would always be a Meagan, or a Carolyn. He couldn't live alone. Each of us needs to be able to live alone. That's the start and end of everything.

'I have been running,' I said softly. 'Ever since Rosie. I couldn't stop, but now I think perhaps I can. Here, with Robin. And if I can't, then that's all right too. I'll never forget her but I won't ruin my life over it, not any longer. Joe . . .' I wanted him to look at me, but his eyes slid away. 'You shouldn't let it ruin yours. Meagan thinks she has you, forever. And I'm afraid of what you'll do to break free. Because I know you, Joe. You won't be trapped, not forever, not even for a while.'

He wet his lips, but wouldn't look at me.

'You're afraid, and it makes you dangerous in a way Meagan will never understand.' And Carolyn too, although I didn't speak her name. 'She's right, all the same.'

His eyes were unfocused, wavering from the lamp. 'How is she right?'

'I want to help you. But I want to help Robin too, because I can. I'm strong, and kind, and careful.' I placed a space around each word. 'I know my worth. I wish you knew yours.'

'You mean *that*?' Joe pointed at the rota. 'That's what you're worth?'

'I'm not saying he's perfect.'

'Good. Because he's a control freak. At best.'

'You don't know him.'

'Don't I? She told me enough, that night she picked me up in the club.'

'Carolyn is a liar.'

My face was burning, not wanting to believe it any more than I had when Carolyn herself told me her stories of Robin.

'And I know *you*,' Joe insisted. 'You won't let yourself be happy. You'll wreck this, the way you did with Brian, with everyone. Anyone who ever tried to help us.' He sounded bitter, but his eyes were sad. 'You think you don't deserve to be happy. Because of what happened, what we did—'

'What *we* did, Joe?'

He shut his eyes. 'I know what she likes. Carolyn. It won't be hard. It'll be over soon.'

'You should leave.' I put back my chair. 'I can give you thirty pounds, it's all the money I have. Go to a hostel for the night. I'll find you in the morning. I'll help you, but not if Meagan's part of it.'

It was no good, I knew. Joe was gone from me. Back to her.

'She took me back. She won't do that again, not if I let her down.' He lifted a hand and sucked at the skin on the side of his thumb. 'Anyway, we owe her.'

'Is that what she said?' My heart hurt.

'It's true. Two years. More, if you count the ones before. I owe her.' He bit at the skin until tears came into his eyes. 'We both do.'

'I don't owe her anything,' I lied.

This whole evening was lies and tricks and who taught me that, if not Meagan?

'It's just one night. Then you'll be rid of us, for good.' He spread his hands flat on the table between us. 'Just one night, Nell. Please.'

Carolyn made the first move. Meagan must have counted on that, on Carolyn's need for control. I imagine she'd lectured Joe on how tonight must look like Carolyn's choice.

'There you both are!' Swaying into the kitchen in her high heels, one hand wringing the neck of an empty wine bottle.

We'd heard her coming. Joe was at the sink, pretending to dry the dishes I was washing. He half turned, showing off his waist in the new jeans. I felt the hungry tug of her stare.

'Hello again' – smiling with her voice – 'have you had a nice supper? It was delicious, a true feast, but . . . !' A schoolgirl laugh. 'We've run out of wine.'

'I'll bring another bottle.' I shook suds from my hands, reaching for the tea towel.

'It's good to see you again.' Joe held the towel out to me, addressing Carolyn. 'Thank you for this, letting me see Nell before I head off home.'

'But you're not drinking? Oh, you must have a glass! Come along.' A dip in her voice at the last moment as if she'd tasted the cutting edge of something. 'Nell? There's another bottle of this, yes?'

I nodded, folding the tea towel over the rail on the stove, taking my time. Showing her I wasn't in a hurry, that I didn't feel the same desperation she felt. It was the first time she'd used my name, but of course she had no choice after Joe used it. She'd pushed the silver streak behind her ear. Her dress was a vivid midnight blue, ruched at the waist to give the illusion of softness. She'd been afraid to wear black, knowing her sleek lines would be reduced to sinew. She'd worn a black satin coat the night she took Joe home with her, but that was different. She'd seduced him, that night. This second time must feel like an invasion, his coming to her house. But she wanted it to happen, or perhaps her pride insisted on it; like me, she had to feel in control of the situation. I felt for her, the brave dash of silver wilting under her fingers, her need exposed by the greedy light that sought out all the places she'd fought to fill with a highlighter pencil and a bronzer brush.

'I'll bring another bottle.' I selected one from the wine rack.

Perhaps my pity was too obvious because she tilted her chin at me, saying sharply, 'Come upstairs. We should have a drink together, the four of us.'

She gestured at the table. 'This is too . . . primitive. We can do better.'

Primitive. Servants in the kitchen, eating alone, when what she was suggesting was so civilized: four adults getting drunk and fucking. I didn't want to go with her. Joe had collected a pair of long-stemmed glasses and was following her up the stairs, but I wanted to stay down here in the warmth of the kitchen where the scent of bread lingered. Upstairs, Robin was waiting, alone. I didn't know what he'd do when Carolyn and Joe stopped drinking and started kissing. He might be appalled, or aroused. I didn't know, and I was afraid to find out. He might blame me for Joe's presence in the house or he might accept it, watching as his ex-wife took Joe by the hand and led him away to the guest bedroom. Or to his room. She loved to play games, he'd told me that. And Carolyn had said the same, but of the pair of them. What if she played with Joe in front of Robin, if that was her idea of fun? I couldn't bear the thought of him sitting alone, cuckolded. So I followed, up the stairs and across the tiled floor to the drawing room, carrying my bottle of wine in both hands.

The drawing room had clearly been Carolyn's province, with its velvet cushions and curtains. She'd curled herself at one end of the sofa, nodding at Joe to set the glasses on the low table where a single stained glass already stood. Robin wasn't in the room.

Joe sat where he was told.

Carolyn met my eyes over his head. 'He's in the library.' She reached to pull her shoes from her stockinged feet. putting her whole attention on Joe. 'Pour the wine, would you?'

It was shocking, how blatant she was. I'd expected an opening act where the four of us pretended politeness, asking one another about our days, discussing the meal or the wine. Instead, Carolyn dismissed me with a handful of words, wanting Joe to herself, imagining I wanted Robin in the same way. I stood for a moment, an awkward adjunct until she flapped a hand, swatting away my unscripted attempt to alter the shape of the room, and the night.

Joe leaned to pour the wine, his wrist exposed, still brown from the summer. I was afraid to take my eyes off him. Then Carolyn leaned towards him, the tips of her fingers dark with polish. I couldn't look any more.

In the library, Robin was waiting by the window, his white shirt blue with shadow.

I walked away from the door, towards him. I understood that this was necessary – *we* were necessary – to make sense of Carolyn and Joe. I didn't speak, grateful when he too stayed silent.

He put a short glass into my hand. Ice and raw vodka, setting my tongue on fire. More honest than wine. I was grateful for that too, the way he shed any pretence of seduction, even though it meant the stories Carolyn had told were true – he liked to take charge. I should let him take charge, play the master of the house. Meagan would approve of that. It was the quickest way to win her game. But I'd wanted this, for days now. To be alone with him, to be touched by him. It wasn't a game, to me. It wasn't one night, bookended by blackmail. It was my whole life.

Robin and I were so close we made a single shadow on his desk. He reached to untie the apron from my waist, setting it aside. The whiteness of it dazzled the edge of my eye.

We leaned into the wall, away from the window where the night's neon was stretched on the street's stone. Hardly moving, my neck turning loosely to the left when he wanted more of it under his mouth. No kissing, no scent from him other than clean skin and ink, a hot press of light against my lids when I shut my eyes. I thought of the bathroom upstairs, raw and white, the mirror where I'd held my own gaze as if it were a stranger's.

When he moved away, I shivered, feeling the cold in the room for the first time. The loss of his heat was unbearable, the worst loneliness I'd ever felt. I shut my eyes against it then made myself look. My apron was limp on the desk, already losing its starchiness. I was his servant. He'd backed me into this wall – he and Meagan both – and I should stay where I'd been put.

He was adding ice to fresh drinks, sharing the glasses between us. Vodka again, smoother this time. I swallowed it, setting the empty glass on the edge of his desk. The slim spines of his books set their words in my head: *Narrow Wave. Love and Barley. Lips Too Chilled.*

His hands again. His mouth. I knew I felt good; nothing beat a three-storey-house workout. I tried to set it all aside, as if this were happening to the stranger in the mirror, but it was no good.

Lips too chilled, heated by his kiss. Meagan's way was the easier; I was too afraid of being lost, of what it would mean for me and Robin tomorrow, and the next day. I tried to focus on the thought of what was happening in the drawing room, the narrow wave of silver in Carolyn's hair coming loose under Joe's touch. Joe wasn't in danger because he was not in love. He was playing by the rules, Meagan's rules, but I couldn't do the same. It meant too much. One night. My life.

Robin's hands held me in the room, taking his time. A lesson in self-control, or to pleasure me, I couldn't tell. His fingers snagged, and his mouth, finding out a slim ribbon of muscle in my throat. Enjoying what was different about me.

What was she like in bed? Like this?

I'd been passive, thinking that was what he wanted. But now I pushed away, reaching for the back of his neck, pulling his mouth to mine before he could issue any protest or counter-command.

Kissing him, tongue and lips, tasting him for the first time. Salt and vodka, smooth as glass. He put his hands on my shoulders, a warning pressure but I kept kissing, deeper, knowing my mouth felt good. His hands moved to my throat then up through the fall of my hair to the shape of my skull, the bones of me.

This was what I wanted. Skin, taste; the heart of him. I could make this man – smooth as glass, distant as the horizon – lose control before I did. But I wanted more than that, more than Meagan's vicious bargain and more than my cure for loneliness, or the need to hold my old fear at bay. I wanted Robin, all of him, no part held back by either one of us.

I backed us away from the wall, to the sofa, pushing him down with the pull of his hands at my waist. My hair fell forward, covering his mouth for a moment before I swept it aside with my lips.

Curling my hands around the heat of his skin, I let him move his mouth back to the ribbon of muscle in my throat and on, to all the places where I was different, and new, like nothing he had ever touched before.

Afterwards, I watched him as he slept.

Secrets were packed under his skin, too deep for Carolyn to reach. I wasn't her, I didn't know who I was.

I wasn't there, in the library. There was only my reflection trapped in the small surfaces, the rim of our glasses and the spines of his books, squirming to break free.

28

Four of us now in Starling Villas. Five, if I counted Rosie. Meagan must have known her vengeance didn't need any other weapon but this – my memories, and my conscience. The night after I slept with Robin, I opened the attic window wide and let the memory of Rosie in.

Gulls had woken me that morning, their cries sounding loud in my bedroom. I turned in the sheets, and smelt the sea. Rosie turned too, bumping me with her small body, a freckle of sweat across her shoulders. She'd been sick last night, clutching her tummy until she finally fell asleep, soothed by a cup of warm milk. I curled around her, despite the heat.

That summer was so hot, even the nights. She'd be hungry when she woke, and cross if her breakfast took too long to prepare. I'd been saving an egg for her but she'd rather have a big bowl of puffed sugar. Last night, I'd hidden the milk at the back of the fridge where it stood a chance of staying cold. Joe and the other boys could drink a pint in seconds, hips propping the fridge door, throats working fast before Meagan could catch them and read the riot act. I'd told her we should buy more milk but she refused to believe it was growing pains, just the boys getting greedy, taking advantage. She was so fast to think the worst of us.

Shutting my eyes, I breathed in the sticky sweetness of Rosie's skin, trying not to think about shopping and meals, money and washing. Just for a minute, before it was time to get up, I wanted to be a child myself. How would most fifteen-year-old girls be spending their summer? Sunbathing on the beach or shopping with their friends, sucking giant iced coffees from plastic cups. I'd seen them in town, always in twos or threes, tanned legs and long hair, giggling into their phones or at the gangs of boys who followed them everywhere. Back home, I bet no one shouted at them to make supper or beds, to put the washing on or get the ironing board out. Some of the girls were pushing prams already, but they had their mums with them. It was rare to see anyone my age on her own. When I went into town with Joe, the girls stared at us. They knew who we were, everyone did. Lyle's kids, foster kids. Some were scared of us, others hated us, but mostly they just stared, like the man at the harbour wall that day. Joe never seemed to noticed, and they stared hardest at him.

Rosie snorted in her sleep. If it wasn't so hot, I'd tickle her awake, the pair of us rolling in the bed, smothering our shouts for fear of Meagan's wrath. Roughness pricked my foot and I fished with my toes for Mr Bear. His funny face, button-eyed, winked at me. I rubbed his fur against my cheeks and lips, remembering a toy my mum gave me, a donkey glove puppet with a strip of fur for a mane. The glove had been too big for my hand but I'd liked to cuddle the donkey, happy to have a gift from her. The glove puppet was in the cupboard now, in the playroom. Meagan said it was only fair to let the little kids play with it, since I'd outgrown toys.

Gulls beat past the window, heading out to sea. It would be too hot for the beach today. Rosie's pyjamas stuck to her skin, and mine. I lay and listened for the church bell. Meagan made a rule at the start of the holidays about not getting up until the bell rang eight, but the hours before eight were the only cool ones, when the kids could play in the garden. As long as they didn't wake Meagan, it was allowed. Sometimes I thought she'd allow anything as long as it didn't disturb her. The bells were quiet but I could tell it wasn't yet six o'clock, maybe as early as five.

'Nell.' A whisper from the doorway. 'Let's go to the lake before it gets hot.'

No shade at the lake, but I smiled across the room. 'Give me a minute.'

Rosie stirred in my arms. 'Me too,' she whimpered. She hated it when we left without her. It was why she slept so close to me. I unpeeled myself, propping Mr Bear under her neck so she could tuck into him instead. 'Me too . . .'

I loved her but if I didn't hurry, Joe would leave without me. I slid from the bed in stages, freeing myself without waking her. She hunched away, seeking a cool spot in the sheets, and I stripped off my vest top to strap on a bra before pulling an old sundress over my head. The curtains hung limp at the open window. It would take less than ten minutes to reach our lake. I thought of its chill, and shivered deliciously.

Joe was waiting at the top of the stairs.

He cut his eyes in the direction of Meagan's room, shaking his head. We were serious, unsmiling, treading in one another's footsteps around the creaking of the house.

Outside, the air was honeyed. A seagull sat on the gatepost, its wings folded along the bullet of its body. The sea was beyond the hump of the hill, but we turned inland.

Every house we passed was silent and curtained, people still in bed. These were the only hours cool enough to let you sleep. No one but the gull saw us going.

The road bent away from the houses, narrowing to a lane that ran behind the walls of the school where Joe smiled at the teachers to stop them examining his work too closely. I helped him when I could, but none of that mattered now because it was the holidays. Six long weeks stuffed with our whispered plans to never go back. We'd run away, taking Rosie with us to start a new life.

'Her dad was round again.' I fidgeted a stone from my sandal. 'Talking with Meagan. He wants her back. He's got a new girlfriend who loves kids, that's what I heard him saying.'

'They'll never let him.' Joe shrugged, shouldering the beach bag. 'If it was her mum maybe. But not her dad, not without hundreds of interviews and questions. He'll get fed up of it.'

I turned and looked back in the direction of Lyle's, lost behind the hill of houses. Joe walked on a few paces then stopped. 'Nell. The lake.' I could taste it in his voice, the coldness of the water, the slate beach when the sun sat in purple splinters. An ache reached up my legs to ripple through the pit of my stomach. I turned away from Lyle's and followed him.

The way down to the lake was closed off. Signs warned that this was private land, the water dangerously deep and subject to strong tidal currents. We found our way in through a gap in the fence, the same gap we slipped through every day, its edges worn smooth by our shoulders.

The pool was sunk deep between the slag heaps, glinting green.

We worked a circle of slate, flattening it with our hands before digging a shallow trench where we'd lie the whole day if we could get away with it. The beach bag opened flat into a groundsheet under the towel, softening the worst of the slate. We worked swiftly because we wanted to swim before the lake heated up. The sun was already strong in a cloudless sky. When the towels were down, we stripped to our underwear and walked into the water. We didn't run or splash, wanting the slow push of water against our ankles and shins, its icy tongue at our thighs.

The slate ended abruptly, stubby grasses stabbing our toes, weed strangling our ankles as we pushed out until the lake swelled, lifting us onto our toes. Spreading our arms, we balanced on the points of our feet until the first wave took us. I shuddered, shutting my eyes at the brisk chill in my armpits, then ducked beneath the surface, greedy for more, opening my eyes to the cut-glass heart of the lake, brown and green as bottles.

I swam deeper, feet shoving, arms scooping, leaving the surface behind. Down, down, until my chest burnt with held breath. Bubbles squeaked past my lips like kisses. I saw the shallow slope that fell away to the deep base of the pool and pushed harder, wanting its true heart. The pressure stacked in my chest; I knew I'd never make it. My feet kicked as if at a wall. The lake thickened, resisting my efforts to dive deeper, drilling its fingers into my ears. At the last second, with my chest about to burst, I turned back. Up, up, to where the sun was moving in silver bars across the surface. Joe was a long shadow in the water over me. His feet turned so slowly I wondered how he kept afloat.

I was in the throes of panic but it was thrilling, gripping me like a lover. I knew I'd make it and if I didn't, Joe was right there to save me, hauling me through the surface into the golden air.

It was mid-morning before I felt the first itch of guilt. Meagan would be waking to find us gone and the kids hungry, Rosie bawling, the heat making everyone noisier than usual.

Joe was immune to guilt. 'What can she do about it?' He lay on his back, flat under the sun. 'It's not like she can kick us out. And she wouldn't anyway, because she needs us. Needs you.'

'I hid the milk.' I sat beside him, chewing my lip. 'For Rosie's cereal. She'll be hungry.'

'She'll be fine.' Joe brushed a lazy finger at my leg, above the cuff of my shorts. 'Stay with me.'

I ducked my head to sniff at my shoulder, the beer bottle smell of it. 'I'm here.'

'So stay.' He dropped his hand from my leg. 'I want to sleep. I can't sleep back there.'

I rested my head on my shoulder, seeing the water dazzling Joe's fringe. He was so beautiful it took my breath away. That pressure was back in my chest, like being inside the lake.

'We didn't bring any food. We'll get hungry.'

'Nell, come here.'

His mouth tasted sweet and sour, a new flavour. New Joe. Tomorrow, he would tell me it was weed, or whatever he'd been able to buy down at the harbour. He'd be frantic to confess, needing me to understand, and to cover for him. I didn't like the taste but it was Joe's. I shut my eyes, concentrating on the plush heat of his mouth and the hardness of his body against mine.

The slate moved under us, opening and closing in pockets to fit the shapes we made. On our sides as we kissed, then Joe over me, on top of me, inside. The slate sliding, splintering against the base of my spine, digging me deeper into the trench we'd made.

When he rolled free, Joe muttered my name. I turned to look at him, ignoring the flare of pain between my legs. The need to sleep flattened his face, his mouth tight, freckles on his lips.

I closed my eyes and dozed. The sun was soft on my legs, not yet hot enough to burn. Joe didn't move. There was only the stir of the water, whispering. When I opened my eyes, I saw a fly sitting on his cheek. He slept so deeply he didn't feel it, the sun striping him like a tiger.

I let my mind wander back to Rosie waking alone in my bed. She was always wanting to come with us, but Joe always talked me out of it. She was scratchy when she was tired, too big to carry now. When I held her hand she dragged at me, making herself heavier. If I told her to stop, she pulled harder, hanging off me. She was worse with Joe, winding herself around his legs. Last week, I'd found her trying on earrings, struggling to push them through the holes that had healed since her parents pierced her ears, back when she was a baby.

'Don't do that.' I was alarmed, fearing blood, infection. 'Rosie, stop.'

'They're pretty.' She scowled. 'I want to be pretty.'

The earrings were long and dangly, made of cheap pink and blue sequins. She had a new bikini made of red triangles, its strings biting at the baby fat on her neck.

'You are pretty,' I told her.

'No.' She screwed up her face, a furious pug. 'You're pretty. He wants you, not me. I want to be pretty too.' She was talking about Joe.

I knew she was talking about Joe but still I said, 'Who?'

She twisted her head to glare at me, cocking her hip. 'Joe. Joe, Joe, Joe, Joe, JOE!'

The earring popped through her ear, making her jump. Quick as a flash, her eyes were on the mirror, staring at her new reflection. The sequins quivered like her dimples. She curled her mouth into a triumphant smile.

With a chill, I saw the girl she'd be six years from now. Twelve years old, precocious, lips painted to match her red bikini. Hips cocked at Joe, and anyone else who'd look.

'See?' She pointed a finger at her face in the mirror. 'See!'

At the lake, Joe's breathing deepened, settling into sleep.

I lowered myself until I was lying next to him, using his shadow for shade. The lake creaked at our feet. I wanted to watch him sleep but it had been so hot last night, with Rosie rolling in the bed. I was too tired, and the day was too bright. I shut my eyes for a second, and sleep snatched me away.

When I woke, the roughness at my ankle confused me. I was back in bed at the beginning of the day, waking with her teddy bear scratching my skin. I blinked, feeling bruised.

Sun, slate, the shifting of the lake. No shadow at my side.

'Joe?' I moved my hand into the hollow where he'd been sleeping, as if he was there but I couldn't see him, the light playing a trick on me. The hollow was hot but it was the sun's heat, not his.

I rolled upright, reaching to scratch at my ankle, the brush of a bee or a wasp—

It was Mr Bear, Rosie's best friend. She never went anywhere without him. I'd put him into her arms in the bed, before I'd left the house. Hadn't I?

250

I sat up, fear like fine needles in my scalp. 'Rosie?'

She wasn't there. Only the long glower of the lake, scabbed over by the sun. And Joe—

Kneeling at its lip with his hands in the water as it rippled away from him.

29

In the library, Robin was waiting for his breakfast, dressed for the day despite the early hour. I lowered the tray to the side table, carrying the coffee press to his desk.

His wrist rested on an open book, its page marked by his thumb. He'd showered (cool green ferns in a forest) and shaved. No trace of foam for me to wipe away, his skin sealed by the razor's brightness. My stomach stirred with hunger.

'Come and see.' His head was bent over the book. When I didn't move, he looked up with an easy smile. 'Nell, good morning.' He pressed the pages flat with the heel of his hand. 'Look!'

It was a guidebook to Japan, Mount Fuji in the distance, shrouded in blue snow. On the facing page, pink cherry blossom crowded an avenue of trees where lanterns swung in golden flasks of light. Robin's fingers formed twin temples either side of the photos.

'*Mono no aware.*' He pronounced each syllable distinctly. 'The pathos of things, would be the literal translation. Or ... an empathy towards the little things, their fleetingness and how it moves us. What Virgil called *lacrimae rerum*, the pity of things. Impermanence. No, that's not quite it.' He frowned, searching for the right words. '*Sunt lacrimae rerum et mentem mortalia tangunt* – "These are the tears of things, and our mortality cuts to the heart." '

I separated his words in my head, trying to make sense of them. Pity, tears, pain. Was he sorry for last night? Impermanence – telling me it must never happen again? I hadn't seen him like this before, his eyes shining like a scholar's. This was how he'd been as a schoolboy, big with learning and possibility, so much to see and touch and know. A betraying whisper in my head: *He's taking refuge in Latin and Japanese, languages he knows you don't know, to shut you out and make himself safe again. Rebuilding the walls between us, scholar and servant.*

'It sounds like poetry.' I reached to touch a finger to the page.

'It is poetry. I lived in Japan for six months, when I was your age.'

He moved his hand so the ends of our fingers touched, framed in cherry blossom. It was too chaste, ludicrous after last night. I drew my hand back, afraid of being tricked into another emotion.

Last night cannot have meant much to him, I told myself, *or else he'd have said something, not simply shown me pictures and poetry.* But perhaps he was waiting for me to speak first. I'd slept badly, snatching at dreams of walking with my mother in a wet wood with the ripe stink of winter all around us, carrying cans of paint for the new walls in my room, the baby's room.

Behind me, the banknotes burnt in the wall. If only I'd taken the cash and left with Joe. I didn't belong here any more than Joe did, but Joe hadn't left the house. He was upstairs, sharing a bed with my lover's wife. I wanted to laugh. I wanted to weep.

'Sit with me.' Robin reached for the coffee. 'Bring another cup.'

I shook my head. 'I have breakfast to make.'

Carolyn would come down from the guest room soon, with or

without Joe. I had to be back in the kitchen when that happened. I'd make toast for Joe, I didn't care about that, but I couldn't sit next to Robin and pretend it'd all worked out the way she'd wanted it. Her neat, post-coital quartet.

'Please, just for a moment. I want to talk to you.' He waited then added, 'She won't be up for another hour, at least. Perhaps not at all.'

I mistook his meaning for a second, picturing bloodied corpses: Joe and Carolyn slaughtered as they slept.

It was the Latin and the strangeness of the morning, conspiring to put me on high alert for tragedy. But he only meant sex, that Carolyn would spend the day in bed with Joe for sex.

'Please,' he repeated.

'I brought two cups, in case she was awake.'

'Perfect. Use that one.' He crossed the room to bring a second chair to the desk, clearing space for me to sit at a right angle to him.

'Tell me about Japan,' I said, to fill the small silence. 'You lived there for six months?'

'In the mountains. Takayama. You wouldn't believe the stars on a clear night, so many stars packed so close together. I slept outside when I could. The sika deer came right up to the doors.' He'd been happy; it shone from his eyes.

'Sika deer . . .' I fished for what little I knew about Japan. 'Are those the sacred temple deer?'

'Yes.' He smiled and I wondered how much it mattered to him that I could hold a conversation like this, how much more I was to him than a girl he'd seduced. 'I'd have stayed, if I could. For a long time I thought of living there, finding work as an English translator.'

'Why didn't you?'

'Life got in the way of living.' His expression didn't change, as

255

if he'd done all his regretting long ago and had no patience with self-pity. I'd have poured the coffee but he was already doing it, remembering the way I liked mine, gifting me the froth from the milk. 'Now tell me something. Where were you, before Meagan Flack fostered you? You were eight years old?'

'When she took me in, yes. Before then I was with my birth mother, but she wanted to marry and they wanted a new family.'

'You were their family.' Robin passed me the cup. 'Surely.'

'I was a mistake my mum made when she was too young to know any better. She didn't like being reminded of it. She said she deserved a second chance, and so did I. She was honest about it, at least.' I sipped at the coffee. 'She couldn't love me the way a mum should. I was excited to be fostered, I thought it would be different to be picked by someone who really wanted me.'

Robin listened in silence, passing no comment on my mother's selfishness or my naivety.

'I don't remember very much about her. You'd think, being eight, I'd have lots of memories.' I paused, wanting to pick the right words. 'She wasn't neglectful, it wasn't that. It's as if ... my brain got rid of my memories of her, to make room for my new life.'

With Meagan and Joe, and with Rosie. All my memories were of Rosie now. Robin wanted more, I heard it in his silence. There was a flush of colour in his face as he waited. He looked younger and happier than I'd seen him look before. I searched my memory for a suitable story.

'I do remember one thing. A pair of yellow sandals when I was five or six. Just straps really, around the heel and ankle, and a strap across the toes. I wore them everywhere. At Christmas, I was invited to a fancy dress party and I wanted to go as Athena. I'd been reading a book of Greek myths from the library. I'd have lived in the library, if they'd let me.'

I hesitated, wanting to give him a truth, however small. He'd given me the sika deer, a handful of his happiness. 'I suppose I used stories to make sense of my life, and to feel safe. I'd been reading about Arachne, how Athena turned her into a spider for daring to boast about her sewing skills. I thought the outfit would be easy, it was basically a sheet, and I could make a helmet with kitchen foil. I only needed the sandals. My mum bought a can of spray-paint after I begged her, and she sprayed my yellow sandals silver. Only it didn't work, because the silver wouldn't dry. She left them by the radiator for days, but they never dried. In the end, she had to throw them away. She was cross about the expense but she'd done it to make me happy. I remember that.'

'Did you go to the party?' Robin asked.

'Yes.'

'As Athena?'

'Barefoot.' I fished a tiny coffee ground from my cup, black on the pink tip of my finger. 'Of course no one knew who I was meant to be. The best guess was Madonna – the singer, not the other one.' I made a gift of the joke, and he welcomed it.

We laughed together. It was easy, too easy. I should have taken fright, knowing this was wrong, that it couldn't last. At some level, I did know. My stomach wouldn't stop churning, but I pretended because I wanted it to last a little longer. Our closeness.

The Japanese guidebook lay open on the desk between us with its pictures of his vast skies filled with stars, the home he'd made in the mountains. So much of Japan was built on volcanoes, shaped by the shifting plates of the earth. Hadn't it been joined to Siberia, once upon a time? I tried to picture him with cherry blossom in his hair, sacred deer pushing at his hands for food.

'There was an earthquake when I was in Takayama, quite a big one.' He touched a hand to the guidebook. 'I was surprised how little it frightened the people I was living with. Afterwards, they were unsentimental, sweeping everything up, replanting their gardens and starting over. They said it's what you do when you live in a place where earthquakes and tsunamis are a fact of life, "You learn to let go." For a long time, I tried to live by that example. When my grandfather left me this house, I thought it an anachronism. I intended to sell it, perhaps even to return to Japan. Then I met Carolyn, and everything changed.' He smoothed a frown from his face with his fingers. '*Mono no aware,*' he murmured. 'I studied it briefly, at university. A poet, Matsuo Bashō, wrote haiku about it. The tears of things . . .'

'Tell me one of his poems.' I sat to attention, a good student.

'I'm not sure I remember any.' He crinkled the bridge of his nose. 'Let's see . . . "Summer grasses – the only remains of warriors' dreams." Fitting, for Athena.'

And it was all right, that's what I told myself, because he was pretending too. We wouldn't fall out over what had happened last night, even if I brought up Meagan's demand for money. I couldn't break his heart, even if I broke my own. He was so much older than me. I told myself that to him this was just a game such as two strangers might play on the long and tedious journey home after a holiday romance, knowing it's over but needing to fill the time on the plane and during the wait at the carousel for separate suitcases before the short walk away from one another, back into separate lives.

*

In the kitchen, the sun was in the sink, sitting on last night's unwashed wine glasses. I rolled up my sleeves, turning over all the things he'd said, and left unsaid. Did he want me to stay, or was the speech about Japan a farewell?

'*Mono no aware*,' I whispered. 'The tears of things.'

I was weeping as I whispered it, but tears were no use.

Meagan would be coming soon, with her hands held out, wanting his hush money.

I ran hot water into the sink. The sun had no heat this early in the day. I shivered as I told myself the story of what would happen next, here in Starling Villas. Not the story I wanted, but the real one, the only believable story.

Robin and I would sleep together a second time, and then a third. His sheets would start to smell of me and at first he'd like it, but soon he'd want the sheets taking to the laundry. That would be the beginning of the end of it, of us. I'd have no time to attend to his rota, too busy touching him and being touched. There'd be a kind of duty in that to begin with but the neglect elsewhere would start to infuriate him. He'd remember the time he'd put into the rota, its details like stitches holding his life in order. He'd start to resent the blurring of its lines. Dust creeping in, corners being cut.

'That cheese in the omelette, what was that? Cheddar? I prefer Edam, if you must shop in supermarkets.' That sort of thing. And I'd know he was snapping not about the cheapness of the cheese but about the cost of having Joe in the house when I was already here. When I was the one who'd brought Joe back, breaching the rules. Perhaps I was stealing from him too, keeping food for myself, eating it in secret. A little might be tolerated, but where did it end?

'I asked you to let the wine breathe,' I imagined him saying. 'This wine hasn't breathed.'

He'd allowed me to live in his attic, furnished with instructions to make sure his needs were met, day and night. Neither of us had blinked at the arrangement. I'd gone about my work so readily he must have imagined his demands were few. It was my own fault. I'd pandered to his proclivities as if they were nothing unusual, certainly nothing to be remarked upon. I'd given him that – the ultimate luxury of feeling normal.

I pressed the scourer to the wine glasses, water swelling in the sink.

The story took shape around me, as if I'd summoned a stage set. Walls springing up, doors slamming shut. My eyes heated with tears, but I didn't stop. Meagan's voice took up the story in my head: *Found yourself a gaoler, girlie?* He'd wanted a servant, that's what I was. *All* I was. To imagine anything more was vanity. Worse, it was a trap. Secretly, all men want a slave, someone to do exactly as she's told. If they could press a button and make it happen without fear of being judged, even by their own conscience, I think all men would do it.

In this way, as the hot water softened my hands, I hardened my heart to him. Because I didn't believe anything else was possible. When had I ever succeeded in getting what I wanted?

'Remember the Shunt Lounge,' Joe had said, and I did remember.

If Robin found out about that, we'd be over. He wouldn't want to touch me ever again. There would be no pity in him, no tears for the small fleeting thing between us. No *mono no aware*.

30

The Shunt Lounge was a pit. Grungy yet pretentious, everyone faking an interest in the art on the walls, everyone faking everything. Only Joe and I thought we'd found the real London, *our* London. We'd put the past in its place, that's what we thought, imagining our secret locked shut and sunk deep, airtight. This was days after we'd escaped from Lyle's. London was new to us, and we loved it. The big city don't-look-now deadly with danger and vice, mind the gap, police sirens, protests. Fearlessness was our new thing.

I slouched my shoulder to the Shunt Lounge's wall, a beer bottle at my lips, feeling the fever in Joe's gaze as he watched me swallow. I was in charge, tonight. And every night. Meagan would've been proud. She'd trained us to stay on our toes, trusting no one, taking what we wanted from whoever we chose.

In London, hers was the mask I put on. For one night only, that's what I'd thought, that first night when the stares scared me and the streets scared me; everything scared me. I put her on, and I'd not been able to take her off since.

'I paid for that.' I jerked my head at the beer in Joe's hand. 'Drink it, or hand it over.'

Joe put the bottle to his lips. Obeying me, the way he'd always obeyed her. He propped himself against the wall, mirroring my body language. He'd scoped the exits to the Lounge as soon as we saw the sort of people who patronized it. When I shoved away from the wall, he tensed up.

I turned to face him, blocking his view. 'Where're you going?'

Joe shook his head. 'Nowhere.' It thrilled me, the way he was dancing to my tune.

Behind him, a fresh push of people entered the Lounge.

I didn't need to check the crowd to know the man from the train was part of it. Mr Intercity, that was the name we'd given him. He didn't know our names, but he'd followed us when we got off the train. I'd let him follow us.

In the Lounge, I lifted a hand, thumbing at my lip.

Joe knew something was up but he also knew he wouldn't get anywhere by asking questions or whining for attention. It hadn't worked with Meagan, and it wouldn't work with me.

I watched him drink, aware of the skin heating under my ribs. 'Come here,' I said.

'Where?' He took the beer bottle from his lips, wiping his mouth with the back of his hand.

'Here.' I gave him a slow smile, knowing how he loved to be warm.

He crouched to set the bottle on the floor. When he straightened, he was so close I could see the fine grain of his skin. I didn't touch, just held him there with my stare. I knew exactly what I was doing. The rush was like nothing I'd ever felt before.

Joe didn't jump when Intercity groped him. He moved a fraction closer to me, saying, 'Sorry,' across his shoulder, as if he'd put his waist into the man's hands by accident.

I laughed. That froze Joe. It should have frozen me too, because it was her laugh. Meagan's. Joe stared at me, then tried to turn his head to look at Intercity. I grabbed Joe's chin and kissed him, hard. 'It's okay.' I licked the raw corner of his mouth, pulling him closer, laughing before kissing him again, feeling him shudder as Intercity's hands held him between the heat of our bodies.

Across the high angle of Joe's cheek, I smiled into Intercity's eyes, seeing pound signs there like a cartoon: *ker-ching*. He bent his head to lick at the skin behind Joe's ear and I grabbed Joe's hips, pulling him closer. *He's mine.*

When I drew back, I saw the fever in Joe's eyes.

Intercity freed a hand to reach for my neck, pulling me to a kiss that tasted of Joe.

All around us, the Shunt Lounge pulsed indifferently. No one was interested in what we were doing. London didn't care, and I loved that. Intercity and I could've screwed Joe right there, if I'd let it happen. I was giddy with power.

Joe's head fell back, the line of his throat darkening. Intercity was staying hidden, not wanting to make eye contact. Joe was hanging between us like a doll. I kissed the side of his head, drawing it down, away from Intercity, away from everyone.

Mine, I thought. *You're mine.*

London ate us up, and spat us out.

For those first few weeks, neither of us knew what we were doing. The freedom went to our heads. There was always someone happy to buy us a drink or a meal, a bracelet or a phone. London was packed with Intercities.

Later, we found our way to men like Brian who were happy to share their beds or sofas, until they weren't.

Joe and I shared everything. Favours, love, punishment.

I was punishing us, I know that now. Homelessness wasn't enough, I had to hurt us properly. The streets only made Joe cold, which was nothing when you considered what we deserved. What we still deserved.

Robin and Carolyn Wilder were collateral damage, the same as in a war. Because Joe and I had been at war since we left Lyle's, carrying our dead, the burden heavier with every step. We never spoke her name, unless it was in our sleep.

Joe had been my whole world, once. But he was like Robin's deer, pushing their faces into his hands – the soft of him like innocence, sacred and hungry, always hungry.

London was so loud, swarming and seething, showing us its teeth. Joe went back to the drugs. I filled my emptiness with promises and lies, half-formed thoughts of vengeance. And late at night, with her. My arms aching, skin keening, all of me bent double under her weight, the black lip of the lake seeping into everything.

31

'Come to Jesus!' The couple had parked themselves on the pavement outside the guesthouse, a pair of holy rollers in orange anoraks with pamphlets they couldn't give away. 'Make the change!'

They'd settled in for the duration, same as yesterday, when Meagan left Joe and Nell in the posh house and came back here to a dirty bed and dirtier curtains. He'd be lording it up with the mistress of the house, whoever that was. Not Nell, not yet. Carolyn Wilder with her gold bracelets, laughing about Bala, wanting Joe back in her bed. And he was happy enough with the arrangement, never mind how many women like her had interfered with him as a boy. Old habits die hard.

'Come to Jesus, make the change!'

Meagan's old da had been religious, raising God as often as he raised his fists. Religion was just another way to keep things the same as they'd always been – the likes of her at the bottom of the heap, the Wilders at the top. Nothing in between but debt and temptation. Master and servant, Joe said, that was the game they played in Starling Villas. As if there hadn't been enough of that in

Joe's life and Nell's already. Meagan shoved at the window, opening it a foot so she could smoke.

'Make the change!'

'What change?' she wanted to shout. 'We all just go back to what we know.'

Look at Joe and that rich bitch. Nell with her buckets and saucepans. Each one of them heading straight back towards their old trouble. Starling Villas was no different to Lyle's, not really. There was money in the house, though. She'd thought that would be enough. But seeing Nell had set the meanness back between her teeth, a red cloud of rage in her head. So she'd get some money, keep the wolves away for a while, but Joe would run through it fast enough and then what? Neither of them had Nell's staying power, or her talent for starting over. She'd made a home for herself in Starling Villas and so what if she was making a mistake, if Dr Wilder turned out to be a toad when she kissed him? She'd find a way to make it work because that's what she did, who she was. A born survivor, Little Nell. Nothing Meagan did could alter that, it was all just scrabbling at the slag.

'It's not too late, never too late!'

She sucked smoke into her lungs, tapping ash from the window and watching it float to the street below. She was owed more than money, and not just by Joe and Nell. That rich bitch in her big house, her smug husband with his book of rules, what did they know about survival? Not a fraction of what Nell knew, or Meagan. They'd never had to fight for anything, any more than this pair below her with ash on their anoraks, shouting about Jesus, as if he'd ever helped anyone.

'We help ourselves, sunshine.' She drew smoke into her lungs and held it there until her eyes watered.

Seeing London in all its grasping, ghoulish glory laid out like a feast she'd never have. Not even Nell could scratch a living for herself here without resorting to an apron and a stove. What chance did Meagan stand? The money wasn't enough. She gripped the filter with her lips, tasting its bitterness. It wasn't nearly enough.

32

Carolyn was in the garden room, smoking a cigarette. 'Oh.' Her nostrils thinned. 'It's you.'

It was beyond her power to pull a face at me. Thanks to the attentions of her plastic surgeon, she was obliged to wear the same expression, day and night. In bed with Joe, she must have looked the same, vaguely surprised and supercilious. It was strange only because she seemed to think I too was unchanged, that she could continue looking down her nose at me, after last night.

'I'm afraid you missed breakfast.' I watered the nearest plant. 'And lunch.'

'I don't want food.' Her eyes were pink. She reeked of Joe's drugs. 'Bring me coffee.' She pulled her silk dressing gown tighter, sucking on the cigarette. 'A pot of coffee.'

I shook my head. 'I'm busy, helping Robin.'

She let out a brittle laugh. 'That's what we're calling it, is it? *Help*.'

'We're in the library.' I watered another plant. 'Moving books around. Perhaps you could go out for lunch? I'm sure Joe would like that.'

She ground her cigarette into the saucer under the plant I'd watered. Her hand was shaking. I saw her bare feet on the tiles, and that the hem of her gown needed stitching, like her camisole. She folded her arms in an effort to stop the shaking. The sight of the bones in her wrists flooded me with shame; she was just a woman, older than me but no less breakable. 'I'll make coffee when I can.'

She read the pity from my face, her mouth wrenching. The platinum streak in her hair looked cheap, tattered and tarnished. She'd tried to hide it behind her ear. For Carolyn, everything was a deal to be struck, that's what I'd thought. Look how she'd bartered last night. But sleeping with Joe hadn't fixed anything, only made it more obvious, more exposed.

'I'll make coffee. And toast, if you'd like.'

She gave me a look of loathing before shaking her head. 'You'd better get on with *helping* Robin, since it's what you're paid to do.' She wanted her power back, to put me in my place.

I pictured her in the Shunt Lounge, one of a hundred bodies pressed together in a bid to be lost under the thud of the music. Maybe she was there that night we seduced Intercity, and I'd failed to see her, too pleased with my own power. Trading the chill of Lyle's for London's heat, trying on Meagan's mask only to find it fitted too snugly. I'd lost three months to that disguise, wanting to be as tough and manipulative as Meagan, who always got what she wanted, always came out on top. Look where it led me. To a life on the streets, Joe fading at my side, fear taking hold of him just as it had hold of Carolyn now, stiffening her shoulders against my pity. How frantically she wanted not to care, mistaking hardness for strength. But it's the hearts that bend which can't be broken. Had she never learnt that?

'I'd help him,' I told her. 'Even if Robin wasn't paying me.'

'Then you're a fool.' She tilted her chin. 'You know nothing about him. This schoolgirl crush . . . You think you're the first to fall for his professor act? The cardigans and books, the *sadness*?' Her eyes blinked, refocusing. 'It's an act. At least I own it, when I'm playing the game. Robin doesn't even know he's doing it, it's been so long.'

I heard her out, not taking my eyes from her face.

'You've seen his rules,' she insisted. 'His rota. There's nothing he won't control.'

'I don't mind rules.' I set the watering can down. 'I'm comfortable with them. It's what I know.'

'You know *nothing*.' She spat the words.

What did I know? That I couldn't be alone for fear of being consumed or out of control, the way I was when I seduced Intercity, in danger of becoming Meagan – mean, selfish, vicious. I knew that I needed a home, rules, stability. Starling Villas was a refuge from the streets, and it was hard labour, hard won. Did Carolyn imagine I'd stumbled in here blindly, mistaking captivity for sanctuary? If so, she knew nothing about me. We stared at one another. I was waiting for her to slap me, all those casual cruelties leading up to this moment. Outright war.

'You think you're so clever.' She didn't sneer. Her mouth moved, painfully. 'I thought the same thing, years ago. I was too clever to fall for romance, that's what I told myself. I didn't care about good looks or roses or declarations of love. I wanted something serious. He's so serious, isn't he? And so sad.' Her hands fidgeted for a fresh cigarette. 'Except it's not true.' She turned the unlit cigarette between her fingers. 'He's a monster, like me.' She looked haunted, out of focus, as if another woman stood to one side of her. Her ghost, watching everything she did. Watching me. 'You've no idea what we're capable of. What we've done.'

'What have you done?'

'This.' She gestured at the distance between our bodies, hers and mine. 'I tried to tell you. You're not the first, or the last. He likes new people because they don't know the truth about him, but you won't stay new for long. You and me, and *Joe* . . . You think it's normal, or healthy?'

'We're adults.' I heard the echo of my voice, pious as a child's.

Carolyn didn't laugh at me. 'It's different for them. Robin, and Joe. They can survive it. Men always can, they just keep coming back for more. But not me, and not you. Not for much longer. You're beautiful because you're *young*, haven't you realized that yet? It won't last. Not for us.'

'You make their lives sound easy.' Robin's dark head bent over his books, the pale of Joe's wrists where the summer's tan was fading. 'I don't believe that's true.'

'He's got his books. His plants.' She thrust a hand at the garden room. 'It doesn't matter how grey he gets, or how stooped. He'll always have girls like you thinking he's special. Wanting to help him, believing you can make him happy. As if *happy* is all he wants.'

My heart was pinched by cold. 'What about Joe?'

'Joe's an addict.' She moved her fingers, dismissing him. 'Joe's nothing.'

'He's my friend.'

'Don't you mean your cousin?' Challenging me with her stare.

'You knew that wasn't true, yesterday. You knew and you didn't care.'

'Nobody cares in this house. Nothing's real, that's the whole point. It's why we come here, it's why *you* came.' Fretting the cigarette. 'To hide or to punish yourself, whatever it is you're doing.'

She understood that much, then. All about us, the plants breathed, green and black.

'What's that thing they say about old houses?' Her eyes moved across my face as if it were a page she was reading from: 'In an old house, you learn to live with the dead. That's what you're doing, isn't it, learning to live with the dead.' She shut her eyes. 'Joe told me, about Rosie.'

My throat filled with the rotten taste of spores, unbreathable. I reached for the watering can, holding it to my chest as if it might shield me from what she said next.

'I suppose that's when you learnt to be a carer, being a mother to all those children.' She lit the cigarette at last, draughting smoke into a bolt of light where it shimmered, and died. 'Good little girl. Mummy. Servant.' She sucked on the cigarette, running her stare over me again. 'Seducer . . . Hag. Oh, not you, or not yet. That appalling old witch who thinks she owns Joe. God!' Her shoulders shook with a laugh 'Look at us, we're a casting call for the Ages of Women.'

I found my voice. 'Whatever he told you about Rosie, we loved her. We did.'

The idea of her knowing anything at all made me sick. What was wrong with Joe, leaking our secrets to our enemies, not caring who knew her name, or the rest of it?

But Carolyn had lost interest, smoking with her arms folded and her mouth arched, its old smile restored. She had what she'd wanted, the balance of power restored in her favour. 'You'd better run along. Books, in the library. He doesn't like to be kept waiting.'

I climbed the stairs to my attic, wiping my fingers as if I could be free of her words.

A monster, she'd said. Robin was a monster, I had no idea what he'd done. Shutting the door, I stood with my weight against it, breathing in the attic's brown varnish and black chimneys.

Living with the dead. Her words scratched in my mouth, lodging between my teeth.

What was I doing, calling this place home? The rug worn by countless feet, brass camels polished by fingers long since crooked and knotted with age. I'd papered the walls with programmes to plays no one had seen in a century, all the actors gone to the grave, forgotten. Everything in the attic belonged in the past, nothing was mine. Nothing.

He's a monster . . . You have no idea.

I crossed the room and knelt, searching for the pink silk keychain. My hands trembled as I lifted it from its hiding place. The twin faces smiled at me, gap-toothed and pretty. I held the frame in my hand, making myself look at their faces. I'd let myself forget about them, tied up in my new happiness, but they'd been here all this time, smiling patiently, waiting for me to wake up.

I didn't return to the library where Robin was waiting. Instead, I took my coat from the hook by the kitchen door and left the house, climbing the steps to street level.

Traffic flowed in front of me, an unbroken tide of cars. In Hungry's, I could see Gilbert moving between the tables, the weight of him so solid through the clouded windows. I wanted a gap in the traffic to open and let me through so I could sit in the steamy air and drink a hot sweet cup of tea.

Turning east, I walked away from Starling Villas.

After taking a dozen steps, I stopped and turned, trying to see the house. It had vanished, lost between the restaurant and office block. 'In this house,' she'd said, 'nothing's real.'

I was on the lookout for Meagan, knowing she was camped nearby, expecting the stink of her cigarettes or the sickly damp of her dress. Joe would have his instructions, I was sure of that. He might be lying in Carolyn's bed for the day but he'd have to report to Meagan before she paid for another night at the cheap hotel she'd found. She'd want to know what success he was having, and how much of it was headed her way. I thought of Carolyn's eyes on my face, the flat way she'd delivered her warning of the fate of everyone in Starling Villas.

The windows of the cheese shop buzzed with light. Inside, Bradley was handing change to an elderly gentleman in a regimental tie. He did a little dance with me, each stepping out of the other's way until he smiled and shook his head. 'Save the next one for me!'

Bradley shed the plastic gloves he'd worn to serve the man. 'Good morning, Nell.'

'Good morning.'

'It's not your usual day for shopping.'

'I'm not shopping.'

He raised his eyebrows and began tidying the display beside the till, little jars of honey and quince, muslin bags of bay leaves and spices. 'Then how may I help?'

'Did you know the woman who worked for Dr Wilder? His last housekeeper, Mrs Mistry.'

'She shopped in here, so yes. I imagine I must've met her a few times.'

'She had two little girls, twins.'

'Did she?' He shook his head. 'I never saw her with them.'

'These were her house keys.' I held up the pink keychain. 'She left them behind when she went.'

Bradley stacked the jars of honey into a pyramid. There was a new smell in the shop, of musk and damp spicy heat. He didn't speak.

I was waiting for one of the jars to fall, holding my breath for the smash of it, a sticky mess at my feet. 'You said, "I wasn't aware she had left." And you asked me if I was taking care in the house. Why did you ask me that?'

'I was being neighbourly, I expect.' He glanced past my shoulder as if a customer had entered the shop, but it was just the two of us and the beaming pyramid of honey.

'You weren't warning me? Because that's how it sounded. And then this.' I jostled the keychain. 'Turning up at the house weeks after she went. Why didn't she return for it? Where did she go? Did he fire her, does he fire all his housekeepers?'

'I'm afraid I wouldn't know.' Bradley stopped what he was doing, as if by keeping calm himself he could persuade me to do the same. 'I wonder, was there anything you wanted to buy? We have the Boulette d'Avesnes, just in.' He indicated a cluster of fiery cones, new to the cold cabinet. 'An acquired taste but Dr Wilder is a fan, I believe.'

I shook my head, but Bradley continued: 'Very young, quite delicious. With bread and white beer is best. A simple meal, but complex. It stays with you.'

I struggled to decode his meaning, suspecting a message just for me – *Very young, simple, stays with you* – but he was smiling at the cheese, lost in admiration for his work here. The bond between us that first day, as he'd filled the box with white-shelled eggs – I'd imagined it. There was never any connection. No secret messages or special meaning, just the chasms of class and age and occupation. He was only ever being polite, and a good salesman. Why would he know anything of what went on inside Starling Villas?

'Thank you.' I shook my head against the sudden sting of tears. 'I'll let Dr Wilder know.'

Joe was sitting on the stone steps of Starling Villas that led down to the kitchen door. In last night's T-shirt and jeans, with goosebumps on his arms. His hair was flat on one side of his head, pillow creases in his cheek. He was smoking a joint.

'I won't go back to her,' he said.

'Carolyn?'

'Meagan.' He looked down at his bare feet. 'I can't go back with her.'

I sat beside him on the step. Below us, the stone well was spattered with pigeon droppings and cigarette butts. The kitchen looked different from this side of the window, small and drab and ugly. Joe handed me the joint and I took it, tasting him on the roll-up. Last night's supper, and sex.

'What does Carolyn say?' I asked.

'She wants me to stay,' Joe said. He moved his feet on the step, shivering.

I passed back the joint, watching as he took another drag.

I didn't tell him that I didn't believe him, or ask why he'd told Carolyn about Rosie, or what he thought was going to happen here in Starling Villas. He was too sad. And so distinctly separate from the boy I'd known, as if a second Joe sat between us, a ghost-Joe like the ghost-Carolyn in the garden room.

'She wants me to stay.' He leaned into me, shutting his eyes. 'We're going on holiday to Greece or Italy, somewhere hot. She likes the sun as much as I do.'

I looked through the window to where the kitchen waited. Remembering the story I'd told to myself, of how Robin would tire of my home invasion.

I'd decided I needed to harden my heart against Robin, but it seemed Joe wanted to soften his own heart to Carolyn. Stories were how we survived, whether or not those stories were true. I shut my eyes and let Joe tell me his story about Carolyn.

'She hates Meagan, says I shouldn't let her blackmail me. I should call her bluff. Meagan's bluffing, that's what Carolyn says. She won't go to the police and even if she does, we were kids, under her care. She's to blame for what happened, because she was never there for us. She didn't do her job, leaving it all to us when we were just kids and what did we know?'

He rattled through the words, trying them for size against the depth of the trouble he was in. We were in. 'Meagan gave me drugs too, or cash for them. Sleeping pills—'

'Where is she?' I interrupted, shivering. 'Meagan.'

'Not far. Reina Sofia, it's a guesthouse, greasy. Horrible.' He smoked until the paper was ashes, flicking it away with his fingers. 'I can't go back, Nell. I won't. She wants – she hates you, so much.' He rubbed his fingers on his jeans. 'Carolyn wants me to stay.'

'Carolyn doesn't live here.'

'I don't mean here.' He kicked a heel at the step. 'We're going away. You should, too. Before you ruin it, the way you always do.' He shot me a look. 'I'm serious, you should go. Robin's not like Brian. Carolyn told me about his rules . . . It's not safe here.'

'You don't know that.' Last night, his accusations about Robin had angered me but this morning I was calm. 'And anyway, people change.'

'Not you. I know you. You won't let yourself be happy, or even just safe. It's why I had to leave, why I went back to her.'

'Meagan Flack, bastion of safety.'

'At least she lets me forget.' He pushed his hands between his knees, shivering like me. 'You'll never do that. You want us to be miserable for the rest of our lives.'

I considered the truth of what he'd said. 'Once, perhaps. But not now.' I reached to touch his cold hand. 'I wanted us to be together because of what we did, together. I thought . . . I couldn't carry that alone, Joe.'

'You can't put it down, either. But you should. We were kids, we were just kids.'

'We were older than her.' It broke my heart to have to say it. 'She trusted us.'

He pulled free of my hand and bent forward, over his feet. 'You trusted me, once.'

'I loved you, Joe.' I wanted to make him smile, and to remember. He didn't seem able to remember, not the way I did. 'You were my whole world.'

'I wasn't enough, though, was I?' He scuffed his heel at the step. 'Nothing will ever be enough for you, that's what Meagan says.'

'It doesn't matter what she says, if you're not going back to her.'

He turned his head to look at me, propping his cheek on his knee. 'Aren't you afraid of what she'll do? You were, yesterday.'

'Yes.' I couldn't find the words to explain how my fear had changed. 'You see, I wanted to stay here with Robin. I thought that might be possible, before Meagan came.'

'You're in love with him.' Joe watched me. 'Aren't you?'

'It doesn't matter,' I said. 'Because I can't stay now.'

'Has he said that?'

I shook my head. 'But it's true. I can't stay because she'll hurt us, and Robin doesn't deserve that.'

'Even if it's true, what Carolyn says about him?'

I thought of Robin's hands, seeing the sika deer pressing their freckled faces there. 'People change, Joe. I'm trying to.'

He didn't speak for a moment, then he said, 'If I left with her, with Carolyn . . . If we went away, you could stay. If it was just the two of you.'

'I don't see how. Not with Meagan out there. She hates me, you're right about that.'

'Because we ran away. She's lonely, Nell. She's scared, too.' He rubbed his cheek on his knee, looking for a second like the boy I'd been in love with. 'But I can't do it any longer. I can't go back with her because she doesn't trust me. She loves me, but she doesn't trust me. There was this boy at her flat, she thought I was going to hurt him. That's who she thinks I am. I can't bear her thinking it, it makes me too sad.' He blinked, straightening up. 'I'm so sad, Nell.'

'Don't be.' I reached for his hand again, but he was fidgeting in his pockets for another joint. 'You know I'd help you if I could.'

'We tried, didn't we? Running away. Being together, just the two of us. It doesn't work. You're too hard, Nell. Too hard on yourself, and on us. Carolyn . . . She's not like that.'

I wanted to argue, but I could see he was serious and what did I know of the woman Carolyn was, with Joe? She'd shown me cruelty, but she saw me as a threat. Joe was different.

'I can be with her,' he said. 'She trusts me. I'm just a boy, to her. A bit stupid but nothing worse. Not wicked. Not evil. And if she wasn't here, you could be with Robin—'

'No one thinks you're evil, Joe.'

He shook my words away, tilting his head to squint up at Star-ling Villas. 'This place gives me the creeps, I'm glad we're going.' His eyes swam. 'Before the cold comes.'

Robin was in the library in his shirtsleeves, sorting books. He'd emptied two shelves, the ones immediately above the brick of banknotes. The boxes had been pushed to the edges of the room, out of the way of his work. I stood and watched from the doorway, the way his hips and wrists turned. There was such peace in watch-ing him. Then I went to the sitting room and opened a drawer in the bureau, taking out a plain white postcard. Picking up a pen, I wrote out the advert neatly, all in capitals: 'Live-in housekeeper for London home. Usual duties, own room.' I added the contact details before pocketing the postcard, and sliding shut the bureau's drawer.

Climbing the stairs to my attic, I paused on the first floor, lis-tening for the sound of Carolyn and Joe. The door to the guest bedroom was shut but I could hear someone moving in there. Carolyn, I assumed, getting dressed. She'd go out of the house, newly glossy, and she wouldn't come back. That was my version of the story Joe had told. Carolyn would leave Starling Villas and never return. Meagan would come to the door, having no compunction about that, and she'd take Joe away with her to Wales. I'd be alone in the house with Robin.

The thought squeezed the air from my lungs, bending me double, the feeling as fierce as grief. The postcard's stiff corner stabbed at my hip, the banister rail creaking under my hands. I straightened, climbing one step at a time, up to his attic.

I didn't look at the rug or the walls or the mattress. Kneeling, I dragged my red rucksack from its hiding place and began filling it. There wasn't much to pack. I kept my eyes on my hands, unblinking. The slam of the front door stopped me, the sound rolling like a stone inside the house.

I sat back on my heels, listening.

For some reason, I expected shouting, or screaming. Joe not wanting to go, Meagan furious with him for ruining her plans. Or else it was Carolyn slamming out of the house, walking away with Joe's story in tatters behind her, leaving Robin in the library, staying wide of whatever mess the three of them had made. I hoped he was staying in the library.

No further sound reached me. Of course, adults don't shout and scream, not even Carolyn Wilder or Meagan Flack.

I pulled the rucksack into my lap, allowing myself one last look at the beautiful rug and the Tiffany lamp with its tissue paper pane, my brightly varnished walls shining with the faces of long-dead stars, the little caravan of brass camels. The slam of the door had toppled one of the camels. I set her back on her feet, joining the others in the long march across the tapestry desert, their shadows on the wall as intricate as lace. Then I climbed upright and went to the window, checking that it was shut. I searched for my fat white pigeon, but she was nowhere to be seen. Just a gull on the next roof looking out at the Thames, its yellow beak drawn like a dagger towards the water.

Voices from the dining room hissed at me as I passed. Whose, I couldn't tell. Robin and Carolyn, fighting? The hissing had the high, dangerous sound of gas escaping.

I left the house, walking with my head down, concentrating on the task in hand. My rucksack weighed next to nothing, casting a pink shadow on the walls and windows of the shops I passed.

When I reached the newsagent's, I took the postcard from my pocket. 'May I put this in the window, please?'

'Twenty pounds for the month.' The newsagent didn't read the postcard, ringing up the total on the cash register before I could query it or change my mind.

Taking out my purse to pay, I discovered Robin's keys and sixty pounds in ten-pound notes, half the week's shopping allowance. I paid for the advert from my own money, watching the man pin the card in the window. I refused to think about the person who might respond, the next woman or girl at Starling Villas. I couldn't be responsible for her fate, only for my own. It crossed my mind to keep the sixty pounds, feeling sure Robin wouldn't begrudge it, but what if he thought me a thief? Bad enough I was running away without a word of thanks or explanation. I couldn't bear the thought of his bad opinion, even at the cost of stepping back inside Starling Villas. I'd write a note and leave it in the kitchen, together with the money and the keys.

'Dear Robin,' I would write because, 'Dear Dr Wilder,' was too formal after last night. 'Dear Robin, I'm sorry I had to leave so suddenly. Here's the rest of the week's shopping money, and the keys. I've paid for a postcard in the newsagent's so it shouldn't be long before you have a new housekeeper. Oh, and the cheese shop has a young Boulette d'Avesnes, just in.'

The note I composed was more ridiculous with each step I took. By the time I'd reached the Villas, I'd decided not to write anything, simply to leave the cash on the kitchen table, weighted down by the coffee press. He would find it and know that whatever else I was, I wasn't a thief.

Stopping at the railings, I looked down into the concrete well.

Joe was gone, just a wisp of ash blowing back and forth, trapped by the narrow space. I was suddenly scared of being trapped the same way, and abandoned the kitchen steps for the front door.

In the window of Hungry's, Gilbert raised a hand, waving a greeting.

I waved back, then turned and walked by the railings to the front door, climbing the steps where ten days ago I'd seen the girl with the pigtail come swaying down from the house.

The silence inside was oppressive, a blue-black throbbing like the tricks our eyes play in total darkness. I closed the door and stood listening, trying to take the temperature of the rooms. The hissing had stopped, but the silence was somehow worse. The dining room—

That's where the danger was. A stillness, but not empty. Like the cupboards at Lyle's where Rosie would hide for a game, folding herself away, trying to stay quiet. The room was packed with the sound of someone holding his or her breath. My heart beat hard in my chest. The door to the dining room seemed to swell, pressing further into the hall, seeping across the cracked tiles, towards my feet. I walked to meet it, the keys held tight, their metal teeth spiking my fist. 'Robin?'

Reaching the door, I stopped, as if the handle was hot and might brand my fingers.

I breathed through my nose, keeping my mouth clamped shut, because I knew what was waiting behind the door. I'd known for days. Because I'd brought it here.

No one thinks you're evil, Joe.

I shook my head, wanting to turn and run. Out of the house and the street, away. Away with us.

Oh Joe, I thought. *Oh Joe, what've you done?*

33

Carolyn was in the corner of the dining room. Lying at a right angle between the floor and wall, broken. I couldn't look at her, she was just a shape at the edge of my eye, a darkness. Her black dress, that silver streak of hair falling over her face. I opened my mouth, making no sound.

They looked up at me, Robin and Joe, kneeling to either side of her like sentries.

Robin's hands were dark, stained. I hardly saw him.

I couldn't see Carolyn, or Robin.

I could only see Joe kneeling with his hands buried in the shadows at her sides that spread like wetness up to his wrists.

34

I ran from the dining room. I don't know why I didn't run shouting into the street, or to Hungry's where I could've asked Gilbert to call the police or an ambulance. Instead, I ran to the kitchen, a blind stumble down the stairs, to clutch at the table where his rota sat.

The bronze lamp breathed its heat over me. I was shaking, I couldn't stop. When I brought my hands in front of my face, they were blue with shock.

'Nell?' Footsteps on the stairs, coming down.

I spun towards the window, putting the table between us, snatching my hands behind my back.

'Nell.' Robin with his face pale, palms dark. 'It was an accident.'

I shook my head at him. I could smell the lake, like coins.

'Sit down. You're in shock.' He pointed at a chair. Then he looked at the hand he was pointing and his face changed, seeing blood in his palm and across his fingers. 'She was raving . . .' He moved, coming around the table towards me, his temple striking the lampshade lightly, making it swing.

I shrank from him, shaking my head.

'Sit down,' he repeated, clipping the words.

I did as I was told, because he scared me. The blood scared me. He moved past me to the sink, running the taps, rubbing at the stain in his palm. 'Joe's calling an ambulance.'

'No.'

My voice surprised me, sounding so much less afraid than I felt.

Robin turned his head to look at me, scrubbing his hands as steam rose from the sink.

'Joe won't call anyone.' The star-shaped scar throbbed at my temple. 'He never does. He'll leave.'

We stared at one another. Robin flinched, snatching his hands from the hot water with a curse. He reached for a tea towel, wadding it under the tap until it was drenched. Then he twisted it, wringing out the worst of the water. 'Wait here.'

He crossed the kitchen, away from me. The lamp was still swinging and I realized he must've been moving quickly the whole time, it was only that everything had slowed down in my head.

I heard his feet running up the stairs, across the tiles to the dining room. I sat and stared at the doorway, seeing him there, tall and dark, a trick of the light, retinal ghost.

Had they fought? Robin and Carolyn? Had they fought over Joe? Her blood was on his hands but Joe was there too, standing sentry with Robin. Tilting my head to stop the threat of tears, I found myself staring at the ceiling, knowing the room above me was the dining room. I pictured Robin kneeling, pressing the wet cloth to her broken head. Joe rooted to the spot, blinking at what'd been done. Was he begging Robin not to call the police? The whole house shook with her death. I imagined a stain spreading across the ceiling, gathering wetness until it had no choice but to drip, thick and heavy, into my lap. I blinked, and the ceiling was clear.

Robin didn't return to the kitchen. I sat where he'd put me, obedient as a child, waiting for him to come back. An hour passed or longer, I couldn't tell. I was afraid to get up, afraid to turn my head to track the sunlight through the window where traffic ran in chilly bars across the back of my neck.

My postcard was in the newsagent's window, pinned to the sheet of cork. Already a woman might have stopped to read it, searching for the address on her phone, turning her head when she discovered how close it was, wondering why she couldn't see the house when the dot on her phone's map showed it right there between the restaurant and the office block whose fluorescent lights flickered and burnt against the blank of its windows.

You're too late, I wanted to shout to her. *We're all too late.*

It had happened, the thing I'd feared for two years.

Rosie, and Joe. Death. I'd brought it here. The kitchen's shadows lapped at my feet.

The house was sick with silence, and I was part of it. Living with the dead, just as she'd said we must learn to do in an old house, this house. Starling Villas.

When at last I gathered the courage to go upstairs, I found the dining room empty.

Carolyn was gone. Not just her corpse but her smell, that expensive opaline scratch in the air. No body, no fair hair cobwebbing the corner where she died. No Robin, and no Joe.

There was only the russet smell of her blood. I knelt and put my hand to the place. The floor's boards were knotted, indifferent to the chill of my palm. Where was she?

291

I ran my finger along the seam of the boards, searching. Along the skirting and up the wall, but I couldn't find her, anywhere. The wood was damp from the wet cloth Robin had used to wash it. I could smell old coins. He'd left the stained cloth on the floor, the job half done. A stickiness lay there under the cloth, a shadow. I flinched from it then ventured my hand back to the spot, petting the blood as if otherwise it might bite. I waited for my heart to calm in my chest, then I set to work.

Doing what I knew how to do. Cleaning. The floor and wall, the skirting board. Everywhere her blood had splashed and speckled and sprayed, I wiped and rubbed, wrung and rinsed, and wiped and rubbed again. When that was done, I cleaned myself.

In the small sink, in the attic bathroom. My hands first, which were emptier than they'd ever been, scrubbing between my fingers and under my nails. My face next, scraping back my hair in one hand, holding my head under the water until it boomed.

35

I had every chance to leave Starling Villas. No one barred my way,
I could have left at any time. The front door opened onto a street
which was rarely empty, the office block lousy with CCTV. I could
have stopped a dozen cars with a single scream. I don't know why
I didn't. I'd been about to leave before it happened, my rucksack
packed and ready. But now I found I could barely move.

In my attic, I curled on the mattress, exhausted, as if hot tar ran
through my veins instead of blood. I squeezed shut my eyes, willing
sleep to come and take me. I didn't want to be conscious, to have to
think about what they'd done. Robin and Joe. Her head wild with
hair, that silver streak like a blade. Each time I saw her, it was worse.
Bloodier, more violent.

You didn't look, I reminded myself, *you didn't see.*

It was true. I'd shut my eyes after that first glance but she was in
my head, matting the inside of my skull. My scalp itched madly, as
if her hair was growing out of it instead of my own. My hands smelt
of iron, I could taste her blood on my tongue.

'He's a monster,' her voice hissed, flooding my body with its
poison. 'You have no idea.'

Sleep took me, at last. How else could I explain the fact of sunset when I woke, the window red above me? Robin would be wanting his supper. Guilt brought me upright, but it was a servant's guilt, not a human being's; I was thinking of him, not her. I washed my face and hands, smoothing my hair and clothes. The mirror was bleak with my reflection. Yesterday's stranger had gone into hiding. My own face looked back at me, ugly and deceitful.

My footsteps on the stairs were loud, shattering the silence in the house as I went down.

They hadn't come to find me, hiding in my attic. Robin, and Joe. They'd left me alone. What did that mean? I paused on the ground floor, gripping the banister. The black and white tiles swam away from me, the front door dwindling until it was no bigger than a mouse's hole, impossible for me to escape through. Why had I stayed here? Why did I ever come back with his cash and keys, needing his good opinion? I could've been miles away by now, sleeping on the long train journey, my head resting in the dull patch on the carriage window where the last passenger rested her head, knowing nothing at all about what had happened here.

'Nell.' Robin was standing in the doorway to his library, a book in his hands.

I froze, unable to look at him. How I'd loved his books, once. Now I didn't care if I never saw one again. The light was behind him, all the lamps lit in the room. That was my job, but he'd done it. He'd been with his books and his boxes, pretending nothing had happened, nothing had changed. Did he expect me to do the same?

'I'll cook.' I wiped my hands at my waist. It was easier than asking questions or demanding answers. Easier to do as he was doing and pretend. 'You'll want your supper.'

'Nell . . . Come in here a minute.'

I shook my head. 'I'm running late.'

'You're in shock.' He shifted his grip on the book, holding out a hand to me. 'Let me explain what happened.'

'I don't want to know what happened.'

'Please.' He spread his hand wide. 'Let me explain.'

He was so calm and persuasive, as if offering to clear up a mis-understanding over a menu, not the murder of his wife. My ears ached from listening for the sound of Joe in the library, waiting for me. What story had Joe told to make sense of what they'd done, and why was Robin believing it? I hadn't thought them alike, but they were. They had to be, to have done what they did.

'Where is she? Carolyn.' My voice cracked on the second syl-lable of her name.

His face darkened. 'She's gone, for good this time. At least there's an end to that.' His hand was outstretched as if he expected me to take it, to go with him into the library where the lamps were burning. 'Come on, I've something for you.' He crooked his mouth into a smile.

I crossed the sea of tiles, and stepped into his library.

Joe wasn't there. Just the books and the desk, Robin's chair pulled back from his work. A small silk-covered box, fastened with a sliver of ivory, sat on the blotter. Robin reached past me to open the box, taking out a tiny turquoise bowl striped with gold.

'Kintsugi. The art of scars.' He traced the shimmering lines with the ball of his thumb. 'When a precious thing is broken, rather than throw it away the Japanese mend it with gold, or platinum. It's stronger too, less likely to break a second time.' He turned the bowl on the tips of his fingers, the light firing its scars. 'I love how they've made a virtue of the damage. Kintsugi represents a pivotal moment in our life, the point at which we might crack under pressure. But we can stay strong and useful, the accident that broke us is just a step in our journey.'

'It's lovely,' I said truthfully.

He reached for my hand, opening it. 'It's yours.'

He placed the bowl in my palm, where it rested light as an eggshell, warm from his touch. 'Yours.' He lifted a strand of my hair with his fingers, neatening it behind my ear. 'Nell,' he said, a soft breath against my neck. 'Nell.'

He was buying my silence. I couldn't speak, afraid to move in case I dropped the bowl, in case it wasn't as strong as he said it was. I wasn't afraid of him, not quite, but I was afraid of us – the people we were when we were together. The pair of us, pretending.

I had an urge to shut my hand and see if I could crush the bowl, wanting to know whether its scars could take the punishment of my fist. I wasn't to be trusted with precious things, didn't he know that?

Stepping back from him, I reached for the silk box and fitted the bowl into its padded hollow, closing the lid and slipping the ivory through its hoop of thread.

I set the box on his desk. 'I can't.'

'Take it . . . ?' He tensed. 'Why not?'

'You don't need to give me presents.' *You know why.* 'I haven't anything for you.'

'I wasn't expecting anything. I was tidying the library and found this, tucked away. Carolyn didn't care for it, as I remember.' He picked up the box again. 'I want you to have it.' He spoke her name so easily, it chilled me.

I shook my head, trying for a smile, wanting to make it normal. 'What would you like for supper?'

He searched my face for a long moment then dropped his eyes. 'What's on the rota?'

'Cod's roe. But you missed lunch. You'll want something more than that.'

'An omelette?' He held the box in his hands. 'You'll eat with me? You missed lunch, too. Where were you?'

'This morning?' It was such a long time ago. 'I popped out to the newsagent's.'

Leaving you and Joe alone with her.

How could we stand here swapping meal suggestions, giving and refusing gifts, after what had been done? The quiet in the house was insane. Where were the sirens, the tramp of boots, unreeling of police tape? How were we staying so calm? Like a couple in an air-raid shelter, two strangers making polite conversation to pass the time until we could return to see how little of our lives was left standing after the bombs had fallen and the dust had cleared.

'An omelette,' I repeated. 'You'll eat it in here?'

'In the dining room,' he corrected. 'If you'll join me.' He didn't flinch as he mentioned the room, or give any indication that what had taken place there might have spoilt his appetite.

A monster, his ex-wife had called him. Now I was beginning to understand.

'Where's Joe?' I asked.

'He's gone, with Carolyn. He didn't say where they were going. It was a relief, really. I don't want to think about it more than I have to. I'd rather not know the details. You understand, don't you?' He held my gaze, the kimono box between his hands. 'I'd rather not have to think about it.'

In the kitchen, I prepared his meal, washing up as I went, tidying to save time later. It felt vital I should have time later, but if you'd asked me, 'Time for what?' I couldn't have answered.

I worked efficiently, multitasking. I even found time to prepare a fruit cake, my speciality at Lyle's: mixed peel, cherries and almonds, dark rum, and the rest. The cake would be our last meal together, that's what I told myself. All the while I worked there was a hot, hollow spot under my ribs.

When it came time to lay the table, I blanked my eyes at the corner of the room where she died. If I thought of it at all, it was to tell myself I'd need to clean there a second time tomorrow. Bleach, and hot water. Baking soda to get rid of any lingering traces of blood. Like someone at a distance, I watched the girl who laid the table, marvelling at her composure.

What are you thinking? I wanted to ask her. *And how are you feeling? Is this terror or something else? Who is the real monster in Starling Villas?*

Putting my hand into my pocket, I found the lacy camisole Carolyn had given me to mend. I held it for a moment, half-expecting it to move, or to vanish. It was all that was left of her. Joe had taken everything else – her dresses gone from the guest room, her brushes and make-up. I'd searched the room, but it was all gone. Every trace of her had been wiped from the house.

Robin asked me to eat with him so I did, managing small talk, some nonsense about a ceramics class he'd signed up for but never taken. He made another attempt to gift me the Japanese bowl and I declined, again. When the meal was over, he started to help me clear the table.

'That's my job.' I spoke more sharply than I'd intended.

He sat back, disguising a wince.

His eyes stayed on me as I stacked the dishes. I didn't look at him, remembering Carolyn's words, how she'd fallen in love with him because he was so serious and so sad.

For the first time, I wanted to weep. Not rage, but weep. What had I done? How had I fallen in love like this? After Joe, I'd sworn never again. Never. But here I was.

When I brought the coffee, he was standing by the fireplace, looking at the corner I'd cleaned.

I saw Joe kneeling, wrist-deep in her darkness. I blinked, to be rid of the image.

'Stay here with me,' Robin said. 'Please.'

'I'm tired. I need to go to bed.'

'Then come to bed with me.'

I poured his coffee and added milk, carrying the cup and saucer to where he stood. He took it from me, reaching with his free hand but I stepped back, away, shaking my head.

'Goodnight, Dr Wilder.'

In my attic, I barricaded the door, listening for his tread on the stairs.

For a second, I fancied I heard footsteps, not his but Rosie's light skipping. In that moment, I think I was more afraid of her ghost than of him. The back of my neck was wet. My thighs ached as if I'd been swimming in the lake. I backed away from the door, going to the window to see a smattering of stars in the night sky.

I searched for the constellations Joe and I once loved, but couldn't find them. Perhaps they'd died. That's what stars are, after all. Fire from a long-ago death, only now reaching us.

A sound in the street brought my gaze down.

She was standing outside Hungry's with her back to its unlit window, in a pale belted raincoat. Her face was turned up to Starling Villas, blonde hair brushed behind her ears. Her eyes were wiped out by the street lights, their sockets filled with neon.

Carolyn Wilder.

I jumped back from the window, knowing she couldn't be real. Afraid of her eyes on me, who was still here in the house with her husband. As if that was all I had to be afraid of.

When I looked a second time, she had vanished.

I only saw the red tail lights of a taxi, travelling east towards the river.

36

I wish I could say I slept badly that night. But my sleep was deep and dreamless, the best I'd had in years. I woke early, feeling wonderful for the few seconds it took me to remember.

My attic was semi-dark, its varnished walls glistening. Reaching out my hand, I read the programme for a performance of *Tristan und Isolde* in Covent Garden on 17 May 1910. The names made a sort of music: Carl Burrian, Minnie Saltzmann-Stevens, Louise Kirkby-Lunn. Tristan, Isolde, Brangäne. I ran my fingers left to right, trying to stay in this dreamlike state because I was nervous of getting up and going downstairs.

Where had Joe taken Carolyn, and how? You couldn't hide a corpse in the middle of London, it made no sense. But neither did the fact of her ghost last night. Standing in the street, staring up at Starling Villas when I had seen her lifeless body. Any more than I made sense staying here after what had happened, cooking his supper, eating with him.

'In this house, nothing's real, that's the whole point.' Carolyn had tried to warn me, as if the house wasn't warning enough, hiding on the high street, belonging to an age when Minnie and Carl and

301

Louise were stars of the stage and London had no notion of two wars coming to tear it apart.

I'd slept in my clothes. From the window, I watched for early deliveries to the restaurant, seeing grim-faced joggers, a solitary herring gull ripping at a fast-food wrapper. A grey smell lifted from the street, of someone smoking close to the kitchen steps. Office workers or staff from the restaurant next door. I saw their shadows through the railings. I needed to be outside, away from Starling Villas. Something happened when I was here, the house casting a spell to make me obedient, dull and drugged with hunger. I needed fresh air to bring me to my senses.

Robin was asleep when I left the house, curtains drawn at his bedroom window, seemingly unmoved by all that had happened.

In the street, I sucked in a deep breath, glad of the traffic fumes, not caring about pollution or air quality or anything other than being outside. I should never go back inside. Not even for my rucksack. I'd leave it behind, let it all go. I walked for an hour, heading east like the taxi last night.

Dimly, I wished I'd kept the phone I'd found in the kitchen drawer. I'd sold Brian's phone, the one he'd given me as a gift. A woman tried to press a phone on me when I was begging, 'Take this. It's got credit, you can call hostels, job centres. Call home, let them know you're okay. Take it, please. It's a gift.' I hid my hands in my pockets. 'Look, it could turn your life around. I read about it, how a phone can make all the difference.' Her face worked hard. 'At least call home, let them know you're okay. At least do that.' She'd lost someone to the streets. This was her way of keeping hope alive, but why should she have hope when the rest of us had none? I'd refused her gift as I'd refused Robin's last night. I didn't trust gifts.

That was Meagan's legacy, sewn into me so firmly I couldn't breathe without it pinching at my ribs. When Brian began giving us gifts – that's when I knew we had to leave.

The pace was picking up on the street, Londoners heading to work, bluetoothed and caffeinated. The memory of my time spent begging here had me shivering, searching for shelter.

Was Joe coming back to the house? Why had he left without speaking to me? Where were the police? I'd been trained to fear the police but plenty had been kind to us, after Rosie. It wasn't the police who'd whispered about the mad expense of the funeral or the spectacle her parents were making of themselves. She'd been missing nearly two years by then. There was no body to signal the end of the search, just a red jelly sandal washed up on the shore. No one to pay the price that should be paid when a child dies. Just Meagan saying she'd keep us safe, hide us from the police and press. Not for my sake but for Joe's, because she loved him in spite of everything. Because of Meagan, no one would ever pay the price. I couldn't let that happen twice. This time, someone should be made to pay. I began walking back towards Starling Villas.

When I reached the park, I found a bench and sat to catch my breath. Two little girls were racing around the sandpit, their mother seated with a pair of miniature backpacks at her feet. She looked tired, her dark skin lined, black hair threaded with grey, wearing a long green coat belted over black trousers, cheap plastic shoes on her feet.

A girl wandered past in a red blazer and skintight leggings, her face smeared with make-up, lips glossed, brows blackly arched. As she drew close, I saw she was no older than twelve. Her nose was pierced by a pin-head diamond, her walk studied and provocative.

If I squinted, I could see the child underneath – her spindly arms and ankles, her small ears. I wanted to wash the warpaint from her face, bundle her under blankets and let her be a child again. She challenged my stare with one of her own, cocking her head at me, an unspoken, *What?* I nodded a smile, looking to where the smaller girls were playing in matching pink anoraks, hair bobbled at the sides of their heads. When they reached the top of the climbing frame, they swung upside down from the bar, shouting for their mum to look. She lifted her head, murmuring a warning. Something about their faces, cracked wide with laughter, made me hold my breath. Big gap-toothed smiles, identical. Twins.

I sat up straighter, staring across the park.

Even upside down, I recognized their smiles. They were the twins from the keychain. I glanced across at their mum, sitting with their school bags at her feet. She was Robin's last housekeeper, the one before me.

'Excuse me,' I was on my feet without thinking, walking towards her. 'Mrs Mistry?'

She turned towards me, shielding her eyes from the light. 'Yes?'

'I'm Nell. I'm – a friend of Robin Wilder. From Starling Villas?'

She went rigid on the bench, cutting her eyes away from me, towards her girls. They'd stopped playing, standing to watch us, side by side. Unnerving, in the way twins can be.

'I have your keys.' I dug my hand into my pocket, pulling out the pink keychain. 'You left them behind, when you went.'

She stooped to pick up the bags, calling to the girls in a language I didn't speak. I tried to hand her the keys but she brushed past me. I watched her strap the backpacks onto the twins, gathering a small hand in each of her own. 'Please. Your keys? The pictures of your girls.'

She stood her ground, staring at me. The girls began to whine, pulling away from her, but she hissed at them to be still. 'What do you want?' she demanded.

'To give you back your keys, that's all. What else would I want?'

She looked me over, from my tattered canvas plimsolls to my sleep-creased clothes. Slowly, her face unclenched. 'You're the new one. The one who came next.'

I nodded. 'I'm Nell.'

'You're working for him, living in the house?'

'Yes.'

The girls pulled away from her, and this time she let them go. They didn't head for the climbing frame, running instead along the path that led out of the park, their school bags bumping on their backs. Mrs Mistry watched them go, following with me at her side.

'What happened?' I asked her. 'In the house?'

'Not much.' She belted her coat closer. 'Not when he was alone.' She glanced at me. 'You've met her? The wife.'

I nodded, dry-mouthed, handing her the keychain, which she accepted this time.

'When she was there? Parties, all the time. Strangers who didn't care how much mess they made or how much noise.' She stroked her thumb at the silk photo frame. 'They took this, one night. Put it with the other keys. To play a game, they said.'

My mind turned, emptily. She couldn't mean wife swapping, surely the Wilders were more sophisticated than that? But sex didn't need to be sophisticated. Look at Carolyn buying Joe for the night. Sex just needed to be there. And if Carolyn had taken

Mrs Mistry's keys, it wasn't about sex at all. It was about intimidation, and humiliation. Power.

'She took your keys?'

'They did.' Mrs Mistry looked at me, very clearly. 'Both of them.'

My heart hurt in my chest. 'He isn't . . . He's kind to me.'

'I'm sure that's true.' She paused. 'You've been there a very short time.'

We walked on a way, watching the girls dart and skip ahead of us, peeling apart then coming back together like two pieces of the same person.

'Is that why you left, because of the keys?'

'That was the end of it, yes. I needed the money or I'd have gone sooner.'

'Did you sleep in the bedroom at the top of the house?'

'Sometimes, when they needed me to work late. But I tried to get home to my girls whenever I could. He preferred someone to live in.' This time she didn't look at me. 'Now he has you and that suits him very well, I'm sure.'

'I like him.' My voice was small, shaped by protest. 'Not her, but him. I – trusted him.'

She didn't remark on my switch from present to past tense, just nodded to where her girls were walking, slowly now, their heads together. 'Do you know the work he does? Have you seen it?'

'His work?' I could only think of the poetry, the sacred temple deer.

'He's a magistrate, making the rules.' Her eyes tracked her girls. 'All the worst things. The things that trap us, you and me. *His* work.'

I didn't understand her. I thought of his library, the stillness of

306

his books. Then I remembered the boxes, pushed to the edges of the room. Carolyn had said I should search the boxes.

'My sister's children,' Mrs Mistry murmured. 'They were taken. It's terrible.'

'I don't understand.'

'A man like him decided they were at risk. So they took them from my sister and put them with strangers. Foster parents. The littlest hasn't spoken a word in months.' Her face twisted painfully. 'But they know best, these men. These magistrates. They make decisions and the rest of us have to live with it, with the misery and the harm.'

Sparrows darted down onto the path before flitting back into the branches. I tried to process what she was saying. Misery and harm, I understood that much. Dr R. Wilder JP.

We'd reached the end of the park. I wanted to stay with her, to ask a hundred questions about the Wilders and the house, her sister's children. But she was hurrying again, chivvying the girls along to school. 'Thank you for the keys. You should go.'

'Yes, it's time for his breakfast.'

She shook her head, her body already turned away from me. 'You should go from the house. Leave, before they hurt you. Before he does.'

No doubt I should have followed her advice, but then who would answer for what was done to Carolyn? I watched her walk away before I turned towards the house. It was time to end this.

37

In Starling Villas, the stink of cigarettes announced her arrival. Meagan Flack, come for her fair share. She was in the library; I heard the rise and fall of her voice through the walls. I was surprised Robin had let her in the house, but that was my fault for not being here to answer the door. Without stopping to remove my coat, I crossed the hall to the library, pushing wide the door.

Robin stood by the window in shirtsleeves and flannels, his expression as severely formal as I'd ever seen it. Meagan sat in his chair on the other side of his desk, wearing her old coat and a blue woollen beanie pulled down over her hair. She swivelled as I entered the room, a Poundland Bond villain without even a cat to warm her vicious lap. 'Here she is, my little Nellie.'

Seeing me, Robin's face grew stark with relief. He didn't speak but his eyes met mine with more emotion than I'd have thought possible.

'What're you doing here?' I asked Meagan. 'Joe's left, I don't know where he is.'

'So I've been hearing.' She stayed in the chair. Her skin was grey, hair flattened around her face by the beanie. 'I was just talking with Dr Wilder about how I'm going to manage back in Bala.'

'You don't live in Bala.' I made my tone conversational, determined to stay calm. I wasn't afraid of her, but Robin was worrying me. How much did Meagan know of what had happened here last night? Joe was gone, that alone was enough to sound alarms in her grizzled head.

'You know what I mean, love. You know how hard it is back home, it's why you ran off. You and Joe both.'

'And now he's run off again.' I was amazed at my own composure. 'There's nothing here for you, so you may as well go back.'

'After yesterday?' She gave a laugh that was mostly a cough, raspy. 'I don't think so.'

The entitled way she sat in the chair, with her elbows on its arms, made me glance across at Robin. He scratched at his eyebrow with his thumb, a silent plea for me to clean up this mess. I was the housekeeper and I'd brought her here, it was my job to get rid of her.

'Joe's gone. There's nothing for you.'

'And she's gone.' Meagan's smile soured. 'Which suits the pair of you very nicely.'

'Carolyn's not gone.' I fixed a matching smile to my face. 'I saw her last night, in fact.'

Robin was a statue, his face carved with silence. He didn't recognize this version of me. But Meagan did. She pushed upright, keeping hold of the chair. She stank of more than cigarettes, an astringent smell that took me back to Lyle's – disinfectant in the bath, plasters on scraped knees, antiseptic wipes. The scar at my temple throbbed.

'I could go to the police. He knows it.' Jerking her eyes at Robin. 'Even if you don't. I wanted to give him the chance to avoid that trouble but since he doesn't seem to appreciate it, I'll take myself off to the station.'

'The train station.' I nodded. 'Good idea. Because I am not sure what you think happened here, but I would like to see you gone.'

'The *police* station.' She'd turned her back on Robin, concentrating all her attention on me. 'Maybe I'll make a couple of statements, while I'm at it.'

'You should. Two years you've been subverting the course of justice, withholding evidence, interfering with an investigation. It's time you came clean.'

'It's because of you that kiddie's dead.' She clenched her fists. 'You and Joe Peach.'

'No, it's not. You were the adult in charge. You handed me the blame, needing me to be guilty in order to protect yourself. You've had the luxury of that protection for two years. But it's over.'

She gave an ugly laugh, not believing me.

'I was a child.' I looked her in the eye. The next words out of my mouth surprised me because I meant them: 'I forgive myself.'

'You? You'll never forgive yourself.'

'Watch me.' Robin was watching but I was hardly aware of him, only of her. 'You like to think you've no weaknesses, but what about Joe? You'd do anything for him. That's how I know you're bluffing. You won't involve the police, not where Joe's concerned.'

She wet her lips, eyes slitted on my face. Joe had said, *She hates you so much,* but he didn't understand the depth of her loathing. Only I understood, because I felt the same way about her.

'Joe isn't even your real weakness,' I went on. 'That's believing

311

no one can change, that there's no way back once we've seen the worst of ourselves.' I was addressing Robin now, and myself. 'You're wrong. We can change. It's not too late.'

'Too late for Rosie.'

'You covered it up. After I told you what I knew about what'd happened, you covered it up. And now you're attempting black-mail.' I tilted my head at her. 'The police are going to love you.'

Moments passed with Robin like a woodcut against the window and Meagan immobile. Then she laughed and let go of the chair, grinning as she came across the room towards me.

There was a second when she was so close I thought she'd hit me, or pull a knife and bury it in my neck, but instead she fixed me with her bloodshot stare.

'There she is, my Nell with a K. Death Knell.' She bared her teeth. 'I'll leave you two lovebirds together but I'll tell you this, lady. You can do better. Oh, you can do so much better.'

'Goodbye, Meagan. Good luck.'

I followed her from the room, crossing the hall at her heels, holding the front door as she passed through it into the street. No parting shots, just the sight of her limping up the road, away.

In the library, Robin was sitting on the edge of his desk, both hands in his hair.

'Thank God,' he said. 'Thank you. That was – nearly a scene.'

'It still might be.' I removed my coat, placing it in the empty chair. 'There's a chance she'll go to the police. Without Joe, she'll be desperate. She loves him, you know.'

'Funny sort of love!' Robin gave a short laugh, breathless.

'Like ours.' He looked up at me quickly. I met his stare,

unflinching. 'I'm here, aren't I? When I should have been the one to go to the police last night. When I saw what you'd done, you and Joe.'

Which of you, I wanted to ask, *which one of you killed her?*

'That was an accident,' Robin said shortly. He moved to sit behind his desk, twitching my coat from his chair, straightening its papers. 'In any case, as you saw for yourself, she's fine.'

'I saw . . . a ghost.' I couldn't believe he was making light of it. 'I was in shock, I expect.'

Carolyn, I meant. I'd seen Carolyn's ghost.

'What?' He stared at me, puzzlement and exasperation battling for control of his face. 'You just sent her packing! You were magnificent.'

'Meagan?' It was my turn to be puzzled. 'She was bluffing, but if she knows what happened last night . . .'

'Of course Meagan knows. She was right here!'

We stared at one another across his neat stacks of papers and books.

'I don't understand,' I said finally. 'Meagan was here? Yesterday?'

'You know she was. I thought you knew.' He stood and came around the desk, reaching for my hands, stopping when I shook my head at him. 'I tried to explain this last night. She came in here, raving. Joe had told her he wasn't going back with her, and she was furious. Just as you said. She wanted money, or Joe. Both, probably. She was – insanely angry.'

He pushed the knuckles of one hand at the wood of the desk. 'We tried to calm her down but she kept grabbing at Joe, insisting he was to come with her. Then Carolyn intervened.' He drew a short breath. 'And Meagan turned on her. It was an accident,

I imagine; she can't have meant to hurt her, not badly anyway. But she lashed out and Carolyn fell and hit her head then Joe threw a punch at Meagan with a similar result. It was like a scene from a bad film.' He frowned with distaste. 'I'd have called an ambulance but by the time I got back upstairs with that wet cloth, Carolyn was conscious and agreeing to go with Joe, anywhere away from that madwoman. Meagan was gone too, back to the hotel. I offered to pay for a cab but Joe wouldn't let me.'

'Meagan.' My tongue was thick in my head. 'This was all Meagan.'

'Yes. Nell, what did you think had happened? You've been odd since last night . . .'

'I saw the two of you, in the dining room. With Carolyn . . .' I began to shake. 'You and Joe, kneeling next to her. And there was blood, on the floor. You cleaned it up, but I saw it.' I looked up at him. 'Meagan was hurt, too?'

His face cleared. 'You saw her just now, with that hat covering the head wound. It was shallow but it bled a lot. The scalp does, of course.' He reached for me again.

I held him off. 'You said Joe took Carolyn, that she was gone.'

'They weren't going to stay here after that. I gather Joe had been trying to talk her into going away with him. Meagan just speeded things along. God knows if it'll last, Joe and Carolyn, but I have to hope it might. If Carolyn could just – stop, stand still and make a choice . . . Anyway, that's why Meagan came back just now, looking for Joe. When I told her he was gone, she threatened to tell the police about her head injury. Really it was Carolyn she was furious with, and I pointed out she'd caused as much damage to Carolyn. I didn't think the police would have much trouble believing how it unfolded.' He searched my face. 'What did you think had happened, exactly?'

'I thought she was dead.'

'Carolyn?' His face creased in confusion. 'But you told Meagan you saw her last night.'

'I saw something. I thought it was a ghost.' Carolyn taking a last look at Starling Villas before leaving in the taxi heading east. 'I was lying just now, to make Meagan leave. I wanted her gone and I was afraid Joe had told her what happened, how the pair of you—' I stopped, flooded with remorse and relief. No one was dead. What a fool I'd been. If only I'd taken the time to *look* – but all I could see was Joe, Joe kneeling at the side of the lake, and Rosie. A psychotic break, that's what a psychiatrist would call it. Guilt and fear, fighting it out in my gut.

'My God, Nell.' Robin leaned into the desk, his face blank with shock. 'You really thought we killed her? Carolyn?' He tried to laugh but it died in his throat. 'You think I'm capable of that? Murdering my wife, disposing of her corpse and eating an omelette with you afterwards?'

My chest clenched in protest. 'No . . .'

'Yes. It explains why you were so changed, so terrified.' He stared at me. 'Oh God, my God. What did we do? What did we ever do, to make you think that?'

'I didn't want to think it, not of you. But I know *Joe*, and I was scared.'

'You stayed.' He straightened, moving his head as if to get a better perspective on me. 'You actually stayed in the house, thinking I'd done that. And you defended me against that bloody woman and her blackmail. Thinking all the while that I'd done it, imagining me a murderer.'

'I didn't know! I didn't know what to think.'

But he nodded, his stare fixing on me as Meagan's had. 'You thought I killed my wife and disposed of her body. And you stayed in the house, thinking it.'

As if I were the monster. I was the monster.

'I don't know enough about you. You're so secretive, so alone—'

'And that's enough to make me a murderer? You're right, though, I was alone, until you came. And I dared to hope, that if you got to know me . . .' He stopped speaking.

'You wanted me.' Tears burnt the bridge of my nose. 'The night Joe stayed. You didn't mind him being here then. You liked him—'

'I liked *you*.' He lowered his voice, standing like a statue, unreachable. 'I thought I'd made that clear enough.'

'The sex, you mean. Why can't you just say it? You liked having sex with me.'

'It was more than that.' He was so far away now, observing me as if I were a stranger, distancing himself from me. 'I'm sorry you didn't feel the same way.'

'Don't do that.' Anger flared through me. 'Don't pretend you're the better person because you can't call it by its name. It's just sex. You do it all the time, you and Carolyn. Parties, people. And why not? It's your house, your *privacy*, you can do what you want. But don't pretend you're the better person or that you're in love with me, because it's not true. It's not true.'

He blinked slowly, his shoulders up. Making himself narrower, less of a target for my attack.

'You hide money in the house like – like a test.' I couldn't bear the look on his face, the way he was relearning me. 'You said you were ashamed of things you'd done with Carolyn. *You* said that. And she told me not to trust you. Even Mrs Mistry said you played games. Not just Carolyn. You.'

'So you spoke with my former housekeeper.' His voice chilled. 'I'm surprised you didn't decide I'd killed her too. That business with the keychain . . . You have a flair for melodrama.'

'You should've told the truth! Not just stories about Japan, the scared deer, trying to give me gifts! You could have given me the truth.'

'And let you make up a story about that, too? Thanks but as you say, I value my privacy.'

'You don't have to tell me that. All the rules you want me to obey, that rota, everything tied down to the minute, to the second.' When he didn't challenge this, I stuffed the silence with worse words: 'Meagan says she knows women like Carolyn. Broken women who've put themselves back together again—'

'And you've decided I'm the one who broke her. Permanently.' His stillness was full of splinters. 'I see.'

'I don't know what to think, what's the truth, because I don't know *you*. You hide away in here with your books and your boxes, and you expect me to follow your rules. Everything's a rule, it's how you keep control. You're obsessed with keeping control.' I stopped at last, out of breath. My throat was raw, as if I'd scraped this final truth from it with a serrated spoon, everything I'd been keeping inside while I tiptoed around him, scared of making even the smallest mistake.

He reached a hand for the desk, touching his index finger to its polished wood as if marking a full stop. 'You think I'm the one in control, in this house?' His words were soft, his mouth thinned and white. 'That the rules here are for you, or for her?' He gathered a breath. 'The rules are for *me*. To stop me being that man – the one who did those things – ever again. Because you're right. I behaved despicably towards Mrs Mistry, and countless other people besides. I was vile. I made this house vile. The parties, the people . . . Carolyn was only ever happy when we were off our heads, out of control, the pair of us worse than animals. And I let her take charge. I let myself—' He shook with self-loathing.

'Robin . . .' I put out my hand.

'No, let me finish.' His eyes swam darkly. 'You wanted to know what went on in this house before you came. It was a pit. We let anyone in. Strangers, people we'd paid for, friends I can't now look in the face, after the way I behaved. Ashamed doesn't come close.' His face hollowed, his shoulders so stiff it hurt me to look at him. 'I was arrogant, vicious, corrupt. You have no idea.'

'Carolyn—'

'I'm talking about me.' He rapped his knuckles on his collarbone. 'Carolyn can defend her own actions. But you need to know. You have to have the truth. What was it you said that woman believed? *There's no way back once we've seen the worst of ourselves.* Well, the rules were my way of getting back. To something resembling a decent man. Pathetic, no doubt, to you, but there it is. I'm not interested in controlling anyone other than myself. Not you and certainly not Carolyn, which would be a hiding to nothing.'

He shut his eyes, before putting his stare back on my face. I saw the effort it took him not to flinch or look away. 'I can't live alone. I've tried. Loneliness just – I go in circles, straight back to where I was. Then you came and you weren't like the others, that's what

I thought. You looked so different, you were more confident, more certain of yourself. You weren't afraid of me, even after that scene with her dress when I almost . . . You were different.' He tried to smile, but his mouth wouldn't make the shape. Then his eyes heated. 'But of course you came here for a reason, with a purpose. You and Joe. I was forgetting that. When he turned up, it all fell into place. You wanted to scam me, scam us. No doubt you've scammed a lot of people. I was a fool for allowing myself to imagine you were better, decent—'

'So you slept with me, as revenge.'

'No. I wanted you. I took what you were offering.' He squared his shoulders. 'I told myself once would be enough. That I deserved to be taught a lesson, to have my eyes opened. I expect I should be on my own, that's best for all concerned. God only knows what I was hoping for. I suppose I thought if we kept to the rules we'd be all right, you and I.'

'We were.' A part of me ached with pity, and with shame. 'We are.'

He shook his head. 'That's why I didn't want that woman in my house or your friend, Joe.'

'I'm sorry—'

'No. It was my mistake. I should have known it was a game, that you were up to something. I've pulled enough similar stunts myself. It was obvious how it would play out . . . And the art class, you deserve an apology for that.' He took his hand from the desk and folded it away, into a fist. His eyes moved around the room, lost. 'Perhaps Meagan is right and we're not capable of change. I certainly seem incapable of learning from my past mistakes.'

Bitterness now. I felt it flooding my own mouth. 'Don't say that. It isn't true.'

'Yet here we are.' He bent his head, looking at his feet. 'I apologize. For everything.'

He'd gone away, that's how it felt. Given up on all that we had. The old loneliness crowded in, suffocating me. I felt abandoned, as if someone else had told me about it, formally, in a letter: *Your employer has moved away. No forwarding address.*

'What's in the boxes?' I asked it in a whisper, afraid of the answer.

A frown came and went from his face. 'I've no business showing you.' But he reached for the nearest box, pulling out a white envelope. 'Look, if you like. It's all of a piece.'

I pulled the paperwork from the envelope, seeing the royal crest. Family Court, it said. The date was decades old, but I could see names and ages. Children. All the worst things, Mrs Mistry had said, the ones that trap us.

'I'm a magistrate. I suppose you'd say . . . I help decide where children should be placed. Those like you, who can't stay with their own families. But I'm also an academic, and I've been asked to review old cases as part of a study to improve the way the Family Court operates . . .'

I was aware of him speaking, but I couldn't hear or see him standing in front of me. All I could see was Rosie the day she came to Lyle's, so little and lost. And Joe, placed with foster parents who abused him, people who gave him nightmares so horrible he needed drugs to help him sleep. This was his work. Robin's work. *Deciding where children should be placed.* He said it so lightly, as if it hardly mattered, as if he were talking about choosing plants to pot in his garden room, based on which needed least sun and water. Did he put as much thought into deciding which children to give to people like Meagan Flack? She wasn't even the worst of them. Look what was done to Joe, and what it turned him into – an addict who sold himself to predators like the Wilders. Did Robin not see the irony, the pattern? A predator placing children with predators who by their actions turned those children into their preferred commodity? I felt sick.

This was who he was. Robin Wilder. The man I'd fallen in love with, by my accident or his design. How could I tell him it was worse, far worse than the parties or the games?

He hated himself for having sex with strangers, but this was a thousand times less forgivable. What he did for a living – I didn't know if I could ever forgive him for this.

'Were you with Joe, that night?' I looked up from the paperwork. 'I know Carolyn brought him here, from the club. She said you were here. That it was the pair of you together, with Joe.'

Robin's hand clenched on the box of papers. 'Yes. I was here.'

'Did you give him drugs?'

His eyes were black. 'No.'

'Did you sleep with him?'

He shook his head then stopped. 'But I was here in the house. I did nothing to stop it.'

'His bracelet was in your bed.'

'It's where they slept. I was meant to join them.' He waited a beat. 'I gave him a glass of wine and told him to make himself at home. I knew Carolyn had drugs. I don't know why I didn't join them. I usually do – you may as well know that.' He didn't break eye contact. 'It wasn't decency or shame that stopped me. It was disgust. I was disgusted with myself, and with them. And you're right, it doesn't make me a better person. If anything, it makes me worse. It certainly makes me a hypocrite.'

'Drugs are why Rosie died.' My voice sounded strange, faraway. 'A child died. When Joe's high he can't help himself or anyone else. He's a danger. And he gets high to forget what happened to him in the places people like *you* put us. Because we're just names on pieces of paper.' I dropped the envelope onto his desk. 'We're just a job of work, to people like you.'

'Is that why you came here?' He took his hand from the box. 'As payback?'

'I didn't even know you were a magistrate! And anyway,' I demanded, 'what payback? I can't get *payback*. I'm no one. You're the one with all the power, playing God with our lives.' My throat closed on my words. 'I thought Carolyn was my enemy. I came here because she took Joe from me that night, and like you I can't be alone. I wanted to find him, to be sure he was safe. But Carolyn wasn't my enemy, it was you. You made all this – everything we have to live with, and survive. You made *me*.'

Joe must have felt safe coming here, the way I did when I was cleaning and cooking because it was so familiar. It was what we knew, *all* we knew.

Robin dropped his hand to his side. Silence stiffened around us. I wanted to scrub it away, to scour and scrub and burn it with bleach – the silence and the smell of Meagan's cigarettes. Robin was telling the truth, at last. But so was I, or trying to. The only truth I understood. It turned the air into a solid thing, impossible to breathe. There was no room left for me, or for us. Our truth, like our secrets, took up too much of it.

Then Robin said, 'Nell, listen to me. Please.' He was very still and pale. 'You said I hide money in the house. That's true, but it wasn't a test for you. It was for me. I needed to know I could leave, walk out of here whenever I'd had enough. Most of my money's tied up in the property. I kept the cash to remind myself I wasn't trapped, even when it felt that way. Even when *trapped* was what I wanted. I've made so many mistakes. Terrible choices, unforgivable.' He spread his hands on the table. 'But never about you, Nell. Not you.'

I couldn't meet his eyes. His words washed over me. I retreated into silence, shocked by a sudden memory of Rosie's funeral. All those churchgoers, Chapel people. I'd wanted to fall on my knees, dragging Joe down with me to confess. But I didn't, and I couldn't start now. Robin was ready but I was not, too afraid of what it would mean for us, here and now.

'I won't make a meal of this,' he said. 'You know I've made mistakes. I've done things I regret, deeply. But I'm going to try and put that right. With your help, if you'll let me.' He stood in his shirtsleeves with a stain on his collar. I hadn't noticed the stain until now. 'You've done so much for me,' he said. 'I don't want it to be like this between us. I want to be able to thank you, properly, for all you've done.'

He hadn't taken his eyes from my face. His attention was too much, like torchlight shone into the dark corner where we'd been hiding from one another, he with his boxes, me with my cloths and polishes. I must have waxed every piece of wood in the house, greased every hinge. I wanted him to shoulder the worst of the blame but I'd lied too, and I'd cheated. Stolen this job, slipped like a knife into the narrow heart of his house. And here he was, thanking me for everything I'd done.

'Not everything.' It was too much. 'Not accusing you of murdering your wife.'

'That was my fault,' he said. 'For staying quiet for so long. I was hiding, I know that. Carolyn taught me how to hide – but I'm not blaming her. I made the choices to do what I did, all the things I now regret. I need to learn to let it all go and start over, if I can. I'd like to let it go.'

'What if I can't?' Panic clenched my stomach. 'Carolyn, that night. Your boxes, your *work*. The things I'm hiding, or carrying. What if I can't let those go?'

'Then I'd like to help you. To let go, or to carry them.' He stretched a hand for mine, seeing my tears before I felt them wetting my face. 'Nell, please. Let me help, let me carry it with you.'

But I was too deep in my defences, imagining myself at war. I wasn't ready to give Rosie up, or Joe. Not even to this man whose hands I'd trusted long before I knew him.

'These boxes . . .' He gestured around us. 'What I said about my work. It was clumsy of me, and insensitive.'

I looked him in the eye. 'I'd say the last thing you are is clumsy.'

'Insensitive, then. Talking like that, about something that affected your whole life.'

'It did.' I'd misheard for a moment, thinking he'd said *infected*. 'It really did.'

'Then – I'd like to apologize, if you'll let me.'

'You don't need my permission.'

'To apologize, no. But I'd like the chance to explain, if I can.' He leaned forward, elbows on his knees, hands hanging within easy reach of mine. 'If you'll let me.'

'Explain?' I looked at the tidy tide of boxes pushed back against the walls. 'How can you do that, when you don't understand? All you see are pieces of paper, not children. Not *us*.'

'Then – help me to see.' He paused. 'Tell me about Rosie.'

How could I? How could I make him see her, in all her colours? Dazzling and maddening, my Rosie. Not mine, not any more, but who else was carrying her? Not Joe. She was mine, alone.

'No,' I said softly. 'No.'

'She disappeared two years ago, from the foster home run by Meagan Flack. That's what you said.' Robin kept very still, speaking in a steady voice. 'But you never said she died.'

'There was a funeral. Candles and teddy bears and a coffin. There was a coffin.'

Her parents, weeping. The whole village, ashen-faced. Joe with his eyes drugged huge. My skin feeling as if it didn't fit on my face, as if our guilt must be obvious to anyone, everyone.

'But there was no body, isn't that right? They never found a body.' Robin reached for my hands but I shook my head, hating how much he knew. Had Joe told him, or Carolyn? 'The police dredged the pool but it was peppered by caves, passages out to sea. Subject to tidal currents, isn't that what they said?' He placed a space around each sentence, a gap into which I might speak if I could only loosen my tongue. 'They found one of her shoes. Nell . . . Isn't that right?'

'There was a coffin.' White wood with a wreath on top, her name spelt out in roses and forget-me-nots: R-O-S-I-E. A white shoebox inside, with her red sandal. Nothing else, nothing more.

'The funeral was symbolic,' Robin said, as if he understood. 'Her parents wanted a ceremony, for closure. It was intended as a celebration, of her life. Some of the papers said it was too soon, even questioned the parents' motives. I have to confess to looking it up online, after you told me about Rosie. There was the presumption of death, but no body.'

I stood blindly before him. *Rosie*. Little, little Rosie. He watched me, and I knew he saw me. Finally, after all this time, he saw me.

'You know, don't you? What happened to her.'

'Don't,' I warned him.

'Don't question you?' He reached for my hands and this time I let him take them, my skin a distraction from what he was so nearly touching. 'Don't help you?'

'You can't help me. You can't.'

I see Joe kneeling at the edge of the lake where the water stirred, disturbed by a movement under the surface. Ripples running into rings, circling the same spot, swallowing the small hole.

I'd made myself ask, 'Where's Rosie?' but I knew. The answer was in Joe's palms and the sunburnt nape of his neck. He hadn't woken me when she came, hadn't wanted her here with us. She was a nuisance, and told tales. He wouldn't share me, not with anyone. I remember – touching the scar on my forehead, thinking of the ambulance that never came, all the excuses I'd made for him, bloody towels rancid from the sun, smelling of meat. And all the while the sun soaked into the water, joining the ripples circling there. Joe looked up at last and reached a hand for me, wordless.

At the funeral, I was so sure our guilt was obvious to anyone who looked in our direction. The empty coffin, no culprit, no justice. 'We're right here!' I wanted to shout, but I kept my mouth shut, standing at Joe's side. I'd chosen him over Rosie and for that choice to make sense, I had to stay with him. He had to be more than my first love. The centre of my world – I elevated him to that role but Joe couldn't sustain it, how could he? He wasn't big enough or strong enough, even before the drugs. He was just Joe. A boy I once knew, or thought I did. I'd tried so hard to make him carry this, but he couldn't and now there was only me.

'Was it Joe?' Robin asked. 'Were you covering for him, or afraid of him?'

I pulled free, moving so suddenly I nearly knocked a chair over. He reached to save it from falling, and I ran.

Out of the library and up the stairs, not stopping until I reached the attic, tripping on the hem of the rug as I grabbed the nearest trunk, hauling it across the floor to jam against the door. It was heavy but I was frantic, needing to feel safe, shut in. Huddling against the barricade, I listened for the sound of him on the stairs, coming after me. Stupid to have told him Rosie's name, or to have ever texted Joe. Stupid to have held Joe in my heart all this time when he gave me up the first chance he got. I was weeping, sick of myself. I'd done this, brought it all on myself.

'Nell?' He was right outside the attic door, his shadow soaking the gap between the door and frame.

I recoiled, pricked with panic. I hadn't heard him on the stairs.

I watched the handle of the door, waiting to see it rattled by his fist, but he didn't touch it. He said my name again, twice, before he gave up. I saw his shadow lift, and leave.

He'd found us out, Joe and me, and I didn't know what he'd do. I wanted to trust him but after everything I'd said, all the things I'd accused him of doing and being – I didn't dare let him in.

38

'Nell. Nell!'

I'd fallen asleep, my cheek against the trunk which was sliding in stages across the floor, shoving at me.

'Nell!' Robin was shouting, pushing hard at the attic door.

I coughed, coming awake properly. Then I couldn't stop coughing, black soot in my eyes and throat, seeping from the gap under the door where he was fighting to get into the attic. Black soot, burning. Fire.

'Nell, open the door!' Robin was coughing too, the ends of his fingers reaching through the gap he'd made between the door and frame, where smoke was curling. 'There's a fire, the kitchen—'

I hauled at the trunk, my feet skittering on the floor. Robin shoved and I dragged.

Between us, we got the trunk away and then he was in the attic, his face streaked by smuts, tears in his eyes. He grabbed for me and I grabbed back, briefly. Then I broke away, pushing past him to see the fire punching up the staircase, orange fists of flame.

'I called 999 . . .' Robin snatched for breath, a hand at his chest. 'They're coming . . .'

They'd never get through the flames. Its heat was warping the air, buckling and burning. How long was I asleep? I couldn't believe how fast the fire had taken hold but there was the old stove, the cleaning products stashed under the stairs, his boxes of papers and his books. I'd feared a fire, from my first day here.

I ran from the attic to the bathroom, grabbing the towel and bath mat, soaking them in the sink as fast as I could. Robin helped, the pair of us with soot freckling our faces. Together we shut the attic door, rolling the sodden towel and mat along the gap beneath it.

Crossing to the window, I pushed it wide, putting one foot on the ledge outside.

Robin stood and watched uncertainly, but I knew what I was doing. How often had I planned this escape route from Starling Villas to the river and mountains beyond? I waited until he was behind me then dropped from the window to the first of the roofs, sliding down the gutter's edge, finding my footing against the chimney stack where the gulls liked to sit.

The wail of fire engines cut through the fire's roar.

Robin was at my side, following my lead. Treading where I trod, trusting me. A shower of grit and stones rattled under our shoes, down the roof and over the edge into burning smoke.

Our hands were steady, finding holding places and each other, all the way to the restaurant's fire escape where we stood for a second, looking back at the burning house, blood thudding in our ears.

His books and boxes burnt brightest, all that ink and paper, coils of colour coming through the smoke as it swelled into the street. The panes in the garden room cracked like gunshots. The fire spread fast, racing up the polished rail of the staircase, leaping from room to room. I imagined I heard the dull creak of the mirror at the foot of his bed before its glass exploded, his sketch of me curling to a feather of ash, gone in seconds, a puff of black to join the rest.

We stood in the street and watched.

Up and up, the fire pushed. Coiling to the top of the house, retreating from the cold tiles of the box room before bursting into my attic, leaping to lick at the amber walls.

I saw it all, in my mind's eye. The brass camels stayed standing as their tapestry desert caught light, their hard bodies turning crimson with heat. Each pane in the Tiffany lamp chinked free, the tissue paper swallowed in a single fiery bite. Flames ran across the floor and up the walls, varnish sizzling, old theatre programmes curling and falling in hot spots of flame to pierce the beautiful rug over and over again. Downstairs, the Japanese bowl cracked inside its silk box, the chip of ivory blackened and burnt.

Outside, the police moved people back, back. Shouting warnings as the windows began to burst, throwing daggers of glass down into the street.

From the door of Hungry's, Gilbert watched, the fire striping its reflection across his broad face.

Further up the street, I was sure, Bradley closed the cheese shop, drawing down the shutters to keep the smoke from blowing inside and laying waste to his stock.

Starling Villas burnt until its narrow face turned black, and all the rot inside was gone. We stood together and watched, Robin and I, smelling of smoke and flames. I reached for his hand and he surrendered it, our fingers fastening into a single fist.

39

The flat was waiting when Meagan got home from London, litter on its walkway, damp squatting inside. The flat and the boy, Darrell, wanting a cup of tea and a cigarette.

'You stink of fires,' he said.

'So would you,' Meagan told him, 'if you'd been where I've been.'

'To a bonfire?' Cocking his head at her. 'Where's your druggie friend?'

'Taking a trip.'

He laughed as if she'd made a joke, and followed her into the flat. She didn't try and stop him. In the kitchen, he wandered to the stove, fidgeting with its dials.

'Knock it off,' she snapped. 'Don't you know how easy it is to start a fire?'

He threw her a look. 'Are you going to puke?'

A stone thrown through the window, they'd deserved that much. Was it her fault the back door was unlocked? That was Nell's doing. A little fire then, to smoke her out. But fire has a mind of its own, just like the sea, you can't make it do your bidding.

Meagan's hands shook as she remembered how fast it'd taken hold at Starling Villas.

Darrell was watching her. 'What you got there then?' Nodding at the parcel under her arm.

'Fruit cake.' She showed him the tin. 'You can have a slice if you like.'

The cake had been standing out on the table, asking to be taken. She never was able to resist the girl's cakes, and she was owed, wasn't she? Just desserts – would Darrell find that funny?

Where's your druggie friend? On a trip with that rich bitch, gone for good this time. He'd called her, dialling his number on the phone she'd taken from him. They were headed for Dubai, where Carolyn Wilder had friends, and property. Joe was happy, he said. Then he'd said goodbye and Meagan had pushed the phone back into her pocket. Her broken toe told her rain was on the way, a long hard winter on its heels.

'Get the plates,' she told Darrell. 'I'll put the kettle on.'

'Nah, you're all right.' He pulled a face. 'That stuff sticks in my teeth.' He circled the table, looking bored. 'How come you went away?'

'I had business.' She put Nell's cake on the table, her hands shaking. 'But I'm back now.'

She needed a proper meal inside her. The train journey had made her faint and queasy, all she'd eaten all day was a corner of the cake. She needed a strong cup of tea and a proper helping, a big slice of cake on a china plate. The kitchen was smaller and dirtier than she remembered. The damp put a dull pain in her throat. She reached for the table, feeling its tackiness, shutting her eyes for a long second, feeling her age in every inch of her body, toes to teeth.

'I'll be off, then,' Darrell said.

'Stay for a bit.' She was scared suddenly, no good reason for it. 'Why not?'

'Nah, you're all right.' He was at the door, folding his coat around his skinny torso.

He'd taken something. Her handbag? Her purse?

She called after him, 'Don't you bloody dare,' but he was gone.

Footsteps on the walkway, running. Then she was alone in the flat, in the quiet.

She took a plate from the cupboard and a knife from the drawer. The cake smelt good, of rum and almonds. Say what you like about Nell Ballard – Nell with a K – but she could bake a cake.

Meagan cut a fat wedge of it and settled herself in a chair, to eat.

40

I'd said I could never go back, but a week after fire tore through Starling Villas, we caught a train to Wales. The fire investigation team were still at work, but Robin's insurers had released emergency funds. He'd bought matching rucksacks, paying for the train tickets in cash.

We sat at a table seat, sharing sandwiches and wine from plastic glasses with peel-off lids. A strange meal, romantic in its way, but I couldn't manage more than a mouthful.

'Have mine.' I passed the glass of wine across the table, reaching for a bottle of water. 'It's ages until we get there, we should try and sleep.'

Robin nodded, settling himself with his head propped to the window. He was worn out with the talking and paperwork, answering the fire team's questions, arguing with the insurers.

Two little boys raced down the aisle of the train.

'Slow down!' Their mother trailed behind, hands full of shopping bags.

Robin's face was pinched shut with tiredness. He'd lost everything. There was no longer a house hidden on the street where Joe had bartered for drugs. The fire took it all, but I didn't believe in its cleansing power. We weren't free, Robin and I. We were just homeless. Smelling of smoke and ashes, of London and the destruction we'd left behind. My destruction. Nell with a K.

After we escaped the fire, I told him so many of my secrets, unable to stop them spilling from me as we shopped for toothbrushes and clothes. I talked of sofas in London, of Brian and the masseuse, even the Shunt Lounge and Mr Intercity. No matter what I said, Robin didn't get tired or sick, didn't say, 'Enough, that's enough,' but there was still one secret I hadn't shared, or one suspicion. I reached a hand inside my coat, waiting for the slippery sensation to grip again at my insides.

'Rubbish.' A woman was making her way down the aisle, dressed in the uniform of the train staff, hefting a large white bin liner. 'Any rubbish.'

Robin leaned to hand her the empty wine glasses and sandwich boxes, smiling his thanks before settling back to sleep. She looked at me, but I shook my head, 'Nothing, thanks.'

I watched her move down the aisle, hips swinging to the train's rhythm, tidying as she went.

Starling Villas was gone, after all my hard work. A pang of loss made me take my hand from my stomach to grip at the table's edge. Robin cracked open an eye, worry working the muscle at the side of his mouth. I shook my head at him. 'I'm fine, go back to sleep.'

A trolley service would come soon, waking him a second time.

I'd meant us to eat the fruit cake I'd baked, but the cake and its tin were gone in the fire. There was nothing left of what I'd planned in that desperate hour when I'd thought the pair of us deserved no better. All the evidence was burnt or washed away.

With my beeswax and brass polish, I'd made his house shine from top to bottom. To rid the old house of its creaks and groans, I'd worked petroleum jelly into every hinge and loose floorboard, soaking the same into teacup rings on tables, and lipstick stains on bedsheets. In the garden room, I'd sprayed tar to keep the rot from his plants. Wax and petrol and tar.

I'd made everything in the house flammable.

I did that, Nell with a K. Death Knell.

Except – the fire was an accident, they said, almost certainly an accident. No one was to blame. By concentrating all of my attention on Robin's face, I was able to hold the guilt at bay, just.

Across the aisle, a blonde woman stood to let a teenage boy slide out of the seat beside her. She watched him as he idled his way to the buffet car before she sat back down, the swing of her hair like Carolyn's. The boy wasn't like Joe, though. No one was like Joe. Not even Joe. I'd told a story of the sort of boy he was and everyone believed it, even Meagan. Even Joe. Believing he was to blame, that something was missing inside of him, just as Meagan had always said. I was responsible for Joe – the boy he'd become after Rosie's death. That was my doing. But he was out of my reach now, safe with Carolyn. I hoped she'd take care of him.

Further down the train, a man sat alone in cheap dark clothes. I'd been aware of him since we boarded. It's what life teaches us, with or without the aid of someone like Meagan Flack. Beware of men, alone or in packs. Fill your fist with keys, be ready for anything. Be afraid. No one teaches us the same rules about women, but perhaps they should. I think they should.

Under the table, Robin's leg was slack against mine. He was sleeping and I should do the same, on such a long journey.

I settled my hand back under my coat, nestling my head to the wing of the seat, letting the rock of the train draw me down into a dream of keys on a chain with an egg-shaped charm, a gift from Robin. In the dream, he'd hidden the keys in the house and I couldn't find them, digging through dirt in the garden room, under the rubble and soot left by the fire, pulling things up from the ashes – a half-melted hairbrush, perfume in a grenade-shaped bottle, a ruined snowshoe – but still I couldn't find what I wanted. Then Robin returned and put the keys into my hand as the charm split apart, a tiny pink and black bird staggering from the broken shell to peck at my palm.

'It's all right. Nell?' He reached for my hand. I let him take it. 'You were dreaming.'

A baby was bawling in the next carriage.

I listened to the jag of its crying, wondering if it was hungry or tired or scared. Meagan said babies never cried without a reason. You could always make them stop. If all else failed, there was Calpol, or a drop of something stronger. You could always find a way. Me, she meant. I could find a way to make them stop.

On the train, the sound rose and fell, without ceasing. My throat was hot and full, Robin's hand slack around mine. After a time, I slipped free of his grip.

Later, the train windows began to fill with the light that said we were nearing the sea.

I watched Robin sleep and I knew – we could never be together. This was a long goodbye, that's all. I'd been afraid to take the trip on my own, and he'd said he wanted to understand. Not just about what happened to Rosie, but about his work and its consequences. It wasn't that I couldn't forgive him, or even that I could never be entirely sure he wasn't playing a long game with me. It was simply that I'd outgrown him, somewhere between the fire and here. Tonight, though, we would be together. We'd kiss in whatever shabby place we found for the night, a roadside motel. I'd take his face in my hands, and he'd hold me at the waist. It would be a little sad, and a little frantic. We'd smell the smoke on each other's skin and remember how it burnt down before us, his beautiful house and his books, the Japanese bowl I'd refused to take from him. We would talk a little, perhaps, about what we'd lost when we lost our home. The motel's sheets would be slippery like the sensation inside me, which I tried to catch with the curl of my hand. Afterwards, we'd lie side by side in the patchy darkness, each of us listening to the other's breath, pretending to sleep.

We took a taxi from the station, before walking the final mile to Rosie's resting place. It was just as I remembered, the sky stretched broad above our heads. Robin didn't speak. His stride matched mine. We were two tall shadows on the ground, backs huddled by our rucksacks. I could taste copper coins in my mouth.

'There!' I pointed, unable to keep the excitement from my voice.

The lake looked so small, no bigger than a pool. They'd done a better job of fencing it off so that no one could reach it but I knew where to climb through, pulling Robin with me.

Kneeling at the lake's shore, I rested my hand on the water until it settled enough to give back my reflection. The shallows were stagnant and chalky-white but further out it was a deep emerald green, tilting towards me. Clouds shuddered across the sky. I couldn't feel the water under my palm, only the flexing of the lake's skin, the same temperature as mine.

Far below, too far to dive, was our drowned village where fish swam in and out of letterboxes and crayfish scratched, seaweed flying like flags from the church spire. In the house on the corner where the sea urchins lived, I imagined Rosie lying with her toes curled tight, one thumb wedged firmly in her mouth. Her eyes were shut but as the shadow of my hand fell through the water, she smiled, bubbles carrying the smile to where my hand rested, pricking my palm in a kiss.

I shook my hand from the water and straightened, shedding my coat, tugging my T-shirt over my head. 'Let's swim.'

Robin eyed the lake doubtfully.

'It'll be warm,' I lied. 'The water holds on to the heat.'

Stripping to my underwear, I threw my clothes behind me, close to the spot where I'd been sleeping, two years ago. Not looking to see if Robin was coming, I walked into the water, twisting my hair into a knot to keep it out of my eyes.

The lake was shockingly cold.

I pushed on, sweeping it behind me with my hands. When it reached my waist, I shoved with my toes at the stiff, stubby shore then took a deep breath and ducked beneath the surface, pulling the water towards me until I could swim.

As the lake deepened, I dived, lengthening the new muscles in my arms and legs, stronger than I'd ever been thanks to Starling Villas, my three-storey workout.

Down, down into the lake, opening my eyes to air streaming past, swimming the way I always swam, down as far as my lungs would take me. Not panicking as I had two years ago when I woke to find Joe kneeling in the shallows. He'd reached for me but I'd pushed past him, shouting her name, running into the water until it was deep enough for me to dive in.

As soon as I was under the water, I saw her.

It looked as if she was showing off in her new bikini, twisting and turning, sequin earrings flashing. I followed their flashing, down, down, down. Her hands were over her head, fingers starfishing for mine, bubbles breaking, blurring her face. Rosie, my little Rosie. Inside the lake, in my memory, she's six forever. Her face washed free of its ugly scowl, a sweet band of baby fat around her neck.

Robin needed to believe the best of me, just as he needed me to believe the best of him. Neither of us was a monster, not now. The squirming in the pit of my stomach might not be his child. The slippery sensation might be guilt, the same as always; Rosie could have found this new way of haunting me. Because I'd told myself I could have reached her, even as my lungs were crushing and my breath fading out. I could have kicked harder, fought the water with everything I had. Except Joe was up there. I had a choice, that's how it felt in that moment – I could reach her or return to him. I'd convinced myself I'd had a choice, but of course it wasn't true. I had no air left in my lungs. I'd have drowned with her. I know that now, but it was different then. Then, it'd felt so good to turn back, to think about the big breath I was about to take. I was so light and free when I was out of the water, in his arms. Weeping, the pair of us, weeping and shaking. Joe's hands in my hair, his mouth on my neck.

'It was me,' he sobbed. 'I gave her Calpol last night like Meagan said, to help her sleep so we could— She must've been sleepy still, not strong enough to swim—'

I kissed him, to make him quiet.

Because I knew it wasn't Joe who made Rosie's warm milk every night, or the little cakes she loved. It wasn't Joe who knew where Meagan's sleeping pills were kept and wanted him to herself, because he made her feel free and light. I was the one who'd put the pills into her milk and cakes, so she would sleep while I was away with Joe. Night after night. The pills on their own had never harmed her – I'd been so careful with the dosage – but Joe had given her Calpol on top, without telling me.

'You should've told me about the Calpol.' Fear made me fierce. 'Meagan will blame me.'

Meagan didn't care, I knew that. Not about me. She would let me shoulder the blame along with everything else, and she'd do it believing I'd never get better, never find my way back, because people don't change. She'd throw me to the wolves, without a second thought. But not Joe. She loved Joe, would do anything to protect him. If she believed him guilty, she'd do anything at all. I had to convince her that he was the one responsible for Rosie's death. The one in need of Meagan's protection.

Joe's shadow at the surface of the lake, a darkness in the water above me.

Rosie, sinking, the bright flashing of her earrings fading from sight. My hands reaching for her, fingers opening and shutting.

That's inside me, forever. My empty hands, the weight of her, just out of reach. Even when I blank what happened from my mind, my body remembers. The choice I made, what I failed to do. How light I felt coming up from the lake, and how free.

How can I live with what I did? Carry this burden?

I need to choose, again. To swim even deeper, further than my lungs can stand, until my fists are filled by the jag of rocks at the bottom of the lake where no light reaches, into the caves where Rosie could be waiting. Or to turn back to where Robin is standing at the shore, searching the water's surface, trying to stay calm.

In a minute, I think, *in a minute I'll choose*. When there's no more booming in my ears, when the echoes are gone and all I can hear is me.

Acknowledgements

I owe an enormous debt of thanks to Vicki Mellor, my editor at Pan Macmillan, whose patience, focus and gimlet eye turned the first draft of *Fragile* – finally – into this far better book. My agent, Jane Gregory, and her team, especially Stephanie Glencross, who saw me over the hurdles in style; and everyone at David Higham who helped their authors through an extraordinary year. Gillian Green, Matthew Cole and Hannah Corbett, together with the wider Pan Mac family, who welcomed me so warmly. Jessica Cuthbert-Smith, whose copy-edits were the kind authors dream of. Ami Smithson, who gave *Fragile* its beautiful face. Friends, sometimes found in far-flung places: Tama, Anne-Elisabeth, Susan P., Jane S., Paddy and his family, including Lola and Dolly. For solidarity and cheer, I could not have asked for better than Erin Kelly, Jane Casey, Mick Herron and Liz Nugent, who gave *Fragile* their time and attention when the world was demanding so much from each of us. My family, who survived all this with their sense of humour and their love intact. And Alison Graham, whose companionship made all the difference when it was most needed.

Fragile: The Director's Cut

When my editor and I first discussed the possibility of including a deleted scene from *Fragile* at the end of this paperback, I was paralyzed with fear. Scenes are deleted for a reason; did I really want my first stab at the story to see the light of day? But then I remembered how much I enjoy watching the director's cut of my favourite films, especially the commentary explaining creative decisions behind which scenes are cut and which are kept. I began to see readers might be interested in learning how the early draft of *Fragile* was transformed, as part of the editorial process that is crucial to the success of every published novel. And so (*deep breath*) here is my original opening scene, with my 'director's commentary' to follow. Be warned that it contains spoilers, so it's probably best to save it until you've finished reading *Fragile*.

DELETED SCENE

After dark, the house is different. Less strange, more solid. The shadows stand and stretch as if they spent the day as he did, cramped over a desk. The evening's noise drops away as night prowls in, poking its soft muzzle into all the corners as if seeking something to hunt.

During the day, light spears through the house, filling it with holes. Then there's an hour when everything is the colour of skimmed milk and nothing has substance; I'm scared to set his plate on the table, fearing it will fall through, shatter or dissolve. Even the dust doesn't know where to settle during that hour. We have to wait until nightfall for the house to feel real, its furniture filling out, shouldering the dark. I stub my toes on it, which I never do during the day.

After dark, then, I make my way downstairs. Slowly, running a hand along the apple-green wall to my left, sore fingertips finding out the plaster's worms and threads. He hasn't seen the flaws in the wall or he'd have me sandpapering in my imagined spare time, odd jobs to keep me busy so he can forget all over again, make-believe I'm not here. Kept busy, I am invisible.

'Good evening, Dr Wilder.'

I am standing in the library now, where the walls breathe in and out with the apricot light of his lamp. Time ticks by. He doesn't look up from his work. His desk is mahogany, inlaid with oxblood leather, the shadow of his head broken up by books. How I loved those books, once.

'Sir,' I try, tasting the word on my tongue, over-seasoned, under-cooked.

He looks up at last and, from the way he stares, I know he's done it again. Forgotten the ad in the corner shop, the neat little notice that brought me here so many weeks ago. Forgotten too the ways in which he's kept me here ever since, even those which were a trouble to him, ruining his appetite and routine, going against the grain of his indifference. That's what you get, I feel like telling him, for wanting a servant in this day and age, coveting a slave. I'm glad he's uncomfortable, he ought to be, it's what the pair of us deserve. My fingertips throb. I stand and let him stare at me. He's dying to say, 'Who *are* you?' but he won't, and I won't help him. Once, maybe, back at the beginning when things were different and I was eager to please, afraid of losing the roof over my head. And later, when I grew to like him. That is all in the past now.

He stares at me as if seeing a ghost. 'Not a servant,' he'd insisted at the outset. 'A personal assistant. Housekeeper, if you must.'

But he would have to converse with a personal assistant – how else would they know how to assist? No, what he'd wanted was a servant to clean up his mess, make food appear and dirty dishes vanish, to change his sheets and take the stains from his ties before important meetings Outside the House. Someone he could rely upon but ignore, without any breach in etiquette. No need for conversation, no awkward pretence at social interaction. A non-person, to make life less of a struggle. Perhaps secretly we all lust after someone like that.

Just go about your business. That was his instruction, all those weeks ago. *We'll stay out of each other's way. That would be best.*

I'd fallen into the habit of thinking less and less of myself, so it was a relief to find I meant nothing at all to a man like him. I preferred to be invisible, to go about my business undisturbed; we were well-suited in that respect.

'Your cocoa, Dr Wilder.'

As I set the cup on the desk, I hear his soft sound of protest. Empirically, it is his cocoa. Had I not spoken, he would still have it in a cup at his elbow. By speaking I've reminded him that I'm here under his roof, breathing his air, taking up space in his beautiful house. *Being other.*

351

I clear my throat as I retreat to the door, a further, phlegmy reminder that things do not appear and disappear as if by magic here. Not that he believes in magic, or in ghosts. He's a magistrate, dealing in hard evidence. This is how I know that I will win. Sooner or later he will have to talk and touch and look, it's just a question of whose nerve lasts longest. In this war of attrition, clearing my throat is like firing a cannon. The clock ticks, a sly note in the disturbed stillness of the room. I linger by the low table, pretending to tidy his papers. In reality, I'm prolonging the moment of his agony. I want to see him trying to forget who I am, and what we've done. Bad enough that he brought me here in the first place without the rest of it, the hot, ripe mess of it.

Oh God . . . My God. What did we do—? I hear it again, the horror in his voice. All that alien emotion. He wasn't a magistrate in that moment, he wasn't even a man.

The papers riffle under my fingers, their insect sound reaching around the room. I'm tired of playing along, the way I did at the beginning. It takes a lot of effort to be invisible. You can't clean a house from top to bottom and cook three meals a day without making a sound. Yet I took such care to limit the noise, sensing the strain it put on him. You might say that's how I first seduced him: with my silence. Fulfilling his ideal of perfection, being his little woman, neither seen nor heard but here at his convenience, *for* his convenience. That, too, is in the past now.

Tick-tick-tick. The longer I stand here, touching the tips of my sore fingers to his papers, the harder it is for him to keep up the pretence. Soon he'll be forced to put down his pen, acknowledge my existence, and the red raw rest of it, the *Oh-God-What-Did-We-Do* of it.

Back at the beginning, he saw no reason to understand me, no benefit to knowing who I was or where I'd come from, this stranger he'd brought into his home. He asked so few questions, betrayed so little curiosity; all that came later. He may argue with himself that he needs tangible proof of who I am and what we've done. Hard evidence. As if the blood wasn't enough, its stickiness, stubborn on the floor and wall. I've scrubbed and scrubbed but it won't leave. In the end, just as in the beginning, he will have to reach out and connect. His skin and mine, my bones and his.

The clock is ticking.

All around me, the room is bristling with shadows, real.

Full of darkness, full of us.

AUTHOR'S COMMENTARY

This scene, as readers of *Fragile* will know, takes the form of a preface, providing a glimpse of the fate in store for the characters in Starling Villas. It finds Robin and Nell in a state of shocked estrangement, days after an accident involving Robin's ex-wife, Carolyn. Originally, I'd felt this was the perfect place to start. The scene introduces Starling Villas in all its decaying, claustrophobic glory, as well as providing a close-up on the complex relationship between my heroine Nell and Robin Wilder, the man she struggles not to love.

My editor (thank goodness for editors) questioned whether the scene was quite true to the reality of what unfolds in the house. She pointed out my tendency to be overly descriptive, slowing the pace at this crucial stage of the story, and stressed the need to strip back paragraphs for clarity. (Seriously, thank *goodness* for editors.)

I tortured the scene through several re-writes – paring back the wordiness, tightening my focus – before removing it entirely. (My advice when murdering your darlings? Do it swiftly, for their sake and yours.)

So why *did* I want to start the story here, out of sequence and with the characters of Nell and Robin still strangers to the reader? In part, I expect, because I learn my characters through their actions and interactions; there is no script before I begin shooting. This moment, stolen from later in the story, demanded I answer a number of questions critical to understanding Nell's character and motivation. Why does she choose to obey Robin's rules? What makes her want to live in his house, and to keep living there after terrible things take place? Is she afraid of him? If not, why not? How does she feel when Carolyn, his ex-wife, sweeps in? Who ultimately holds the power in Starling Villas? The answers to these questions proved to be very interesting indeed.

Another good reason for starting the story at this point was to plunge the reader into the dark heart of Starling Villas, the narrow stage on which so much of my story is set. While I cut this scene in its entirety, I made sure to retain this sense of strangeness in the house. The ticking of the clock. The feeling that only at night does Starling Villas reveal its true face. The sense in which everyone who enters becomes a prisoner of one kind or another. I set out to write Starling Villas as if it were a haunted house whose ghosts were still living. Full of shadows and the emotions we associate with ghosts: longing, sorrow, regret. I hope, too, that I held onto the sense in which Nell is drawn to Robin even while she is trying to pull away, to free herself from this prison and its warden.

Nell descending the spiral staircase with Robin's cup of cocoa is my favourite image in the scene. It is, of course, a tribute to the films of Hitchcock. Specifically, the moment when Cary Grant carries a (poisoned?) glass of milk upstairs to his terrified wife in *Suspicion*. Hitchcock put a lightbulb inside the glass to make it more dramatic, and lit the scene so the bannister rail cast shadows like prison bars. When I'm writing, I always have a film track playing in my head. It helps me to see colours and textures, and to bring the story alive. Nell's hand trailing the wall, finding out its scars and wounds, sets the prickly, tense tone for the story.

The deleted scene is bookended by references to the dark, and to shadows. The shadows that stand and stretch at the end of the day, and those bristling in the room at the close of the scene. Whatever else was lost when I cut this original opening, the shadows and darkness found their way into the final book. I hope you enjoyed reading *Fragile*.